O9-AID-320

BESTIARY

ROBERT MASELLO

BERKLEY BOOKS, NEW YORK

THE BERKLEY PUBLISHING GROUP
Published by the Penguin Group
Penguin Group (USA) Inc.
375 Hudson Street, New York, New York 10014, USA
Penguin Group (Canada), 90 Eglinton Avenue East, Suite 700, Toronto, Ontario M4P 2Y3, Canada
(a division of Pearson Penguin Canada Inc.)
Penguin Books Ltd., 80 Strand, London WC2R 0RL, England
Penguin Group Ireland, 25 St. Stephen's Green, Dublin 2, Ireland (a division of Penguin Books Ltd.)
Penguin Group (Australia), 250 Camberwell Road, Camberwell, Victoria 3124, Australia
(a division of Pearson Australia Group Pty. Ltd.)
Penguin Books India Pvt. Ltd., 11 Community Centre, Panchsheel Park, New Delhi—110 017, India
Penguin Group (NZ), Cnr. Airborne and Rosedale Roads, Albany, Auckland 1310, New Zealand
(a division of Pearson New Zealand Ltd.)
Penguin Books (South Africa) (Pty.) Ltd., 24 Sturdee Avenue, Rosebank, Johannesburg 2196,
South Africa

Penguin Books Ltd., Registered Offices: 80 Strand, London WC2R 0RL, England

This is a work of fiction. Names, characters, places, and incidents either are the product of the author's imagination or are used fictitiously, and any resemblance to actual persons, living or dead, business establishments, events, or locales is entirely coincidental. The publisher does not have any control over and does not assume any responsibility for author or third party websites or their content.

BESTIARY

A Berkley Book / published by arrangement with the author

PRINTING HISTORY
Berkley edition / November 2006

Copyright © 2006 by Robert Masello.
Cover illustration and stepback art by Mark Gerber.
Cover design by Richard Hasselberger.
Interior text design by Kristin del Rosario.

ISBN: 0-425-21280-7

BERKLEY®
Berkley Books are published by The Berkley Publishing Group,
a division of Penguin Group (USA) Inc.,
375 Hudson Street, New York, New York 10014.
BERKLEY is a registered trademark of Penguin Group (USA) Inc.
The "B" design is a trademark belonging to Penguin Group (USA) Inc.

PRINTED IN THE UNITED STATES OF AMERICA

10   9   8   7   6   5   4   3   2   1

Bestiary: Books that had a great vogue between the eleventh and the fourteenth centuries describing the supposed habits and peculiarities of animals both real and fabled, with much legendary lore and moral symbolism. They ultimately derived from the Greek *Physiologus*, compiled by an unknown author before the middle of the second century.

—Ebenezer Brewer,
Brewer's Dictionary of Phrase and Fable (1870)

PROLOGUE

Base Camp, Outside Mosul, Iraq—
February 2005

SAND. THERE WAS sand in his boots, sand in his clothes, sand in his armpits, sand in his hair. At night, there was sand in his dreams. Greer swore that if he ever got out of Iraq alive, he was never going to see sand again.

If things went right today, he might get his wish.

Sadowski poked his head under the flap of the tent. "Hasan's in the Humvee, Captain," he said. "Cuffed."

Greer nodded, and finished lacing up his boot. There was sand in his sock, but what would be the point of trying to get rid of it? He'd take off the boot, shake it out thoroughly, then put it back on—and find even more sand inside it than before.

"Load up," he told Sadowski, glancing at his watch. "We don't want to lose the light."

Outside, the sun was beating down so hard it made the ground, if you looked long enough, seem to undulate. Greer adjusted his shades, pulled the brim of his cap down, and walked toward the Humvee, parked in the narrow slice of shade provided by a water-cistern truck.

It was a desert-camo model, tricked out as a communications "rat rig," with windows tinted almost black, and hillbilly body armor—anything they could scrounge from the salvage depot—covering it from grille to bumper. Greer got into the passenger side of the front seat, without looking back. He knew who was there.

Lopez, cradling his trusty SAW—short for squad automatic weapon. Donlan, with a map, a laptop, and a GPS hookup. And Hasan, right behind him, in plastic cuffs, clutching his pocket-sized Koran.

Sadowski, in the driver's seat, said, "Captain?"

In reply, Greer simply lifted his chin toward the windshield, a sliver of bulletproof Plexiglas, and the Humvee, its air conditioner roaring, rumbled out of the camp and onto the road past Mosul.

This stretch of road had been officially declared mine-free and under coalition control for three weeks now. But that hadn't kept a jeep from being blown sky-high by an RPG last Thursday, or mortar fire from leaving fresh potholes in what barely passed for a highway to begin with.

No more sand, Greer thought. Ever. Not even on a beach.

"Excuse me? Mr. Greer?" Hasan asked, leaning so far forward that Greer could feel his hot breath on the back of his neck. "Shouldn't we be having more soldiers, more guns, with us?"

Greer just smiled. What was this guy smoking? Was he under the impression that this was some kind of authorized mission, instead of what it was—a nicely subsidized treasure hunt?

"We've got everything we need," Greer said. "You do what you're supposed to do, and you'll be back in time for your next interrogation."

The soldiers laughed; Hasan didn't.

For another hour they drove along what had come to be known as the Saddam Expressway, passing not much but bombed-out abandoned villages and the charred hulks of military transports, taxis, and once, improbably enough, a bright yellow school bus. How the hell, Greer had to wonder, did that get here? Lopez, cradling his SAW, zoned out with his eyes closed, while Donlan kept track of their progress.

"We should be approaching the palace," Donlan finally announced, studying his laptop in the backseat.

"Well, Hasan," Greer asked. "Anything look familiar?"

Hasan pressed his face to the dark glass and peered out. He'd grown up in this area, he'd owned the best grocery, he'd had a wife and two daughters. Now he had his life—and not much more. "Yes," he said. "You will come to a . . . a place in the road that goes two ways."

"A fork," Lopez said, from all the way in back.

"Okay, a fork," Hasan said. He hated them all so much that he was afraid they could hear it in his words, however innocent they might be. "You will turn to the right side. And go ahead for maybe three miles."

"That road going to be cleared for mines?" Sadowski asked.

Hasan had no idea. None of this was his idea.

And no one else answered, either.

"And then what should we expect?" Greer asked.

"You will see the walls—high walls, maybe ten feet high. And great iron gates."

"If they haven't been stolen," Sadowski said with a knowing smirk.

"They will not have been stolen," Hasan said with certainty. "People here are too afraid."

"Of Saddam?" Lopez piped in. "We've got him, or haven't they heard?"

"Not Saddam. They are afraid of the al-Kallis."

"What's so scary about these al-Kallis?" Lopez asked.

What could Hasan say to that? How could he explain to these ignorant men, these barbarians, who the al-Kallis were? But he had to tell them. He had to do something to put them on their guard—as they would have to be—or it could cost him his own life, too. "The al-Kallis are the oldest family in Iraq—and the most powerful. This was once their palace. Saddam took it."

"I guess he took pretty much everything," Greer observed.

"The al-Kallis will be back. They have been here for over a thousand years." He glanced down at his hands, where the cuffs were digging into his wrists. "They have been here perhaps forever."

Sadowski and Greer exchanged a smile. It was just this kind of mumbo-jumbo that made these people such easy pickin's.

"So what?" Greer asked. "So they've been around awhile."

"There are stories," Hasan said, knowing full well that they were mocking him. He tried to turn his hands to increase the circulation. "The al-Kallis have . . . powers. Strange things happen there. You have to be very careful."

"Who you gonna call?" Lopez sang out, shaking his weapon. "GhostBUSTERS!" The soldiers laughed, though Hasan had no idea why. It crossed his mind, for an instant, that if he could just find a way to kill them all himself—and he wouldn't hesitate—he could commandeer the car and escape.

But to where?

The Humvee rumbled on, over a road covered with so much windblown sand that at times it was impossible to see. Sadowski leaned toward the windshield and stared through the glare. He couldn't get the question of land mines out of his head; two of his pals from the 3rd Infantry Division had been in a nineteen-ton Stryker armored combat vehicle that had been hit by a roadside bomb just the week before, and each had left a leg behind.

Far ahead, unless he was imagining it, he thought he saw some whitewashed walls rising like a mirage out of the desert sands. If these were the walls Hasan had been talking about, his estimate was way too low—these walls were more like fifteen or twenty feet high, if he could judge from this distance. And they went on for what looked like a quarter of a mile, on one side alone. Sadowski had already "liberated" two of Saddam's palaces—they hadn't really seemed all that much more spectacular than the houses he saw on MTV's *Cribs,* and nothing like what he thought of when he heard the word "palace"—but this place looked like something else.

"Should be dead ahead, about a half mile due west," Donlan reported.

"I can see it," Sadowski replied.

There were towers, too, narrow white columns set far back from the walls and rising like gleaming needles into the air; the whole compound had to be enormous. Even the roadside began to change. There were date palms lining both sides of the road, along with the desiccated remains of other plants that had died from lack of water. Sadowski could imagine that this was once a very grand entryway.

Captain Greer picked up a pair of binoculars and scanned the walls ahead for enemy activity. But the only sign of life he saw was a flock of evil-looking crows, lining the parapets above the main gate. The gates themselves, as Hasan had predicted, were intact; no telling whether they were locked or not. Just in case, he'd brought along a couple of plastic explosives charges.

"Stop about fifty yards short," Greer told Sadowski, then added, "You'll stay with the vehicle, and keep the motor running."

The Humvee ground to a slow halt on the sandy road, and Hasan said a silent prayer. No one he knew had ever penetrated the al-Kalli palace walls; no one he knew had ever wanted to. For generations, mothers in the region had warned their unruly children that if they didn't behave, they would be sold to the al-Kallis. And whenever anyone went missing, it was darkly hinted that they had strayed too close to the al-Kalli palace.

On some nights, when the wind was right, local villagers claimed that they could hear strange and savage cries.

While Sadowski waited in the Humvee, the others all got out.

"Looks like nobody's home so far," Greer announced as he approached the gates with his Beretta in hand. Donlan stayed a few feet behind Hasan, who had nothing to protect him but the Koran pressed between his cuffed hands as if his life depended on it.

Greer went to the gates, which were also at least twenty feet high, and although they were stiff from disuse, their hinges choked with sand, they weren't locked; he was actually able to push one a few feet back; to work so well now, they must have been made with fantastic precision in their day. There was a design of some kind, elaborate flourishes of metalwork that looked like writing. He turned to Hasan.

"Does this say something?"

Hasan nodded.

"Well?"

How could he translate this properly? Hasan wondered. It was archaic, a few lines of verse that even he could not entirely make out. But the gist of it was clear. "It's a welcome, and it is a warning."

"That's what I've been hearing ever since I got here," Donlan said.

"Just tell me what it says," Greer said.

"It says, 'Welcome to the traveler of good . . .'" He couldn't come up with the word. He'd studied English in school, and he'd even once spent a summer with an uncle in Miami, but he couldn't find the equivalent now.

"Go on."

"'Such a traveler may stay the night inside these walls. But the traveler who does not have a heart so . . . good, he will regret his mother ever gave him milk.'"

"Not exactly *'mi casa es su casa,'*" Greer remarked before slipping through the opening between the two gates.

Hasan looked up at the fat crows above the gate. Their wings fluttered and their hoarse cawing was carried down to him on the hot desert wind. How, he thought, had he come to be in this place, with these men? One night, bombs had landed all over his village; he'd been at the soccer field. By the time he'd run home, his house was a pile of swirling dust and broken bricks—with his wife and children inside. And then he'd been arrested. For what—not dying?

He felt a rifle poke him in the back. "Come on, Hasan," Donlan said, "you might still come in handy."

With Greer leading the way, they entered the palace grounds. First, there was a tunnel, big enough to drive a truck through, which appeared to end in another iron gate, this one with sharpened spikes at its base, raised high above their heads. Their footsteps echoed around them.

"Yo-de-lay-e-hoo!" Lopez crooned softly, and Greer whirled around with his gun pointed straight at Lopez's head.

"What the *fuck*?" he whispered angrily.

Lopez stood, chastened, the gun still aimed at his forehead. He'd just wanted to make a joke—you know, lighten things up a little. It was the way he'd always been.

"You out of your mind, Lopez?"

"Sorry, Captain." He kept his eyes down; he knew Greer was right. He'd been told before that his mouth would wind up getting him killed. "Won't happen again."

"Next time I just shoot."

Greer turned around again, and one by one, instinctively spreading out, they emerged from the tunnel and into what looked like a huge forecourt to the palace. It must have been several acres of land, all covered with something under all the sand that felt as smooth and hard as marble. In front of them, at the top of a wide set of steps, was a huge and very grand palace of pale yellow stone, several stories high, and topped with the kind of dome Greer normally associated with a mosque. He pulled from the inside pocket of his jacket the folded map, sealed in a plastic sheath, that he'd been sent when he accepted this gig. He oriented himself quickly, and determined that this was indeed the main house—there were others in the compound, for servants and the like—and that what he was looking for lay somewhere behind it, off to the right.

He turned and gestured for the soldiers, and Hasan, to follow him. The soldiers looked puzzled for a moment and glanced longingly at the palace, as if to say, "Aren't we busting in there?" and Greer understood their impulse. God knew what stuff might still be lying around inside, especially if Hasan was right, and the locals were too scared to set foot in there—but that wasn't what he'd come to do. He'd come to find, and retrieve, one thing, and once he had that, he was out of here.

It was a long walk around the side of the palace, but fortunately there was a sort of colonnade that provided some shade from the rays of the late afternoon sun. The heat was still nearly unbearable and, apparently, it had been too much for a couple of birds, whose bodies lay sprawled in the dust, their tail feathers spread like fans around them.

"Peacocks," Hasan said. "It was the al-Kallis' favorite."

But these looked like they'd been picked clean with a knife and fork. All that was left were brittle bones and a spray of flattened feathers, a faint vestige of their purple and blue iridescence glinting in the sun.

Greer motioned for the men to keep moving, his eyes swiveling from one side of the grounds to the other. They passed several smaller buildings—in one they could see the dust-choked grillwork of a Rolls-Royce, in another what looked like horse stalls—before coming to a short bridge spanning what was now a stagnant stream of green water. Greer tested the wood, pressing down with his boot, but it seemed solid. They crossed over, and into another vast courtyard, surrounded on all sides by towering palm trees. Underfoot, there was a length of fine meshed chain; Greer bent down to lift it up, but realized then that it was under both his feet—and under the feet of all his men, too. The chain was everywhere.

"What do you think they were trying to catch in this net?" he wondered out loud.

Nobody answered.

Greer look at Hasan, who lifted his cuffed hands to point toward the top of one of the trees. "You see the hook?"

Greer turned to see, and damned if Hasan wasn't right—way up toward the top, there was a large iron hook driven into the trunk of the tree.

"They all have such hooks," Hasan said.

"I still don't get it," Donlan said.

"The net was not used to catch anything," Hasan explained. "It was tied to those hooks and used to keep something in."

"Oh, you mean the birds? The peacocks?"

Hasan shrugged. If that's what they chose to think . . .

"What are we looking for, anyway, sir?" Donlan asked. "It's going to be dark soon."

Greer was studying the map; they were close. Straight ahead, there was a row of what had looked like little boxes on the map, but which he could now see were, in reality, cages, with loose straw thrown around their wooden floors. Some of the cages were small enough to hold a pair of rabbits; some were big enough for a couple of rhinos. All were enclosed at the top, too—and most of them were oddly dented, as if the creatures inside them had been banging their heads against the iron bars. On the last one in the row, the gates had been bent forward so far that they hung open on the twisted hinges.

"What'd they do—keep a zoo?" Donlan said.

There was the smell of a zoo, too, in the air. Although no animals were to be seen, the fetid scent of manure, rotting hay, and mangy fur still lingered. Behind a row of eucalyptus trees, and nearly concealed by dead vines and wilted flowers, Greer saw what he'd been looking for—the structure that was highlighted on the map with a yellow pen. It looked like an oversized mausoleum, made of the same yellow stone as the palace.

"Follow me," he said, striding up its steps and stopping at a pair of massive wooden doors, studded with iron bolts; with his gun still drawn, he pushed his way inside.

The place was built like an atrium—circular, with ladders and rails made of olive wood running along all the sides. There were hundreds of shelves, many of them with old leather-bound books still on them, spiraling upward toward a domed ceiling; in its center, there was a stained-glass window that cast a pale purple light over everything below.

"Nothing but books in here," Lopez said. "I say we go back to the palace."

"I say shut up," Greer said, folding up the map and slipping it back into his pocket; from here on in, he knew what to do.

Mounted on the front wall was a big iron bird—okay, a peacock—with its wings spread wide. "Come here, Lopez," Greer said. "And take hold of one of these wings."

Lopez looked confused, but he leaned his rifle up against one of the bookshelves and did as he was told. The bird was about six feet high and four feet wide, and the metal was warm in his hands. Would this thing be worth anything, he wondered, back in the States?

"When I say so," Greer told him, "press the wing forward."

"You want me to break it?" Now it'd be worth nothing.

"Just do it. Now."

As Greer pressed on his side, Lopez pressed on his, and after some initial resistance, the two wings began to give way.

"Keep pushing," Greer said.

Gradually, the two wings began to come together, and as they did so, dust began to crumble from the wall just below the peacock's feet.

Lopez, seeing the dust, started to ease up, and Greer said, "No, that's what's supposed to happen."

"The whole place is supposed to fall down?"

Donlan, though he kept his rifle loosely trained on Hasan, was rapt.

As the ends of the two wings touched, a narrow space below the peacock's feet was partially revealed. According to his instructions, something should have opened up completely, but this was close enough for Greer. He crouched down and dug his fingers into the wall. Loose bits of brick and sand fell away, enough finally for him to reach inside—the slot was no more than ten inches high and perhaps a few feet across—and touch something. It was a metal box, covered with dust, and it was what he'd come for. When he pulled, he could hear the crunching of the sand underneath it, but moving it from this angle was tough. He pulled his hand out, brushed it clean, then reached in again and pulled the box another inch or two forward; it must weigh twenty or thirty pounds, he guessed.

"You need some help, Captain?" Lopez asked eagerly. Maybe Greer knew what he was doing, after all. Maybe this was the treasure!

Greer didn't need any help—not now. Leaning back on

his heels, he pulled the box out of the hole. It was matted with grime, and for all he knew, the damn thing was made of lead. Huge iron clasps were sealed on both sides, with antique padlocks that looked like they took a key the size of a fist.

Lopez looked at the locks gleefully and said, "We can pop those—no problem."

Greer stood up, cradling the box in his arms. "Time to go."

Lopez and Donlan just stood there. Hasan was afraid of what might happen.

"What do you mean, sir?" Donlan asked. "You mean, we open it back at camp?"

"I mean, we go. Now."

Greer stepped around them, giving Hasan a shove toward the door. Donlan and Lopez traded a glance—*what gives?*—then slouched behind.

Outside, the shadows were lengthening. The sun had fallen to the height of the walls, and a night wind was already beginning to kick up.

Greer was marching Hasan past the rows of empty cages, then onto the wooden bridge. Hasan was only too glad to go. He didn't know what those cages had once held, but he did not want to find out. Nor did he wish to know why the al-Kallis would have needed a fine mesh net large enough to have created an aviary a hundred feet high and ten times as wide.

As they passed the garage with the Rolls parked inside, Lopez cast a covetous glance inside. What if the thing still ran? Why couldn't he drive it back to camp, right behind the Humvee? Wouldn't that be something?

But then, he could swear he saw something move inside the garage. No, not that he'd actually *seen* something, but the light in there, the shadows, had changed. He glanced ahead at the others—was it worth calling out an alarm? He looked again, his rifle leveled at the front of the Rolls. But now there was nothing, and the others were even farther away.

He picked up his pace, his head turned to keep an eye on anything behind him. He was sorry he'd listened to all that bullshit from Hasan. Strange cries in the night, people disappearing. But he was even sorrier that he'd listened to Greer. What was all that crap about a treasure hunt? The only treasure he'd seen—and who knew what was inside that box?—was now gripped in Greer's loving arms.

On his left, he saw what he took to be the stables—there were empty stalls and unidentifiable pieces of harness hanging from the half doors. Lopez was from Santa Fe, and he'd actually worked summers at a ranch, but he'd never seen tackle like this. Maybe the al-Kallis kept those famous Arabian stallions he'd heard so much about.

As they approached the back of the palace, he scanned the many narrow windows, wondering what lay behind them. Christ, did people really live like this? The palace reminded him of pictures he'd seen of places like the Taj Mahal. By joining the army he thought he'd see some of them. But so far, this was it.

There was a cry, a loud, prolonged cawing from somewhere in the distance. It sounded like a baby being strangled.

"Jesus," Lopez exclaimed. "What was that?"

They'd all stopped in their tracks.

"It was a peacock," Hasan said. "They cry for rain."

Lopez swallowed hard—his mouth was suddenly as dry as the desert. "They ever get it?"

"Not often."

In the colonnade, the shadows made a kind of zigzag pattern on the floor. The sun had fallen now to just below the top of the outside walls. Their footsteps echoed here, too, but Lopez knew enough to make no *Ghostbuster* jokes this time. He pulled the damp collar away from his neck, and as he did so, he thought he heard breathing behind him, a low rasping sound. He whipped around, his finger on the trigger of the rifle, but there was nothing but a row of stone columns, glowing like burnished gold in the dying sun.

"Hey," he said, and the others stopped and turned toward him.

"What?" Donlan said.

"I thought I heard something."

"Hasan already told you—it's peacocks."

"No. Something else."

Greer wedged the box under one arm and took out his gun. "Let's keep moving.'"

The back of Lopez's neck tingled, and it wasn't the drying sweat. He felt as though he were being watched. Tracked. He thought of the coyotes he'd shot back in New Mexico—and he felt like one of them.

"When we get around front," Greer said, "spread out in a—"

And then it was on top of Lopez. A running shadow, a huge black stain, it lunged out from behind one of the columns and snatched him like a wolf picking off a stray lamb. Donlan panicked and sprayed a burst of automatic fire around the colonnade; Hasan flattened himself against the inside wall, but Greer suddenly felt something like a splash of hot water on his left leg. He knew he'd been hit by a ricochet, but he didn't have time to look. He needed to get himself, and the box, out of there.

He tried to run, but his leg was barely able to hold him up.

Donlan was still firing as they fell back. Hasan was probably hiding somewhere back there. Screw it—who needed him anymore?

Greer hobbled across the marble forecourt, leaving, he knew, a trail of blood. Whatever the hell that thing had been, it would sure as hell pick up this scent. He forced himself to keep moving—the adrenaline, blissfully, was keeping the leg from exploding in pain, but that wouldn't last much longer. He could hear Donlan reloading. Night was falling fast, the way it did here—he could just make out the gates.

Keep moving, he told himself. *Keep moving.*

He dragged himself into the tunnel, shouting ahead to Sadowski, "We've been hit!"

But he doubted his voice would carry into the closed Humvee.

Donlan was firing again—was he shooting at something, Greer wondered, or just shooting?

The headlights were on, and Greer careened into their glow, waving one arm.

Sadowski spotted him, and leapt out of the vehicle.

"Help me!" Greer shouted.

Sadowski tried to take the box from him, but Greer said, "Just open the damn door!"

Sadowski threw open the passenger door, and Greer tossed the box onto the floor.

There was another crackling round of shots, and then Donlan raced up to them, panting.

As Greer clambered, bleeding, into the front seat, Donlan jumped into the back as if there were a tiger on his tail.

"Where's Lopez?" Sadowski shouted, and Greer said, "He's gone. Let's move."

Sadowski slammed the door after Greer, then ran around to the driver's seat. *Lopez was gone? Dead?*

He threw the Humvee into gear. "What about Hasan?"

"I said move!"

As the vehicle started to turn in a wide circle, the headlights picked up something else—a figure running toward them, arms extended as if in supplication.

Hasan, in the handcuffs.

Sadowski glanced at Greer for his orders. Surely he didn't plan to just leave him here?

But a second later, something descended upon Hasan like a frenzied black cloud. Sadowski heard a scream, saw Hasan's terror-stricken eyes widen in the glare of the headlights, before the thing had yanked him off his feet and into the night. All that was left in the headlight beams was that little black copy of the Koran.

Sadowski's hands were frozen at the wheel.

"Drive," Greer barked at him, wincing and clutching at his leg. "Can't you see I'm bleeding?"

CHAPTER ONE

Present Day

CARTER COX DIDN'T have to be down in the bottom of Pit 91. As a visiting fellow to the George C. Page Museum of Natural History, and head of its paleontology field research department, he could have been sitting in his comfortable, air-conditioned office overlooking Wilshire Boulevard. Instead of wearing overalls and a Green Day T-shirt, he could have been in a suit and tie—well, maybe not a tie, not many men wore ties in L.A., Carter had noticed—and his hands could be clean and his hair combed and his shoes shined.

But then he wouldn't have been half this happy.

Right now, at the bottom of the tar pit, the temperature hovered in the high eighties, his hair was gathered under a sweaty headband, and his hiking boots were covered with a viscous coating of warm, black tar. Asphalt, actually. Even though these were called the La Brea Tar Pits, it was asphalt, the lowest grade of crude oil, that had been bubbling up under this ground for the past thirty or forty thousand years; those were methane bubbles that still rose lazily to the surface of the pit, swelling up like bullfrogs, before popping without a sound. And those were prehistoric bones, miraculously preserved in this thick, black goo, that he was still able to excavate with a chisel, a brush, and a lot of elbow grease.

The pit itself was about fifty feet square, with wooden boards propping up the walls on all sides (in case of a cave-in or an earthquake), and rusty iron girders supporting the boards. It was open-air, about twenty-five feet deep, with a slanted plastic roof overhead to keep off the sun (or the rain, though in May in Los Angeles rain wasn't much of a problem), and that was about it. Rows of heavy black buckets were stacked on the north wall for glopping out the bottom of the pit, and a thick red chain hung down from the pulley above.

Today, Carter had a crew of three working for him. These were all volunteers who'd been trained by the museum. Claude, a retired engineer, was working on a three-foot grid in the east quadrant; Rosalie, a middle-aged teacher taking a year off, was working beside him; and next to Carter—where he usually seemed to find her—was Miranda. Miranda had just graduated from UCLA with a bachelor's degree in anthropology, and she was trying to decide if this kind of work was what she really wanted to do.

At the moment, it didn't look that way.

"I think," she said, "I'm stuck again." She was kneeling on the boards that crisscrossed the floor of the pit, just above the area she was excavating, with her hands deep into the muck. Too deep, Carter knew. When you reached down to pull out the tar—and yeah, he had to concede that he called it that, too—you had to be careful not to dig down too far or to try to take out too much at one time. The stuff had been trapping animals of all kinds—from woolly mammoths to saber-toothed cats—for thousands of years, and it wasn't done yet.

"Just relax," Claude called out. "Pull slowly."

"I am," she said nervously, glancing up at Carter, who sat back on his haunches and wiped the sweat from his brow.

"You're pushing down with one hand while you're trying to pull out the other," he said. He inched along the board until he was shoulder to shoulder with her. "That means you're getting one hand trapped after the other." He put his hands on her forearms, then began to pull them up, slowly, with equal force. The tar was especially warm today, which made it even more resistant than ever. Their faces were just inches apart, so close he could smell that she'd recently popped a couple of Tic Tacs into her mouth.

"There's something down there," she said. "Something big. I can feel it."

"There's always something down there," Carter said, as her arms slowly emerged from the hole. "So far, they've got about two million finds catalogued in the museum."

"How many from this particular pit?"

"A lot," he said as her hands emerged, black and glistening with goo; the stuff was too thick to drip. "That's why we keep digging here."

She leaned back with a sigh. "Thanks. You're a lifesaver."

"Not a problem," Carter said. "I had to promise the museum I wouldn't let any of my crew get swallowed in the pit."

"What happens if one of us does?" Claude asked.

"There's a ten-dollar fine," Carter replied, "and I lose my parking privileges for a week."

"Good thing we signed up for your shift," Rosalie said, as she plopped a handful of wet tar into a waiting bucket, and they all laughed.

GETTING THE STUFF off your hands and out of your hair always took at least half an hour. There were showers installed in a trailer parked right next to the pit, equipped with loofahs, pumice stones, sponges, long-handled brushes, shampoo, and enough skin scrub to clean a battleship.

Your work clothes you left hanging on a wooden peg. You were never going to wear them for anything else as long as you lived.

Carter got into a fresh pair of jeans, a blue Polo shirt, and white sneakers. Although he'd never been what you'd call formal, this was still a far cry from the way he'd dressed when he held the Kingsley Chair in Paleontology and Vertebrate Biology at New York University. There, he'd at least have worn a shirt with long sleeves. But everything in L.A. was more casual, and it was one of the things, he had to admit, that made the city appealing.

So did the weather. It was late afternoon now, and even though the pit tended to trap the heat, the air outside it, in the surrounding park, was mild. A breeze was stirring the tops of the palm trees, and squirrels were scampering up the trunk of a California oak. Carter hadn't ever planned on living in L.A.—he'd always nursed the standard-issue Eastern prejudices against the glitz and superficiality of the place—but when he looked at it objectively, as the scientist he was trained to be, he had to concede that the climate was advantageous, too.

As were the job opportunities, if it came to that.

After the lab disaster at NYU, he'd become pretty much persona non grata in the department. He had tenure and an endowed chair, but he didn't have anybody's faith or loyalty. In fact, people hardly knew where to look when they passed him in the halls. So when his wife, Beth, got the call from the Getty art museum, inviting her to come and work for them in L.A., the two of them only had to think about it overnight before deciding she should take it.

The only question had been what Carter would do. But with his scholarly credentials still as impressive and unchallenged as they'd been before the accident, it hadn't been hard for him to find a post on the West Coast himself. The tough part, in fact, had been sorting through all the offers.

But their lifestyle here couldn't be more different. In New York, they'd lived in a cramped apartment on Washington Square Park; here they rented, from a museum trustee who was generous enough to take a loss, a fully furnished house in a private, gated community called Summit View. To get there you took a main artery, Sepulveda Boulevard, which wound along beside the San Diego Freeway. It was a looping, dipping, four-lane highway with brushy hills on one side, and the freeway up above on the other, and while most people preferred the freeway because you could move a lot faster (when it wasn't slowed to a crawl), Carter liked the Sepulveda route because it felt more like a road to him. It wasn't predictable, it wasn't jammed with traffic, it had character (including a tunnel through the Santa Monica Mountains that you had to pass through to get to the San Fernando Valley). Today, for a Friday afternoon, the traffic wasn't bad, and he'd only had time to listen to maybe forty-five minutes of a taped lecture on the Galápagos Islands before he was pulling into the Summit View drive.

The minute you hit the drive, it was like entering another world. It was a broad, empty concourse that swept up into the hills, past neatly cropped lawns and a pristine community center. Halfway up, as always, Carter spotted the private patrol car parked on the right. Carter gave the cop a wave—at this time on a weekday, it'd be Al Burns—then continued on toward the top of the rise.

Their house was on the left, with a flagstone drive in front of the garage. It was a modern house, white, with a sloping red-tile roof, and coming home to it was still a new enough experience to Carter that he felt out of place parking in its driveway.

But it wasn't just the unfamiliarity of the place that struck him every time; it was the silence. All the houses that lined both sides of the wide, winding street were neat and orderly and silent as the grave. Not a kid playing in the street, not a lawn mower growling, not a light on in any of the windows, not a stereo blaring anywhere. And not a soul on the immaculate, new sidewalks.

To be honest, it felt a little creepy. But he told himself he'd get used to it.

"I'm home," he called out, coming through the door. He dropped his backpack, heavy with books and papers, on the parquet floor of the foyer. "Hello?"

No answer. He'd expected to hear from Robin, the nanny they'd hired to help out with the baby.

"Robin? You here?"

He climbed the stairs—thickly carpeted by the owner when he learned that Carter and Beth had a one-year-old—and headed for the nursery. Beth was in the corner rocking chair, her sweatshirt hiked up, nursing little Joey. "I didn't want to shout," she whispered.

"Where's Robin?"

"I didn't go in today, so I gave her the day off."

"Still got that cold?"

"I can't seem to shake this one."

"The prince looks happy."

"Oh yeah—nothing bothers this guy." It was something they joked about—Joey had yet to have a cold, an ear infection, colic, you name it. They'd been prepared by all the baby books for a litany of problems and complaints, but so far . . . nada. This kid was made of steel.

"You want me to make some dinner?" Carter asked.

"I'm not hungry. But there's still some of that salmon from last night."

"That's fine," Carter said. "I'll leave you to it," he said, nodding at the busy Joey.

Downstairs, he took a Heineken out of the fridge and, as there wouldn't be any witnesses, drank it straight from the bottle. The mail was on the counter—some bills, a couple of catalogues—but what looked like a more interesting pile of papers lay scattered on the butcher-block table in the breakfast nook. Carter pushed out two of the chairs, rested his long legs across one, and turned some of the papers around so he could read them.

The cover letter, addressed to Beth, was from Berenice Cabot, an important administrator at the Getty, asking her to examine the contents enclosed and prepare for a meeting with the owner of the work of art displayed there, a man whose anonymity Mrs. Cabot had been asked at this point to maintain. That wasn't so unusual, Carter knew; museums often dealt with wealthy donors who didn't want their names made public until they chose to do so themselves.

By now Carter felt he should probably stop snooping. This was between Beth and the Getty, he thought as he took another swig from the bottle. But then, she *had* left it all out in plain view. In a court of law, wasn't that justification enough? And what harm could it do just to take a little peek at some of the photos enclosed? Even a quick glance told him they were pretty unusual.

He put the letter aside and looked at the glossy eight-by-ten that lay on top of the pile. It showed a massive old book, with what looked like an ivory cover, studded with jewels. A ruler, laid beside it in the shot to offer scale, indicated that its pages were large—perhaps two feet long and almost as wide. Although Carter was no expert in this sort of thing, it reminded him of ancient books he'd seen in Europe, most notably the Book of Kells at Trinity College, Dublin. That volume dated from the eighth century, and this book looked, to his unpracticed eye, to be in the same league.

The other photos, their colors muted by what Carter guessed to be insufficient light, were of the book's contents. And most appeared to be of fanciful creatures, mythological beasts made up of strange composites—the heads of lions on the bodies of snakes, a chicken's beak on a lumbering bear, a towering giraffe with eight legs and a prominently displayed set of curving tusks. They were all rendered in the primitive, but forceful, medieval style Carter had seen in some of Beth's textbooks from her days as a student at the Courtauld Institute of Art in London.

"Snoop," she said as she padded into the kitchen in her stocking feet.

"You caught me."

She plopped onto his lap and leaned her back against the edge of the table.

"Looks like they've got you working from home."

"Mrs. Cabot messengered those over this morning." She was wearing matching sweatpants, too, and had her black hair tied up hastily in a ponytail.

"What's she want you to do?" Carter asked innocently.

She smiled. "Didn't you read the cover letter first?"

Carter laughed. "So when are you supposed to meet with Mr. Mysterious? It failed to specify that."

"Who knows? Whenever he chooses to come forward."

"Looks like a very interesting project."

She snuggled closer. "I think so, too. It looks like one of the earliest and most complete bestiaries ever found. I can't wait to get my hands on it."

"And I can't wait to get my hands on you," Carter said, wrapping his arms around her; she smelled of Dove, Prell, and milk, a combination he would never have thought could be so heady. "You know, with the prince asleep . . . ," he said suggestively, running his hand up the front of her sweatshirt.

"And the queen so sore," she said, taking his hand away but kissing the knuckles. She laid her head on his shoulder, and as he held her, Carter's eye fell on a photo lying upside down on the table. He reached out and turned it around, to see what at first he took to be a beautiful illuminated picture of a peacock. Its head was turned to one side, its tail feathers were fanned out in a wide display, but unlike any peacock he'd ever seen, this one was bright red and had an unmistakable aura of menace. Its eyes glowed like rubies, and its talons looked as sharp and gnarled as thorns. It reminded him less of an ornamental creature than a prehistoric bird of prey.

CHAPTER TWO

THE VETERANS ADMINISTRATION hospital was just off Wilshire Boulevard, but most motorists never even noticed it. They were too busy looking for the on-ramp to the 405 freeway, and traffic at this spot as a result was almost always a nightmare—even by L.A. standards.

The hospital access ramp was separate from all the others, and every time Greer took it he felt slighted. As his beaten-up Mustang convertible left the other cars, he felt afresh his injuries. All those bastards driving by, he thought, had no idea of the pain he'd suffered, and the wounds he had borne, fighting for his country in Iraq. It was just so damn easy to drive on by, in your Mercedes or your SUV, babbling into your cell phone, and never give another thought to guys like himself who had made the big sacrifices.

And for what? That was one question that had kept him up more nights than he cared to count.

By now, he knew the VA routine inside out. He parked his car in one of the few spots that offered any shade, checked in with the security guard, who always demanded that he show his credentials every time he came in (one more way for the military to still stick it to you), and then hobbled down the hall to the physical therapy clinic.

Most of the other patients in there he knew—there was Gruber, who'd lost both hands to a booby trap in Tikrit; and Rodriguez, who'd stepped on a land mine outside Basra; and Mariani, who'd never talk to anybody about what had happened to put him in that wheelchair. Greer would look around at all these other guys, many of whom had suffered far worse injuries than he had, and try to make himself feel better. See, he'd say, you could be pushing yourself around like Mariani, or using clampers for hands like Gruber, or clomping around like Rodriguez on a carbon-fiber leg. But it never worked the way he wanted it to; he was just as pissed and bitter when he left as when he arrived.

Indira was his usual therapist, and today she had the table already prepared for him. "How are we feeling, Captain Greer?" she said, smoothing the paper cover on the table nearest the windows. "Are we grumpy as usual?"

He never knew how to answer stuff like that. *Affirmative?*

She patted the table with a smile, as if she were urging a dog to jump up onto the sofa. "Come on and get ready. I'll get the towels."

There was a changing room to one side, and he went in there, put most of his clothes and valuables in a locker, and came back out in his clean T-shirt and running shorts. He refused to wear those open gowns.

Indira was waiting, and as soon as he levered himself up onto the table, she slipped a small pillow under the crook of his neck, another one under his knees, then gently wrapped the hot towels around his left leg. He tried not to let her see him studying her as she did all that, but he suspected that she was aware of it. The first time he'd seen her, he was so consumed with pain and rage that he'd hardly noticed her. But the next time, and the time after that, he'd been able to take a good look.

She wasn't like anyone he'd ever known. She was small, with dark hair and dark eyes, and her skin was a kind of copper color. Kind of like the Iraqis'. She didn't talk a lot about herself, but over the many sessions he'd had, he'd learned a few things. She was from Bombay, which accounted for that kind of singsong way she spoke, and she was something called a Zoroastrian. It was some ancient religion (he'd looked it up on the Internet) that believed in cycles of fire, or something like that, lasting millions of years. She lived somewhere in West L.A., with her parents and a bunch of brothers and sisters. He could never figure out a way to ask her how old she was, but he was thirty and he knew that she had to be younger than that.

"Let's give it fifteen minutes," she said, setting an egg timer and leaving it by his feet. "Tell me if it gets too hot."

The heat was used to limber up the leg, before they tried the exercises designed to increase the muscle tone and range of motion. He'd never told her how his leg had been injured, and she'd never asked; he wondered if that was part of their training. Wait till the gimp volunteered the information; don't press him on it. He knew a lot of the guys—like Mariani in the wheelchair—didn't want to talk about it. And in his case, he was just as happy to keep quiet. When he'd been brought into the camp's medical tent outside Mosul, Sadowski had corroborated his story; they'd been conducting a perimeter patrol when a sniper had taken a potshot. In those days, not a lot of questions got asked; everything was up for grabs, and sniper attacks were an hourly occurrence. The army had given him his Purple Heart, his honorable discharge, and a monthly disability check that didn't go nearly far enough.

He lay on his back, staring at the ceiling, listening to the ticking of the timer and the grunts and groans and murmured conversations of the other vets talking to their therapists and going through their agonizing drills. Still, he kind of looked forward to these sessions; the government paid, and Indira took care of him.

When the timer went off, she came back, unwrapped the towels and tossed them into the bin, then told him to bend the knee. At first it wouldn't go.

"I'll help," she said, lifting the leg slightly. "Tell me if you need to stop."

Her hands were cool and smooth, and the leg felt better just from her touch. He tried to flex the knee, but sometimes it felt like the damn thing had just locked in place. Like right now.

"Just relax," she said, "let me bend it. Don't you try to do anything."

He closed his eyes, and willed himself, or tried to, into a state of passivity. Indira gently flexed the knee, a few degrees at a time, then went through the other exercises, bringing the leg slowly to one side and then the other, to make sure he wasn't losing lateral motion. She had him do some standing exercises, a couple of squats that were more like crouches, and finished up, as usual, with the ultrasound, designed to penetrate the muscles and break up the scar tissue.

"Are you doing your exercises at home?" Indira asked, as usual, and Greer, as usual, lied that he was.

"Are you okay on your meds?"

"I'm running low on the Demerols, and I'm out of the Vicodin."

She gave him a puzzled look. "Didn't we get you a renewal on the Vicodin last time?"

"Yeah, but I spilled 'em. Most went down the kitchen sink."

She frowned. "You know, those can be addictive," she said. "We're limited on what we can prescribe."

"Oh yeah, sure, I know that," he assured her. He could never tell if she knew he was lying, or if she was just doing what she could to help.

"I'll see what I can do," she said, and as she went off to the clinic dispensary to see if she could get him a new prescription, Greer got dressed and checked the time. He was due to meet Sadowski at the Blue Bayou, the strip club where Sadowski's girlfriend danced.

Indira, God bless her, got him the pills—"They were very suspicious," she told him, "and next time we will have to get an okay from Dr. Foster"—and he slipped them into the breast pocket of his shirt on the way out to the parking lot. The sun had moved, and the steering wheel had come

out of the shade; it was blazing hot when he tried to hold it.
He flicked on the radio, and used a crumpled page of the
L.A. Weekly to hold the wheel.

Going against traffic, it took him only ten minutes or so
to drive down toward the ocean and pull up in front of the
club. He hung his Handicapped placard on the rearview
mirror, and noticed that parked right behind him was a
Silver Bear Security Service patrol car. Sadowski was already here.

Inside, the place was nearly empty. The stage lights
were off, and a guy with a mop was washing down the runway for tonight's show.

Greer got a Jack Daniel's at the bar from Zeke, who
asked him in a low voice, "That it?" Zeke also sold him his
drugs, especially the ones the VA would never prescribe.

"Yeah," Greer said. "I'm set."

Zeke nodded and moved off.

Sadowski was sitting in the back booth, with a beer and a
copy of some gun catalogue spread out in front of him. He
was a big guy, with a slack face and closely cropped, bristly
hair—Greer had once kidded him, when he first got the job
at the security service, that he looked like a silver bear, so
how could they have turned him down? Sadowski had kind
of liked the joke.

"What are you shopping for now?" Greer asked, easing
himself into the booth. "An anti-aircraft gun?" Sadowski,
he knew, already had a private arsenal better than the one
they'd had in Iraq.

"Ammo clips, Captain."

"I told you, you don't have to call me that anymore,"
Greer said. "And what, they don't give you ammunition to
go with your piece?" He gestured at the pistol strapped in
its holster to Sadowski's side. He was wearing his full
uniform—silver-gray shirt, pants, and sidearm.

"Nah, this is stuff I need for home use. Steel-jacketed
shells."

Greer didn't even ask what he'd need them for. Sadowski was part of some secret militia that was arming itself
and getting ready for Armageddon, and whenever he tried

to tell Greer about it—or get him to enlist—Greer would just nod, then turn the conversation back to business.

As he did now.

"So, what's the big rush? You said you had something?"

Sadowski took a swig of his beer and pushed the gun catalogue to one side; under it, there were some folded papers.

"Owner's leaving tomorrow morning, be gone for one day," he said, opening the top paper and showing Greer a color photocopy of a Colonial-style house behind a red brick wall.

"Jesus, you could have given me a little more warning."

"I only found out today."

Greer wearily reached out and turned the papers around to see them better. Under the picture there was a blueprint, with several points circled in red.

"I have to do any cutting?"

"No, I can give you the codes, if you want 'em."

"Isn't that going to be a little obvious?"

"There's one entrance, in back, that's not wired yet. It's part of an addition that was just put on. You can't see it in the picture."

Greer studied the papers. For over a year now, he and Sadowski had had a nice little business going on the side. Sadowski would hand over information about Silver Bear clients whose homes were going to be left unattended—clients were instructed to tell the firm whenever they were going to be away for more than twenty-four hours—and Greer would burglarize them. Sadowski received a 25 percent finder's fee, based on whatever the value of the fenced goods turned out to be.

"Any idea what's inside?" Greer asked, washing down a couple of Vicodin. He liked to know what he was looking for, and what he might expect to find. He worked alone, and he was not about to start carting out big-screen TVs and desktop computers; he was strictly interested in the small and the portable. Cash, jewelry, maybe a laptop if it presented itself.

"The guy's a doctor," Sadowski said, unhelpfully. "They like to wear Rolexes."

"Then he'll probably have it on, wherever else he is."

Sadowski pondered this, then brightened. "But these guys always have more than one watch."

Greer sighed, folded up the papers and slipped them into his jacket. "He married?"

"No."

So there might not be much jewelry. Unless . . . "He gay?"

"Don't know. Want me to ask around?"

"Christ, no, I don't want you to ask around."

Sadowski looked stumped, which wasn't out of the ordinary. "So you gonna do it or not?"

"I'll think about it."

"Because he's only going to be—"

"I said I'll think about it," Greer repeated, leaning in close. Then he slipped out of the booth before Sadowski could invite him to a meeting of the Minutemen, or the Friends of the White Race, or whatever the hell it was he kept stockpiling his ammo for.

CHAPTER THREE

THERE WERE ABOUT twenty-five kids in the group, all sixth graders from a local school, and the docent was having a bad first day. She'd been carefully trained by the museum, given a lengthy test to make sure she knew her stuff, but she'd never actually been in charge of a group, all by herself, and peppered with quite so many questions.

"Where are the dinosaurs?"

That was an easy one. "There aren't any. The fossils from the tar pits date from the Ice Age, when the dinosaurs were already extinct."

"What about saber-toothed tigers?"

"Actually, they're not tigers at all; we call them saber-toothed cats, and yes, we've found many of those."

"How big were they? Were they as big as dinosaurs?"

"No, they were about the same size as a modern-day lion." She knew she had to move the group along, but there were always stragglers who didn't want to leave the life-sized re-creation of the giant sloth, or the glass dome covering the plungers immersed in tar. "If you'll just come this way," she said, looking in vain for their teacher—wasn't she supposed to be there, too, for the entire tour?—"we're coming to an exhibit of one of the most—"

"Could you talk louder? I can't hear you."

"Yes, of course," she said, raising her voice and detecting a surprising quaver. "We'll see an exhibit of one of the most successful predators in this region."

"A predator like in the movie?'"

For a second, she didn't even know what that meant. Then she remembered her boyfriend talking about a movie called *Predator* versus something else bad. Alien?

"Probably not. By predator, I simply mean a creature that hunted and killed other animals, for its own survival. A carnivore."

"A what?"

"A meat-eater. Like all of you."

"Not me; my mom's a vegetarian, and so am I."

"That's very laudable," she said, still trying to shepherd them to one of the Page Museum's most startling displays—a wall where 404 skulls of a creature called the dire wolf were mounted and displayed against a glowing golden light. As the kids approached, some fell silent, and some muttered things that sounded like approval. The questions were just starting to come—"Are those from a dog?" "Why are there so many?" "Did you dig those up around here?"—when she spotted her salvation walking by, in a hurry, toward the main exit.

"Dr. Cox?" she called out, and then, when he didn't seem to hear her, "Dr. Cox? Over here." She actually waved one arm feebly over the heads of the kids. "Would you like to tell these students something about the dire wolf?" To the students, she confided, "Dr. Cox has dug up several of these himself. He's a very famous paleontologist."

Carter had been on his way out to Pit 91—his crew would be assembling there in a few minutes—but he could never resist a chance to talk to students, especially when it looked like a new docent was drowning.

"Sure, the dire wolf is a good friend of mine," he said, striding to the front of the group, "and at one time he

roamed in packs all around here. Up and down Wilshire
Boulevard, all over the Farmers' Market, in Hancock Park
and Koreatown and Century City." He knew from experience that it always helped to place these extinct creatures
in the modern context at first—not only to get your listen-
ers' attention, but to bring the experience closer, to make it
clear that the animals didn't live somewhere else, as if on a
movie set, but on the very spot where, today, everyone was
walking and talking and, like the kids all the way in back,
goofing around. His comments already seemed to be having the desired effect.

"Why's he called a dryer wolf?"

Carter wanted to laugh, but he didn't want to risk em-
barrassing the questioner. "Actually," he said, keeping a
straight face, "he's called a *dire* wolf; the word 'dire'
means dreaded, frightening. And these wolves were."

Carter stood in front of the prehistoric skulls—starkly
black against the yellow light, displayed in four massive
panels sixteen shelves high—and explained how these
wolves differed from the wolf we know today. More heavily built, with a deeper chest, wider hips, shorter legs.
Originally from South America, but scattered all over Central and North America by 130,000 years ago. The domi-
nant carnivore in the New World by the Late Pleistocene.

"The late what?" one of the kids asked, and Carter had
to remind himself that he wasn't talking to NYU students
anymore.

"The Pleistocene is what we call the period of time
from about two million years ago to ten thousand years
ago." And then to make sure he had their attention again,
"The dire wolf may have had a smaller brain than any wolf
today, but he also had much bigger and more deadly teeth.
The jaws of the dire wolf were so powerful he could jump
on and bring down a much bigger animal than he was—a
bison, say, or a camel—and crush its bones with his teeth."

There was a moment of silence.

"And now I have to leave you so I can go and try to dig
up one more!" He turned to the grateful docent and said,
"They're all yours."

* * *

THE PIT, LOCATED on the museum grounds, was a two-minute walk away, and by the time he got there the afternoon crew was already at work. Claude, the retired engineer, was toiling in one corner, Rosalie in another, and Miranda had her arms up to the wrist in the goo.

"You're late," she said, teasingly. "I'm telling."

"Who are you going to tell?"

"Oh yeah, you're the big cheese."

"A quick lesson in life," Carter said. "There is always a bigger cheese."

Claude snorted as he slopped another handful of tar into his bucket. "You can say that again."

Rosalie mopped her brow with the back of one chubby arm and said, "I think I can feel a lot of stuff over here."

"Me, too," Claude said.

"Me three," Miranda chimed in. Today, she was wearing a pink tube top and a necklace of little silver beads. Not exactly what Carter would have recommended for fieldwork.

Carter glanced around; they were all working in different quadrants, carefully marked off pieces of the grid, and they were all at almost exactly the same depth.

"It's like I told you last time," Miranda said. "I can still feel something really strange down here."

Carter began to suspect they'd hit a lateral "pipe"—a section of the pit where a particularly dense concentration of fossils had accumulated. Sometimes this could happen. A large beast, perhaps a giant ground sloth or a long-horned bison, had ventured too far into the tar—which might have been concealed beneath a layer of brush and leaves, deposited by a running stream—and become trapped; just a few inches of the tar could do the trick. The youngest and strongest animals might have been able to extricate themselves, but the older ones, or the infirm, or the ones that exhausted themselves bellowing in fear and frustration, would not. Their cries would hasten their doom, in fact, drawing predators from far and wide. Packs of wolves, or saber-toothed cats, or American lions—who, unlike their African counterparts, traveled in pairs not prides—would have leapt on the trapped beast and tried to kill and devour it.

And many of them would have been trapped in turn.

Carter had seen evidence of such mad scrambles before, piles of broken bones and fangs and claws, but glancing over the wide expanse of the pit, nothing quite so broad and focused as this. What was at the bottom of it? What had attracted so many creatures to the kill, and dragged so many to their own death?

"What have you got over there, do you think?" he called to Claude.

"Can't say for sure," Claude replied, "but it feels like a neck or collarbone. I can show you right where it is."

The surface of the pit was crisscrossed with narrow wooden walkways, perched just inches above the tar; Carter walked carefully to Claude's corner, then knelt down beside him. He was wearing shorts today, and the wooden boards were sharp and hard on his knees.

"It's a few inches down," Claude said, pointing to a spot right between them.

Carter leaned forward and put one hand into the glistening black muck. It was warm and viscous, as always, and gave him a slight shiver as he plunged his hand deeper into it. His fingertips grazed something hard and angular, exactly where Claude had indicated.

"You feel it?"

"I do." But it was still so immersed in the tar, and out of sight, that he could only guess what it was. "Right now, I'd say it's a machairodont of some kind."

"A what?" Rosalie said.

"Miranda," Carter threw out, "can you answer that?"

Miranda bit her lower lip. "I'm not sure they covered that at UCLA."

"What if I said it was probably a *Smilodon fatalis*?" Carter prompted her.

"Oh, that I know!" she piped up. "It's a saber-toothed cat." Claude tried to applaud with hands coated with tar, and Miranda laughed. "I remember the name because it sounds like the cat is smiling."

"But how can you tell it's not some other cat, like a scimitar or a western dirktooth?" Claude asked. He'd been reading up on his paleontology, and Carter knew he liked to try it out.

"I can't," Carter admitted, "with any certainty." He let his fingers probe a little deeper. "But something tells me I'm touching the hyoids, or throat bones. The fact that the saber-tooths had these is what tells us they could roar like a lion." Along with the wolves, they were one of the most commonly excavated fossils at the site—a ruthless killer, with especially powerful forequarters for holding their prey while their massive fangs did the rest. While it had been commonly assumed that the cats attacked their prey by biting and breaking their necks, Carter believed they actually preferred to attack from below, ripping into the soft belly of their victims and then patiently waiting for the creature to expire from blood loss before devouring the remains. Over seven hundred saber-toothed skulls had been found at the La Brea site and only two of them had shown teeth broken with wear; if the cats had been lunging at other animals' hard and strong-muscled necks, Carter reasoned, there'd be more missing and broken teeth.

But his was the minority view so far, and he hoped soon to finish the paper that would lay out his case in full.

"What about mine?" Rosalie asked. "What have I got?"

There were moments, like right now, when Carter felt a bit like a grade school teacher, with a bunch of eager, brown-nosing students. But he also knew that this was part of the deal: In return for their volunteer service glopping out the pit, folks like Claude and Rosalie and Miranda were promised a sort of tutorial, with a real-live scientist.

"I think it's a limb of some kind," Rosalie ventured, and not to be outdone by Claude, "maybe a femur."

Carter doubted she would be able to distinguish a femur from a tusk, but he would never say anything to deflate their enthusiasm. He got up and walked slowly over to her quadrant, studying the mottled, lumpy surface of the pit as he went. It *did* look unusually uneven and, though nothing was moving but the occasional bubble of methane gradually

swelling up and then bursting, it looked somehow agitated.
He wondered if his little crew had come to some signal
event, something that had triggered a feeding frenzy of extraordinary dimensions.

"It's about six inches over, and the same distance
down," Rosalie said. She leaned back on her haunches, in a
dirty madras shirt and what looked like green slacks that
had been cut off at midthigh. "You can't miss it."

Carter knelt down again—he was tall, with long arms,
which gave him greater reach but sometimes left him precariously balanced, like a crane hovering over a construction site—and slipped his hand into the pit. The tar parted
with an audible glug, and he slipped his hand farther down.
He felt nothing so far.

"More to the left," Rosalie said.

Turning his wrist to the left, he stretched his fingers out.
Still nothing. A series of methane bubbles rose, iridescent
in the sunlight, and broke with an especially gassy pun-
gency. And then he felt it—and moved his fingers slowly,
against the protesting sludge, along its length. Rosalie was
right—it probably was a leg bone of some kind, and possibly from what was known as a short-faced bear, a precursor of the grizzly, who had entered the contiguous United
States, and departed it forever, sometime toward the end of
the last ice age. Though they stood even taller than grizzly
bears—eleven feet when rearing up, and weighing up to
eighteen hundred pounds—their legs were surprisingly
long and slender, giving them the ability to break into a fast
run for short distances and, presumably, catch inattentive
herbivores, such as horses and camels. People were always
surprised, when Carter happened to mention it in a lecture,
that most of the evolution of camels had taken place in
North America.

"Am I right?" Rosalie asked. "Can you feel it?"

"Yes, good job," Carter said. "It could be from a bear."

Rosalie beamed, like a kid who'd just been told she was
head of the class.

"But we won't know for sure, of course, until we've
glopped the rest of this out, and actually removed the fossil."

Even then it often wasn't easy. Carter had an uncanny knack for guessing where a fossil might be located, and what it might turn out to be—that knack had served him well when excavating the Well of the Bones in Sicily, where he had first made his reputation—but he also knew that lab work was a painstaking business, where your initial assumptions could all be turned upside down with the discovery of one molar, an unexpected alveolus, or, as had happened to him on one occasion, fossilized blowfly larvae lodged in an ulna. Larvae could tell you a lot, if you were paying attention.

He pulled his arm back out of the pit, and held it up to let some of the goo dangle and then plop back down. By now it was clear that they had definitely hit a very fertile layer of the pit—a big cat and a monstrous bear, a dozen other sharp anomalies perceptibly (at least to Carter's trained eye) disturbing the surface of the presently un-worked quadrants. Carter felt a prickle of excitement, the feeling he'd had on so many other digs, in places far more exotic than this, where discoveries far more significant than this was likely to be were begging to be made. But it was the same old feeling, nonetheless, and he suddenly re-alized how much he'd missed it. The post at the Page Museum was a great one—most paleontologists would sali-vate at the chance to fill it—but office work wasn't what appealed to Carter. Even writing up his monographs and reports and arguments was less interesting to him than the sheer pleasure of being outdoors, in fields and mountains and long-lost riverbeds, surveying a strange landscape and making his best guess as to where its secrets lay hidden. The world, to Carter, had always been a kind of treasure chest, filled with odd things—stones and bones, shells and shards and petrified bugs—that most people didn't even notice, much less want.

But that he did.

Miranda, who'd been patiently waiting, said, "I wonder what that leaves me with."

"Pardon?" Carter said, who'd been lost for a moment in his own thoughts.

"If Claude has a saber-tooth, and Rosalie has a bear, I

wonder if I've got something different over here." She gave Carter her most dazzling smile—he knew she had a crush on him, and wondered what he could do to discourage it—and looped a finger under her silver necklace, unwittingly leaving a smear of tar on her neck. "Maybe a lion?"

Carter smiled and, stepping over Rosalie's buckets, made his way to Miranda's work spot. By now, his forearm was so crusted with muck it felt three times its normal weight.

"You've got to wear more sunscreen," he told her, gesturing at the pinkish skin of her neck and shoulders. She blushed even redder, and he said to himself he should have kept quiet. Anytime he noticed something about her, particularly something so intimate as her skin tone, it only gave her hope. "And get yourself some cheap T-shirts like mine," he said, showing off today's Old Navy logo. "The paleontologist's best friend."

Miranda mumbled that she would, but hardly budged when Carter knelt down next to her. He'd expected her to make a little room, then kicked himself for thinking that. "So where's your find exactly?" he asked.

"In the center of the square," she said, "kind of deep."

"If you glop from the side," he advised, "it's easier, and just as effective."

Then he leaned forward and reached down, one more time, into the pit. He could feel Miranda's eyes on him, and when she volunteered to hold on to him—and grabbed the back of his belt—he had to tell her it was okay, he wasn't in any danger of falling in. He could only imagine the look that Claude and Rosalie were exchanging from their respective corners.

His own eyes flicked self-consciously to the upper observation deck—a small enclosure behind a Plexiglas shield—that allowed the general public to see paleontology in action. Today, they had but one spectator, but he was a regular—a Native American man in a buckskin jacket that he wore no matter what the temperature was.

The tar at first seemed to be fighting him, even more than usual; it was especially thick and sludgy here. But then, as if he'd hit a pocket of gas and looser material, he

felt his wrist descend into the mire. Still, he hadn't encountered anything of any substance. He reached deeper; the
farther down he went the warmer the tar became, and as
the methane was released, mephitic bubbles speckled the
surface and released little exhalations of gas. Miranda gig-
gled and said, "What'd you have for lunch, Carter?"

"Very funny."

And then he did feel it. Or, to be more accurate, *it felt
him.* His breath caught in his throat, and his arm stopped
moving. His own fingers were spread wide, and for all the
world it felt as if another hand—someone else's fingers—
had just slipped into his own, the way a drowning man
might grasp the hand of his savior. Carter could feel the in-
dividual bones, the metacarpus, the phalanges. And, though
he could never have even imagined such a thing, it didn't
feel inert. It didn't feel dead and lost, as if it were lying
there, inanimate, and waiting to be lifted from oblivion. To
Carter, it felt as if the hand—too large to be a woman's—
had found his own, had sought it out, in order to be raised,
after a silent eternity in the earth, from the dead.

CHAPTER FOUR

GREER COULD HEAR the TV blasting in the living room—sounded like Conan O'Brien—as he gathered his stuff together for a last check. He had his flashlight, with brandnew batteries, his wallet with complete fake ID (just in case he got pulled over or got into any trouble), a large black Hefty Sak with drawstring top, a pair of surgical gloves, glass cutter, and, finally, his Beretta handgun, loaded.

He was wearing black jeans and a black shirt, under a dark blue windbreaker with a lot of pockets for all his gear. He took one last glance in the mirror on the back of his bedroom door and thought, *Jesus, with a mask I'd look like Zorro.*

He'd hoped his mother might be asleep when he came out, but she wasn't. She was propped in her easy chair, with one hand on the cat in her lap and the other in a bag of Trader Joe's soy chips; since the soy chips were low-cal, she thought that meant you could eat as many bags of them as you wanted. It sure didn't look that way to Greer. She was getting fatter all the time.

"You're going out?" she said, without taking her eyes from the big-screen TV.

"Yeah."

"Where?"

Christ, he felt like he was sixteen again. "What do you care?"

"Derek, why would you say that?" she said, doing a good imitation of sounding hurt.

"I'll be back in a couple of hours." He went to the apartment door, then said, dryly, "Don't wait up."

It was a California-style building, with an open courtyard in the middle and open hallways that looked down into it. But the place had been on rent control for years, and everything now was falling apart at the seams. The concrete floors were stained with God knew what, the plants in the courtyard were mostly dead, and the elevator stalled if more than two people had the nerve to get in at the same time. He wondered if his mother could stall it on her own now.

When he'd come back from Iraq, he'd moved into her back bedroom—where she normally kept her "collectibles"—with the full intention of staying just a few weeks, until he could get his act together and find a place of his own. But the weeks had gradually turned into months, and his disability payments sure lasted a lot longer when he only had to split the rent on a cheap apartment. His mother, who'd been a little put out at first, had also come to accept the idea—along with his cash. She lived on disability, too—for a bipolar disorder that made her no longer able to work for the Social Security Administration in Westwood—so between the two of them, they had things pretty much covered.

But not completely.

Greer had picked up some nasty habits—he liked to blame it on Iraq, but it wasn't as if he'd been clean before going over there—and he could always use more money than he had. But a regular job would mess up his government money, so the way he looked at it, he was driven to this . . . sideline.

He'd studied his Thomas Guide before leaving the house, just to make sure he had the route down (along with a couple of ways out, if things went wrong), and he'd even checked to see if there was going to be a full moon that night. There was. That wasn't actually all that bad; you had to use *something* to see where you were going, and a flashlight beam wasn't exactly subtle. Besides, he only worked in the best neighborhoods, where most of the houses were pretty well concealed from any neighbors, anyway.

This place—Dr. Hugo's, as Greer had learned when he told Sadowski he'd do it—was in the middle of a block with wide lots in Brentwood, just north of Sunset. The problem was always where to put the car; you couldn't exactly leave it in the driveway, but you didn't want it so far away that you had to run there dragging a Hefty bag full of stuff in your hand. In this case, Greer decided to park the Mustang across the street, a few doors down. He picked a spot under a shady tree and in front of a house under construction, making sure to angle the wheels away from the curb and to leave the doors unlocked.

The street was perfectly quiet, and Dr. Hugo's house was dark, except for some stair lights in front that nicely illuminated the little sign that said SILVER BEAR SECURITY— 24-HOUR PATROL. Greer looked up and down the street, then casually strolled to the side of the house; he'd taken his painkillers and the leg wasn't bothering him much at all right now. He put on the surgical gloves.

There was a wooden gate, with a Beware of Dogs placard showing a barking German shepherd. Lots of people, he knew, just put out the signs for effect, and Sadowski had assured him there were no guard dogs on the premises—at least according to the file. Still, Greer was going to keep an eye out for any telltale sign like a water bowl, a leash hanging on the back of a door . . . or a pair of snarling jaws.

The side of the house sported an immense Weber gas grill, and in back, where the addition had been put on, it looked like a lap pool had been added, too. Some people had all the luck. The walls and window frames of the new room were still unpainted, and the whole place, even out here, still smelled of fresh wood and sawdust. The yard, Greer was pleased to see, was surrounded by trees and, in the rear, a high wall. This was going to be a piece of cake.

Just for the hell of it, he gently rattled the doorknobs of the French doors—you never could tell, some people were really asking for it—but they were locked. Taking out the glass cutter, he neatly removed a pane of glass just above the knob (the putty was still damp), placed it on the lawn, then reached in and opened the door. This was the moment when he'd normally have to be worried about an alarm, but he was trusting Sadowski to be right—though how dumb was that, he thought.

Inside, the wooden floor creaked as he made his way, in new black high-top sneakers, across it, and then into a kitchen, where rows of copper pots hung, gleaming in the moonlight, above a center island. There was a hallway off to the left, with a few rooms opening off it. He had his flashlight in one hand, and the Hefty bag, unfurled, in the other. One room was a den, the next a bathroom, and the third looked like a home office; there was a laptop computer, a printer, stuff like that. If he had time, and room in the bag, he'd check it out on the way back out. No reason to carry anything heavy up and down the stairs.

The master bedroom was what he was looking for—90 percent of what you wanted was always in there. He mounted the stairs slowly—they made a turn on a wide, carpeted landing—and at the top he played the flashlight beam around. Again, there were several doors, but the master bedroom, he figured, would be in back, overlooking the pool and the yard. The walls had mounted, glass-covered photos on them, glamour shots of old movie stars—this Dr. Hugo guy had to be a fag—and at the end double doors stood open to what had to be the master suite.

As Greer approached it, he could see a dresser, with what was unmistakably a digital camera sitting on top. He'd been wanting one of those! The bed, against the far wall, was one of those canopied jobs, with heaps of bolsters and pillows. He was already dropping the camera into the plastic bag when a dog barked.

Not a loud bark—just a yip, really. But it was in the room, very close.

It yipped again, and Greer turned the flashlight beam to

the corner. A sleepy old cocker spaniel was sitting up on a dog bed.

Not a problem, Greer thought with relief.

"Brian?"

He flicked off the light and froze in place. *This* could be a problem.

"Bri?" It was a girl's voice; she was in the bed. He heard the covers rustle. "You up?"

Shit. He gauged the distance to the door.

"What are you doing?"

Greer didn't answer. Was she looking at him, or just mumbling from her pillow?

Could he manage to get out? he was wondering, when the bathroom door swung open and a white kid with his hair in dreads came out, in an open robe.

"You say something?"

Greer turned the flashlight on, and shone it right into the kid's face. "Who are you?" he demanded.

The kid didn't answer, or move.

"Who are *you*?" the girl asked. She was sitting up now, with a sheet in front of her.

"Security," Greer declared. "Silver Bear. Now, answer me!"

"I'm Julia," the girl said, terror in her voice. "The dog-sitter."

Greer wasn't sure what to say next. "Nobody's supposed to be here."

"Sometimes I stay over," the girl said. "Dr. Hugo knows."

And then she turned on the bedside light. And Greer found himself standing there, wearing a pair of rubber gloves, with the Hefty bag in one hand, the flashlight in the other, between the two of them. There could be no mistaking what was really up.

"You," he said, waving at the kid—Brian—with the flashlight. "Get on the floor, on your stomach! Now!"

The kid got down on the floor. "And you," he said to Julia. "Lie down on the bed."

"Don't hurt us," she said, very softly. She was about eighteen, in a football jersey.

The dog yipped again, but didn't move from the corner.

Greer was thinking fast. He dropped the sack, put one foot on the small of Brian's back, and yanked the cotton belt free from the robe. Then he went over to the bed and told Julia to put her hands together, behind her.

"Please don't hurt us."

"Shut up." *God damn,* he thought. What a fuck-up this was. God damn that Sadowski.

He looped the belt around her hands, a couple of times, then, dropping the flashlight on the bed, knotted it.

And that's when Brian made his move; the kid was fast, up on his feet and running for the door.

Greer lunged for him, but missed. He caught just the end of the flapping robe, which burned through his fingers.

He grabbed the flashlight and raced after him, his bad leg juiced by all the adrenaline. The kid didn't know the house any better than he did, and flew past the stairs, before having to whip around and tumble down them. Greer was just a couple of steps behind.

The kid wheeled at the bottom and made not for the front door but the back, down the hall, through the kitchen, into the addition. At the French doors he had to stop and fumble with the knobs, and just as he got them open, Greer was able to grab him by the collar, spin him around, and club him in the face with the heavy-duty flashlight.

The kid fell backward, into the yard, but he didn't fall. There was blood all over his lips. He kept back-pedaling, toward the lap pool, and Greer smacked him again. The kid kept going.

Christ, Greer thought, wasn't he ever gonna stay down?

The grass was slick, and the kid started to slip. Greer saw his chance and shoved him toward the pool. Just before he toppled over, Greer hit him again, hard, across the cheek.

The kid went in, with a huge splash, and Greer, panting, stood by the side of the lighted pool, waiting. The kid floated, a cloud of blood seeping into the water. Greer waited. Was he dead? Was he faking? The blood began to disperse in the water.

Christ almighty, was he going to have to get into the goddamned pool?

The girl was screaming now; he could hear her even out here.

Greer knelt down and snagged the kid by the collar of his robe, pulled him over to the side. With one huge tug, he had him levered onto the grass again . . . where he left him, sputtering but alive, before snapping off the rubber gloves in disgust, stashing them in his pocket, and heading back to his car.

Sadowski was going to hear about this.

And his leg, he just knew, was going to give him hell later that night.

CHAPTER FIVE

BETH WAS SO deeply into her work, studying an ancient parchment page through a magnifying glass, that at first she didn't even hear the phone ring. It didn't help that she'd accidentally laid a sheaf of reports from the Getty conservation lab on top of it.

When she unearthed it, on the fifth or sixth ring, she was happy to hear it was Carter—until he said, "What are you doing there?"

"What do you mean?"

"Shouldn't you be at the press party?"

She glanced up at the wall clock. He was right.

"I was just going to leave a message for you," he said.

"Saying what?"

"That I'm stuck on Wilshire, going nowhere. Start drinking without me."

"Okay, I will," she said. "But you're right—I've got to run."

"Run," he said, and she could hear several car horns honking in the background before she hung up.

She dropped the magnifying glass, replaced it with a hairbrush from her bottom drawer, and, using the mirror on the back of her office door, did a quick once-over. She pulled the clasp off her ponytail—it was easier to do close work with nothing hanging down in your eyes—and brushed her thick, dark hair out and onto her shoulders. Then she touched up her makeup, or what little of it she wore, grabbed the jacket that went with her skirt, slipped out of her flats and into her heels, and hurried out. Her boss, Berenice Cabot, would be livid if she was any later than she already was.

Especially as the reception was in honor of an exhibition—"The Genius of the Cloister: Illuminated Manuscripts of the Eleventh Century"—that Beth had been the chief curator on.

Tonight was the press reception, designed to introduce some of the local art critics, connoisseurs, and friends of the museum to the new exhibition, drawn from the voluminous holdings of the Getty Center. Beth had spent countless hours poring over the exquisite and rare manuscripts in the museum collections and culling the precise examples that would best illustrate her thesis and story. An exhibition couldn't just be a random sampling of things, however related; it had to have a point of view, and a point. That was one of the first things they had taught her at the Courtauld Institute, where she'd done her graduate work after Barnard.

Beth stepped out of the elevator, pushed through the ponderous glass doors of the research institute, and then scurried across the outdoor court toward the gardens, where the party was being held; it was going to be a balmy and beautiful summer night. And the Central Garden, as it was known, was going to provide the perfect setting for the kickoff event. Entered through a circular walkway, shaded by London plane trees and traversing a running stream, the garden contained hundreds of different plants and flowers, from lavender to heliotrope, crape myrtle to floribunda roses, all gradually descending to a plaza with bougainvillea-covered arbors and an ornamental pool; the water in the pool sparkled blue, under a floating veil of azaleas.

Tables had been set up, covered with gold damask cloths, and waiters circulated with trays of champagne, Perrier, and whatever else anyone requested. About two dozen guests had already toured the exhibit in the museum, and were now, some of them still clutching a program, enjoying the artfully arranged hors d'oeuvres.

The first person who caught Beth's eye was Mrs. Cabot—an older woman, she had no use for the Ms. business—and she did not look pleased. She was standing with the Critchleys, a prominent couple on the Los Angeles art scene. Beth grabbed a glass of champagne from one of the passing trays and went to join them.

"We were hoping you'd stop by," Mrs. Cabot said, with a smile that only Beth knew wasn't genuine.

"So sorry," Beth murmured, nodding hello to the Critchleys. "I got immersed in something, and lost track of the time."

"Oh, I do that all the time," Mrs. Critchley said; she was a dithery sort of woman, but right now, Beth was glad to have her there. "I once forgot to go to my own birthday lunch because I was so busy planning my daughter's."

Mr. Critchley, an old-school gentleman in a seersucker suit, looked on, beaming. He never said much, but Beth always felt he radiated goodwill.

"The *Los Angeles Times* sent that Rusoff woman," Mrs. Cabot confided to Beth, "and the *Art News* writer is over there, in the bow tie." Beth turned to look—at events like these, bow ties weren't that uncommon. "The red one," Mrs. Cabot said, intuiting her question.

"Oh, fine, I'll be sure to speak to him."

"I'm sure the Critchleys won't mind if you do that now," Mrs. Cabot said. "I believe he said something about having to go to a LACMA event after this."

Beth knew when she had her marching orders, and left to go introduce herself to the red bow tie. This was the part of her job she didn't relish. She loved doing her research, she loved studying the Old Master drawings, the antique manuscripts, the precious incunabala that the museum possessed in such abundance; she loved working with the expert conservators on preserving and protecting the invaluable works of art that time and tide had begun to decay.

But she didn't love doing public relations work.

The *Art News* writer—who told her his name, Alexander Van Nostrand, through a mouthful of puff pastry—was indeed going to a second engagement. But upon seeing Beth, he lit up and decided he definitely needed to hear more about the genesis of the exhibition.

"The Getty Museum, as you know, has one of the most extensive collections of illuminated manuscripts in the world," Beth said, "and these ecclesiastical works, most of them dating from the eleventh through the thirteenth centuries, were produced for English priories and monastery libraries." She was doing her standard spiel, parts of which she had recorded for the audio tour, but Van Nostrand didn't seem to mind a bit. "These manuscripts were considered prized possessions, and many monasteries—including Abingdon, Waltham, Worcester, and Christ Church in Canterbury—kept a list of exactly what they had in their catalogue. They also kept their books chained, literally, to pulpits and lecterns."

"Yes," Van Nostrand said, "the exhibition made all that quite clear. What I was wondering, though," he added, a pastry crumb still clinging to his lower lip, "was what fascinated *you* about them? What makes a beautiful young woman, if I may say so—"

He waited for a reaction, and Beth simply smiled, saying nothing.

"—decide to devote herself to such an arcane and, some would call it, dusty, subject?"

Should she tell him about the crumb? She elected not to. "Their beauty, I think, was what first attracted me to illuminated manuscripts."

"All that glitter and gold?"

"In some cases," she said, warming, despite herself, to her subject. "Many of these medieval works are pretty spectacular, especially the ones made for emperors and kings. But many of them are more humble than that; we call them illuminated, using the term loosely, but technically they're not. They don't have the metallic gold or silver decoration that the word 'illuminated' connotes. But they're still quite beautifully made, and beautifully written, objects."

"And how did you make this selection, for your current exhibition?"

Beth had the uncomfortable feeling that he hadn't heard a word she'd said, that he was just asking these questions to keep her there and occupied. But if the alternative was to return to Mrs. Cabot and the Critchleys, she would stay.

"I had noticed some interesting things about these particular manuscripts. Although they had been owned by different monasteries, sometimes in quite different parts of the country, they all had a distinctive writing style and decoration. These books, as I'm sure you know"—it never hurt to flatter your interlocutor—"were generally unsigned, written anonymously by monks in open cloisters and drafty scriptoria. But the books in this exhibition all displayed, to my mind, a common creator."

"How? The text was always pretty much the same, wasn't it? Bibles, patristic commentaries, Gospels?"

So he was paying some attention, after all.

"Yes, that's true, though even in that respect there was greater latitude than is generally accepted. There's a lot of room between the Lindisfarne Gospels and the *Très Riches Heures* of the Duc de Berry. Room for Livy's *History of Rome* and Aristotle's *Ethics*, Virgil's *Aeneid*, and the *Adventures of Marco Polo*. In fact, King Charles V of France was such a Marco Polo fan that he had five copies of the book, one of them bound in gold cloth."

"But those books span centuries."

"That's correct, but the monk, or scribe, to whom I'm attributing the works collected in this exhibition, lived in the mid to late eleventh century, and he wrote, whatever his subject, with a distinctively sloping script, tilted slightly to the left. He might have been left-handed, or he might have had a problem with his vision. His illustrations are remarkable—they have a rare psychological acuity to them." Where most such figures were stiffly drawn and without expression, Beth felt that this unknown scribe had found a way to convey feeling and nuance to his work.

"Hold on," Van Nostrand said. "I bow, of course, to your superior wisdom in these matters, but weren't the scribes, who did the text, and the illuminators, who did the artwork, two different people?"

"Yes," Beth said. "Generally they were. But something tells me that this one man—the Michelangelo of the illuminated world—did both. When I called this exhibition 'The Genius of the Cloister,' I meant the phrase to be taken in two ways: as a tribute to the talents of the monks in general and as a nod to the one man I believe surpassed them all."

Van Nostrand still looked dubious, so Beth decided to give him something more tangible to hang on to. "And this man, this artist, was proud of his achievement. Even though the work was generally done anonymously, he always managed to insert something of himself, somewhere, into the written text."

"Surely not into the Bible?"

"Oh no," Beth said, "he wouldn't have done that. That would have cost him his job, or his place in the religious order. No, he had a more unusual way of making himself known."

"And that was . . . ?" The crumb, hanging off his lip, finally relinquished its hold and drifted off on the evening breeze.

"He cursed."

"He what?"

"He laid a curse on anyone who stole or defaced his work."

Van Nostrand laughed, and Beth did, too. It was the very thing that had made her first connect the various books now in the exhibition. On the top of a Reading Abbey manuscript roughly a thousand years old, it said, *Liber sancte Marie Radying[ensis] quem qui alienaverit anathema sit.* Or, in other words, 'Cursed be he who tampers with this book.' On other manuscripts, drawn from all over the British

Isles, there were similar curses, some of them even more colorful and elaborate. In fact, though it was difficult to date all the manuscripts exactly, it seemed to Beth that the unknown monk had grown more obstreperous all the time, until at some point he abruptly vanished from the scene— as did his work. Had his health failed? Had he died? Was he no longer commissioned to do such work? And who, finally, was he?

This exhibition was Beth's first concerted attempt to find him.

"Sorry I'm late," Carter said, slipping up behind her, then extending a hand to Van Nostrand. "Carter Cox."

"Alexander Van Nostrand. *Art News*."

Beth turned to her husband—no red bow tie here, just an open-collared blue Oxford-cloth shirt, a navy blue blazer, and khaki pants. She used to kid him that he simply bought his outfits off the Brooks Brothers mannequins.

"Ah, so you are the lucky husband?"

Carter smiled and said, "I hear that a lot."

Even now, after several years of marriage, Beth always enjoyed looking at her husband—at the way his brown hair flopped over his forehead, the way his dark eyes focused so intently on whatever, or whomever, he was looking at, the way he carried his tall and rangy frame. He was to her mind the perfect combination, with something of the professor and something of the cowboy in him.

"I'm sure you do," Van Nostrand said. "Because she's as erudite as she is beautiful." Van Nostrand took her hand in a mock courtly fashion and said, "Unfortunately, LACMA calls. But I would love to talk to you some more about your exhibition. I'll call later in the week, if that's alright."

Beth assured him that it was, then, slipping her arm through Carter's, turned back toward the other party guests. The gold damask tablecloths were rippling softly in the evening breeze.

"Where's the ogre?" Carter asked.

"Watch what you say," Beth murmured. "She's right over there, under the trellis, with a couple of museum patrons."

In fact, at spotting Beth, she began to wave wildly, and then started stumping across the lawn in their direction.

"Did you do something wrong?" Carter asked in low tones. "Am I not on the guest list?"

"I have no idea."

Taking the bull by the horns, Carter stepped forward and said, "Good evening, Mrs. Cabot. It's a pleasure to see you."

"None of that," she said, dismissing his comments with a wave of the hand, "it's Beth I need."

"I just finished talking to the *Art News* writer, and—"

"Mr. al-Kalli is coming; he'll be here any minute."

"Mr. al-Kalli?" Beth asked. "I don't believe I know him."

"*The Beasts of Eden*," she said, peremptorily, "the bestiary. I messengered the photos to you."

"I'm still not following."

"Mr. al-Kalli is the owner of the book! The man who is asking us to study and restore it."

"Oh," Beth said, at last making the connection. But the cover letter from Mrs. Cabot had never named the owner of *The Beasts of Eden*, and she wondered now if she should bring that up in her own defense.

When Carter did. "Oh yes, honey, don't you remember that you told me there was an exciting new project for you, but that the owner of the work had chosen to remain anonymous?" He turned to Mrs. Cabot. "Beth was very pleased"—he knew enough not to divulge to Mrs. Cabot that his wife might have shared any details with him—"but I thought she was purposely concealing the owner. Now I guess she wasn't."

Mrs. Cabot was momentarily stymied. "Oh yes, that's right," she conceded, "he *had* asked to remain anonymous." Then, quickly picking up the cudgels again, "But I've just been told that he has decided to come here, quite unexpectedly, tonight. He expressly wants to meet you, Beth, as you will be the person in charge of the project."

Beth wished that she'd been given more notice—it might have been nice to prepare some thoughts and a few remarks about how she planned to proceed—but she was

pleased, too. The few photos she'd been given of the mythical creatures depicted in the manuscript had been striking,
beautiful, and even, in a way, haunting. The fact that the
book was of Middle Eastern origin—the information so far
provided to her had been fairly sketchy—made it all the
more intriguing. Not many manuscripts from that region
had survived so well, and for so long.

"In fact," Mrs. Cabot said, glancing up at the top of the
stairs leading to the garden, "that's Mr. al-Kalli now."

Beth and Carter followed her gaze. A bald man, somewhere in his fifties perhaps, wearing an impeccably cut
black suit, was standing with military rectitude on the top
step, surveying the party as a general might survey a battle-
field. He was flanked on one side by a surly teenage boy—
Carter could see his scowl even from here—and on the
other by a stocky man, clearly a bodyguard, who hung one
deferential step back.

Mrs. Cabot raised a hand to signal their whereabouts,
and the guard, spotting her, leaned toward his employer.

As Mr. al-Kalli approached, he took off his sunglasses
and slipped them into the inside pocket of his suit coat; the
waning sunlight glinted off his eyes, reminding Carter of
the glittering obsidian on the beaches of Hawaii. His skin
was a burnished gold, and the perfect dome of his head
looked as if it had been buffed to a high sheen with a cham-
ois cloth.

He introduced himself and his son, Mehdi—who
shrugged and looked away—but said nothing of the guard,
who now stood several feet back, his head turning slowly
from side to side, taking in everything and everyone, in
close proximity to his boss. Mrs. Cabot seemed flustered—
odd, Carter thought, for someone whose job brought her
into such close contact with the high and mighty all the
time—but Beth remained poised and collected. One of the
countless things Carter admired about her.

"I know quite a lot about you, Ms. Elizabeth Cox," Mr.
al-Kalli said with a slight smile.

"You do?"

"Oh yes," he said. His voice was very smooth, and he

spoke with an upper-crust English accent. "And all of it, I may say, is good."

Beth put the back of her hand to her brow, as if in relief.

"It's why I came tonight. I wanted to meet the woman who is going to take charge, as it were, of my family's most precious possession."

"From what I've seen of it," Beth said, "it's a beautiful piece of work."

"Oh, it's more than that," al-Kalli said. "It's the legacy of my family, it's the source, some would say, of our . . . enduring."

Beth didn't know quite what to make of this, but she said, "We'll take every precaution to make sure no harm comes to it."

"I know you will," he said. "I have had a thorough study of your career done—you graduated with highest honors from Barnard College, you did exceptional work in London, you have dealt, scrupulously, with some of the finest Old Master works in the world—"

He *had* done his homework, Beth thought, though his recitation was starting to give her the chills.

"—and your previous monographs on medieval manuscripts have been both accessible and intelligent." He glanced over at Carter, "And I don't need to tell you how inaccessible, to the layman, many of these scholarly works tend to be."

Now Carter found himself in the spotlight—and he didn't know why.

"You, too, I know something about." He listed several of Carter's accomplishments—from the discovery of the Well of the Bones to his appointment to the Kingsley Chair at NYU, and on to his recent post at the Page Museum—before adding, "I do my homework, you see."

His lips curled in a tiny, self-satisfied smile, as if he'd just performed a popular parlor trick. Carter sensed that he liked to do this, to gain the upper hand.

"You forgot to mention the fact that I won the American Legion Good Citizenship medal in my senior year of high school."

"At Evanston Township High School," al-Kalli replied. "You were also the valedictorian," he added, and now Carter really was nonplussed. "But may I borrow Beth for a few moments?" he continued. "There are just a few things I want to go over with her." To his son, he said, "Have something to eat, and Jakob"—to the guard—"make sure he does not drink anything but soda."

Beth felt herself taken by the elbow and steered toward the less-tenanted portion of the garden. The Getty Center was built high atop a hill on the west side of Los Angeles, and from here it commanded a panoramic view of the city below. Sometimes, when Beth had been closeted all day in the galleries or the conservation lab, she would come out here just to breathe the air and look out into the far distance; she felt like she was exercising her eyes, giving them a chance, after hours of intensive work, to range freely over a great distance, all the way to the soothing blue of the Pacific Ocean beyond. Tonight, with the sun going down, the view was especially magnificent.

But her focus right now had to remain on al-Kalli, who was busy telling her what methods he wanted employed to restore the manuscript, what methods he definitely did not, and what information he hoped to glean from her study of the manuscript. She also had the distinct impression that he just wanted to spend a bit more time in her company, making sure of his decision, getting a feel for her. Everything he was telling her could just as easily have been written in a cover letter or introductory document—indeed, she was sure it had—but al-Kalli seemed to want something more than that. He was like a climber who wanted to make sure of his partner before a difficult ascent. Can I rely on you? Are you trustworthy? Although she knew he wasn't actually putting his life in her hands, she sensed that he wanted her to feel that way.

When he had finished, Beth said in her most reassuring tones, "It's an extraordinary manuscript, and there's no better place than the Getty to have this work done." She felt like a summer camp director taking responsibility for someone's child.

CHAPTER SIX

THE CAR, A Mercedes-Benz limousine, looked like any other of its kind—long and black, gleaming and powerful. But this one had a secret: It was built to withstand almost any attack. Its entire chassis—posts, columns, door frames, roof—had been buttressed with high-hardened steel, reinforced fiberglass, and ballistic nylon; under the burgundy-carpeted floor lay a bomb-suppressor blanket. The tires were equipped with "run flat inserts"; the front and rear compartments housed satellite global phones, klaxons, and loudspeakers (to call for help, or to negotiate with terrorists if necessary); the windows had been transparently armored with a layer of dense ballistic glass, laminated to a sturdy inner spall shield of resilient polycarbonate. Overall, the car maintained a B-7 armor level, enough to survive even a concerted assault.

Mohammed al-Kalli always wanted only the best—especially after what had happened to his family in Iraq.

Even Saddam Hussein had thought twice about taking on the al-Kalli dynasty. Not only because of their inestimable wealth and influence, but also for a reason less rational, less plain. Saddam, like all Iraqis, had grown up hearing the stories, listening to the legends of the al-Kallis' strange powers and even stranger possessions. As a youngster, he had listened no doubt to the warnings about what happened to bad children (the al-Kallis got them!), and to the tales of what befell anyone who crossed the family in any way. There were rumors of dungeons and torture chambers, of terrible rituals, deadly sacrifice, and, finally . . . of creatures beyond imagining.

For years, Saddam had bided his time, and he had even done a bit of business with the al-Kallis now and then. But eventually his avarice and his ego had gotten the better of him. Whether it was at Saddam's express order or not, al-Kalli never knew. It could have been a lower-level functionary who sought to curry favor by perpetrating what his leader had only wished. But either way, a plan was put into action. A celebration was to be held at one of Saddam's many palaces, and the al-Kallis were all invited. Mohammed had no desire to go, nor did his wife, his brothers, his children, but the invitation was more of an order than a request. So, in the interest of keeping the peace and observing the political realities, Mohammed had acceded.

The celebration was in honor of some trumped-up event in the grand and mythical history of Saddam's family—as Mohammed recalled it, Saddam had traced his lineage back to Nebuchadnezzar, or maybe it was the Prophet himself—and the al-Kallis had dutifully come from their own various palaces and compounds. The event was expectedly lavish, sprawling over a dozen acres, with more than a thousand guests. There was a Western orchestra playing Beethoven and Wagner under one immense, air-conditioned tent, while in another Middle Eastern music, and a bevy of belly dancers (reputedly handpicked by Saddam's son Uday) held sway.

At first, all went well. Mohammed, who'd been suffering from a stomach flu, had simply sipped club sodas, while his family, assembled on a special dais reserved for honored guests, had dined. But even then, something had struck Mohammed—the waiters who were serving at their table were not very efficient. They did not seem used to this kind of work; in fact, they looked more like soldiers. But then, he thought, perhaps all of Saddam's staff looked like this.

It was only when his wife began to look pale, and dropped her soup spoon on the table, that Mohammed began to grasp what was happening. His younger brother had also stopped eating. His daughter suddenly gasped and groped for her water glass. The waiters stood, with napkins badly folded over their arms, around the rim of the tent. Mohammed stood up, took his son, Mehdi, who was sitting next to him, by the hand; fortunately, Mehdi never ate soup. One of the waiters stepped into his path, but when Mohammed said, "My son must use the bathroom," the man stood aside. Mohammed saw him flash a look at one of his superiors, undoubtedly wondering what to do, but Mohammed was able to walk slowly, as if he had not a care in the world, out of the tent.

Once outside, he lifted his son, then just a child, into his arms and raced for the limousine that had brought them. The driver was smoking a cigarette and lounging in the shade, but when he saw them, he instinctively knew what to do. He leapt into the car, started the engine, and drove right over a potted palm to get onto the driveway again with the car pointed toward the main gates. Several people had to jump out of the way. The car jolted to a stop and al-Kalli and his son threw themselves into the backseat. They slammed the door, and the car hurtled off in a cloud of dust.

But by the time they had reached the main gates, the sentries had been notified, and as guests screamed and ducked for cover, the soldiers opened fire on the racing car. Mohammed ducked down, covering his son's head with his hands, as the windows exploded; slivers of glass shot through the car. Bullets thudded, with the sound of hammer blows, into the doors. The driver swerved, keeping his head down, and the car drove straight into one of the sentries, who was thrown over the hood, his automatic weapon still firing in the air.

Once the car was beyond the gates, the driver sat back up—his hair was standing on end, Mohammed remembered—and asked what he should do. Mohammed told him to drive back to their own palace as fast as possible.

"What about . . . the others?" he asked.

But Mohammed knew there was nothing that could be done to save them. Whatever poison Saddam had administered would no doubt be lethal . . . and even if it wasn't, what other recourse was there? To take them to a hospital in Mosul or Baghdad? They would never survive the trip, or the tender ministrations of the doctors there, who would assuredly be under their own orders from Saddam.

Mohammed got on the cell phone and instructed his staff to implement the plan that he had long held in reserve. The walls of the compound were fortified by his own militia, his helicopter was readied for immediate takeoff, and his most prized possessions—what was left of them—were loaded onto the waiting cargo trucks, to begin their own long journey out of Iraq. There was no time right now even to mourn. For that, he knew, he would have a lifetime . . .

His revenge, too, he knew would have to wait.

As the Mercedes now drove under the arched gateway into Bel-Air, Mohammed stared out the bulletproof window at the elaborate facades of the great houses they passed, the filigreed ironwork fences, the manicured hedges and expensive landscaping. (The drought warnings had not left Bel-Air any less green.) Up and up they went, on silent winding streets, with fewer and fewer cars—and then almost none—as they rose toward the top of the hills. Now there were no houses visible at all; just closed gates, occasionally with a guard in a lighted kiosk reading a magazine or listening to a radio. The road became darker and more silent the higher they went, until at the top of the crest it stopped altogether, at a lighted stone guardhouse; in addition to the sentry on duty there, a small sign, newly planted on the lawn, announced that any intrusion would bring an instant, armed response from the Silver Bear Security Service.

The gates swung open as the limousine drove through, up a long and winding drive, past an elaborate fountain modeled on the Trevi in Rome, under a canopy of towering elms, and into a porte cochere. Mehdi, who'd been dozing in the car, woke up.

"Go to bed," his father said.

"Why? It's not even nine o'clock."

"You're tired."

"What are you going to do?"

"That's none of your business."

Mehdi smirked. "Don't think I don't know."

"Go to bed."

Jakob was holding open the rear door, and Mohammed got out. "You can put the car away; we're in for the night." And then, before turning away, he said, "Check on our guest, too."

Jakob nodded.

It was a warm night, with a dry wind blowing. One of the peacocks, who roamed the grounds at will, cawed loudly. Al-Kalli took a flagstone pathway, carpeted with soft purple jacaranda blossoms, toward the rear of the estate. It was the largest single property in Bel-Air, twenty-five acres on a hilltop—and he had expanded it by another dozen acres or so by buying up the adjacent properties (for far more than even they were worth) and leveling the houses.

His own house—a massive affair of gray stone and timber, referred to by the real estate broker as the Castle—had originally been built by a silent film star, who'd used it, by all accounts, for wild orgies and bacchanals. When he had died in the middle of one—found floating in the pool, in fact, naked except for a dog leash around his neck—it had been purchased by an oil tycoon, who'd added on to the house even more. That's when the ten-thousand-bottle wine cellar, the gazebo, and the stables had been built. Even now, one of the horses had his head hanging out the stable door, sniffing the night air.

Beyond the stables, past the wooden footbridge, lay the single greatest addition al-Kalli had made to the property—a vast riding ring and equestrian facility that had required him to get a dozen different permits from the zoning commission to erect. From a distance, it looked like a rusticated airplane hangar, with whitewashed board walls and a massive sloping roof, but up close it began to give a different impression. The windows were triple-paned and thermal-sealed; the barn doors weren't wood at all, but galvanized steel with more locks than a bank vault and several security cameras mounted just above them, surveying the scene in all directions.

The doors magically unlocked as al-Kalli approached—he could hear the thunking sound they made, followed by the whir of the blowers—and as he entered, his black suit billowed briefly around him. Then the doors swung shut again, his suit subsided, and he was in the midst of his kingdom.

Or what he had been able to salvage of it.

At this hour, it was mostly quiet, except for the rustling of the bird. For him, an aerie had been constructed, high above what passed for the dirt-floored riding ring. All along the far wall, behind a shoulder-high, white tile barrier with iron bars that rose, improbably, another fifteen feet in the air, al-Kalli could hear, and smell, his creatures. There was the occasional yelp or howl as he passed by—they could sense he was there—but he had no desire to stop and observe them tonight. Tonight he had more urgent business, with the man—Rashid—who was waiting nervously, in a soiled white lab coat, at the far end of the facility.

"Is it no better?" al-Kalli asked.

Rashid swallowed hard. "No, sir, I cannot say so."

Al-Kalli came to the farthest cage—a large pen easily a thousand feet square. The floor was dirt that looked as if it had been heavily raked, or pawed by something with powerful claws. A couple of small trees and bushes had been planted inside, around the lip of a private wading pool. Some bleached bones, snapped in half like twigs, lay on the ground. Although the air in the facility was changed constantly, there was still the unmistakable odor of a great beast here. An elephant, or a buffalo.

Al-Kalli looked through the bars. At first, it was difficult to see the creature. A kind of cave had been built in the back, from the same gray limestone that had once been used to build the main house. In the deepest recess of the cave, looking at first like nothing more than an immense black shadow, lay al-Kalli's most treasured possession—more valuable even than the book he was going to entrust to that young woman at the Getty.

"Did he take the medicine?"

"No, you can see for yourself, sir." Rashid pointed to an enormous joint of bloody meat that lay to one side of the cave entrance. "The medicine is inside it."

Al-Kalli had no great faith in it, anyway, or, increasingly, in Rashid. Rashid's forebears had, for time immemorial, tended to this bestiary; it was a job that was passed down, from one generation to the next, for as long as the al-Kalli family, too, had existed. And to that, there was no clear answer—the dynasty had gone on forever. It had fought the Crusaders, it had reveled in the gardens of Babylon, it had roamed in battle dress through the fertile crescent of the Tigris and Euphrates valleys. For all al-Kalli knew, it had plucked the fruit from the trees in the Garden of Eden.

And Rashid's ancestors had been its most loyal and faithful retainers for all that time. To them alone had been confided the secrets of the bestiary; to their care, the animals had been entrusted. Rashid's father had shared with him the ancient wisdom that his own father had shared with him, and his father before that. And the al-Kallis had then sent Rashid to a veterinary college in Cairo, to augment his knowledge with all the modern methods of animal care and husbandry.

But all of this, now, was proving to be of no avail. This beast, the last of its kind, was ailing. And Mohammed, to whom the legacy had been passed down, felt as if he were failing a thousand previous generations. He felt that the torch, which had burned so bright forever, was going to be extinguished on his watch. And with it, quite possibly, the power and wealth of the al-Kallis. Legend had always had it that the power of the family was inextricably tied to its strange inheritance. And though al-Kalli himself had been brought up in a secular world, schooled in England at Harrow and Sandhurst, he could no more shake this superstitious dread than a lapsed Catholic, at the moment of his death, could refuse absolution.

What was bred in the bone could never be taken from it.

"Has he eaten anything?" he asked Rashid.

"Not for days."

"Get a goat."

Rashid nodded his head and left. Al-Kalli brooded. What could be done? He could no more bring in an outside vet than he could have called a doctor in Iraq to care for his poisoned family. Once word of this got out, he would never be able to retain control. Once word got out, he would be found in violation of a hundred different codes, from the unauthorized importation of animals to the manifold lies on his immigration documents. His papers would be revoked; he and his son would be deported. And the bestiary? The bestiary, in the name of science, would be stolen.

The creatures would be dispersed, to God knew where, and the al-Kallis, too, would fade into history.

He could not let any of this happen.

Rashid returned, dragging a mottled gray goat by the horns.

Al-Kalli pressed the stainless steel release button, and the first of two gates slid open. Rashid dragged the goat into the small enclosure, left it there, and then scurried out again. Al-Kalli pressed the button one more time, the second gate slid back, and the goat was now left defenseless in the large pen.

Even if it hadn't seen anything yet, the goat could tell that it was in grave danger. It raised its head, scenting the air anxiously, and kept its hindquarters backed up against the gate. The goat pawed the dirt, lowered its head, sniffed at the soil. In the gloom of the cave, al-Kalli could see the beast stir. The goat, perhaps catching something on the breeze, suddenly defecated in fear. The beast lifted its monstrous head. The goat bleated, and first pranced to the left, then the right. Then stood stock-still. Al-Kalli was looking straight into the beast's eyes. They were a deep, smoldering yellow, overhung by a low crocodile-like brow.

"Eat," al-Kalli urged him in a low voice.

The goat bleated again, and looked all around for any means of escape.

"Eat."

The creature raised itself on its stubby front legs, but instead of lumbering out of its lair, it chose instead to turn—its haunches displayed the glistening scales of a reptile, tufted here and there with fur—and move farther into the shadows. Al-Kalli could hear it settling itself, out of sight, in the black recess of the cave.

It was not going to feed.

"You see," Rashid said, timidly. "It is like it no longer wants to live."

"It has to," al-Kalli said, more to himself than Rashid. "It has to."

CHAPTER SEVEN

GREER STOOD WITH his legs slightly apart and both hands on the pistol grip. He raised the gun, sighted, and squeezed the trigger.

A neat round hole appeared just to the left of center on the silhouette.

He adjusted his grip, aimed, and fired again—the barrel of the gun burst into orange flame, the gun gave a short recoil, and, as the smoke dispersed, he saw another hole, this one dead center in the light green silhouette of the man on the target fifty feet away.

He still had it. He'd been the best shot in basic training and the best in the field. And the Beretta 92FS—or, as it was known in the military, the M9—remained his weapon of choice. A lightweight semiautomatic with an aluminum alloy frame, it also featured a delayed locking block system, which provided a faster cycle time and exceptional accuracy. The reversible magazine release, positioned next to the trigger guard, gave a rightie or a leftie the same chance to drop the spent magazine clear and reload rapidly. More than once in Iraq, that little feature had come in handy.

Of course, the only times he carried this gun now (a duplicate of the one the army had issued him) was when he went on his home burglaries, and so far he'd been careful enough that he'd never had to use it. He only hoped things stayed that way.

Greer had never been to this place—the Liberty Indoor Firing Range—before. Sadowski had suggested they meet there, and to blow off steam Greer arrived early, and checked into lane 1 against the far wall. That way, he'd have nobody firing on his left side; ever since sustaining the damage to his left leg, he liked to keep things clear on that side of his body.

He fired a few more rounds, and when the extractor no longer protruded, he released the empty magazine and slapped a new magazine into the chamber. That was another good thing about the M9—you could feel for that protruding extractor even in the dark, and if you didn't feel it, you knew it was time to reload.

The door to the rear of the shooting gallery opened, and in walked Sadowski, wearing yellow goggle-style eye protectors, matching yellow noise-suppressing headphones, and carrying—why was Greer not surprised—a CX4 Storm. A state-of-the-art carbine, the CX4 was the perfect step up for any army vet who'd served in the Middle East. It took the standard Beretta pistol magazines, and the controls were immediately familiar to anyone who'd ever used the M9 models. But Sadowski's rifle, Greer could see, had a few extra options, like a vertical grip, a fore-end rail, and tactical lights attached on top. This guy was equipped to take on a whole SWAT team.

"You got time?" Sadowski hollered to Greer. "I want to do some shooting."

Greer nodded. He had some ammunition left himself, and he wasn't in any rush; there'd be plenty of time to ream out Sadowski afterward.

Sadowski, who'd set up in lane 2, clamped his target up, then pressed the button that sent it fluttering down the rails past the twelve-foot line, past the twenty-one-foot line, past the fifty, and all the way down to the far end of the range. Seventy-five feet. Greer might have expected that.

There was a dull popping noise from the only other shooter on the range, a Latino in lane 10, whose pants, Greer had noticed on the way in, were perilously close to falling off altogether.

Then Sadowski opened fire; even through his headphones, Greer could hear the loud bark of the semiautomatic and see the bright muzzle flash. He couldn't make out the target through the drifting smoke, but with all the extra sights and lights and whatever else Sadowski had attached to the gun, it would be hard to imagine him missing.

Greer finished off his own ammo, recalled his target—he'd shot a perfect little heart shape into the center of the silhouette—and went to wait inside the shop. There were glass display cases loaded with everything from holsters to hunting knives, racks of gun videos, stacks of boxes of small arms ammunition. Across from the restrooms—Greer had to wonder how much use the ladies' room got here—there was a combination classroom and lounge. At the front of the room a few folding chairs had been set up, facing a poster outlining the basic rules of gun safety. In the back, under a hand-lettered sign that said KUNG FU MY ASS—TRY TO KARATE CHOP A BULLET, there were a couple of beaten-up sofas and a coffee table covered with catalogues and dog-eared copies of *Field and Stream*.

Greer was leafing through one of them when Sadowski came in, his CX4 nestled away in a custom leather carrying case.

"You still using an M9?" Sadowski asked as he popped some coins into one of the vending machines. A Sprite clattered down. "You want a soda, Captain?"

"No, I do not want a soda."

Sadowski, still determined to pretend everything was right with the world, plopped down on the opposite sofa. The cushion bulged up on the other end.

"You want to tell me why?" Greer asked.

Sadowski took a sip of his Sprite. "Why what?"

"Why was there a dog-sitter in that house? Why was her

boyfriend in that house? And most of all, why didn't I *know* there were going to be people in that house?"

"I didn't know either," Sadowski protested. "That doctor hadn't put anything like that in the file. I checked."

"You checked. When? After I nearly had to drown that kid?"

"He's gonna be okay. We got a full report from the cops."

Greer snorted, and was about to continue when the guy from behind the front counter, who'd checked Greer's ID, waddled in; he was a fat guy dressed for the beach in flip-flops and shorts. He unlocked a vending machine, took out a few candy bars, and stuck them in the side pockets of his Hawaiian shirt.

Sadowski jumped at him like he was a life preserver. "Say, Burt, this is the guy I was wanting you to meet. Captain Greer, my old officer in Iraq."

The fat man came over and extended his hand. "Burt Pitt," he said, before adding, "no relation to Brad Pitt, in case you were wondering about the resemblance."

Sadowski laughed, and looked from Greer to Pitt, to make sure they had hit it off. "Burt owns this place," Sadowski said.

"So I gathered when he stole the candy bars," Greer replied.

"Stan's told me a lot about you."

Oh yeah, Greer thought—although he never used it, Sadowski did have a first name.

"Said you were the best commander he'd had in Iraq." He unwrapped a Twix bar and took a bite. "Said you took a hit over there, too. That why your left leg is sticking out straight?"

Greer didn't answer.

"You shoulda said something at the desk. I give a ten percent discount to vets."

Greer noticed that he had a Liberty Bell tattooed on his right arm.

"Stan tell you about our group?" Burt asked.

"Not much," Greer said. Was this guy ever going to leave? He wasn't done chewing out Sadowski. Stan.

"He ought to. You might be interested."

"I'm not what you call a joiner."

"You don't know till you hear. Stan, I'll give you some papers on your way out. You try to get your pal here to look 'em over."

"I will, Burt, I will."

"Nice meetin' you," he said, and Greer waited for the sound of his flip-flops to recede before starting up with Sadowski.

But he had no sooner begun than Sadowski raised a hand to stop him and said, "Captain, I've gotta tell you, I've got something you're really going to want to hear. Trust me."

"If it's about this fuckin' group of yours—the Nazi Brethren or whatever—I don't want to hear."

"No, no, you're gonna like this."

Greer sat back and waited.

"Remember, in Iraq, that little mission we went on?"

"God damn it, Sadowski—"

"And that palace we went to?"

"There's no one else here. Just spit it out."

"Well, Silver Bear just bought out another security firm."

"So? What's that got to do with Iraq?"

"So guess who one of their clients is? Who's now one of ours?"

Greer waited, but Sadowski, the idiot, was clearly expecting him to guess. "George Bush."

"Better. Remember the name of the guy who *owned* the palace?"

"Yes," Greer said, getting interested now. "His name was al-Kalli."

Sadowski just grinned.

"He's a Silver Bear client?"

Sadowski nodded his head yes.

Greer's mind was racing. "He lives here?"

"Top of Bel-Air, biggest fucking house up there."

Greer had to admit, he was taken by surprise. He sat up too quickly, and his leg suddenly twanged like a guitar string. Al-Kalli, here? In L.A.?

"He's got more land than anyone else up there, too."

What do you know, Greer thought. Sadowski had actually said something that might prove useful for a change; it was enough to make him forget about that little fiasco in Brentwood. And although he hadn't yet figured out how it was going to play out, he felt as though he had just heard the distinct sound of opportunity knocking.

CHAPTER EIGHT

AT THE TOP of the page, all in caps, it said FOR IMMEDIATE RELEASE.

Below that, the press release began: "As part of their on-going research into the world of prehistoric Los Angeles, paleontologists at the George C. Page Museum of Natural History have made a groundbreaking discovery, one which is sure to rewrite for all time the anthropological record of the western United States."

Carter's heart already began to sink.

"A team led by Dr. Carter Cox, Visiting Fellow and head of its Paleontology Field Research Department, has uncovered in an active dig site of the La Brea Tar Pits the fossilized remains of a human being . . ."

Carter put the paper down and looked up at Mr. Gunderson, the museum director. He was leaning back in his high-backed leather chair, with his hands folded across his belly.

"This hasn't gone out yet, has it?" Carter asked.

"You haven't even finished reading it. Go on."

Carter dropped his eyes to the page again; the glare in the room from Gunderson's bank of windows—washed at his insistence, according to the scuttlebutt, three times a week—made it difficult to read. The text made it even harder.

"Although the museum already contains over two million finds, ranging from mastodons to giant ground sloths, saber-toothed cats to camels, only once before have human remains been unearthed."

That much at least was true.

"Known as the La Brea Woman, she was approximately eighteen years old, stood a mere 4'8", and died, based on radiometric dating, 9,000 years ago. Although the cause of her death and how her remains came to be entombed in an asphalt seep (commonly referred to as tar) are questions that still beg an answer, one thing is now clear."

Carter could guess what was coming.

"La Brea Woman is no longer alone."

Why was this starting to sound more and more like a "Bride of Frankenstein" scenario? And did that make Carter the God-defying Victor Frankenstein?

"Discovered in what is known as Pit 91, an open dig site with an observation station open to all museum visitors, these early remains have yet to be dated—" Carter stopped and looked up again.

"It says here the remains have yet to be dated."

"Which is true," Gunderson replied.

"But only because they haven't even been excavated yet." Carter waved the press release in his hand. "This whole thing is premature. Not only haven't we removed the fossil, we haven't even gotten a good look at it yet. It's still buried in the tar."

"Dr. Cox," Gunderson said, leaning forward in his chair now, "we've made a marvelous discovery here, and I don't see any point in hiding our light under a bushel."

It didn't escape Carter's notice that Gunderson had included himself in the discovery.

"Do you know," Gunderson went on, "what museums and research institutions, just like this one, need to survive?"

Before Carter could tell him—it wasn't exactly a riddle worthy of the Sphinx—Gunderson went on.

"Money. And do you know what keeps the money flowing?"

"Prehistoric human remains?"

"News. And yes, in this case, prehistoric human remains happen to be the news. Big news, I might add."

Carter could see his point—he hadn't been raised in a cave—and Lord knows, he'd spent a fair amount of his own time chasing research grants and funds. But what he didn't want—what he never wanted—was to go off half-cocked.

"I understand what you're saying. But couldn't we just hold off a bit? All I need right now is a couple more people on my crew—experienced people—and some extended hours, a second automated pulley to remove the buckets, maybe even night lights. It's cooler at night, and we could get some more mucking-out done then."

"You make my point," Gunderson said. "Everything you're asking for costs money. And right now, the museum is strapped for funds."

Maybe he should have his windows washed only *twice* a week, Carter thought.

"And we have several grant requests that are currently under review. A discovery of this magnitude, given the proper play, could bring in a lot of additional monies. Not to mention the revenues from increased attendance alone. Can you imagine the number of people who will flock to the observation station to watch this drama unfold?"

Yes, Carter could well imagine that, and it was one of the main reasons he was so distressed at this press release. It was one thing to have a few faces, in a tour group, peering down from the observation platform, but it was another to have a raucous crowd tapping on the Plexiglas windows or trying to shout questions down into the pit. He was used to working in out-of-the-way places—the hills of Sicily, the Utah desert, the rural provinces of northeastern China—accompanied only by his fellow scientists and perhaps a few local workers. He wasn't yet accustomed to doing his fieldwork in the middle of a city, with an amateur crew, and gawkers wearing iPods and Nikes up above.

"Does this release," he said, "mention Miranda Adams?"

"No," Gunderson said, "who's Miranda Adams?"

"She's the young UCLA grad who actually first found the fossil."

"I thought you did."

"Not without her help."

Carter could see Gunderson's gears turning. How did this affect the story? Did it needlessly complicate it? Did it somehow lessen the museum's role?

"The news media would love that," Carter threw in. "A young woman, planning a career in paleontology, stumbling upon something so startling."

Gunderson pursed his lips and nodded. "Is she still working on the site?"

"Yes."

"She attractive?"

Carter should have seen that one coming. "Yes."

"Let me run this by the PR people. You could be right." Gunderson's phone rang; he glanced at the flashing light. "I've been expecting a call; this could be it."

Carter stood up, the press release still in hand. "Can you at least give me a few days to proof this before sending it out?"

But Gunderson had already picked up the phone and swiveled his chair to face the sparkling windows. He was saying something about a future exhibition; please, Carter thought as he folded up the release and stuck it in his pocket, don't let him be planning the "La Brea Man" exhibition quite yet.

T**HAT AFTERNOON, HE'D** planned a special treat for Miranda Adams.

As she had been the first to come upon whatever it was still lurking in the muck of Pit 91, Carter thought it would be a good idea to give her a firsthand tutorial on how the process worked. If she was thinking about becoming a physical anthropologist, there'd be no better introduction than this.

He'd arranged to meet her in the interior garden of the museum—an enclosed space where visitors could walk through a lush, verdant landscape, not so different from what it had been in the prehistoric era. Today, the garden was almost untenanted, apart from an elderly couple speaking German, and that Native American man Carter had seen at the observation window of Pit 91 many times before. Once you saw him—laden with silver and turquoise jewelry, a long black braid hanging down the back of his buckskin jacket—you didn't forget him. On at least one previous occasion, as Carter recalled, he'd become obstreperous with a museum docent and had been escorted off the grounds. Right now, he was just muttering to himself as he stared down into the running stream that coursed through the garden.

The security staff, Carter knew, had code-named him Geronimo.

When Miranda breezed in, twenty minutes late, Carter quickly escorted her down into the bowels of the museum, where few ever went. Down here were long, linoleum-floored corridors, with endless rows of numbered metal cabinets, each one divided up into a dozen separate drawers containing different plant and animal fossils from the region. Excavation had been going on since the turn of the twentieth century, and with such success that the area had actually lent its name to an age—the Late Pleistocene time in America, when man first appeared in the New World, had been officially designated the Rancholabrean Land Mammal Age.

Miranda wasn't really dressed for this excursion; the air down here was kept cool and dry, and she was wearing a light cotton blouse and a pair of culottes. Carter should have warned her in advance to wear a long-sleeved shirt, or even a sweater.

"Spooky down here, isn't it?" she said, as their footsteps echoed in the empty hall.

"Why would you say that?" Carter replied facetiously. "Underground, almost alone, surrounded by thousands—millions—of bones, from ancient animals that once hunted humans for lunch." A fluorescent tube hissed and flickered overhead. "And don't forget the state-of-the-art technology."

At the end of the corridor, Carter stopped at a cabinet like all the others, bent down, and slid out a wide, shallow drawer. In it, Miranda could see a collection of artifacts, all of them looking, even to her less practiced eye, man-made.

Carter slid the drawer entirely clear and carried it to a steel-gray examination table. There were several stools, and Miranda perched herself atop one of them.

"Who made these?" Miranda asked, just to prove she knew that much already.

"La Brea Woman," Carter said, "the one and only human so far found in the La Brea Tar Pits. And she was found in 1915. Now you may have come upon the second."

"That's not really true," Miranda said, though she couldn't restrain a bashful smile. "I only said there was something there. You're the one who found it—and knew what it was."

"We'll share the record books," Carter said, "and only after we do know what we've got."

He lifted one of the items, a rough-hewn stone, from the tray. "Ever seen one of these?"

Miranda had, but only in a slide from one of her UCLA lectures. "It looks like some kind of grinding stone."

"Very good," Carter said. "It's called a mano. But do you notice anything else about it?"

He handed it to her, and Miranda examined it more closely. The stone was chipped and scratched. "It's in pretty bad shape?" she guessed.

"You've just won the washing machine," Carter said. "It's been deliberately defaced."

"Not by a staff member, I hope."

Carter smiled. "No, the damage was done thousands of years ago, by one of the original aboriginal people. We think that it was part of their burial practices."

He put the mano back, and gave her a broken basalt stone the size of a brick. "See that kind of notch in the stone?"

She did.

"This is called a cogged stone. It might have been used

for weighting down fishing nets, or it could have been used with digging sticks; we really don't know."

"It looks kind of ornamental to me."

"Say, anybody ever tell you that you could be an anthropologist? There's a theory that cogged stones were used for some kind of ceremonial or symbolic purpose."

Miranda was very pleased with herself, and she glanced up at Carter.

"One more," he said, "before we move on to the main attraction."

He held up an abalone shell and said, "This might have been part of La Brea Woman's business."

"She sold seashells?"

"Not exactly, but she might have traded to get them."

"For jewelry?"

"Nope, this was a practical woman. She used shells like these for scooping up the hot tar and transporting it."

"What'd they use it for?"

"All sorts of stuff. It made a good adhesive, and we've also found it on the remnants of early canoes; tar was good for waterproofing."

Carter pushed the tray to one side of the table, then retrieved another, equally wide but deeper.

Deep enough to house the skull of the woman herself.

Miranda, he could tell, was impressed. And that was a good sign. If you were going to work in anthropology or paleontology, it was good to have a sense of wonder; most of the scientists he knew had never really lost it. No matter how many digs they went on, and how many bones or fossils they recovered, there was always something miraculous and breathtaking about it. Especially when the bones were those of an early hominid.

The skull of the La Brea Woman was small—she'd been diminutive by modern-day standards, standing well under five feet tall—and osteologic studies, based on the skull and the dozen or so other skeletal fragments that had been recovered, had revealed not much more about her. The pelvic bones did suggest she'd already given birth. But there was one thing that was not in any dispute.

"How come there's a different-colored patch here?" Miranda asked, indicating a section on top.

"Because her skull had been crushed," Carter replied.

Miranda paused, and brushed a wisp of blonde hair out of her eyes. "Do we know how?"

"It's possible it happened during the excavation; the left side of the lower jaw is also broken."

Miranda, hearing something in Carter's voice, said, "But you don't think so."

"No, I don't."

"You think she was . . . murdered?" It was odd, but Miranda had to wonder for a second if a person could be murdered long before that crime might have technically existed. Was there some anthropological term for the killing of a prehistoric human?

"I think she was struck with a heavy, blunt object," Carter said. "The discolored patch on top is plaster; it was used to fill in the missing portion of her skull."

He looked steadily into the empty eye sockets and the gaping jaws. In today's world she'd been only a teenager, but in the ancient and dangerous world in which she lived and died—was she a sacrifice of some kind, or a casualty of war?—the La Brea Woman was well along in life. A natural life that was, in the famous formula of Thomas Hobbes, nasty, brutish, and short.

Little different, Carter thought, from the life led by La Brea Man, who'd stretched out a poor, solitary hand to him from the depths of Pit 91.

"I'm getting kind of cold down here," Miranda said, with a visible shiver.

And Carter nodded; she wasn't reacting to the temperature alone, he knew. He put the specimens away and said, "Let's go back up into the sunlight, shall we?"

Miranda nodded eagerly and clung like a puppy to Carter's side until they were once again in the atrium garden, with nothing but blue sky and palm fronds overhead.

CHAPTER NINE

TURNING UP THE long private drive to Summit View, Beth's heart lifted; in just a few minutes, she knew, she was going to have her baby, Joey, in her arms again.

When she'd taken the job at the Getty, she'd made it clear that she could not work a full weekly schedule, that she expected to have a lot of flexibility and to be able, once or twice a week, to work from home. But so far it hadn't worked out that way. Mrs. Cabot expected her to be at the Getty Center nearly all the time, and whenever Beth was plainly not there—when she had to field a call from her house, for example—Mrs. Cabot sounded distinctly displeased about it.

And now, with the al-Kalli project under her supervision, Beth suspected things were only going to get worse.

To her surprise, Beth actually saw three people on her way up to the house. True, two of them were security personnel, but the third—a woman in a tracksuit and headphones—actually looked like she lived in one of the expensive, cookie-cutter houses that lined the broad streets of the development.

Beth parked her Volvo in the short driveway, next to the

nanny's Scion; the bumper stickers, which she'd never noticed before, said WAR IS NOT THE ANSWER and OIL EQUALS BLOOD. Who said young people weren't getting involved anymore?

On the way in, she also noticed, of all things, a cereal bowl resting on the grass not far from the front door. What, she wondered, was that doing there?

"Robin?" she called out, but she got no answer. "Robin?" A warm breeze, blowing from the rear of the house, beckoned her out back.

The French doors on the ground level were open to a small patch of now desiccated lawn; the drought restrictions made watering your grass a capital offense. Robin was on a beach towel, reading a magazine, and Joey was happily bouncing in his red and yellow playpen. He positively chirped when he saw his mother.

"Oh, hi," Robin said, putting down the magazine. "Didn't hear you come in."

"And how's my little angel?" Beth said, reaching down to pick up Joey. She nuzzled her cheek against his, marveling all over again at the smoothness, the perfection, of his little face. She knew all new mothers thought their own babies were the cutest in the world, but in her case she felt the empirical evidence was there; this *was* the cutest baby in all the world, with perfectly sculpted features, delicate blond ringlets, and eyes . . . eyes that seemed somehow wise, as if they were taking in everything at one glance.

"How's he been today?" Beth asked, expecting—and getting—the usual answer.

"Good as gold."

"Did I see a cereal bowl near the front door?"

Robin chuckled, and said, "You did. We've had a visitor the past few days."

Holding the baby in her arms, Beth waited for more.

"I hope you don't mind, but he looks so pathetic. A big yellow dog, mostly Lab I'd say, who kind of hangs around. It was so hot, I put out a bowl of water for him."

"Is he a stray?"

"Yes, I didn't see any collar on him."

Beth was torn—she loved animals, but she wasn't so sure she liked the idea of a stray dog hanging around the house where she had to leave Joey all day.

Robin, guessing what Beth was thinking, said, "He's friendly—kind of skittish, but friendly. And I never let him get anywhere near the baby."

Beth knew Robin would act responsibly; she might be young—twenty, and just out of community college—but she was a nice kid, and a real find. Already Beth had heard enough nanny horror stories to last her a lifetime.

"Are you in a rush?" Beth asked, "or could you hang around while I take a quick bath?"

"No problema," Robin said, taking up her magazine again—now Beth could see it was *In Touch Weekly*—"it's nice to see the sunsets from here."

Beth had to agree—the houses here were built along a ridge, facing the Santa Monica Mountains. From the tiny backyards, you had a staggering view out over the canyon, toward the looming, chaparral-covered mountainsides, and the sun setting behind them.

Beth put Joey back in his playpen and went upstairs. She started filling the tub, but not with hot water. The temperatures in L.A. had been running in the low nineties, and nothing would feel better than something cool and cleansing and refreshing. When she got in, she felt as if she were shedding everything from the hot, gritty city to the pressures at work.

She could hear her cell phone ringing on the bed. She'd pick up the message—probably from Carter—when she got out. She hoped he'd say he was bringing home some food. One of the things she found so strange about living up here, especially after so many years in New York City, was how removed it was from everything. There were no delis, no dry cleaners, no pizza parlors, no newsstands. You couldn't just walk out your front door and get something. You either had to get it delivered or you had to drive way back down to Sepulveda, and from there head back toward Brentwood or down to the Valley. It meant you had to sort of organize your time and errands; when you were out, you had to remember everything from the post office to the pharmacy, because once you got back home again, it was too late. Once you were home, in the quiet confines of Summit View, you were just plain home.

Like most things in life, Beth reflected, Summit View had its good points—this tub alone was twice the size as the one in New York—and its bad—she missed having neighbors she knew and liked.

She put on a sky blue silk robe—her first Mother's Day gift from Carter—and picked up her message. It was indeed Carter, and he was calling, God bless him, from Dynasty Chinese, where he'd just picked up some dinner. How'd she get so lucky?

She went back downstairs in bare feet. And though she'd always thought wall-to-wall carpeting was kind of tacky, now that she had it, she had to admit that it sure felt good under your feet. Carter was just coming through the door, white plastic bags in hand.

"You get my message?" he said.

"I did." She kissed him hello. "Robin's in back with Joey. I'll go and tell her she's released from her bondage."

"Say, did I see a bowl on the lawn?" he asked as he took the bags into the kitchen.

"I'll explain later," Beth called.

They ate in the breakfast nook, with Joey propped up on the window seat, a cushion or two keeping him from rolling off. Carter had picked up her favorite—shrimp with glazed walnuts—and a couple of other things just to lend some variety to the feast. Over a glass of cold white wine, she told him about the stray dog, and he told her about ex-huming the La Brea Woman's bones from their drawer in the museum. He also told her that he'd used the occasion to teach Miranda Adams something about doing anthropological work.

"Uh-huh," she said, "isn't this Miranda kind of a babe?"

Carter knew he had unthinkingly sailed into treacherous waters. "Some men might think so."

"Some men?"

"Okay," he conceded, "men with eyes."

She tossed the uneaten half of her fortune cookie at him. The fortune was still inside.

Carter unfolded it and read it aloud: " 'Patience is a virtue worth waiting for.' "

"What's yours?"

He unwrapped another cookie, read it, then paused.

Beth had her feet propped up on his thigh and said, "So?" She wriggled her toes. "What's it say?"

"It says, 'Fear is your friend—learn from it.' "

"Whoa," she said, with a laugh, "that's pretty heavy for a fortune cookie."

"You're telling me," Carter replied, oddly discomfited by it. "Maybe I should complain to the management." He couldn't help but think of the skeletal hand, reaching up from the pit. What was he meant to learn from that, he wondered?

The sun had gone down behind the mountains, and they turned on the lights to clean up and do the dishes. Beth carried Joey up to the nursery—he seemed pooped, and felt like a sack of potatoes in her arms—while Carter got undressed and took a shower. When he came out, looking dashing as ever in a pair of boxers and a *T. rex* T-shirt (Beth had never guessed one person—much less a grown man—could own so many dinosaur-themed clothes), Beth was already turning out her bedside light.

"Not so fast," Carter said, plopping himself on the bed beside her. "You're not planning on going to sleep so soon, are you?"

Beth could hear the hopeful note in his voice, and much as she wanted to keep him happy, the fatigue was washing over her like a tide. "I'd like to, you know that, honey . . ."

She heard the drawer of Carter's bedside table open, and she knew what he was taking out. Carter drew the sheet down off her body—it was too hot these days to sleep under anything more—and then he was removing her nightie. Beth didn't fight it, in fact she tried to cooperate, but her limbs felt like lead, and she wished she hadn't had that wine with dinner.

There was a splooshing sound as he squirted the lotion

into his hands, then rubbed them together to warm it up. "Roll over on your belly," he said.

That much she could do. She rolled over in the dark, and felt Carter's hands rest gently on her shoulders. She could smell the sandalwood scent of the body lotion. And then she felt his hands moving, first in small circles on her shoulder. Then in widening circles. It felt wonderful . . . too wonderful in a way. If she wasn't careful, she could drift off into unconsciousness. And she knew that was not what Carter was aiming at.

"How's that feel?" Carter asked, kneeling now with one long leg on either side of her.

"Good," she mumbled into the pillow. "Very . . . good."

His hands moved lower, down her back. Then out to her sides. He was being very gentle, very solicitous. Beth thought, *I've got to stay awake. I've got to get with it.* His hands moved lower, caressing her waist, and then below.

He moved down the bed, and adjusted his weight above her. The mattress squished down, then up again. She sensed, without even having to look up, that he'd somehow managed to get his T-shirt and shorts off.

Wake up, she told herself.

He was lying beside her, his hands still moving on her body. He was aroused, too—she could feel him nudging her hip, anxiously. Damp already.

But something in her was still failing to click. Ever since the baby, she'd been slow to arousal, and quick to sleep. Maybe it was the pressure of everything, from having a baby to moving to L.A., from the new house to the new job. He slipped one hand between her legs, parting them.

She was still dry, and knew it. He'd know, too, in another second.

"Do you not want to do this?" he said, his voice husky. He was trying to sound okay with that, but she knew he wasn't.

"It's just that I'm so tired."

He moved his fingers against her, in one last-ditch attempt. And Beth willed herself to squeeze down against them, to rub herself on his fingertips. He licked them, and tried again.

He was kneeling now between her legs. Lifting her hips.

Her hair hung down in her eyes, her face pressed down against the pillows. She spread her knees.

He reached past her, grabbed the pillows, and pushed them under her. She let her belly rest on the cool, smooth cloth.

His hands gripping her, holding her in place, he pressed himself against her from behind, first probingly, then hard. But she was still dry, and she could tell it must be chafing him as much as it did her.

"Should I get some . . . lubricant?" he said in a strained voice.

"No," she said, arching her back, "just go on."

"You sure?"

She didn't answer, just nodded her head.

And he pushed harder—slowly, then deep. He was in, but to Beth it still felt rough and tight. She wasn't really ready, she wasn't really receptive.

He pushed again, even deeper, and it felt—to both of them now—like every centimeter was a battle.

"Can I . . . ?"

"Yes," she said, "yes . . ."

She knew his rhythms, she knew what he was asking. And where she used to want him to wait, to wait as long as possible—and he was good at that, very good—right now all she wanted was for him to finish.

And she knew he knew that.

His hands clenched her hips, and he pulled her back against him. She moved her knees as wide as she could. He moved into her, then out, then in again, several times. Faster. Suddenly, he groaned, and grew very still, arched, immobile, against her hot skin. She, too, stayed still, waiting for him to subside. A few moments later, he bent forward, resting his head between her shoulder blades. She could feel his breath, ragged, on the nape of her neck. She let her knees, starting to ache now, come together.

Carter rolled off of her and onto his back, one hand resting flat on his chest.

Beth moved the pillows out of the way, and lay on her side, facing him.

His eyes were closed.

"I'm sorry," she said. "I'm just—"

"It's okay," he said, his eyes still shut.

"No, it's not, I—"

"Beth," he said, "it's alright. I shouldn't have pushed it."

She moved closer to him, and he draped one arm around her head and shoulder. She did love the smell of him. Now if only she could get that . . . *feeling* back.

She wanted to tell him that, she wanted to explain, and make it up to him somehow, but before she was really aware of it, before she was able to utter another word, she was fast asleep.

And Carter could tell—her breathing went suddenly low and steady. Her lips were slightly parted against the pillow-case.

He lay on his back, in the dark, thinking. While, most of the time, sex left him nicely drowsy, it wasn't having that effect tonight.

He knew that new mothers often had some trouble getting back into the groove; he'd read the articles, he knew about the bonding process she was going through with Joey. He would have liked to have the old Beth back—their sex life had always been vigorous, to say the least—but he understood that he was going to have to give it some more time. No, that wasn't really the reason his mind was still churning.

What was keeping him awake was everything else—Pit 91, the La Brea Woman, Gunderson's publicity plans. He wanted to turn it all off, but the longer he lay there, the more his mind continued to go over it all. He envied Beth the deep, untroubled sleep she seemed to be enjoying. There was no way, he knew, that he was going to get there himself, not this early. Without waking her, he moved her head away from his shoulder, brushed the long dark hair away from her lips, and got out of bed. He put on some jeans, the *T. rex* T-shirt, and his rubber thongs, and went across the hall to check on Joey.

The moonlight was coming through the blinds, but even without that, he would have known Joey was awake. Not that he was making any noise; he seldom did that. But as Carter leaned over the edge of the crib, he could see that Joey's eyes—a kind of gray blue—were open, as if he'd been simply waiting for his dad to come in. It was nearly always like this, and Carter often wondered if that was the way babies were—were they such finely tuned instruments that they woke up the minute anyone got near them? Never having had one before, he had no means of comparison.

"Don't you ever sleep?" Carter whispered.

Joey wiggled his legs, wanting to be picked up.

Carter leaned in and lifted him. "How was your day?" he asked, as if expecting an answer. "You and Robin have some fun?"

The baby calmly studied Carter's face.

"You think your daddy's good looking? Someday I'll show you my whole T-shirt collection." He bounced his son on his arm; Joey was wearing white cotton pj's with little red roosters all over them.

Carter carried the baby downstairs to the kitchen, where he deposited him in the high chair, while he finished off some of the Chinese food leftovers. But he still wasn't feeling sleepy. What might help, he thought, was a short walk and a cigar.

Beth forbade smoking in the house, and wasn't crazy about the fact that Carter did it at all. But Carter had been hoarding a fine Macanudo that Gunderson, of all people, had stuck in his pocket when Carter had first told him about the find in Pit 91.

"Want to take a walk?" Carter asked Joey, who was forming a small bubble between his lips. "I'll take that as a yes."

While he'd have thought twice about a late-night stroll with a baby and a cigar anywhere else, in Summit View it posed no problem; who was gonna see him? There was never anyone on the streets even during the day. And at this hour, on a hot night, he could count on seeing no one.

The street they were on—Via Vista—was the last one in the development, and it dead-ended in the hillside just above. It was wide and curving, and dimly lighted by the lampposts, which were fairly few and far between. One of their neighbors had once told him that the homeowners' association had voted to keep it that way; they wanted it to have the feel of living out in the country—which, to some extent, they'd done. Although the 405 freeway was just a few minutes away, up here it was dark and quiet, and the air smelled of the dry brush in the canyon behind the houses.

That was another thing Carter found so surprising, and unexpected, about living in L.A. Yes, you heard all the time about the traffic and the sprawl and the smog, but no one ever told you about how intimately nature was woven into the fabric of the city. In New York, you had Central Park, and the occasional green pocket here and there, but in L.A. you had mountains and canyons, beaches and ravines, everywhere you went. Looking off to his left, there was a tennis court—several of them dotted the development— but just beyond its fence the land fell away, and quite steeply, into a dense forested valley. All Carter could see in the summer moonlight was a deep, dark cleft, with the rolling flank of the Santa Monica Mountains in the distance. The only sign of civilization in there were the towers that rose up, well above the treetops, to carry the high-power lines. Atop each one a red beacon light went on and off and on again.

Carter strolled slowly, careful to blow his cigar smoke away from the baby. Joey rested his head against his father's shoulder, but if Carter had to guess, he'd bet the kid's eyes were still open. What did babies think about? What *could* they think about? Without a sufficiently developed cerebral cortex, it was unclear how much they could process, and what, if anything, they would ever be able to remember. When would it be, Carter thought, that he'd be able to tell his son about the man he'd been named after? Giuseppe—or Joe—Russo, Carter's close friend and associate. The Italian paleontologist who'd brought into Carter's life the greatest discovery he'd ever made—and who had paid for that discovery with his own life.

Carter took another puff of the cigar, and scanned the windows of the neighboring houses. The only lights that were on were over the garages. Was anybody home, he wondered, in any of them?

Joey stirred in his arms.

And would his son ever understand just what a miracle child he was? Carter had been told it was impossible for him to father a child, that a boyhood illness had rendered him sterile. And then, in defiance of all the odds, Beth had become pregnant after all. Carter could still recall the surprise on the fertility expert's face.

Via Vista stopped, on the south end, where the scrub-covered side of the hill rose up. Carter turned around, and leaving the sidewalk, headed back down in the center of the street. It's not like there were going to be any cars up here. Looking all the way down the wide, curving road, he saw only one thing moving, and at first he thought it was just a shadow.

Then it moved again, and he knew it wasn't.

From here, it looked like a medium-sized dog, maybe a collie. The first thing that occurred to him was that it might be that stray dog Beth had told him about. It had come up from the canyon side; maybe it lived in the brush somewhere.

Carter continued on, his flip-flops slapping the concrete street, enjoying his cigar . . . when the dog stopped and looked up the street at him.

And now he could see it was not a dog. The snout was too narrow, the bushy tail was held straight down from the body. This was a coyote, the first one Carter had seen since his fieldwork in Utah.

And the only one he'd ever seen in the middle of a street.

Nor, he suddenly realized, was it alone.

Several other shadows slowly emerged above the lip of the scrubby hillside. Skulking low, along the ground, walking on their toes—digitigrade—with that distinctive gait of their species.

Carter stopped in his tracks; his grip on Joey instinctively tightened.

One of the pack was loping toward Carter's front lawn.

The bowl. With the water in it. They'd come up looking for water. In Utah, Carter had once seen a coyote leap an eight-foot wall to get to a cattle trough.

He'd also seen one take down a lamb with a single savage bite to the throat.

He quickly surveyed the area. The nearest house on his left was black and the low fence in front of it would offer no protection at all.

To his right, there was only the tennis court. But it did have a high Cyclone fence around it—high enough even to keep a coyote from leaping over it.

Carter moved slowly to his right, the cigar still clenched and glowing between his teeth.

The first coyote was still watching him; normally, coyotes were afraid of humans and would run for cover, but for all Carter knew, these had become acclimated. Or bold. Maybe the drought conditions had forced them to try some new survival strategies.

He inched his way up onto the curb—the watching coyote took a step in his direction—and edged toward the tennis court, never taking his own eyes off the animal. Coyotes were great stalkers, he knew—they would follow or chase their prey indefinitely, until the poor creature, exhausted, gave up. And then the pack would descend upon it.

Carter reached out one hand to the tennis court gate and tried the latch. For some reason, it didn't go down. He tried again, then, looking away from the coyote for an instant, he glanced at the handle. Which had a padlocked chain around it.

They locked the courts at dusk, so hard-core players wouldn't keep their neighbors up at night.

The coyote that had loped onto his lawn came out again, licking its chops. Two others followed it. And they, too, smelled—then saw—Carter up the street.

They fanned out, approaching slowly. Carter would appear formidable to them, but the scent and sight of a baby they would find irresistible. Their tails, Carter noticed, had extended horizontally from their bodies—a clear sign of aggression.

He could try a run for it, but he'd never make it through them to his own front door. And it might just encourage them to attack.

He looked in vain for any sign of the nightly patrol car. But there was none.

Fear is your friend, he suddenly thought. Learn from it.

But what? Learn what?

Fire. Fire is your friend, too.

And the coyotes' enemy.

He anxiously looked around. A bush, with scraggly, dry branches, was a few feet away. He went closer, puffing madly on his cigar. The tip glowed hot and bright, and Carter took it from his mouth and touched it to a brittle leaf.

The leaf burst into flame, and then the flame raced down the withered branch.

Carter reached below it, into the bush, and snapped off the now burning branch. It wouldn't burn long so he had to work fast.

Holding the branch in front of him, waving it just enough to let the smoke drift their way, he moved down the street toward the coyotes. Still they stood their ground. Carter went closer, toward what he perceived to be the leader of the pack—a scraggly gray beast with glaring eyes and raised ears. The branch was snapping and crackling in his hand, but the flame was also burning perilously close to his fingertips. He wouldn't be able to hold it for more than a few seconds.

Joey turned his head to look at the coyotes, but didn't know enough to be afraid.

The gray coyote bared its fangs and growled softly. The others gathered closer, moving forward with their bodies close to the concrete, their black-tipped tails rigid.

The fire singed Carter's thumb, and before it went out altogether, he tossed the smoldering branch at the leader. Who jumped back.

And Carter ran, his thongs flapping, toward his own

front door. He was clutching Joey under his arm like a running back carrying a football.

He broke through the line of coyotes, and kept on moving. But he could sense at least one of the animals turning, and dogging his heels. He could hear panting.

And then he felt fur, brushing his leg. The coyote was going to try to leap up and snatch the baby from his arms.

He raced along, one thong flying off his foot, and then the other. Now he could run faster. But it still wasn't fast enough. He could tell another coyote was easily keeping pace with him on his other side. They were hunting as a pack.

He had just made it to his own driveway—Beth's Volvo was still parked there, but he knew it would be locked—when he felt a rush of air hurtling toward his neck. And a raging snarl. Something struck him between the shoulder blades, but he didn't turn around. He heard an angry yelp, and the sound of two animals tearing at each other in a mad frenzy.

He got to his door and threw it open, then kicked it shut behind him. There was a scrabbling sound, something clawing at the door, accompanied by wild barks and growls. A fight was going on, right outside the door. Carter, still clutching Joey, went to the window, where he saw a furious tussle of fur and fangs. But why would the coyotes be attacking each other?

He stood, gasping for breath, and realized, to his shock, that one of the battling animals was a dog—a yellow dog. That stray.

Three of the coyotes had given up and were strung out in the street; the gray one, caught up in the fight, suddenly gave up, too, and scooted away, yelping, his tail down.

The yellow dog barked ferociously, and stood, with his tail batting against the door, like a sentinel.

The coyotes took one long backward glance, as if saying *we'll be back*, then trotted behind their wounded leader back toward the ravine.

The dog barked again and again, making sure they knew who'd won.

And Carter, catching his breath, wondered what to do next.

A light went on in the upstairs of the house across the street—the first time Carter had ever seen that happen.

Beth, alarmed and standing at the top of the stairs, said, "What's going on? Carter—what's happening?"

"We're okay," he said. "We're all okay."

He flicked on the lights so that they flooded the front lawn and driveway.

Beth hurried down the stairs, fastening her blue robe around her.

"You've got Joey?" she said, puzzled.

"Take him," Carter said, handing over the still unperturbed baby. For all Carter knew, Joey had thought this whole thing was a grand adventure.

Carter went to the door. He could hear the yellow dog, not barking anymore, but panting.

He opened the door cautiously. The dog had blood on the crown of its head.

It turned around and looked at him.

"You okay?" Carter asked. It was a mutt, but mostly lab.

The dog took a second, then wagged its tail in reply.

Carter went outside, pulling the door closed behind him, and knelt down by the dog. "You saved my neck," he said, "you know that, champ?"

The dog, still breathing hard, just looked at him. He had no collar, no tags. He looked pretty beaten up.

"I don't suppose you can tell me your name," Carter said, tentatively holding out the back of one hand.

The dog sniffed the hand, waited.

"How about Champ? Can you live with that?"

The dog looked like he could. He licked the sweat off Carter's fingers.

Carter stroked the dog under the muzzle, where the fur was damp. Then he rubbed the dog's back. The gash on the top of its head would need stitches.

"It's been a long night," Carter said, getting up. "What do you say you come inside?" Carter swung the door wide open and waited, silently, to one side. Beth, holding Joey in her arms, was standing in the foyer, looking as if she had no idea what was going on. "Honey," Carter said, as the dog hesitantly stepped across the threshold, clearly unsure if this was allowed, "I want you to meet Champ."

CHAPTER TEN

DEAR MR. AL-KALLI.

No, that didn't even look right.

My dear Mr. al-Kalli.

Nah, how would he know that Greer was being sarcastic?

Dear Sir.

Christ, it sounded like something from a bill collector.

Greer stared at the computer screen, a cigarette hanging off his lower lip. If he couldn't even get past this part, how was he ever going to figure out what kind of letter he wanted to write? Or just what it was he wanted to say?

Ever since Sadowski had told him about al-Kalli living in L.A., Greer had been consumed with questions and plans and possible schemes. He knew there was money to be made out of this, somehow, but he wasn't sure how to approach it.

On the one hand, he could simply start with a strong appeal. After all, Captain Greer, as he had been known then, had led a patrol into dangerous territory, solely to execute a mission commissioned by al-Kalli. And in the course of that perilous mission, he, Greer, had been sorely injured. Handicapped. For life. Surely that was due some special compensation, above and beyond the fifty thousand dollars Greer had been given to cover expenses. (He'd arranged to share out twenty thousand with the soldiers he took along, but since Lopez hadn't come back, Greer had hung on to his cut.)

But that would be counting on al-Kalli's generosity and charity. And Greer had no reason to expect he was either generous or charitable. For starters, he was an Arab; for another, Greer had never even met the man. All of his dealings had been through some guy named Jakob, who had given him just enough information—maps and all—to proceed, but not a single thing more. Greer was a pretty good judge of guys like Jakob, and the guy's demeanor positively screamed secret service/martial arts/M1/Savak/Mossad, one of those. Greer had gotten back to camp, and even before he was airlifted to the army hospital in Germany, Jakob had showed up to claim the mysterious box. Greer had never even had a chance to try to jimmy it open.

Or, Greer thought, sitting back in the chair and taking a long drag on the cigarette (his mother hated him smoking in the apartment—she claimed she was allergic, but Greer didn't buy it for a second), he could simply go straight for the shakedown. "Dear Mr. al-Kalli, I recovered some of your private property—under color of U.S. military authority—from your palace in Iraq, and unless you come across with some additional money in the amount of . . ." How much, Greer wondered, would be reasonable? One hundred thousand dollars? Five hundred thousand? An even million? If only he knew what it was he'd smuggled out for him. ". . . I will be forced to report you to . . ." Who? The immigration office? The State Department? The L.A. City Council?

God damn it. Greer didn't even know what he could threaten him with. A man like al-Kalli probably had most people in his pocket anyway. And what if he turned the tables on Greer? It wasn't, after all, a sanctioned U.S. army mission. And it could open a further investigation into the disappearance of Lopez, who'd first been listed as AWOL, and then, when he never showed up at all, as missing in action. Greer had pushed to make sure that the MIA status happened; that way, Lopez's wife at least got the death benefit. He was proud of himself for having gone that extra mile for one of his men.

The computer screen was still mostly blank, waiting for him to come up with something. He went onto the Internet instead, visited a couple of his favorite porn sites, then figured he'd need to give it some more thought. Didn't writers always say bullshit like that all the time—that their best ideas just came to them out of nowhere, when they weren't even thinking about it?

"Derek, didn't I ask you not to do that?" his mother called out from behind his bedroom door.

"Do what?" he said, waving the smoke toward the open window.

"I can smell it out here. You know I'm allergic."

He stubbed out the cigarette and logged off. It was almost time to leave, anyway; he had a date in Westwood, with his physical therapist.

He'd been sort of considering it for a long time, but he hadn't gotten up his nerve to ask her until the last session. And he couldn't tell whether she was really interested or just being nice to a gimp. She'd said she'd meet him there, at the California Pizza Kitchen, a place he'd never set foot in. He was more of a Carl's Jr. kind of guy. But he hadn't been on what you'd call a date for a very long time, so maybe that was what you did these days.

In Westwood, he circled the area several times until he found a spot on the street—no way was he going to pay those parking garage fees—so by the time he got to the restaurant, Indira was already waiting outside. It was the first time he'd ever seen her when she wasn't wearing her white coat. She had on a pair of black slacks and a striped blouse; her hips were bigger than he thought they'd be—that white coat was pretty good camouflage—but she looked good. He walked toward her slowly, so his limp would be less pronounced.

"You look hot," he said.

Indira looked confused, touching her face to see if she was perspiring. "I'm not," she said.

"No, I meant you look . . . sexy."

"Oh. Thank you," she said, but it didn't sound to Greer like she meant it.

Maybe that hadn't been the right thing to say to her.

"You want to go in?" he said, holding open the door to the restaurant. Indira went in, and Greer quickly checked out her ass. Ample, but he was okay with that. They were shown to a table pretty near the door.

The waiter came by, took their drink orders—a beer for Greer, and a white wine spritzer for Indira—then left them to what should have been their own conversation. It's just that there wasn't one. Indira sat silent, pretending to study her menu, while Greer searched for something to say. How come it was no big deal at the clinic? There, he'd talk about what he'd seen on TV the night before, or the Lakers game, or what his mother had done to piss him off. True, Indira never said much in return, just sort of smiled and nodded from time to time, but he was sure she was paying attention and wanted to hear more. Now, he couldn't think of a thing to say.

"Parking was a bitch," he finally said.

Indira nodded. "Yes, in Westwood it's very hard."

"Where'd you park?"

"I didn't. I took the bus."

Huh. Maybe physical therapists made even less money than he thought.

"They're very convenient, the buses in L.A."

"Never knew that."

The waiter brought their drinks, and Greer started in on his before thinking that maybe he should have clinked her glass or something. Indira didn't seem to mind.

The waiter came back to take their order, and Greer had to tell him to come back; he hadn't even looked at the menu yet.

"The Thai Crunch Salad is very good here," Indira volunteered.

Greer knew that the salad was at least one thing he

wouldn't be ordering. The place was called a pizza kitchen, so he was expecting to get a pizza or maybe a sausage calzone. He glanced over at a couple of college kids sitting at the next table; the girl was eating a mound of greens and sprouts and the guy had what Greer guessed they called a pizza here—it was a delicate-looking thing, with all kinds of shit on top but nothing that looked like green peppers or pepperoni. And the guy was actually eating it with a fork and knife.

The waiter returned; Indira asked for her salad, and Greer ordered a grilled chicken sandwich with lettuce and tomatoes. What could they do to fuck up a chicken sandwich?

"How is your leg feeling?" Indira asked, and he was sorry she had. The whole point of this was that it was supposed to be like a date; she wasn't supposed to act like his PT and he wasn't supposed to have to act like a patient.

"It's okay," he said. He had it sticking out kind of straight, under the table.

"Are you doing your home exercises?"

Christ. "You bet."

Another uncomfortable silence fell. Indira looked around the restaurant, and Greer followed her gaze. The place was filled with UCLA students and tables occupied by young women laughing and gabbing away. He knew he wasn't actually much older than they were, but he felt like there was a canyon about a mile wide between him and them. They all looked so damn happy and young and, well, not exactly rich, but like money was no problem at all. They looked like they'd never seen anything all that bad happen . . . and, though he knew this was the kind of thought that would land him right back in psychiatric counseling, it made Greer want to show them something . . . something like the shit he'd seen on the "Highway to Hell," as they'd called it, between Baghdad and the main airport.

"So, what have you been up to?" Indira asked, smoothing her napkin in her lap.

"This and that," Greer replied. "Went to the shooting range the other day." While he told her a little about the firing range and his pal Sadowski, his thoughts kept returning to what he'd really just been up to—trying to compose a blackmail note. He really needed some solid advice here—how did you turn a profit on this whole al-Kalli connection?—but for obvious reasons it wasn't the kind of thing he could bring up to Indira. At least not now. But maybe if they got something going . . . later on . . .

Things got a little bit better while they ate—Indira told him about growing up in Bombay, and how she went back there every other year to see her grandparents—and Greer had two more beers, which definitely helped his mood. He'd actually started to feel halfway friendly toward all the other customers trooping in and out of the place—maybe he didn't stand out the way he thought he did—when some chick in high heels tripped over his foot.

"Sorry," she said, but in an exaggerated way, to prove that she really wasn't.

Greer's leg had twisted against the base of the table, and now it felt like his toe had been jammed in a light socket. He didn't say anything, but Indira could tell from his face that he'd really felt it.

"Are you alright?" she asked him.

"You really shouldn't stick your feet out into the aisle," the woman said. "I could have killed myself."

"If you don't get your ass out of here," Greer muttered, without looking up, "I will fucking kill you myself."

The woman looked stunned. One of her friends, also leaving, took her by the arm and said, "Come on, Emily— the guy's a nut job, let him be."

"He's not a nut job," Indira shot back, whirling around on them. "He is a United States Army veteran and you should show him some respect."

The women were speechless now; other people were watching.

"You should be giving him *your* apology," Indira said. "Now get out."

And they did: One of them turned to throw a defiant glance back, but Indira froze her out with a glare.

Greer could hardly believe it; it was like a mother lion rearing up to defend one of her cubs.

"I'm alright," he said, to calm the waters. "No harm done."

Indira turned back to him, her eyes down, and busied herself with her drink and her salad. The show over, the other diners went back to their meals.

Greer gently massaged his leg under the table until it no longer felt like an electrical conduit. Man, he would never have expected that outburst from Indira; she was always so under control. But there was fire under that hood; he could see it now.

When she excused herself to go to the ladies' room, he quickly dug down deep in his pocket and took out the little foil packet with his private stash of OxyContin. There were only two left; he'd need to hit up Zeke at the Blue Bayou for some more. He swallowed them both quickly with the last of his beer.

Indira came back, and Greer threw some bills on the table.

"No, no, I'll pay for myself," Indira insisted.

"Come on," Greer said, "it's the least I can do for my public defender."

"No, you should not have to pay," Indira said.

But Greer simply levered himself up and out of the chair, and Indira let it go.

"Thank you very much."

Greer nodded and started for the door. Outside, the streets were crowded; it was a hot night, and the Bruin and the Fox—two of the old, big-screen theaters in Westwood—had long lines snaking down the sidewalks.

"You want to see a movie?" Greer asked, already starting to feel the numbing effect of the drugs.

"No, thank you. I can catch the bus over on Gayley."

"What bus?" Greer said. "I'll drive you home."

Indira started to protest again, but Greer just turned and headed back toward his car. He was hoping he hadn't left anything incriminating out on the seat in plain sight. But when he got there, the worst of it was some burger wrappers and a few flyers from some strip clubs, all of which he tossed into the backseat.

Indira lived with her family way over on the west side of L.A., in what turned out to be a Spanish bungalow on a narrow lot; a white van, with ELECTRICAL REPAIR AND INSTALLATION written on its side, was parked on the concrete patch where a lawn had probably once been.

"Your dad an electrician?"

"In Bombay, he was a civil engineer."

All the lights in the house were on, and he could hear somebody's radio playing.

What, he wondered, was he supposed to do now? Even when he was a teenager, he hadn't done a lot of this stuff— the girls he knew then just met you down at the beach, and you screwed around under the lifeguard stand at night. Since then, he had largely been in the company of professionals; if he'd been with one of them now, he'd be halfway done already.

He put the car in park, and started to lean across the seat. But Indira, reading his intentions, backed away with her hand on the door handle.

"Thank you very much for dinner, Captain."

Captain? That was a bad sign.

"But I must go in now."

Greer pulled back; fortunately, the OxyContin was making him feel nice and mellow right now. "You don't want to . . . ?" he asked, without even finishing the sentence. He shrugged, like it was of no consequence. "That's okay."

"But I will see you next week, for your regular appointment."

All of a sudden, it seemed to Greer that she was all business. It was as if she were wearing her lab coat again.

She got out of the car, and he watched as she opened the door of the house. The radio got louder; it was playing 50 Cent. What the hell, he thought. Maybe that's all this had been, after all; a PT being nice to a crip. Letting him practice his social skills.

Fine. No problem. He had places to go.

He put the car back in gear, let the engine roar once or twice to signal his departure, then took off for the Blue Bayou.

By the time he arrived, all the spots out front were taken, but Greer took his handicapped placard out of the glove compartment, hung it from the rearview mirror, and parked the car under a Permit Only sign. When he was just driving around, he didn't like to leave the sign out, advertising his condition, but at times like this it came in real handy.

Inside, the lights were shining on the runway, and a woman with black hair, cut short and straight across, was swinging around the pole in a G-string. It took a second for Greer's eyes to adjust, then he saw that it was Ginger Lee, Sadowski's girlfriend. She was half-Chinese or Korean or something, and Greer had always wondered how that jibed with Sadowski's general attitude toward anybody who wasn't white.

At the bar, Zeke was pulling a beer, but spotted Greer, nodded, and made him his next stop.

"What can I do you for?" he asked.

"Make it a Jack Daniel's, a double," Greer said, "and a taste of what we did last time."

"How big a taste?"

Greer peered into his wallet, and said, "Make it a hundred."

Zeke poured the drink, palmed a tinfoil packet into Greer's hand, and said, "My team won the semis last week."

"That so." Zeke was a tall blond volleyball player, who was only bartending—and dealing—until the big volleyball money started to roll in.

"Yeah, you ought to come to the finals. We play down on the beach in Santa Monica."

"I'll do that."

"Seriously, you ought to—you got to get some sun. You need sunlight to make vitamin D, and vitamin D is good for your bones."

This was some night, Greer thought; everybody was looking out for his welfare. "Sadowski here?"

"Haven't seen him." Somebody called out for a Black Russian, and Zeke went back to work. Greer turned on his stool so he could see the runway. Ginger was upside down now, with her feet, in black spiked heels, wrapped around the pole. How'd she do that? The music was blasting Prince, "1999," and the stage was littered with tightly crumpled bills. Greer knew that routine; you wanted to look like a sport, but you didn't want to spend too much, so you crumpled up your bills—ones, maybe a five now and then—and tossed 'em to the girl, hoping she wouldn't notice what they were until she'd already given you a little personalized attention.

He had a nice buzz on just now, and maybe that was just what he needed. Personalized attention.

He sipped his drink, and thought about Indira—that was going nowhere, what had he been smoking?—and then he thought about Ginger, bending down now to scoop up the bills lying around, and then, after she left the stage and another girl, dressed in a red, white, and blue bikini, came out, he thought about al-Kalli again. And how he could make that pay.

"Hey, Derek," Ginger said, popping onto the next barstool. He hadn't seen her coming.

"You catch my set?" she asked.

"Most of it." She was wearing a sequined tube top and high-cut black panties.

"What'd you think of the new music?"

"Prince is old."

"I mean, it's new music for my act. I think a lot of these guys like the oldies."

Greer wondered how old Ginger was—nineteen, twenty? "You could be on to something." And she looked good in what there was of the outfit. What was she doing with Sadowski?

"You want to buy me a drink?"

Greer snorted. "Why don't you use some of that cash you just picked up?"

She raised a finger toward Zeke, and he brought her a glass of something green.

"Stan's not here," she said.

"So I noticed."

"He doesn't come in till later. After his shift."

If only Sadowski weren't so stupid, Greer thought, he'd be somebody he could discuss the al-Kalli angles with. But knowing Sadowski, he'd just recommend that Greer kidnap the guy and hold him for ransom.

"You want a dance?" she said, tilting her head toward the Blue Room in back, where the lap dancing went on.

Greer gave her a look. "What about Stan?"

"What about him? He doesn't care." She licked the rim of her glass. "Only rule he's got is, you got to be white."

"How's management feel about that?" Greer asked, looking around. Maybe half the men in the room fell something short of that high standard.

"Who cares? I do what I want anyway."

Maybe she and Sadowski did deserve each other. She put a hand suggestively on his knee.

"I'll make it special for you," she said. "Other guys can't touch, but I'll let you."

Her hand slid up his thigh. "What about it?"

What about it indeed. For the first time in ages, Greer felt something in his thigh that wasn't an ache or a pain. He swallowed the last of his drink. She spread her fingers, letting them fall between his legs.

She didn't say another word—maybe she knew she didn't have to. Instead, she slid off the stool, taking Greer by one hand, and without looking back led him, the way you'd lead a horse by the reins, toward the Blue Room. A burly guy with a clipboard stood in front of the silver Mylar strips that made up the entryway, reeled off the prices, and checked them in. Then Ginger guided him to a big, plush wing chair in the corner. Another guy was already being serviced on a love seat. The music in here was slower, lower. You were paying for the privacy, of sorts, and the romantic mood.

Ginger playfully pushed Greer back into the chair—he could tell she was already going into her regular act—and ran her hands across his chest and onto his shoulders. She unbuttoned the top button of his shirt, while Greer, who knew the usual rules, sat back passively, with his hands resting on the arms of the chair.

"Oooh," she cooed, as if she'd never laid eyes on him before. "You are so . . . sexy. You make me want to come, and we haven't even got started yet."

Greer put his head back against the chair; the fabric was still warm from the last guy's head.

"Do I make you want to come?" she whispered, leaning in so close her lips actually brushed his. Was that, Greer wondered, part of the special service he was going to get? He could taste something sweet—left over from that green stuff she was drinking—on his own mouth.

"Yeah," he said, just to keep things rolling along, "you sure do."

"That's good, 'cause what I want is for us to come together."

Greer wondered if anybody ever fell for this nonsense. Even in his present state—with a few drinks in him and several pharmaceutical products still percolating through his veins—he was well aware that he was being played. Ginger rubbed her cheek against his—"oh, it's rough," she said, "I like rough"—and then she playfully nipped at his ear. Only she really got it between her teeth and gave the lobe a sharp little tug.

"I call that my Mike Tyson," she said, giggling.

Greer had to smile. Despite himself, he was starting to get into it. She had a very tight little body, and she knew how to use it. Her fingernails, painted different colors, were a few inches long, and she used them to rake his forearms and his pecs. Her breath was warm and her lips were sticky; she planted another little kiss on his chest, in the space where she'd opened his shirt. "You really do turn me on, Derek," she said. "You know that, don't you?"

He was momentarily confused. The use of his name wasn't supposed to be part of the game; he had just gotten used to the fact that she was playing him—and he was okay with that—and now she had to go and make things personal. He wished she hadn't.

"I've wanted to do this," she said, "ever since Stan brought you in here that first time."

She kissed him again, lower down, then whipped herself

around. Her ass, straining against the black panties, gyrated in front of him. His hands wanted to reach out and grab her, but he knew the rules.

She was doubled over at the waist, moving her ass, and looking back at him now. "You want to touch it?" she said.

Greer didn't have to answer.

She glanced over at the entryway—the burly guy was talking to somebody just outside—and, pulling the panties up so that only a tiny strip of fabric ran right up the middle, she said, "Go for it."

He lifted one hand and cupped her butt cheek. The skin was smooth and taut; she pushed her ass back against his hand, and it was just then that Greer happened to glance over at the entry.

Sadowski was standing there, still talking to the burly guy, and watching the whole thing. When their eyes met, Sadowski laughed, gave him a thumbs-up, and went on talking.

Greer felt his own temperature drop about ten degrees. He took his hand back, and Ginger said, "I told you, he doesn't mind." She turned around again and, propping herself on the arms of the chair, leaned into him. "You're white, aren't you?"

Yeah, she was right about that. But it still wasn't until Sadowski stepped back outside that Greer could really focus on Ginger again. It had been years since Iraq, but something in him still felt as if he'd just betrayed one of his soldiers—even though the soldier himself clearly didn't give a damn. Ginger, perhaps sensing his diminished involvement, exerted herself doubly hard.

Greer let her do her stuff, but his thoughts had gone back to other matters. He was back on that al-Kalli business, and he suddenly saw what it was he should do. Sadowski, of all people, had shown him the way.

He should go back out on patrol!

Why was he worrying about writing letters and making shakedown demands? The first thing to do—had the army taught him nothing?—was to reconnoiter the terrain, to figure out where your enemy was, what he had in his own arsenal, and what you could do to defeat him. Maybe he could even find out what had been in that damn box he'd retrieved. Once he thought of that, once he knew that he had a plan, however rudimentary, Greer was finally able to focus again on the urgent business at hand.

"We've only got till the end of this song," Ginger warned him, "and then you get charged all over again."

Greer had no intention of being overcharged.

CHAPTER ELEVEN

"**M**R. **AL-KALLI HAS** arrived," Mrs. Cabot said excitedly, popping her head in the door of Beth's office. "Security is showing him upstairs."

Beth was just on the phone to Robin—who was telling her that little Joey had eaten two big bowls of applesauce—but she nodded her head in a serious fashion and continued to pretend that she was on a business call. "That's very interesting," she said to Robin, "and I would like to hear more about the acquisition." Robin was used to this kind of charade and would surely catch on. "May I call you back for more details? Thanks so much."

She hung up the phone and said, "He's bringing the book with him? The bestiary?"

"Why else would he be here?" Mrs. Cabot said. "Are you prepared?"

Beth wondered what exactly that meant. She'd studied illuminated manuscripts, among other things, for nearly ten years. If that didn't do it . . .

"I think so," she said evenly. But then, just to show some effort, she lifted a pile of monographs off the top of her blond wood desk and put them out of the way on the window

ledge. Way down below, she could see the cars on the freeway, gleaming in the hot sun.

"Perhaps we should call in one of the conservators,"
Mrs. Cabot said with a look of concern.

"I think that can wait a bit," Beth said, slanting the
blinds so that no direct sunlight might fall on the manuscript when it arrived.

Mrs. Cabot pursed her lips, still debating. But by then it
was too late—Beth could hear footsteps approaching, and
voices in the hall.

Beth stood up behind her desk as Mr. al-Kalli stopped to
greet Mrs. Cabot. He was wearing a cream-colored suit today, with a scarlet pocket square, and his right-hand man,
in funereal black, stood just behind him, holding a cumber-
some, antique iron box.

"Would you like to put that down?" Beth asked, indicating the broad expanse of her cleared desk. "It looks heavy."

The man waited until al-Kalli said, "Yes, Jakob, go
ahead."

Jakob came in and lowered the box like a baby onto the
desk; even so, it made a pronounced thump. The box was
still closed, with huge, rusty hasps. At a glance, Beth esti-
mated the box alone, like others she had seen, was as much
as a thousand years old.

Jakob stepped back silently and hovered in the open
door, as al-Kalli turned to Beth. "Just as I promised," he
said, shaking her hand across the desk. His skin was as
smooth and dry as silk. He sat down in one of the guest
chairs, taking care to pluck up the knee of his trouser leg,
and Mrs. Cabot—a bit to Beth's surprise—commandeered
the chair beside him.

"I wanted to see where my precious one would be," he
said, surveying her office. "Is this where you do your work?"

"Some of it," Beth replied, sitting back down. "The research library is actually in the institute, which is just
across the plaza. The conservation work is done in what's
called the East Building."

"So many different buildings," al-Kalli observed.

"Yes," Beth conceded, "the Getty can be confusing at

first." She remembered her own introduction to the place, and having to learn just where various collections were housed in the cluster of galleries and pavilions that made up the sprawling complex.

"But *The Beasts of Eden*," al-Kalli said, "will never leave this hill?"

To Beth, his English accent made him sound like Rex Harrison on her old *My Fair Lady* album. "No, it will always be up here," she said, "safe and sound."

He appeared satisfied, and Beth could no longer contain her very genuine excitement.

"May I?" she said, gesturing at the closed, but unpadlocked, hasps.

"I thought you would never ask," al-Kalli replied with a small smile.

Beth loosened the hasps—some flakes of rust fell onto the clean desk—and then raised the lid; the box was almost three feet square, and inside, it was lined with musty, threadbare red velvet. But in its center, neatly cradled—the box must have been built expressly to house it—rested the single most exquisite book she had ever seen.

And she had seen hundreds.

She paused, unwilling even to touch it yet, and al-Kalli noted her amazement with pleasure.

"You may remove it," he said.

Beth still didn't say anything, but reached in, reverently, to lift the book out. It, too, was very heavy, and it was no wonder why. As she took it out, into the light of the office— my God, she thought, it must weigh twenty-five pounds— the fantastically tooled and bejeweled cover winked and sparkled, as if happy to be seen and admired once again.

Jakob silently came forward and took the box out of her way; Beth laid the book down again.

Although the covers of most such manuscripts were made of leather or vellum, this one was far more valuable. This one was ivory. Elephant ivory. Not whalebone or walrus tusk, with their buttery yellow color and tellingly coarse grain. Ivory. Almost white, finely grained, one of the most precious materials in the ancient world. The only cover Beth had ever seen that even approached this one in beauty had once adorned the *Psalterium Latinum* that belonged to Melisende, the wife of the Comte d'Anjou, who succeeded his father-in-law to become the King of Jerusalem in the twelfth century.

But this one surpassed even that. The *Psalterium* was decorated with garnets and turquoise; *The Beasts of Eden* was decorated with deep blue sapphires and glittering rubies. They studded the four corners of the cover, and marked the borders of the six roundels—the carved circles—that formed most of the design. In each of these roundels, a stunningly intricate creature had been carved. Griffins, gorgons, dragons. Beth would have to study them further to determine what each one was meant to be. In the very center, in a larger circle carved in the shape of a serpent, was a bird that looked a lot like a peacock, with an elaborately fanned tail and a high proud beak.

"Oh, it's magnificent," Mrs. Cabot put in, "and didn't someone tell me the peacock is on your family crest?"

"That's true," al-Kalli said, though his eyes were still on Beth, "though this is not a peacock."

The flames that curled up around its feet had already told Beth that much. This was the mythical phoenix, the bird that never died, but instead made its own funeral pyre, and then emerged, reborn, from its own ashes.

"From what I know of your family," Beth said, still absorbed in the beauty of the cover, "the phoenix would be apt. As I understand it, the al-Kallis have survived, under difficult circumstances, for many centuries."

"That we have done," Mohammed admitted, though there was a surprising note of something—resignation? doubt?—in his voice. "And this book has survived with us." He cleared his throat and looked directly at Beth. "And that is why it is so important to have the book restored . . . and thoroughly translated."

"Oh, surely the book has been translated before," Mrs. Cabot put in.

"It has," al-Kalli said, but without even bothering to look her way. "But not reliably. The Latin is difficult, the text has faded, and the peculiar hand of the scribe makes some of it hard to decipher."

Beth hadn't opened the book yet, so she couldn't comment on the text. Still, she wanted to put his mind at rest. "We have some of the most advanced computer programs here," Beth explained, "that are capable of scanning small sections of text, breaking them down, and then extrapolating that information to the rest of the book. In other words, once we know how this scribe tends to form each letter, the computer will be able to identify all further examples of that letter, or word, or design element, wherever and whenever it appears."

"How long would such a process require?" al-Kalli asked, with an urgency that surprised Beth. After all, the book had been around for a millennium or so—what could be the big hurry now?

"It depends," Beth said. "But the job could probably be done in a few weeks."

She thought he would look pleased, but his brow remained furrowed. "Not sooner?"

"It's possible," Beth said. Already she could see that this project—enticing and enthralling as it was—would also have its political dimensions. Al-Kalli would not be an easy taskmaster. "We have to handle every step with extreme caution. Just this binding," she said, lifting the front cover less than an inch, "is extraordinarily fragile—and rare."

"Of course it is," Mrs. Cabot said, "inlaid with such beautiful gemstones."

"It isn't just that," Beth said. "Something like this— what we call a treasure binding—is almost never found on the book it originally belonged to."

Mrs. Cabot looked confused—the esoterica of illuminated manuscripts was not her forte or her field. But Beth guessed, from the expression on al-Kalli's face, that he knew a great deal about his *Beasts of Eden*; she also felt that he enjoyed hearing her expatiate on it. "No, these covers were so priceless they were often recycled," Beth continued. "They were removed from the wooden boards that were used for backing, and then reused on later books or codices. This one, however, is still wedded not only to its backing, but to the book itself. That alone makes it a near miracle."

Al-Kalli had a half smile on his face now; he liked hearing his legacy praised. "Go ahead and open it," he said with a tilt of his chin, and Beth, feeling a little like a kid on Christmas morning, did so.

Even though the centuries had indeed taken their toll, the book was still resplendent. The ink had faded, the colors had dimmed, the vellum leaves were creased and cracked, but Beth had never seen such a vibrant, rich, and original work. As she carefully turned each page, it crackled in her hand, and once or twice, she felt a tiny grain of sand . . . a gritty reminder of the book's Mesopotamian provenance.

The text was inscribed in gold ink, on what had once presumably been an imperial purple background; now it was a very faint lavender. The script was so intricate and compacted that it was impossible for Beth, without much closer inspection, to pick out more than a word here and here, but what she did see confirmed her opinion that the book dated from the eleventh or perhaps twelfth century; the style of the script was somewhere between the Carolingian—promulgated by the emperor Charlemagne hundreds of years before—and the Gothic, which gradually came to the fore in Western Europe thereafter. Even with the help of the advanced computer programs that the Getty employed, decoding the densely inscribed and miniscule writing—much of it entwined or overlaid on elaborate drawings and illustrations—would be extremely difficult and time-consuming. Al-Kalli, Beth knew, was not going to be happy about that.

"Have you ever seen anything like it?" al-Kalli murmured now, leaning forward in his chair. Beth picked up a scent of expensive cologne.

"Yes," she said, to be perfectly professional, "it reminds me of the Vienna Coronation Gospels and the Xanten Gospels in Brussels."

He looked deflated. Mrs. Cabot looked annoyed.

"But this is, if anything, more exquisite."

Both al-Kalli and Mrs. Cabot appeared mollified.

"What I am particularly struck by," Beth said, thinking aloud, "are the illuminations." Indeed, she was trying to come to terms with her own opinion of them; they were not quite like anything she had ever seen before, especially in a work of this age. While many such manuscripts displayed artwork that was finely controlled—almost mathematical in its precision—these illustrations were bolder, more impressionistic. They were executed with bold, blotchy swatches of color, and imparted to the animals they depicted a cunning sense of movement and life and reality.

Which, given that this was a bestiary—largely a catalogue of mythical creatures, unseen by anyone, ever—was particularly impressive.

Beth turned another heavy page of the book, and was greeted by the baleful glare of a manticore, a legendary creature with the head of a man, the body of a lion, and the scaly tail of a serpent. In most such illustrations, the creature was shown in a static pose—often while being skewered by a party of equally static hunters—but not in this one; here, the manticore was in motion, leaping from a stand of palm trees, its head turned to the reader. Below its claws, drenched in vermilion, lay the remains of its prey—what might have been a camel, perhaps. It was surprising, even shocking in a way, to see such a fluid, powerful rendering in a manuscript so old. Most of the pictures from this era were drawn and colored by monks who worked from other, previous versions. And even when they depicted an actual creature, one that the illuminator might *conceivably* have seen—a crocodile, a whale, even an elephant—the work was formal and postured.

But in this book, the manticore, the chimera—a fire-breathing goat with a serpent's tail—the unicorn—a horse with the horn of a rhinoceros—all were drawn in a style that seemed far more sophisticated, more expressive, than anything else from their time. It was as if, Beth thought, the creatures in the al-Kalli *Beasts of Eden* had been drawn from life.

And she said so.

Mrs. Cabot beamed, pleased to see Beth pay their guest such a compliment, but al-Kalli didn't smile, budge, or react in any way. His lack of reaction was in itself puzzling; he looked to Beth as though he were suddenly filled with too many feelings to sort through, too many thoughts to express just one. He looked as if his mind had traveled to some far distant place . . . perhaps the desert that his family had inhabited—and ruled—for so many centuries.

"It will be my honor to work on this book," she said. "It's simply magnificent."

But he still said nothing; he just offered a small, cryptic smile.

And when she closed the book—very carefully, and using both hands—on her desk she saw a fine silt of white sand glinting in the overhead light. Even the sand she wanted to preserve and keep with the book. It was as if it had come, like the strange beasts depicted in the illuminated pages, from a place as old as Eden.

CHAPTER TWELVE

IT WAS PRECISELY the carnival atmosphere Carter had predicted—and dreaded.

Gunderson had issued the press release to the media, the *L.A. Times* (among many others) had dutifully written up the story of the early human, only the second one since 1915 to be unearthed at the La Brea Tar Pits, and the public imagination had in fact been captured.

Today, looking up from the bottom of Pit 91, Carter could see dozens of faces pressed against the glass of the upper observation deck, all waiting to see the grisly skeleton of their ancient ancestor released from its unmarked grave. Security guards occasionally moved them along to make way for the next wave, but the faces kept coming. Carter could tell it made Rosalie and Claude, normally two of his most reliable workers, self-conscious: Miranda, on the other hand, it seemed to have sprinkled with stardust. Gunderson had gone along with Carter's suggestion to share the credit for the discovery with the budding young paleontologist, and now Miranda had transformed herself into some interesting cross between Paris Hilton at the MTV awards and Louis Leakey in the Olduvai Gorge. She was dressed in tight khaki shorts with many zippers and velcroed pockets, a sleeveless green T-shirt that simply said PIT 91 EXCAVATION TEAM (where, Carter wondered, had she had that thing made?), and clunky black work boots that served chiefly to show off her long, tanned legs. Periodically, she leaned back on her haunches to dramatically wipe the sweat from her brow, and scan the upper deck for admirers.

Right now, the most dedicated of the observers was a La Brea regular, the Native American the museum guards referred to as Geronimo. Carter had seen him glaring down into the pit most of the morning, his lips moving in what seemed like some kind of inaudible chant.

"If I'd known I was going to be on Eyewitness News," Rosalie said, glopping out another handful of muck, "I'd have gone on a diet."

Claude chuckled, and said, "I'd have bought a toupee."

"What can I tell you?" Carter replied, wiping his own hand on the edge of a black bucket. "You're celebrities now, and there's no going back to your ordinary lives."

Eyewitness News had indeed sent a crew the day before; they'd clambered down into the pit with a camera and a mike, and shot some "spontaneous" footage of Carter and his crew continuing to disinter what the anchor later called "the first man ever to walk down Wilshire Boulevard." The coanchor had wondered if, back then, traffic was any better than it was today.

"Careful you don't cut yourself," Carter said to Claude, who was digging deep in the quadrant where the human bones lay. In order to facilitate the dig, extraordinary measures had been taken—discretionary funds, Carter discovered, could be found when they had to be—and one of the first things Carter had done with the money was install slim steel plates to keep the tar from neighboring quadrants out of this one; the plates were inserted, to a depth of ten feet, on all sides, and though nothing could be done to keep the tar from welling up from below, it did help to keep the surface area relatively clear.

At Gunderson's own insistence, high-power hoses,

hooked to a massive turbine that now rumbled on the lawn up above the rear of the pit, suctioned off debris and what was called the matrix—the rocky, gooey material that surrounded the find. Carter had strenuously objected, on the grounds that this material could be ineffably important to deciphering the remains, but Gunderson had only partially relented; he wanted these human bones unearthed *now*, but he was willing to let the matrix be stored in a massive holding tank, steam-cleaned beforehand from top to bottom. Part of Carter had wanted to weep, but another part told him to be practical—this was a momentous find, and if he didn't want Gunderson to hijack it completely, and turn it over to some hack who would unwittingly do it great damage, he had to compromise.

Still, it wasn't in his nature—and he tried not to focus on the hoses.

"Don't you think we're ready to start plastering?" Miranda asked, innocently. The glopping could be fun, and photogenic, for only so long. The next step, once the fossils had been exposed, was usually to plaster them *in situ*, to protect and preserve them during the extraction process.

But they were days away from that, at best. "Not yet," Carter replied. "First we've got to clear away more of the tar."

Miranda exhaled, loudly.

"And then we've got to ascertain where, and how deep, these remains go. We don't want to chisel away anything germane."

Miranda looked even more deflated.

"Then we can think about how to extract them safely."

"What are our choices?" Claude asked, pushing his bifocals back up onto his nose with the knuckle of one tarry hand.

"We've got several," Carter replied, though he was reluctant to go into it now. Yes, there were the usual methods of fossil preservation—plaster of paris casting, transparent resin application, polyurethane foam over aluminum foil—but he hadn't yet decided on how he wanted to proceed. He knew that this find was special not only in the scientific sense, but in a political one, too. These were human remains, of an aboriginal ancestor. As a result, they had to be treated, at all stages, with a heightened degree of responsibility and tact.

As if in response to his thoughts, there was a sudden thumping from above. Carter looked up at the observation deck to see Geronimo banging his fist against the Plexiglas and shouting something indecipherable.

"I knew he'd go off one day," Claude said.

"But why now?" Carter said.

"Maybe," Miranda said, "because of this." She was pointing at a spot in the quadrant where, miraculously, the top of a skull now protruded. Only minutes earlier, that area of the grid had been covered with tar. Now, a human skull, its empty eye sockets staring upward, emerged like a swimmer coming up for air.

Even Carter was speechless.

The banging got louder, and Carter could see a security guard grabbing Geronimo's arm and pulling him away from the window. The other spectators backed off, too, though not before one or two had snapped photos of the fracas.

"Where'd that come from?" Rosalie said, her voice filled with awe.

"I don't know," Carter mumbled. "I've never seen anything just show up like that." Was it the steel plates he'd inserted into the grid? Was it the hoses, making what would normally take weeks of excavation transpire in a matter of hours? His crew had been digging around in the region of the hand, the fingers that Carter had once felt entwined in his own. But they hadn't expected to see the skull for some time; Carter had figured it was still at least a foot or two down.

The body must be lying almost horizontally in the tar.

"What do we do now?" Miranda asked.

Up above, Carter could see the remaining spectators being herded out of the observation platform; he could also hear some muted protests.

Claude and Rosalie waited, with Miranda, for orders. And Carter gradually focused his attention again on the

blackened skull. He rubbed a clean rag across his forehead
to mop the sweat from his eyes; the temperature today was
in the eighties, and in the bottom of the pit at least five or
ten degrees hotter than that. The surface of the tar looked
more fluid than usual; it reminded Carter of the expression
used by fishermen to describe a spot where fish were active; they called it "nervous water." This looked like nervous tar.

"Let's keep the suction hoses away from the quadrant,"
Carter said. "And start a new bucket for anything you glop
out now; we don't want to lose anything that might turn up,
no matter how insignificant it might look." Carter knew
from experience that tiny shards of diseased bone, the pulpy
parts of leaves, even insect exoskeletons, could still be found
and extricated from the pits. The asphalt, immiscible in water, impregnated everything, staining it black or brown, but
protecting all the organic compounds that might have otherwise been leached out and run off by groundwater or replaced during petrifaction. The asphalt, deadly to so many
creatures for thousands of years, could also preserve them
in a way no other medium could; as a result, the fossils
found here, and almost nowhere else, included the auditory
ossicles of mammals, the delicate bones of birds, beetle
wing covers that retained their iridescent hues. Fossilized
wood from the pits looked fresh when it was broken in two,
and if you lit it with a match, it would burn.

The four of them went back to work, under a kind of
constrained silence. The nearness of the skull, its empty
orbs, its black and grinning teeth, made any kind of conversation feel . . . disrespectful. Even sacrilegious. Carter
had to keep his eyes on the close work in front of him, still
struggling to free the hand he had felt days before, and he
was nearly succeeding when he heard, off in the distance
somewhere, strange sounds that he couldn't identify.

First, it was like chains being rattled and shaken.

Then more shouting, in words that made no sense.

And then Claude, his eyeglasses glinting in the sunlight
as he looked up at the back wall, cried out, "Carter! Look!"

Carter turned, just as a man—Geronimo, in his buckskin

jacket—clambered onto the steel ladder that led down into the pit. He was chanting something—no doubt in some Native American tongue—and swiftly descending the rungs. When he was a few feet from the bottom, he abandoned the ladder altogether and leapt to the wooden boards that ran around the perimeter of the pit. Carter felt them lurch and buckle under his own feet.

The guy must have been released by the security guards—were they nuts?—and then come back to vault over the rear fence surrounding the enclosure.

But what was he supposed to do now? Carter jumped to his feet, his hands dripping tar, and shouted, "Get the hell out of here!"

"No!" the man shouted back. "These are the bones of my people!" He walked stealthily in a pair of moccasins down the wooden catwalk, toward the quadrant where they were working.

Carter quickly stepped past Miranda to cut him off; Rosalie and Claude stood, in shock, on the other side of the grid. Carter wondered if he should be picking up a weapon of some kind. But what—a bucket of tar?

"You can't be down here," Carter said, hoping to calm him down.

Geronimo threw his black braid back over his shoulder and lifted his chin in defiance. "You leave," he said, "all of you. Now!"

"That's not going to happen," Carter said.

"Yes, it is," Geronimo said, and for the first time Carter saw what he held in one hand—a hunting knife with a gleaming blade.

Miranda must have seen it, too, and screamed.

"Carter, look out!" Claude cried. "He's armed."

Worse than that, Carter could see that he was utterly unhinged. The look in his eyes was black and fierce and beyond reason; his throat muscles were flexing against a necklace of turquoise stones.

"Okay," Carter said, putting up his hands in a placatory gesture, "why don't we all stop what we're doing, and go back up top? We don't need to talk about this down here."

Geronimo came one step closer and swung the knife in a broad, flashing arc.

Carter fell back, bumping into Miranda. "Go to the other side," Carter said to her over his shoulder. "Go up the stairs to the observation deck." It was how they usually came and went, on a narrow set of wooden steps. Out of the corner of his eye, he saw Claude stooping to a bucket, and Carter said, "No, don't do anything. Just leave—all of you. Right now."

Rosalie was the first to turn and scurry toward the steps, but Claude waited.

"Just do what I'm telling you," Carter said.

Geronimo was getting what he wanted, so far. Some of them were leaving. He stood on the catwalk, one foot on either side of the suction hose, his chest heaving. He kept his eyes on Carter.

"Miranda," Carter said, in a low voice, "go around the other side. Get out."

"I'll call the cops," she said.

Good idea, he thought. But what was he going to do until then?

Miranda came out from behind Carter, and Geronimo flicked his gaze her way. It might have been something about her blonde hair, the tight T-shirt and shorts, but something suddenly set him off. His lips curled in an angry snarl.

"I saw you on the TV—you're the bitch that started this!"

He made a move to head her off, and Carter had no choice; he lunged forward, grabbing the hose between Geronimo's feet and yanking it up. Geronimo teetered back, but immediately regained his balance, slashing at Carter now and catching him on the forearm.

The sight of the blood, dripping down Carter's arm and into the black tar, seemed to momentarily rivet him.

Carter saw the gash, but he felt next to nothing; the blade was so swift and so sharp and his adrenaline was so high.

But he knew he had to get out of there, fast; Rosalie and Claude were already out, and Miranda was thundering up the steps in her heavy work boots.

He glanced up at the observation deck, hoping to see a cop or security guard.

But all he saw was Rosalie's ashen face, calling out something he couldn't hear.

He simply had to make a run for it; he feinted to one side, enough to make Geronimo move a few steps to the other side of the grid separating them, then bolted for the ladder on the back wall. If he could just scale it fast enough . . .

But Geronimo was too quick; Carter hadn't gone more than a few steps when his attacker was on him. Carter had to stop and wheel around. He caught the hand holding the blade, and forced it back.

"You disgrace my ancestors!"

Carter pressed him back; the catwalk shuddered under their feet.

"You've got to die!" Geronimo shouted again, the spit flying into Carter's face.

They were both struggling to keep their balance on the narrow boards above the tar. Carter didn't dare let go of his arms; the rage in his eyes boiled like fire.

And suddenly, the hand with the knife wriggled free. Geronimo smiled—and Carter slugged him so hard he went reeling back, his moccasins scrabbling on the wood. For a second, it seemed as if he would manage to stay upright, but then he tilted back and toppled into the pit with a thick, wet splash.

The tar spread like a wave to either side, then sloshed back.

Geronimo hung there, on top, like a leaf on a stream.

Carter bent double, breathing hard.

And then the tar bubbled and seethed.

Geronimo's eyes went wide as he felt himself starting to sink.

Carter lifted his wounded forearm to impede the blood flow.

Geronimo's legs were out of sight, the black asphalt seeping inexorably over them.

"I'm sinking!" Geronimo screamed in terror. He started

to flail his arms, but the fringe on his buckskin jacket was stuck in the tar.

He wouldn't really sink, Carter thought; the tar wasn't quicksand. It would just do what it always did—entrap the unwary until they simply gave up the struggle.

"Stop moving," Carter said.

"Fuck you!" Geronimo cried.

"If you stop moving, we'll get you out." Or, Carter thought, the fire department will.

"I'm sinking!" he shouted again, and now Carter could see that the asphalt was indeed more liquid, more agitated, than he had ever seen it. Geronimo's waist was now submerged—and methane bubbles were rising all around him.

"Just hang on," Carter said, looking around for something to throw him.

The hose. Carter started to drag it over. But it wouldn't go that far.

He looked desperately for something else.

"Get me out!" Geronimo shrieked. The tar was edging up onto his chest. "Get me out of this shit!"

Carter quickly undid his belt. "Throw your knife away."

"I can't!" Geronimo said. His hand, the knife still clutched in his fist, was coated with tar.

Carter would have to take the chance. He pulled his belt from the loops, lay down on the catwalk, and flipped the buckle end toward Geronimo's free hand.

Geronimo missed it.

Carter pulled it back, then tossed it again.

This time, Geronimo was able to snag it, but the tar was up to his shoulders now and showed no sign of stopping.

"The police are coming!" Miranda called from the top of the stairs.

"Get me a rope!" Carter shouted.

"Help me!" Geronimo cried. "Help me!" All the anger had gone out of his eyes now, replaced by mounting fear.

Carter looped the belt around his hand, and tried to drag Geronimo toward him.

"Help me," he said, in nothing but a plea now.

"I'm trying," Carter gasped, pulling again. But it was like pulling against a powerful current.

The tar was up to his neck now, the methane popping in tiny acrid bursts.

"Hold on," Carter said.

But he could tell Geronimo was running out of strength; the tar was too strong, it was sucking him down, down toward the bottom of the pit.

Like a black tide, it rose up to his chin, then over his lips. Geronimo tilted his face upward, struggling to keep clear. His single black braid hung down in back, most of its length already lost in the mire. His turquoise necklace disappeared. He tried again to raise his arms, but the tar dragged them down.

"No," Geronimo sputtered, "no," as the tar climbed up his face.

Carter tugged on the belt, but there was no resistance; Geronimo had let go of his end.

His head began to sink, the tar touching his nose, then his eyes—he stared at Carter with mute incomprehension as the bubbling black asphalt covered his eyes. It was the look of a rabbit caught by a stoat.

And then it covered his forehead, until all that was left visible was the crest of his head, the black hair shiny and neatly parted in the middle.

"The cops are here!" Miranda cried, and Carter could hear the crackling of their walkie-talkies and the commotion as they clattered down the wooden steps.

"Where's the guy with the knife?" one of them shouted at Carter, just as the tar made one last, irresistible grab. The belt slipped off Carter's hand, and the top of Geronimo's head sank swiftly beneath the surface of the pit.

The tar seethed for a moment, as if digesting its prize, then instantly grew as still, as silent, and as satisfied, as the grave it had just become.

CHAPTER THIRTEEN

"JAKOB," AL-KALLI SAID, from behind the easel.

"Yes, sir?"

"You see where I've placed that wheelbarrow?"

Jakob looked down the line of jacaranda trees, their branches in full purple blossom, to the rustic wheelbarrow artfully positioned at the far end.

"Could you move that forward, more into the frame of the picture?"

As Jakob went to do as he was bid, Mohammed sat back in his canvas lawn chair, under the shade of the towering beach umbrella. In the afternoons, he often liked to set up his easel somewhere on his estate—it afforded him so many different views and scenes—and paint, quickly and with as free a hand as he could muster, a watercolor impression. He had a good eye—his art instructor at Harrow had thought he should pursue a career in art—but he did it chiefly to relax, to take his mind off more troubling things, things that might be preying on his mind.

He was given, as had been all the members of his family, to dark fancies.

Jakob moved the wheelbarrow a few inches forward, and al-Kalli cried out, "More! More!"

It was an old wooden barrow that al-Kalli had seen in a plant nursery and purchased, though it hadn't been for sale. He had immediately spotted its potential.

"Right there—stop." Al-Kalli sat back, studied the composition of the scene one more time—the row of jacaranda trees, the winding flagstone path, the worn-out wheelbarrow placed as if about to be put to use—and nodded his head. He idly rinsed his brush in the Baccarat crystal vase he used for that purpose, dried it, then dabbed it against his palette; it was so hard to get a color that matched the gorgeous purple and lavender, with an undertone of blue, that the blossoms took on at this time of year. Their flowering lasted only a matter of weeks, and al-Kalli wanted to capture it, as well as he could, on his canvas.

But even as he made a few tentative strokes, a cloud passed overhead, subduing the colors of the scene, and al-Kalli checked his pocket watch. It was four-thirty in the afternoon, and the light was becoming too sharp, too slanting. He'd really have to start again tomorrow.

"We'll leave everything just as it is," he said to Jakob, placing his brush and palette back on the supply table and standing up. But it was a promising arrangement that he would return to tomorrow.

He wiped his hands on the linen cloths, drained the last of the Boodles gin in the chilled glass, and turned toward the house. Jakob, as usual, was three steps behind him.

"Why don't we pay a visit to our guest?" al-Kalli said without turning around.

Jakob didn't answer; he knew it wasn't a question.

"Perhaps he has some new stories he wishes to share."

Al-Kalli skirted the black-bottomed swimming pool, crossed the wide portico behind the main house, and was just about to go inside when he bumped into his son, Mehdi, who was sauntering outside with a towel, emblazoned with the al-Kalli peacock on it, thrown over his arm.

"Have you done your homework?" Mohammed asked him.

"If I said yes, would you believe me?"

"No."

"Then what difference does it make?"

Al-Kalli had to concede the point, but not the actual battle. "Have you done it?"

"It's not due till next week; it's a long report. I have time."

Mehdi scooted past before they could go another round. Mohammed loved him with all his heart—he was literally all of his family that he had been able to spirit out of Iraq—but ever since the boy had become a teenager, he had been surly and argumentative, and their relationship had become one of bickering and evasion. Mohammed wondered if that was how it was in all families; he wondered if his own parents had felt the same way.

But there was no one left to ask, was there?

Al-Kalli led Jakob to the back servant stairs, but left it to him to open the padlocked door. After they had made their way through several storage rooms beneath the house, they came to another sealed door; this was the wine cellar, built in this cool, out-of-the-way spot decades before, by the oil tycoon who had once owned the Castle. He had designed it to hold ten thousand bottles of his finest wine. Al-Kalli had never been much of a wine connoisseur, but now, quite unexpectedly, he'd found a novel and imaginative use for this cellar.

Jakob flicked on the overhead light—an incongruous chandelier—and the room suddenly sprang from utter blackness into twinkling, bright light. There were indeed a few hundred bottles gathering dust on wooden racks along one wall—after all, al-Kalli did do a fair amount of entertaining—but the most startling feature of the room was the metal stool against the back wall, on which al-Kalli's guest was seated. His head was thrown back against the concrete, his eyes closed, and a chain, bolted to the wall, shackled his hands. Jakob had gone to a lot of trouble, and asked a lot of odd questions at Home Depot, in order to find out how best to install the bolt and chain.

"Sleep well, Rafik?" al-Kalli asked, in Arabic. The room reeked from the chemical toilet stashed in the far corner.

Beside it lay several plastic bottles of Calistoga water and the remains of a sandwich. His guest didn't seem to have much of an appetite.

"You can open your eyes," al-Kalli said, again in the tongue he had barely used since leaving the Middle East. He was rusty, but it came back well enough.

Rafik didn't respond. He was as still as death—though al-Kalli hadn't decided to bestow that gift on him yet.

"We're just here to talk," al-Kalli went on, in entirely reasonable tones. "To pick up where we left off." He cocked his head at Jakob, who slapped Rafik on one cheek, and then the other; his head lolled forward, his eyes slowly rolling open.

"That's better," al-Kalli said.

The prisoner's face was bruised, and his lip had been split. His black hair hung down over his forehead in limp tendrils.

"Do you remember what you were telling me the last time we talked?"

Rafik's head kept lolling around as if it were barely connected to his neck.

Al-Kalli nodded at Jakob, who picked up one of the Calistoga bottles, opened it, and then held Rafik's head back; he poured the water over his broken, half-open mouth, and only stopped when the prisoner began to sputter.

"We were talking about that party at Saddam's palace."

Rafik's tongue touched his parched, cracked lips.

"The one where you served my daughter her soup."

Rafik's head dropped, but held steady.

"I was asking if you knew that the soup had been poisoned."

Rafik didn't move.

"You were saying, as I recall, that you were just doing what you were told."

"Why," Rafik muttered, in barely audible Arabic, "don't you just get it over with?"

"Because we're not in any rush," al-Kalli said, sharing a half smile with Jakob, who stood, hands folded, to one side of the metal stool. "And I still want to know who the other waiter was—the one with the mustache, who served my wife."

"I told you," Rafik croaked, "I don't know."

Al-Kalli barely had time to signal his desire to Jakob before the bodyguard lashed out, knocking Rafik off the stool with a single punch to his face. The man fell, the chain dangling, to the concrete floor.

"Oh, I don't think Saddam would have entrusted such an important job—murdering my family—to strangers." Al-Kalli shook his head, as if debating the point with himself. "No, I think you were all well trained, together. I think you were specially chosen."

Rafik didn't stir.

"I've already found the other two." He didn't say what he had done with them. "And I went to a lot of trouble to track you down."

Indeed, the search had cost him nearly a million dollars in bribes, and as much again in transportation costs. Rafik, at the time he found him, was living in Lebanon, under another name, working as a garage mechanic. He had been smuggled across several borders tied in a sack, under the floorboards of a van that had been in the shop for repairs.

"Straighten him up," al-Kalli said; Jakob bent down and, with unexpected care, righted Rafik with his back against the wall. Above his head, hung there many years earlier, was a framed Campari poster, covered with dust.

Al-Kalli crouched down in front of him, so he could look directly into his eyes. What he saw there was defeat, resignation, even the acceptance of death. What he didn't see—and had hoped for—was fear. Out of fear, he would talk.

But that could be remedied easily enough.

"Rest," al-Kalli said, first in English, and then, remembering himself, again in Arabic. "You're going to need your strength."

CHAPTER FOURTEEN

WHEN SADOWSKI SUGGESTED that Greer rendezvous with him at the Liberty Firing Range that night, Greer smelled a rat. And once he got there, he knew he'd been right.

About a dozen men—all of them white, all of them service vets of one kind or another—were milling around in what Burt Pitt called the classroom. But between the poster for gun safety and the one that showed you how to clean your weapon, there now hung a banner showing the Liberty Bell and proclaiming SONS OF LIBERTY — ARISE! It was the same image Greer had seen tattooed on Burt's arm.

The table in back had some chips and salsa, a cooler filled with cold beer, and a thick pile of stapled materials. Greer had the impression they were expecting more people. He picked up one of the packets; it was a hodgepodge of stuff, xeroxed copies of speeches by guys like Tom Paine and Patrick Henry and Pat Buchanan—wasn't he that guy with the funny, high-pitched voice that Greer sometimes saw on TV?—along with pictures taken at Sons of Liberty rallies held in Green Bay, Wisconsin; Butte, Montana; Gainesville, Georgia. The last page was a picture of Charles

Manson, with the words HELTER SKELTER across the bottom. Greer was still mulling that one over when Sadowski stepped up and said, in a louder voice than necessary, "Brew, Captain?"

He was holding out a can of Coor's, and Greer noticed that several bystanders perked up—as Sadowski no doubt had hoped—at his saying "Captain." It was as if Sadowski wanted credit for bringing in an officer.

Greer took the beer.

Burt waddled to the front of the room and called for order. Everybody but Greer, who had commandeered the sofa in back, took a seat on the folding chairs.

"First of all, I want to thank you all for coming," Burt said. "I know you're busy guys."

Yeah, Greer thought, looking around at the motley crew nursing their free beers. These were guys who'd come straight from their delivery trucks and factory jobs, or, better yet, the local welfare office.

"Some of you already know all about us"—a couple of heads nodded sagely—"and some of you are here tonight because you're wondering. You're wondering who we are, you're wondering what we stand for . . . and you're wondering what the hell is happening to our country."

Oh boy, Greer thought, here it comes. And he was right again. Burt launched into a long speech (better, actually, than Greer thought it would be) about the founding of the country by our noble forefathers, about the contributions made by men and women from all over Europe and Scandinavia (Greer noticed that Burt glanced at a guy in the front row who looked like a Viking when he said that), about how the culture was built on Christian values, and about how that culture—"once the highest in the history of the world"—was now in terrible danger.

"What is it in danger of?" Burt asked, looking around the room. Everybody stopped crunching on their chips or sipping their beers. "It's in danger of falling apart."

Not even a chair squeaked.

"And from what?" Burt asked. "Why is it gonna fall apart?"

"Because you can't carry a gun anymore," someone called out.

"That's true," Burt said. "In L.A., they've got more laws about guns than you can shake a stick at. But that's not what I was talking about."

"Pornography," another guy threw out. "Ever'where you look, there's nothin' but porn, porn, porn."

Especially under this guy's bed, Greer thought, sipping his beer in back.

"That's a problem, too," Burt said, "but I'm getting at something else." He clearly felt he had led his audience to the brink and then started to lose them. When another guy said something about divorce law and the rights of fathers, Burt jumped in and said, "Race, gentlemen, race."

They all got quiet again.

"We're in a race war, and most people don't even know it."

That dog's too old to hunt, Greer thought.

"We've got a border with Mexico that's nearly two thousand miles long, and it's about as protected as . . ." He paused, trying to figure out how to complete his thought. "About as protected as anyone here would feel at midnight, on the corner of Florence and Normandie."

A few obligatory chuckles, but his hesitation had killed the joke.

And, Greer considered, he was mixing his message. Who were we supposed to be worried about? Blacks in South Central L.A., or wetbacks sneaking into America through the back door?

"Every day hundreds—hell, thousands—of illegal immigrants just wade across the Rio Grande, stroll into San Diego or up here to Los Angeles, and flood our systems. Our schools, our hospitals, our highways."

Now he was back on the more likely track. You could always get people fired up about the border, Greer reflected. If they weren't worried about terrorists coming in, they were up in arms about all the spics taking those great jobs picking tomatoes and mopping floors. You could see Burt warming to his task, too.

"Just look around you the next time you go to the mall. I was out in Torrance last night, at a Denny's, and I was the only white guy in the place. And I counted—there were sixteen customers, and maybe three waitresses—and I was the only authentic white guy in the whole damn place."

He waited for that alarming news to sink in. But if Greer was any judge, only half the crowd—probably the ones who were already charter members of the Sons of Liberty—seemed moved. Two or three others glanced down at the sheaf of papers they'd picked up from the table, one glanced at his watch, then stared blankly out the window, undoubtedly wondering if he could have one more beer before getting the hell out.

But Burt was just hitting his stride. For another twenty minutes or so, he outlined the darkening skin, and the resulting decline, of the United States of America. Most of his warnings were about the Mexicans, the Guatemalans, the Salvadorans. Greer had never been able to tell one from the other, not that it mattered. For a second, he thought about Lopez, the guy he'd lost on that mission outside Mosul. The guy who'd just been . . . carried off in the night. Had he felt one way or the other about him? As opposed to, say, Donlan, or Sadowski, or anybody else in his unit? He took a long pull on his beer, and decided that he had not; there were even times when he felt bad about having gotten the guy killed.

As if he'd been reading his mind, Sadowski was now turned around in his chair, smiling at Greer, with an expression on his face that said, *Isn't this guy Burt great or what?* Greer just tapped his wristwatch. Sadowski, looking disappointed, turned around again.

But Burt was finally wrapping up. "I hope you'll all take a copy of the Sons of Liberty membership packet—you'll find a new members form inside—and if you've got any questions, or you just want to shoot the shit, I'm here . . . all the fucking time!" He laughed, and a few of the audience members, maybe just because they were so happy to be free again, laughed along. "And don't forget, when you join, you get a ten percent discount every time you come to the range." Same discount Greer was offered as a vet.

While a couple of interested candidates milled around the front of the room with Burt, and the others grabbed a beer or headed for the men's room, Sadowski ambled back to the sofa. "You got any questions for Burt?"

"Yeah. How come he talks so much?"

Sadowski started to look pissed. "You didn't believe him? You don't think it's time we woke up and smelled the coffee?"

"I think it's time we got in your little patrol car and did what we're supposed to do tonight."

Greer got up—damn, his leg had locked again, and he had to stop to rub some life back into the knee—and headed for the door. He saw Burt, busy recruiting a guy in a UPS uniform, look his way, and Greer raised a hand, giving him a thumbs-up. *Yeah, right—he'd be joining up real soon.*

In the parking lot out front, Greer waited by the Silver Bear Security car until Sadowski, after muttering something about the Fourth of July to another Son of Liberty, came over and unlocked it. He still looked pissy.

"I don't know why you won't listen," Sadowski said as they got into the car and strapped their seat belts.

"Because it's a crock of shit."

"It's not."

Greer wondered if it was his turn to say, "Is, too." Instead, he said, "Just give me the jacket."

Sadowski, pulling into traffic, said, "It's in the bag."

There was a Men's Wearhouse bag on the seat between them. Greer opened it and took out a gray Silver Bear windbreaker, with epaulettes and silver snap buttons, and a visored cap. A growling bear, rising up on all fours, was emblazoned just above the brim. He put the cap on and turned the rearview mirror to check himself out.

"I need that," Sadowski said, turning the mirror back.

Greer laughed. "What, did I hurt your feelings?" he said.

Sadowski, his jaw set, just kept driving.

Greer shook his head; it was too weird. Sadowski didn't mind Greer getting a lap dance from his girlfriend, but he got bent out of shape if you dissed his secret society. He looked out the window, trying to focus himself; there wasn't time for this bullshit right now. He had to concentrate on what was ahead. He reached into the pocket of his dark gray jeans—as close to the jacket color as he could find at the Gap—and took out a couple of pills; one to kill any pain from the leg, and another to raise his internal alert level. This wasn't like that job in Brentwood, when he'd stumbled into the dog-sitter at the doctor's house. This was big time.

This was the al-Kalli estate.

And he would need to be as hyped and vigilant as he had ever been.

Once they'd passed under the arched gateway to Bel-Air, Greer started to take careful mental notes on the terrain, the street layout, the avenues of escape. He'd already studied the map of this area in his Thomas Guide, and pulled it up on MapQuest, too, but there was nothing like checking out the lay of the land for real. And the maps didn't tell you just how dark—he guessed the locals would call it tasteful—the street lighting in here would be. No high-crime, low-sodium glare here, no rows of towering poles, humming softly, their heads bobbing in the ocean breeze. The street lamps were few and far between, and the light they cast was more like amber pools. As far as Greer was concerned, that was ideal.

The higher they went, the darker it got, and the less Greer could see from the patrol car. If there were houses back there, behind the high hedges and brick walls and iron driveway gates that bristled with warning signs and intercoms and surveillance cameras, you'd never know it. Once in a while, especially when they passed a Silver Bear sign, Sadowski told Greer what movie star or pop singer or athlete lived there. Greer could only imagine what kind of pickings those houses would provide. Why had he been bothering with guys who were just doctors, in Brentwood? He'd have to discuss that, later, with Sadowski.

"See that? Sadowski said, slowing on a narrow curve, beside a high stone wall.

"See what?"

"The gates."

Greer saw an unmarked solid steel-plated gate, and a door, barely visible between some thick bushes, set into the wall beside it.

"That's the back service entrance to the Al-Kalli estate. That's where I'll pick you up."

"How do I get out without setting off an alarm?"

"Only the driveway gates are alarmed, and the door can only be opened from the inside," Sadowski said, driving on. "You see any other car come by, just hide behind the bush."

"I haven't seen another car for the last fifteen minutes."

"Yeah, but up here, almost any car you do see is a security patrol."

Greer nodded, as Sadowski completed the curve, then took them back up around a wide bend—Greer had the feeling that they were basically making a big circle around the top of the hill crest—before entering a long, dimly lighted, dead-end street. Greer hadn't even seen another driveway gate, on either side, for a while—just ivy-covered walls, with impenetrably thick and high hedges rising right behind them. So all of this was one property? And all of it al-Kalli's?

"Okay, that's his gatehouse up ahead," Sadowski said. "A guy named Reggie's usually on duty."

Greer straightened his cap and collar. "You're doing the talking."

"Yeah, I'll get us in," Sadowski said. "After that, it's up to you."

Sadowski flashed his headlights as they approached the lighted gatehouse. It looked like the kind of stone cabin you'd see when you were entering some national park. A black guy holding a magazine in one hand stepped out as Sadowski pulled to a stop and lowered his window.

"What's up, dude?" Sadowski said in a friendly tone.

What happened to the coming race war? Greer wondered.

"Not much," Reggie said, resting his hand on the door of the car. He looked into the car. "Who's this?"

"This, my man, is our sensor expert."

Greer lowered his head, nodded, but said nothing.

"Your what? Your sensei, like in *Karate Kid*?"

Sadowski faked a laugh. "No, this is the guy that checks out all the motion sensors around the house and grounds."

"Whatever you say," Reggie replied.

"Anybody home tonight?"

"Everybody."

"Okay, then, we'll get this done as fast as we can."

Reggie stepped back and batted a lever with the end of the rolled-up magazine. The gates swung back smoothly.

Sadowski raised his window again as he steered the patrol car up the long, winding drive. Greer didn't particularly like the sound of that—everybody home. He always hoped to hear that his targets were away on business or off on vacation. But he would work around it.

But he still couldn't see any sign of a house. What he did see, standing by the side of the drive and staring silently at the car, was a pair of peacocks. When one of them, suddenly caught in the headlights, cried out, the sound took him right back to Iraq. To those eerie cries, at dusk, when he'd first ventured into al-Kalli's palace grounds.

"Yeah, those fuckin' birds are all over the place," Sadowski said. "I don't know how anybody gets any sleep up here."

Greer wasn't going to worry about it. "Is there a house somewhere, or are we just out for a ride?"

Sadowski snorted. "Yeah, it's coming." And then, under his breath, for no particular reason, "Fucking A-rabs."

The car passed a lighted fountain, with lots of carved figures and water jetting up on all sides. Greer started to feel like he was in an amusement park—but he wasn't amused. Maybe it was that damned peacock cry, maybe it was just the fact that it was al-Kalli's place, but he was already getting a bad vibe about the whole mission. He'd had enough bad nights, nights when he bolted up in bed sweating, thinking about endless colonnades, slanting desert sun . . . and empty cages with bent bars. Just a couple of weeks earlier, he'd actually screamed in his sleep, so loudly his mother had poked her head in the door and asked if he was all right.

At first, he hadn't been able to answer her; his mouth was that dry. And he hadn't been able to shake that image . . . of a black fog, but stronger, and more substantial, rolling toward him, starting to envelop him. He'd been struggling to get free, to get out, before whatever was in that fog—and he knew there was something in it, something terrible—discovered him. He could hear its breathing, a low rumble, and he could smell it—the smell of putrid fur and dung and blood.

"Yeah, yeah," he'd finally said to her, wiping his damp palms on the sheet. "I'm okay."

"You don't look it."

"I said I'm okay."

"Well, you don't need to snap at me," she'd said, before jerking the door closed.

He'd swallowed a couple of Xanax and spent the rest of the night in a stupor in front of the TV.

The wheels of the car had moved off the smooth concrete now and onto a rougher, cobblestoned surface. The car made another turn, and suddenly the house loomed into view. Greer had to lean forward in the seat to see all the way to the top of its spires and gables, silvered in the moonlight.

"They call it the Castle," Sadowski said.

"No shit."

To Greer, the place looked like a cliff of stone and timber, with here and there a shaft of yellow light creeping out of a curtained window.

Sadowski stopped the car short of the house and turned to Greer. "Okay, the pool and tennis court and all of that are back behind the house. Off to the left, that's where the stables and some kind of barn are. That back gate, the one where I'll pick you up again, is just past that; you can't miss it, just follow the service drive."

Greer didn't move, and Sadowski waited. "Captain?" he said, maybe because they were back in reconnaissance mode.

"Yeah," Greer replied, still taking in the sprawling house. "I got it."

"How long you want?"

"Give me an hour, but stay on your cell in case I need you sooner."

"Affirmative."

Greer hated that military crap.

He got out of the car, making sure to close the door quietly; no point in emphasizing that you were there. The night air was warm, and a light breeze was blowing. He waved Sadowski off, and the patrol car backed up slowly, then made a slow turn back down the drive. Because the car would exit on the other side of the guardhouse, they were counting on Reggie not to notice that there was now only one occupant. If he did, Sadowski was going to tell him that Greer was working on a broken motion detector and he'd come back for him later.

Once the car was gone, Greer surveyed the house, which had a wide flight of stone steps leading up to a massive wooden door, and big, several-storied wings extending out on either side; dense ivy covered much of the walls. All the way on the left there was a garage with about six bays in it, and a weather vane on top shaped like, what else, a peacock.

What was it with this guy?

Greer approached slowly, but taking care not to look furtive. He straightened his cap, removed the flashlight he'd looped on his belt, and sauntered up the front steps, as if on a routine patrol. He tried the door handle—locked, big surprise—and glanced up at the surveillance camera neatly tucked above a stone gargoyle. This one, a grinning demon with a monkey's snout, reminded him of gargoyles he'd once seen, when he was a kid, on an old church in downtown L.A. The last time he'd gone by the site, the church was gone and a parking garage was standing in its place.

But where, Greer wondered, did these cameras feed to? Was there some underground command center, with round-the-clock attendants, or did it just feed to Reggie in the guardhouse? Sadowski told him he'd checked the Silver Bear files, and there was nothing to indicate anything more than the usual camera setup. But Greer had been burned by Sadowski before, and knew enough not to rely on his information.

Keeping to the shadows, but at the same time doing nothing to appear suspect, Greer walked the length of the house, then moved into the porte cochere, where a golf cart, with a little fringed roof, was parked next to a top-of-the-line black Mercedes limo. Greer glanced inside the car, and he could see that this model was fully tricked out, with better body armor than his army Humvees had ever had. Al-Kalli knew how to travel . . . and he knew how to live.

Greer tried the side door to the house and it, too, was locked; Greer could even tell, just from rattling the knob, that there was a thrown dead bolt, with a metal reinforcement plate behind it. Brass lamps that cast a yellow glow were affixed to the exterior walls, and Greer followed them around to the back.

The estate really opened up back here, with a wide portico giving on to long rows of trees in full bloom, and beyond that a pool, and one of those little garden houses that reminded Greer of the open bandstands where old guys in straw hats would play Sousa on the Fourth of July. A wooden easel was set up next to a table with brushes and stuff all over it.

Turning back to the house, Greer saw a few lights on inside, some on the upper stories and some on the ground level; staying just out of range, he walked across the flagstones to peer into the first-floor windows; they were the casement kind, with lots of little diamond-shaped panes. Inside, he could see the back of a kid's head, with curly black hair; he was bent over what had to be a PlayStation or an Xbox or one of those things. Greer could even make out, on the giant plasma TV screen, some kind of battle scene, with guys in camouflage blowing away guys who looked like Taliban. He had to laugh—his life was a video game now.

Suddenly, the kid looked up, and the action on the screen stopped; the kid was talking to somebody just out of Greer's sight. Then the screen went dead, and the kid pushed himself up off the sofa. It wasn't hard to figure out what this was all about. Greer glanced at his watch—it was almost midnight, on a school night. Greer moved back a bit, and to one side, and now he could see who the kid was talking to—a man with a bald head, in a black turtleneck, and a scowl on his face.

And Greer knew instantly that he was seeing, for the first time, Mohammed al-Kalli himself.

He had Googled him and surfed the Web, but for a guy with his money and power, al-Kalli kept a very low profile. The only photos Greer had been able to find showed a young man in a riding outfit in England, a couple of grainy shots taken at Arab summits, and one where al-Kalli was holding up a hand to hide his face as he stepped out of a limo in Paris. But this, now, was definitely the guy—Greer would have known it just from the way he held himself, like that emperor named Saladin in *Kingdom of Heaven*.

The kid shuffled out of the room, and al-Kalli followed right behind. The lights went out. And then another light went on, upstairs. The kid in his bedroom? Greer waited, for another light. Or a sound. But all the windows were closed, and there was little chance of hearing anything emanating from inside the house.

But then there *was* a noise from the area where the car and the golf cart had been parked. The sound of a bolt being thrown, a door opening, low voices. Greer quickly retreated into the shadows of the trees.

Al-Kalli was standing outside, holding a riding crop. The door stood open, and a moment later, Greer saw why—a muscular man in a dark blue tracksuit hauled a guy who looked half-dead outside. He dragged him over to the golf cart—the guy looked way past fighting back—shoved him into the seat, then squashed himself in, too. Al-Kalli took the driver's seat.

Jakob, Greer thought—that was the muscleman's name. And he was the guy Greer had given the box to in Iraq!

A second later, the golf cart jolted to a start, and Greer cursed to himself. This was way too interesting to miss, but how was he going to keep up?

The cart rumbled across the flagstones, then onto the

lawn. Greer knew his leg would kill him tomorrow, but right now, all he could think of was keeping them in his sight. He hobbled along through the trees. The cart slowed down, as the lawn dipped, then picked up speed on the other side. Greer smelled horses, and sure enough, a stable showed up on his right. He could hear a horse neigh, softly. But that wasn't where the golf cart was going. It glided past the stables and toward that back service entrance Sadowski had showed him.

Greer had to stop, to catch his breath and rest his leg. The cart disappeared into the trees. But what the fuck—it was a golf cart. If they were going far, or beyond the walls of the estate, they'd have gotten into the car.

He set off again. The grass was thick and lush under his feet; the rest of L.A. might be suffering from a drought, but al-Kalli was keeping his own lawn nicely irrigated. A narrow stream ran through the grounds, and though he hated to be so exposed, Greer crossed it over a little wooden bridge. Way up ahead, he could see, rising above the trees, the top of what looked to him like one of the massive ammo sheds in Iraq. He remembered Sadowski saying something about a riding ring; that must be it.

Rather than head right for it, Greer moved deeper into the trees and approached the ring at an oblique angle.

And he'd been right.

Because at one end, where there were two big doors, the kind you'd see on a barn, the golf cart was stopped. Al-Kalli was still at the wheel, but the prisoner was scrambling across the ground, aimlessly, while Jakob plodded after him, clearly not worried that the guy would get away. In fact, the prisoner stumbled and fell, and Jakob reached down, grabbed him by the collar of the jumpsuit they had him in—one of those orange jobs you see convicts wear—and hauled him back to the cart like a sack of laundry.

Whatever was going on here, it didn't look good for the guy in the jumpsuit.

Al-Kalli turned and said something to the bodyguard. Greer couldn't make out the words, but the tone told him it was an order. Al-Kalli reached up to the visor of the golf cart, where there must have been a remote; the doors to the ring—the biggest damn thing Greer had ever seen on a piece of private property—slowly swung open. Greer moved closer.

They were going to go in . . . but should he try to follow? Or would that be the biggest mistake of his life?

There was the sound of blowers—huge fans blowing out cool air from the interior—as the gates spread wide.

Greer moved closer.

The golf cart lurched forward, with Jakob firmly clutching the prisoner.

The gates held steady as the cart entered. Greer could see a vast open space in the center, with mountains of crates and equipment stacked along the near side and, more interestingly, what looked like barred enclosures along the far wall.

Even bigger, and more high-tech enclosures, than he'd seen in the palace outside Mosul.

And that's when he made his mind up. He had to know. Keeping low to the ground, as if avoiding sniper fire, he scurried into the building, the massive fans nearly blowing his cap off, and then cut to the side where some crates would afford a hiding place. The ponderous doors swung shut with a thud behind him.

CHAPTER FIFTEEN

BETH DIDN'T KNOW what woke her, or how she knew she was alone in the bed. But when she opened her eyes, moonlight was streaming in through the window, and Carter's side of the bed was nothing but a twisted sheet and crumpled pillow.

She slipped on her blue robe, and padded across the hall to Joey's room. She had barely crossed the threshold when she suddenly stepped on something soft, heard a yelp, and she jumped back, startled.

Champ was sitting up, watching her.

"Oh my gosh," she said, letting out a breath. "I didn't see you there."

The dog waited, his ears up, tongue out. She could see the glistening scar on the top of his head from his fight with the coyotes; the vet had said it would heal in a few months. But ever since that night, Champ had appointed himself the unofficial companion and protector of little Joey, keeping tabs on him during the day, sleeping by his crib all night. Robin, the nanny, said he was like a sheepdog, tending to his flock.

"We're going to have to get you a doggie bed, aren't

we?" Beth said. Right now, he just slept on the carpeted floor. "And maybe put it farther out of the doorway."

Champ appeared to have no opinion, but watched silently as Beth went around him to look into the crib. Joey's eyes were open.

"Oh, did I wake you, pumpkin?" she said, leaning down. Although she had nothing to compare him to, Beth thought that he must be the most sensitive baby in all the world; he always seemed perfectly well rested, but he never seemed to sleep. Anytime you so much as approached him, he was wide awake. She'd even mentioned it to the pediatrician, who'd said he couldn't see any problem or adverse effects.

"If anything," he'd said, "he seems ahead of the curve—growing fast, thriving. I'd put him in the top one percentile on almost any measure."

Beth checked his diaper—no problem there—and kissed him on his forehead. His eyes, crystal clear and pale blue, remained fixed on her, and she had the odd sense, as she often did, that he was about to say something to her. That he *could* say something to her, if he wanted to, but that he just hadn't decided to do so yet. She knew it wasn't really true, but even as she drew back, she felt it.

"Someday," she whispered, "you're going to tell me what that's all about. Okay?"

He wiggled his feet in reply.

As she left, she could hear Champ turning around and around in a tight circle as he settled back down at the foot of the crib.

Downstairs, the house was dark. Had Carter actually gone out somewhere, at this hour? And after what had happened with the coyotes the last time? She glanced at the digital clock on the microwave; it was almost one in the morning. Going to the kitchen window, she looked out into the tiny yard, and she could see him sitting there in a lawn chair, facing out over the canyon. He had a beer in one hand.

Opening the double doors to the yard, she said, "Drinking alone again?"

He turned his head toward her. "Couldn't sleep."

She gathered her robe around her, walked barefoot across the short, mostly brown grass, and sat down in the chair next to him. "Was it the arm?"

After the attack in the tar pit, Carter had been taken to USC University Hospital, where they'd sewed up his forearm with a half dozen stitches. Now he had a narrow white bandage running down his forearm.

"No, that's okay." He was wearing a California Science Center T-shirt and a pair of Jams.

Beth sat back on the plastic strips of her chair, its aluminum frame creaking. The moon was full, etching the trees and brush below in a cold silver light.

She knew what it was; she knew Carter well enough by now to know what he would be thinking after such a terrible day.

"You know," she said, gently, "it's not your fault."

He didn't answer.

"The man was crazy."

"I know that," he conceded. "But now he's dead."

"Through no fault of yours. He attacked you, with a knife, and all you did was defend yourself."

He shrugged, as if to say, I know you're right . . . but it doesn't matter.

And it occurred to Beth that she had had this conversation before . . . back in New York. After the lab assistant had misused the laser, and set off the fatal explosion, Carter had blamed himself for everything. How strange, she thought, that even here in L.A.—where they'd gone to start over—such awful accidents were haunting them again.

"So, how come you're up?" Carter asked, as if to change the subject.

"I don't know. Just woke up, to an empty bed."

But Carter could read her as well as she could read him. He could see the concern in her eyes. It was one reason he'd gotten up and come outside; he didn't want her to be disturbed by all his tossing and turning. He'd tried to sleep—God knows, it had been a long enough day—but every time he closed his eyes, all he could see was the terrified face of Geronimo as he sank, slowly, to the bottom of the pit. He kept thinking that there was something else he could have done, some way he could have saved him.

And he wondered what the man's real name was.

No one knew—and there was a good chance no one ever would. Even if his body was recovered from the tar one day, there was no guarantee he'd have identification—that was still legible—on him. He'd become just another anonymous victim of the pit.

"At least it's not so hot out anymore," Beth said.

"Yeah, that's a relief," Carter agreed.

Another silence fell.

Carter finished the bottle of beer. "How's your work coming? On that bestiary."

"Good," Beth said, sounding as chipper as the late hour would allow. "The book is spectacular—the most beautiful I've ever seen—and I can't wait for the script analysis to come back. Trying to read it right now is an ordeal."

"How come? You were always pretty good with Latin."

"This text is so archaic, and the handwriting so peculiar, it would take me months to translate it on my own. Not to mention the fact that in some places it's very faded, and in others it's so intricately woven into the illustrations that it's hard to separate out."

"But apart from that," Carter said, with a laugh, "it's a piece of cake."

Beth smiled. "At least on my job I don't have to worry about getting attacked with a knife."

"But you do have to worry about the mysterious Mr. al-Kalli." A breeze blew through the canyon below, rustling the dry leaves. "Is he breathing down your neck?"

"Oh yeah," Beth said with a laugh. "He acts as if he's waiting for a doctor's report to come back from the lab."

Carter nodded companionably.

Beth levered herself out of the lawn chair. "I guess I'll try to get some sleep."

Carter reached out, took her hand, and drew her down onto his lap. Beth's robe fell open. "Hey, what'll the neighbors think?" Beth said.

"That's the great thing about this place," Carter said, gesturing out over the wide, dark canyon. "There aren't any."

He bent his head and kissed her. And for the first time in a long while, Beth felt herself . . . go with it. Maybe it was just the shock she'd had, hearing how close Carter had come to being killed in the pit, and maybe it was something else entirely, but right now she wasn't thinking about anything but her husband—not the baby, not her work—and the way his lips felt on hers. His hand moved up onto her breast, and she felt the nipple, usually so sore, stiffen under his fingertips. She let out an inadvertent moan, and his tongue went into her mouth.

Together, they slipped out of the chair and onto the parched grass. Carter pulled the robe off her shoulders as she shoved his Jams down. He pressed himself on top of her, and she opened her eyes, gazing up at the moon and stars—in L.A., you could actually see the stars at night—then closed them again. She didn't want to be distracted, even by something so beautiful; she didn't want to miss a moment of what was happening.

CHAPTER SIXTEEN

THE GOLF CART rolled to a stop at the far end of the facility. Overhead, a bird swooped and cawed, making lazy circles around the perimeter of the high, slanting roof.

Al-Kalli waited as Jakob pulled Rafik out, then said, "You know what to do."

Indeed, Jakob did—it wasn't the first time. Holding Rafik by the collar of the orange jumpsuit, he dragged him to the gate of the last pen and shoved him inside. He slammed shut the outer gate, leaving the prisoner boxed as if in a shark cage. Until the inside gate was released, Rafik still had some small measure of protection.

There was no sign of the pen's occupant, and that was a good thing. There was information that al-Kalli still needed to glean from his prisoner, and if he was already out of his mind with fear, it might prove difficult.

Al-Kalli drew a gold cigarette case from the pocket of his trousers, tamped a cigarette on the lid, then lighted it. Normally he would never allow such a thing in here, but on these special occasions, it seemed the right thing to do. Weren't the condemned always given one last cigarette?

He held it out to Rafik, who shrank back as far as the

cage, roughly the size of a phone booth, would permit, and regarded him warily.

"It's a Marlboro," he said, the most popular brand in Iraq before the war. To prove it was safe, al-Kalli took a draw on it himself, then exhaled the fragrant smoke. He held it out again, and this time, Rafik extended a shaky hand through the bars and took it.

Al-Kalli let him savor the moment—and perhaps hear the denizens of the facility as they stirred themselves awake. The overhead lights were blazing, uncharacteristically at this late hour, and some of the creatures were so sensitive that they might have already detected the smell of the cigarette. They would know something was afoot, and they would be curious. A yelp came from one of the nearby cages.

Rafik's eyes did dart in that direction, as he no doubt wondered what animal had made the sound. A hyena? A jackal? A coyote? Al-Kalli gave him time to run through the possibilities, knowing that he would never arrive at the right one.

"Now," al-Kalli said, calmly and in Arabic, "we still have some things to clear up."

Rafik, pinching the cigarette hard and holding it to his cracked lips, said nothing.

"There were four of you, to the best of my recollection."

Rafik had been through all this before.

"And three of you I have now come to know."

Rafik knew what that meant. His life had been nothing but torture and imprisonment since he'd been kidnapped in Beirut.

"But I want to know you all."

"You want," Rafik said, lowering the cigarette, "to kill us all."

"Not necessarily," al-Kalli said. "I am not without mercy." The same mercy, he thought, that had been extended to his own murdered family.

"Do you have a wife? Children?"

Rafik, he could see, was debating how to answer.

"Just tell me the truth," al-Kalli said, in reasonable tones.

Rafik finally nodded; yes, he had a wife and children.

"Then I'm sure you would like to see them again."

Rafik was sure that he never would. But the tiniest flicker of hope nonetheless stirred in his breast.

"I can send you back to them, or I can bring them here. To this country."

Al-Kalli was surprised that the beast, no doubt sleeping in his cave at the rear of the enclosure, had not yet made an appearance. He began to worry that it might be even more gravely unwell than he thought.

"What," Rafik ventured, "do I have to do?"

Ah, that pleased al-Kalli. He hadn't been sure that at this stage of the game he would be able to ignite any hope at all in the prisoner—surely the man would know his fate was sealed. But the human spirit was a strange and wondrous thing—even in the face of the obvious, it could harbor all kinds of illusions.

"Very little," al-Kalli said. "I know that it was Saddam himself who ordered the executions."

Rafik had never actually said so—what was the hold that Saddam, now a toothless lion who would never again walk free, held over these men?—but he hadn't bothered to deny it, either. In his dreams, al-Kalli imagined what he would have done if Saddam himself had ever fallen into his hands.

"But I wish to know how he chose you, and your comrades, for such a delicate task. Were you part of an elite squad? Were you handpicked?"

Al-Kalli had no real interest in the answers to these questions. He simply wanted to get Rafik talking. To give him time to think about his predicament—locked in some wild animal's cage—and to let him think that there might possibly be some way out.

"We trained together," Rafik said.

"Where?"

Rafik shrugged. "Baghdad." Both of his eyes were black and blue, and his nose, slightly askew now, was clearly broken.

"So you must have grown close. Training together, enjoying all the special privileges that only Saddam could provide."

Al-Kalli gave him a conspiratorial smile, and for a split second Rafik seemed to acknowledge it with a smile of his own. Al-Kalli was delighted.

"The others," he said, "were all from Tikrit originally. Were you?"

"Yes."

Saddam had always relied upon his fellow Sunnis for his most important tasks.

"And the man with the mustache," al-Kalli said. "Also from Tikrit?"

Rafik stopped talking.

"Who served the soup to my wife," al-Kalli said helpfully, though there could be no confusion about whom he was referring to.

"I didn't know him."

Right back where they'd started, al-Kalli thought with disgust. And he didn't disguise it. He turned to Jakob, standing with his hands folded, and with his chin gestured at a paint bucket lying by the gate.

Jakob lifted the lid off the bucket, walked to the gate of the enclosure, and threw the contents of the bucket all over Rafik.

For a moment, it might have been mistaken for red paint. But then the smell came—the smell of fresh blood.

Rafik dropped the cigarette and stared down at his blood-soaked jumpsuit.

From the next enclosure, the yelping suddenly surged into a series of frenzied barks. From even farther off, a low growl arose. On a perch high above, a huge bird loudly screeched.

Rafik's eyes went wide with the sudden cacophony—and the shock from his drenching.

"The man with the mustache," al-Kalli said, his words now as hard as flint.

"I tell you, I didn't know him!"

Al-Kalli pressed the release button for the inner gate, which opened wide. Rafik was now exposed to whatever lay within the enclosure.

And he knew it.

"What was his name?" al-Kalli asked.

Rafik looked frantically around the large enclosure, taking in the wading pool, the stunted trees, the low shrubs . . . the broken bones, covered with dust. *What lived in here?*

"I can close the gate again, as easily as I opened it," al-Kalli said.

A lion? Rafik thought. A tiger? All the way in back, he saw a cavernous stony grotto, raised a few feet off the hard-packed earth.

"All I need is a name."

What harm could it do? Rafik thought. He could give him a name—any name at all—and it might buy him time. But what if al-Kalli guessed that he was lying? What if, the clever bastard, he already knew the name, or had his suspicions, and was only waiting for Rafik to confirm them?

From within the lair, Rafik thought he saw a shadow move. Something was awake now. Something was alive.

Al-Kalli saw it, too, and was greatly relieved.

There was a long, soft sound of exhalation. A creature was struggling to its feet. And sniffing—Rafik could hear the echo from inside the cave as it sniffed the air appreciatively.

He looked down at himself. Covered in blood. And his hands flew at the zipper of the jumpsuit.

Al-Kalli laughed and glanced over at Jakob to share the joke. "He's smarter than the last one."

Rafik stripped off the suit as fast as he could, wadded it into a ball, and hurled it away; unfurling in the air, it caught on the branches of the nearest tree and hung down like a banner.

There was a growling from the cave.

"It's Ahmed!" Rafik cried out. "His name was Ahmed!"

"That's a start," al-Kalli said, suspending his hand above the control panel that could open—or close—the entry cage.

And then, they could both see the creature's eyes—blinking as they adjusted to the bright lights outside.

"Ahmed Massad!"

The name was familiar, and then al-Kalli realized it was Rafik's last name, too. "Was he—"

"He's my brother! Yes, he's my brother!"

Al-Kalli felt a warming glow. This would explain Rafik's reluctance for so long, and it impressed al-Kalli as the truth.

But now the beast had lumbered into the opening of the cave. Even after all these years, al-Kalli never failed to be moved by the sight of it. Its massive head, with a long, low snout and large, lizardlike eyes mounted on either side. Its cruel jaws, lined with dozens of sharp incisors, and over-hung, like a saber-toothed cat, with two curving fangs.

Rafik was frozen with fear.

The creature smelled him and moved its head, slowly, from side to side. Al-Kalli had never been sure how well the beast could see.

Rafik screamed, but the beast did not react. It had, al-Kalli knew, no visible ears—just triangular holes set well back behind the eyes—though he knew from experience that it could indeed hear. Quite well, in fact.

Rafik whipped around and clutched the bars. "Let me out!" he shouted in Arabic. "In the name of Allah, let me out!" His hands clenched the metal so forcefully, al-Kalli noticed, that the knuckles had turned as white as ivory.

"First," al-Kalli said, taking a deliberate pause, "I'll need to know more."

The beast had moved its forequarters out of the cave now and was standing on the lip of the rocky ledge. It was, in al-Kalli's estimation, a prize beyond compare. The size of an overgrown rhinoceros—and a very large and strong one at that—the creature was covered with scales, the kind you might see on a snake. Black, but with a dull green un-dercast that made them flash in the sun. Under this artifi-cial lighting, that effect was not as pronounced.

"What? What else do you want to know?"

"I want to know," al-Kalli said, drawing out his words, "where this brother of yours—this Ahmed Massad—lives now."

"I don't know!" Rafik cried, "I don't!"

"That's too bad."

The creature stepped forward on its stout front legs, longer than its rear legs, an anomaly that gave it the appearance of always rising up. As if perpetually lifting its fearful head in search of prey.

Which was not, al-Kalli knew, inaccurate. When well, when it had lived with its companions in the desert heat of Iraq, the beast had been a mighty and voracious predator. It could, and would, kill anything that came within its range. Al-Kalli had personally seen it attack and devour everything from a water buffalo to a hippopotamus with frightening dispatch.

Except when it wanted to play.

Like the cat whose fangs it shared, the beast sometimes liked to taunt its prey, to play with it and wear it down, before suddenly tiring of the game and slashing it to pieces.

Now, it hesitated on the ledge, its legs splayed out from its body, like a crocodile's, before deciding which way to leap.

"No idea?" al-Kalli said.

Rafik was staring at the monster, speechless now.

"Then I'd run if I were you," al-Kalli advised, softly, in Arabic. He didn't want the game to end too soon.

The creature sprang, like a lizard, off the ledge and landed on all fours with a loud thud. Dust plumed up around its broad clawed feet. Its long reptilian tail swished first one way, and then the other, in the dirt. Like a broom, it flicked some crumbling bones to one side; the pieces rattled as they rolled along the ground.

The beast knew where Rafik was now, and it slithered forward, its fanged head still held high. Among its scales sprouted incongruous clumps of filthy hair.

Rafik saw it coming and took al-Kalli's advice. He suddenly raced from the open cage and ran, naked, for the far end of the enclosure.

The creature turned its head to watch him with one large, unblinking eye.

Was it hungry at last, al-Kalli wondered? Would it feed again?

Rafik was frantic, leaping at the white-tiled wall that surrounded the enclosure to shoulder height; above that, thick steel bars rose much higher, higher than he would ever be able to climb . . . or to hold himself. Each time he fell, he whirled around to see where the beast was.

And now it was coming toward him again. Past the wading pool, with its smooth, sandy bottom. Past the stunted olive trees, with their gnarled, barren branches . . .

"Where is he?" al-Kalli called out.

Rafik could barely spit out the words. "Afghanistan."

"That's a big place."

"He went there to fight."

"Not good enough."

"It's all I know!" Rafik cried, his voice breaking with fear and anguish.

The beast jerked its head and squirmed forward. Al-Kalli knew it could move slowly . . . and, when it wanted to, as fast as a shot. Over short distances, he had seen it bring down gazelles.

"How will I find him?" al-Kalli said, with weary annoyance. He wanted Rafik to know that he was at the end of his patience.

The beast was close enough now that Rafik had to run again. Would he try to hide in the cave? al-Kalli wondered. No, that would be too absurd; he'd never do that.

Instead, he ran to the taller of the olive trees, leapt into its lower branches, and scrambled, screaming, all the way to its fragile top.

Al-Kalli smiled and turned toward Jakob, who smiled back. They had both seen this particular ploy before . . . and knew how it would turn out.

"How long," al-Kalli asked, "do you think you'll be able to stay there?"

Rafik simply screamed again, the other animals in the facility joining in. There were barks and yelps and lonely howls from the other enclosures.

"He has . . ." Rafik started to say, "he has . . ." But he couldn't finish. The beast had turned and was moving toward the base of the tree.

"He has what?"

"He has a girlfriend!"

"Who?"

"Fatima. Fatima Sayad."

"And where would I find her?"

"Tikrit!" he wailed in terror, and clung to the swaying branch. "On the Avenue of the Martyrs."

Al-Kalli glanced back again at Jakob, to make sure he was jotting this down. He was, in a small leather notebook.

"That's good," al-Kalli said. "That's very good."

"Mercy!" Rafik cried out. "Have mercy!"

But the creature had come to the trunk of the tree now, and did just as al-Kalli expected it to do. Rising up on its stubby back legs, it stretched its long scaly body to its full length—nearly fourteen feet—and lifted its head toward Rafik's dangling heels. He yanked them up, just out of reach, and the beast let out a guttural blast of fury. Today, it was tired of the game already.

Its long tongue shot out, flicking at Rafik's ankles, and its fangs snapped at the empty air.

Rafik clung to the top of the tree.

"Please!" Rafik cried. "I've told you everything I know!"

"I believe you," al-Kalli said. "I believe you have."

And then he waited. The beast stretched, with its powerful limbs, another foot or two up the trunk, enough to catch one of Rafik's feet in its jaws. And to drag him, shrieking in terror, back down to the ground. He sprawled in the dirt and managed to free himself, bleeding and torn. He ran wildly, in a wide circle, and when he came within a few yards of the cave, the beast suddenly sprang, with the power of a lion but the splayed legs of a lizard, on top of him. Rafik was crushed under its mighty bulk, and before he could scream again, the creature's jaws had fastened on his throat.

Al-Kalli sighed; from here on, it became far less interesting.

Rafik's legs kicked out, his heels digging into the dirt.

The monster shook him, like a plaything, and sank its fangs deeper. The legs stopped kicking, the feet flopped to each side.

"You got it all?" al-Kalli asked over his shoulder.

"Yes," Jakob said. "I will send the information to our people tonight."

Good. It shouldn't be hard to find the girlfriend . . . and from there . . .

As al-Kalli watched, the beast dragged the body by the throat toward its lair. It liked to dine in privacy. It climbed up onto the rock ledge, never letting go of its limp prize, and then, flicking its thick tail, disappeared into the cave with it.

Al-Kalli was happy to see it acting so much like its old self again.

CHAPTER SEVENTEEN

"**I**'**VE ASKED THE** police to move them back another hundred yards, but they say they can't do it," Gunderson fumed, glaring out the window at the picketers chanting and beating their drums on Wilshire Boulevard.

"The street is public property," Carter said.

"Not the sidewalk in front of the goddamn museum!"

As Carter followed Gunderson's gaze, he saw a TV station truck pull up outside. No doubt there'd be another evening news story, focusing on the tragic death of the unidentified victim they had dubbed "the Mystery Man," a Native American driven to violence by the desecration of his people's remains. Ever since the accident, the local news had been featuring the story prominently, following the search (so far unsuccessful) for the man's body, along with lots of talking heads debating the pros and cons of anthropology: "Where does science end," as one fatuous commentator had intoned, "and respect for the dead begin?"

Carter could only listen to so much of this gibberish. These were bones he excavated—not people. These were fossils—not souls, or spirits, or sacred vessels. Whatever immortal elements they might ever have possessed—and he wasn't a true believer there, either—it was long gone, into the air, into the ether. There was nothing deader than a petrified bone.

"We've had another interview request," Gunderson said, wheeling away from the window as if he couldn't bear to witness that spectacle another second. *The Vorhaus Report.* It was a serious-minded cable TV show—so serious almost no one watched. "I said you'd do it."

"You said what?" Carter blurted out.

"I said," Gunderson explained coolly, "that the head of our paleontology field unit—the man who not only discovered the remains of the La Brea Man, but who was in the pit when this unfortunate man fell to his death—would be happy to represent the museum and explain our interests."

"Why did you do that?" Carter said. He'd been ducking reporters, interview requests, even mikes shoved in his face when he got out of his car in the museum parking lot, for days.

"Because I'm tired of taking the heat, and because, frankly, this is your mess."

Carter had to bite his tongue, or he knew he'd say something fatal. What had really happened here, he could see, was that Gunderson, who'd been only too happy to stand in front of the cameras initially, with a sorrowful face and a beautifully folded silk pocket square, had gotten burned. He'd thought this would be a little blip of a story, a chance to make his own name and face synonymous with the museum, but it hadn't gone that way. The story had "legs," it wasn't going away overnight, and the more Gunderson talked, the more trouble he got himself, and the museum, into. Finally, he'd come to see that, and now he wanted to set up a new fall guy—Carter.

"But that's not why I sent for you."

Carter waited for the rest.

"I want to know what's happening in Pit 91 now. How long is it going to be until we find that man, that Geronimo's, body?"

Nobody liked calling him Geronimo—and on the air, and in public, they simply referred to him as "the victim," or even "the Mystery Man"—but in private, they reverted to the early shorthand.

"We're doing everything we can," Carter said, "but it's extremely difficult, for reasons I've already gone into." And reasons Gunderson kept conveniently forgetting.

The body of the Mystery Man had been sucked down into the pit in a way Carter had never before seen, and even now could not explain. The tar normally didn't work that way; hell, it hadn't worked that way for tens of thousands of years. It *trapped* animals, it didn't devour them. But something had changed; maybe it was a result of the high-power suction hoses (insisted on by Gunderson) or the steel sectioning plates that Carter had installed, or something else entirely—there was a theory that heavy construction work on nearby Curson Street had altered the underground geology—but whatever it was, it had caused the pit to behave in a totally anomalous fashion. And now, just when he was about to excavate one of the most fascinating and important finds of his career—the bones of only the second human being ever to be discovered in the La Brea pits—Carter had to find a way first to recover the body of a man who had somehow, impossibly, become its only modern prey.

"I simply do not understand this," Gunderson went on. "Why can't they just dredge the pit? How far down does it go? How far down can the body be?"

"We don't know," Carter said, as calmly as his growing impatience would allow. "Nothing here is going according to form. The pit has been agitated in a way we have never seen, and it's possible—though unlikely—that the body has somehow shifted laterally."

"What the hell does that mean?"

"It means, the body may have been dragged sideways, into a subterranean pocket or asphalt seam that we didn't even know was there."

Gunderson ran his hand over his carefully groomed gray head. "So how do we ever find it then?"

Carter had wondered about that himself. "It's possible," he said, "that we could try some kind of ground-based sonar." He'd actually started investigating the possibility, just in case everything else failed.

"Good Lord," Gunderson muttered, more to himself than Carter, "what's that going to cost?"

Plenty, Carter thought. But there was no point going into that now. He knew that there was a new Emergency Rescue Team, on loan from the San Bernardino Fire Department, down at the pit today, and he was due there to help oversee their activities. In fact, glancing at his watch, he realized that he was overdue.

"I've got to go down there now," Carter said.

"When you leave the building, try not to call any undue attention to yourself."

What would they have to do next, Carter thought—wear masks?

THE MOMENT HE left the air-conditioned confines of the museum, the pounding of the drums became louder. It was another painfully hot and arid day, and in the pit it would be at least ten degrees hotter. He didn't relish what he would have to do there.

As he walked past the pond of black asphalt near the entrance to the museum, where the life-sized replicas of a family of mastodons stood, someone shouted, "Grave robber!" at him. What grave? Carter thought. The La Brea Man had died a terrible, and probably solitary, death, either stuck in the tar and dying slowly of dehydration, or torn to pieces by predators, who had likely then died with him. For all anyone knew, he might have been happy to be found.

The LAPD had set up barricades that allowed visitors to the museum to go in and out, but blocked off all access, for now, to the parklike grounds where Pit 91 was located. Carter had to show the official pass that hung on a laminated card around his neck before the cop at the barrier would let him pass.

The pit, from here, looked like some kind of triage site. Where there was usually just one trailer, for changing and showering, there were now several, for coordinating the work of outside agencies, dealing with media requests, community outreach. The coroner's department had a person there at all times, to make sure the body of the Mystery Man was handled with kid gloves, whenever it might finally be found. To Carter, it was all a massive case of overkill.

Down in the pit, there were maybe a dozen workers now, none of them his usual crew. Rosalie and Claude had been relieved of duty for the foreseeable future, and even Miranda—the poster girl for enterprising UCLA graduates—had been informally banned. The workers now were postdoc paleontologists, and even a retired professor or two, who knew how to do the painstakingly close labor that the extraction of the La Brea Man now required. This was delicate, highly skilled work that was tough to do right under the best of circumstances. But to do it now, with firemen and cops and coroners looking over your shoulder, and rescue workers trying to figure out how to dredge a nearby quadrant of the site for a recent victim, was nearly impossible.

Carter could tell there was no news as soon as he started down the ladder into the pit. The San Bernardino crew had installed some kind of rope and tackle assembly, and their generator rested precariously on one of the wooden walkways; its operator, dripping with sweat, had stripped down to his navy, SBFD T-shirt and suspendered overalls. It made Carter sick to his stomach to think of what damage all this equipment might be doing to the as-yet-unrecovered finds that lay below.

The operator glanced up at Carter, and it appeared he knew who he was. Carter was having to get used to that, people knowing who he was without his ever having met them. "Nothing so far," the guy called out over the thrumming of the motor.

Carter nodded.

Several neighboring sections of the grid had men and women with piles of tools and paraphernalia all around them. Most were on their knees, using chisels and hand picks and stiff brushes to isolate the fossils that had been partially revealed. Others were carefully applying the burlap strips, soaked in plaster of paris, to the areas already exposed; once the cast had hardened, the fossil would be removed, hopefully intact, to the labs, where the finer work would be done.

A couple of the workers looked up as Carter approached, but under their hats and headbands, and with their goggles over their eyes, it was tough to tell who was who. His friend Del, however, he could always pick out. A middle-aged guy with a mane of prematurely white hair (tied up today, quite sensibly, with a thick rubber band), he leaned back on his haunches and pushed his goggles up onto his head.

"Hey, Bones," he said, using the nickname Carter had acquired years before. "Where you been? We've hit the mother lode."

Carter had to smile. He and Del went way back, to grad school; Del had already been an assistant professor at the time, and he had helped to get Carter on a couple of prize assignments. Now he was a full professor up near Tacoma, and when he'd heard about the situation in L.A., he'd been among the first to heed the call.

"Hell," he'd said upon arrival, "I was on sabbatical anyway, and I *still* wasn't writing my book." It was a running joke between them that Del had been working on his book—a revolutionary theory of the Permian extinction—all his life.

"Oh yeah? What have you found?"

"We've pulled up a six-pack of Tab—you know how hard that is to find these days?—and a Partridge Family lunch box."

Carter laughed and said, "Don't forget to catalogue them." Crouching down, he said, "It looks like you're making progress." A thick white layer of plaster was coating a section a few feet square.

"Yeah, we're getting there. But this plaster's a bitch to work with in this heat."

"Foam would have been worse." A more modern method, which Carter had rejected, was to apply polyurethane foam to an aluminum sheath.

"Would have made a lighter cast," Del replied.

"But the fumes would have killed us all down here."

"True," Del said. "But it's a small price to pay . . ."

Carter took off his shirt, draped it over a rung of the rear ladder—the very one that Geronimo had descended—and borrowed a pair of safety goggles from one of the workers too hot to continue. He picked up a chisel and began to work away at an area just beyond the plaster, where what might have been a scapular was still concealed. He felt better the second he started. He felt like himself again—a scientist, doing fieldwork—and not a bureaucrat dodging interview requests. With his head down, and the chisel in his hand, he could forget about all the other distractions and concentrate instead on what he loved . . . and what he did best.

For the next hour, Carter simply worked, occasionally trading a word or two with one of the other diggers, swigging regularly from the Gatorade bottles that made the rounds, glopping tar into the heavy black buckets. As if by some unspoken consent, the other workers had left the prize area of the La Brea Man's skull and upper torso to Carter, while they worked in the region of the man's extremities. Overall, the bones appeared to be remarkably connected still, especially considering the wild frenzy that the man's entrapment had apparently inspired. Bears, wolves, lions, every predator for miles around must have heard his cries, or seen him flailing to get out, and come running. Ordinarily, they'd have torn a limb loose, and dragged the meaty bone off to consume in safety elsewhere, but in this case the conditions must have been disastrous for all. The tar must have been heated and thick, the temptation of human prey too irresistible, and the fight for a piece of him too violent. All across the pit, the signs of an epic struggle were more than evident.

So why, Carter wondered, were the man's bones laid almost horizontally? It was quite possible, of course, that they had just been pushed and pulled into that configuration over thousands of years in the tar—bones were scraped and scattered and broken and abraded all the time—but there was something about these that still struck Carter as strange. Out of the corner of his eye, he glimpsed again the plastered dome where the skull now resided. He tried not to look right at it—skulls still had a peculiar resonance that made them hard to ignore, even for Carter—but looking now, he had the impression that the face had indeed been turned up toward the sky at the time of his death. That he had lain flat, surrendering to the tar . . . and offered himself to the animals that had come to kill him.

Had he just run out of strength and been pinned down by the hot tar? Had he simply given up and resigned himself to his fate? Or had he, out of some primitive atavistic sense, sacrificed his body and his spirit to what he might have perceived as the great chain of being?

"Now this might be interesting," Del said, prolonging that last word.

Del, sort of the unofficial second-in-command now, had been working a few feet to his left, in the area of the hand.

Carter pushed his goggles back on his head to get a better look.

To a layman's eye, it would appear to be no more than a lump of tar-covered rock, but to Del, or Carter, it was more than that. It had a special shape, a man-made shape, and it appeared to be cradled in the palm of his hand.

"Looks like something that mattered to him," Del said, and Carter couldn't have agreed more. He scooted closer. It might have been a weapon, used in his final struggle. Or simply the last thing, as the breath left his body, that his dead fingers had closed upon.

Or was it something the man might have cherished?

Carter had no more time to consider the possibilities before there was a shout from the other side of the pit. "Yo! We've got something."

Carter turned and heard a high-pitched whine from the generator on the walkway as the pulley chains drew taut.

The other workers all stopped, too, took off their goggles, and waited.

The drag chain, with a steel claw on the end, had been submerged to a depth of twenty-five feet or more. The operator, his damp T-shirt clinging to his body, waved up to another fireman standing at ground level.

The generator rumbled, the chain tightened again and then, slowly, began to pull.

"We've got something, that's for sure," the operator said, staring down at the now turbulent tar. Methane bubbles pocked the inky black surface.

Stepping around the other workers, Carter crossed to the section of the grid where Geronimo had gone down. The chain was still pulling something up, and Carter found himself thinking, to his own shame, that he was worried it might be a priceless fossil, now damaged beyond repair. Lucky, he thought, that the media could never guess what was going on in his head.

"Hold it a second," the operator shouted. "We've got a snag."

The guy up top signaled back, and the operator actually leaned out over the pit and shook the heavy chain, the old-fashioned way, before kicking up the generator again. A tiny plume of smoke, or steam, escaped from a valve on top.

"Should it be doing that?" Carter shouted over the whine.

"Does that all the time," he said, before looking back into the pit.

Carter looked, too, as the chain, swathed in black asphalt, continued to rise. The fireman appeared pleased, like a fisherman who's just caught a big one. Carter's feelings were certainly more mixed—relief, if it came to that, and dread, at the grisly sight that was probably about to unfold.

"Okay, any time now," the operator shouted as he watched the clanking chain. Coated in tar as it was, Carter could only guess how he knew they were about to reach the claw end at last. Across the pit, Carter could see Del, his white hair blowing loose now in the afternoon breeze, waiting expectantly.

And then something emerged from the mire. Something caught in the claws of the dredge.

A slender object, wedged between two of the prongs. Carter leaned closer. What was it?

The chain pulled up, slowly, another few inches, and now Carter could see that it was a foot. In some kind of shoe.

A moccasin.

The fireman looked at Carter, who said, "Keep on going."

Another prong had apparently snagged the end of Geronimo's trousers.

The body emerged gradually, the tar seeming to reach up and hold on to it until the last possible second before rolling back off and plopping into the pit. The corpse, hanging upside down like a slaughtered animal on a meat hook, was glistening black from head to toe, the arms hanging listlessly in the fringed buckskin jacket. It twirled languidly on the hook, until it had come around to face Carter at eye level.

The fireman quickly looped a nylon cord around its waist to keep it from slipping off the hook and into the pit again.

Geronimo's long black braid had a knot at one end and hung straight down, like an exclamation point, all the way to the surface of the pit. His face was entirely covered in tar, which only now began to ooze and drip off the skin. As Carter watched, transfixed, the man's features began slowly to emerge. The chin, the nose, the cheeks. The hot tar gleamed in the late-day sun.

Apart from the whine of the generator, there was no noise in the pit. Everyone was dumbstruck by the horror of the sight.

Then, just as the fireman reached out to pull the dangling corpse over the walkway, more of the tar seeped off the face—and the eyes, sealed tight, were slowly revealed.

Carter was reminded of the slitlike eyes of a mummy.

And then, perhaps due to the pull of the falling tar, or simply gravity, the eyelids opened.

In the blackened, slack, and silent face, the whites of the eyes were now like slivers of light. Carter looked directly into Geronimo's eyes; he couldn't stop himself—and it felt, in some strange way, as if he owed him that.

But as he stood there, in the stifling confines of the pit, a sudden chill coursed down his spine. He knew it was impossible—what could be more so?—but it seemed as if Geronimo, even now, was looking back at him.

CHAPTER EIGHTEEN

"**J**ESUS," GREER SAID, "that hurts."

Indira laid the leg down slowly onto the table. "You must not neglect your home exercises."

How many times had he heard that? But it wasn't as if the damn leg hadn't been getting a workout lately.

"Maybe we should do some ultrasound," she suggested.

"Yeah, ultrasound," Greer said, "that's always good."

In honesty, he couldn't say it ever accomplished a thing. But it didn't hurt, which was one thing you could say for it, and it didn't require any exertion on his part, which was another.

Indira first went to get some hot packs and wrapped the leg in them, while Greer lay flat on the table. He knew he should say something, there was a lot of stuff hanging in the air, but he just didn't know where to start. Indira's feelings were hurt, he could see that without even asking. She'd probably been wondering why, after their first "date"—if you wanted to call it that—he had never suggested they go out again.

But Christ, hadn't she been there, too? It had been a mistake, right from the start, and Indira had acted like it wasn't a date at all. And then there'd been that humiliation at the restaurant, when the girl tripped over his leg and Indira flew to his defense . . . well, shit, did she really think any man was going to want to relive an experience like that?

"Thanks again," he said as she bent over the leg, tucking in the hot towels.

"For what?"

"Having dinner with me, you know, the other night."

Even under her coppery skin, he thought he saw a slight reddening. Shit, maybe he should have just let it go. It wasn't as if she'd thrown herself at him or anything. God, he could not read women.

"I was happy to do it," she said, still not looking him in the eye. "Now, I will be back in ten minutes for the ultrasound." She set the egg timer, and he turned his head to see where she was going so abruptly. Mariani, in his wheelchair, was having some trouble navigating out of a tight spot.

He adjusted the neck rest, closed his eyes, and tuned out the rest of the noise in the room—the clanking of the machines, the moans and curses of the other vets as they suffered through their various therapy routines. What he wanted to do was sleep; he reminded himself to hit up Indira for some more sleeping pills before he left. But if he thought he'd been having trouble before, it was nothing compared to what went on in his head ever since that night on the al-Kalli estate.

Now, every time he closed his eyes, he saw that guy, that prisoner who was coated in blood, running for his life in the huge animal pen.

And the creature that had hunted him down and dragged him, screaming, out of the tree.

Now he knew what had lived in the empty, broken cages of Iraq . . . now he knew what he'd glimpsed in the headlights the night Lopez had been snatched.

And now he knew what kind of man he was up against.

Which still didn't tell him what to do about it.

After al-Kalli and Jakob had left in the golf cart, Greer had slunk out from his hiding place, behind a pile of feed crates, and with shaking legs stumbled to the doors. He had tried not to look into the other cages lining the west wall of the facility—he'd seen enough already—but he could hear an occasional grunt or growl, and once something had lunged at the bars and its spittle had hit his neck like hot oil. He didn't have the remote control that he'd watched al-Kalli use to open the doors, but after a few frantic seconds, he'd found a mounted panel with a door release handle built into it.

Once outside, he'd hauled ass, as best he could, for the back entrance; he found it by following the rear service road that ran along the northern perimeter of the estate.

Sadowski, thank God, was parked across the road in a patch of deep shadow. Greer looked both ways to make sure nobody was coming, then sprinted, his leg blazing, to the car and climbed in.

"You're late," Sadowski said. Then, "And you're sweating like a pig."

"Just get out of here."

Sadowski started the car. "What's that shit on your neck?"

Greer felt where he'd been spat on; it was thick as mucus and when he glanced at his fingertips, he saw it was pale green, too.

"It stinks."

"Will you just shut the fuck up and drive!" Greer snarled.

Sadowski knew enough to do that, though he kept glancing over in Greer's direction. Greer knew what he was looking for—some sign of booty. Some indication that the night hadn't been a complete bust.

Greer didn't feel like relieving his curiosity just yet.

They'd made it all the way down to Sunset Boulevard before Sadowski dared to break the silence. "So," he said as they waited for the light under the Bel-Air gate, "what happened?"

What happened. Greer still hadn't decided that for himself. His eyes could not believe what they'd seen. His brain couldn't process it. His hands couldn't stop trembling. He reached up and took off the Silver Bear Security cap, which peeled away from his sweaty temples like a strip of adhesive, and tossed it onto the floor.

"Hey, I've got to return that."

Greer gave him a withering glare.

The light changed, and Sadowski took a left. "You get into the house?"

"No."

Sadowski smacked the steering wheel in irritation. "So you didn't actually get anything?"

"That wasn't the purpose." Greer had told him that this was simply a reconnaissance mission, but he knew Sadowski hadn't understood that. Maybe he'd thought it was just Greer's way of cheating him, of pocketing some cash or jewelry and then claiming he'd come away empty-handed.

"So what did you do?"

"What I did was, I watched a guy get eaten by a creature out of your worst nightmare."

Sadowski just glanced at him, not knowing how to take this. "Yeah, right," he said, returning his eyes to the road. "What did you really see up there?"

Greer wondered whether he should even bother to try. Whether he could ever make what he'd seen believable to someone who hadn't seen it with his own eyes. He still hardly believed it himself.

"What I really saw up there," Greer repeated, in a deliberate manner, "was a zoo out of *The Twilight Zone*."

"I love that show," Sadowski said, hanging a left. "I've got the whole thing on DVD."

Greer gave up. What was the point of trying to convince Sadowski of something he'd never understand?

"Mind if we stop at the Blue Bayou?" Sadowski said. "I gotta check on Ginger."

Greer nodded that it was okay.

"You can give me the real 411 when we get there."

But Greer had already decided to keep his own counsel. In the meantime, the idea of a noisy strip club, with lots of people, and naked girls, and a fully stocked bar, was a very good one right now.

"In the meantime, you better take off that Silver Bear jacket, too."

Greer wrestled the jacket off his arms and shoulders.

"Man, I hope none of that crap on your neck got on the jacket."

Greer would have liked to deck him. But he held himself in check, not saying another thing, until they got to the club, and he had the first of several Jack Daniel's doubles in front of him. He drank the first one as if it were water.

"Burt Pitt was asking about you," Sadowski said, as they huddled over a small table not far from the runway. A topless girl in a pair of bicycle shorts and skates was rolling around the stage to the tune of Avril Lavigne's "Skater Boy."

"Let him ask."

"We're getting close," Sadowski confided, leaning in conspiratorially, though there was no chance of their being overheard. Between the blaring music and the fact that the drunks at the nearby tables were firmly fixed on the skating girl, their privacy was pretty much complete.

"Close to what?"

"I can't exactly tell you that," Sadowski said. "Not until you join up."

Greer threw down the rest of his drink and didn't answer, which drove Sadowski crazy—as Greer knew it would.

"Okay," Sadowski said, "and you've got to promise that you won't say a word about any of this to anybody, because if you do, my ass is grass, and I mean that seriously. I will be dead meat if word of this gets out."

Greer just waited.

"You know how a lot of people like to set off fireworks on the Fourth of July?"

"Yeah," Greer said, "I've heard a rumor to that effect."

"Well, this year there's going to be some really major fireworks in L.A., if you know what I'm saying. We're going to really start something up."

Greer looked at him, while signaling for another round. "Why?"

"So everybody'll finally get pissed off about what's happening in this country, so they'll finally get off their fat asses and help us do something about it. Before it's too late."

Greer had been hearing this vague, apocalyptic shit from Sadowski forever, and tuned him out now. Fortunately, the next girl on the runway was his lady love, Ginger Lee, and Sadowski had soon lost himself in admiration.

Which allowed Greer to go back to ruminating on the horrors he had seen that night. A few more shots of Jack Daniel's and it had all begun to take on a weird, surreal glow . . .

A timer went off behind his head now, and Greer realized he'd been dozing on the therapy table. Indira's hands were quickly removing the no-longer-hot towels, then coating the leg from thigh to calf with a lubricant designed to make the ultrasound wand move more smoothly over the skin. The thing looked like vibrators Greer had seen in ex-girlfriends' apartments, but it didn't make that loud humming noise. It was fairly quiet, and all Greer had to do was lie back and let Indira move it around over the trouble spots. Supposedly, though Greer thought the whole thing was bullshit, the ultrasound helped to break up the scar tissue.

Greer remembered what he needed and what he'd come for. "Say, Indira, I'm still having a lot of trouble sleeping, and I was wondering if you could get me—"

"No, Captain. You have already exceeded the dispensary limits."

"But all I need is—"

"I cannot get it for you," she said. "I strongly suggest that when we are done with the ultrasound, you use your time to do some stretching exercises on one of the machines."

Greer realized that he had broken one of the cardinal rules of the drug user—he had alienated his supplier.

"And I do not believe that you are doing your home exercises at all."

She had him there, too.

CHAPTER NINETEEN

"**T**HAT'S A *G*," her assistant said.

"It's a *q*."

"No way."

"Way," Beth said wearily. "Just put it in the Q file."

Beth pushed the chair back from her desk and rubbed her eyes with her fingertips. How long, she wondered, had they been at it? She glanced at the clock, nestled between the framed photos of Carter and Joey, and realized it had only been an hour. But such close work made the time crawl by.

Not that Elvis seemed to mind. He was twenty-three, she'd been told, but he looked like he was about twelve. And he also looked like he had never been out in the daylight. His skin was dead white and smooth as marble, his hair was jet black, and he had long, narrow sideburns running halfway down his cheeks. She suspected that Elvis was a name he had adopted on his own.

"That makes three variations in the Q file," he said.

"It wasn't uncommon for medieval scribes to do slightly different, more or less ornate versions of each letter, often in the same manuscript. One might be used as a large initial to signal the beginning of a chapter or section, one might be simply a capital, one might be in the lowercase. And sometimes they just got fancy."

"Must have made it tough to read," Elvis said, entering the letter in question into his database.

"Now you see the problem."

For days they had been hunched in front of the computer screen, going over scanned pages of *The Beasts of Eden* and laboriously picking out and entering each variation they could find of each letter or numeral—each grapheme—and then cataloguing it in the master concordance. The idea was, once they had a solid and broad enough selection of the letters and numbers, the computer program would be able to immediately identify all the characters; after that, all you had to do was let the program run and it would translate the entire manuscript in a lot less time than it would take Beth, armed with a magnifying glass and a Latin dictionary, to do the same.

But before you got *there*, you had to stay *here* for at least a few more days.

"You want a caffè latte?" Elvis asked. "I'm going to get one."

For a second, she wondered if he should risk it; it meant going outside, in the sunlight.

"Sounds great. Charge it to the conservation department."

"In that case," Elvis said, "can I get some other stuff, too?"

"Go to town." She hoped he'd get something healthy. He looked like he lived on candy bars and soda.

While he was gone, she stood up, did some stretches, then phoned home. The nanny picked up, and in the background she could hear Champ barking.

"Anything wrong?" Beth said.

"No, no," Robin said with a laugh. "I think a bird had the nerve to land on Joey's windowsill."

"Guess we don't need a security service after all."

"Long as you've got Champ, you don't."

Joey, it turned out, was upstairs in his crib for nap

time. But would he be sleeping? Beth wondered. Sometimes she had the feeling he just lay there, thinking deep thoughts he wasn't yet able to express. But with all quiet on the home front, she could turn her attention back to the work at hand.

Which was coming along. At first she'd debated how to go about it, then decided that the best way might be to focus on what were known in medieval manuscripts as the catchwords—words that were written at the bottom of each gathering, or quire, and then repeated as the first words at the top of the page in the next quire. It was a technique used to make sure that the separate sections, when they were all illuminated and ready to be bound together into the actual book, were placed in the right order. It was also a convenient handwriting test, a good way for her to see the scribe writing the same words twice, in close proximity.

But it was grueling work, not only because the dense script was extremely difficult to decipher, but because portions of the book had faded, or been worn away. Most of it, it was true, was still remarkably well preserved and vibrant, the colors leaping off the page, the metallic gold glinting in the light. But after nearly a thousand years, nothing could be expected to remain entirely intact and undamaged.

Elvis came back with two caffè lattes and what looked like a grocery bag filled with sandwiches, fruit drinks, yogurt cups, cookies, and who knew what else. "I think I went a little crazy," he said.

Beth couldn't have cared less. Elvis was considered the boy genius of the Getty's computer world, and whatever it took to keep his motor running was well worth it. And it was nice to hear his boyish enthusiasm as she showed him page after photocopied page of the ancient book and explained what it all meant. Or at least what she *thought* it all meant.

Even the catchwords, she'd noticed, were a little strange. The text occasionally seemed to end a little short, or run a little long, all in order, as best she could surmise, to make sure that certain words appeared naturally at the bottom of the page. And although they weren't the words she might have expected to land there, she had the distinct impression that the scribe had gone to some trouble to see that they did.

While Elvis went about eating with one hand and maneuvering icons all over the screen with the other, Beth began to look idly at the list of preliminary catchwords, in the order that they showed up in the book so far. And something funny struck her. The first two catchwords, which closed out the first quire, neatly matched up to the three words that closed out the second one. They started to make a sentence, which, roughly translated from the medieval Latin, said, *Brought here / to this land.*

"Huh," she said, under her breath.

But Elvis, sitting right next to her at the desk, said, "Huh what? I do something wrong?"

"No, nothing's wrong," Beth said. "I just noticed something kind of funny."

"Share," Elvis said, taking another big bite out of a sandwich that smelled like it had pesto in it.

"Could you make a quick list of all the catchwords we've translated so far, in the order they appear?"

"Not a problem."

His fingers flew across the keyboard, and a minute later he said, "It's printing out now. Want me to go get it?" The printers were in a central station down the hall, something Beth usually found to be a total nuisance. But right now, if it meant getting away from that blast of pesto, she'd happily walk a few steps.

"You eat. I'll go."

She got up and went out into the hall. She could hear Mrs. Cabot haranguing someone in an office down the hall. Why, she thought, did God create bureaucrats? Ducking into the printer room, she found her sheet, still warm, waiting on top of a stack of other, legal-looking documents in the tray. She didn't have to study them to know what they were about. The word "provenance" jumped out three times on the top page alone; the Getty, like all major museums, had to be scrupulously careful about where its acquisitions came from, and whether or not the seller, or donor, had legal title in the first place.

Fortunately, *The Beasts of Eden* was just a loan, in for conservation and study, the way you might bring in a car for a thirty-thousand-mile tune-up. So that was one paperwork blizzard Beth had not had to slog through. Not yet.

Elvis had printed out each set of catchwords on a separate line, first in Latin, then with the English translation (these would have to be refined later on) right after it.

Reading down the page, Beth could easily put them all together, and what they said, as she stood there between the sleek machines, which had already begun to work on other jobs that had been remotely transmitted, was either a fantastic coincidence or a game of some sort.

Or—a third possibility, and one she should not rule out—a startling discovery that had waited almost a thousand years to be made.

Right now, reading through just what they had so far, the combined catchwords said: *Brought here / to this land / honored guest / now prisoner / laboring in obscurity / my name to sleep* (or was it really "to vanish"?).

Beth just stood there, reading the words over and over again, as if to convince herself that they really did fall together in such a neat and logical order. And as she did, the notion of a coincidence was discarded altogether. Which left the other two alternatives: On the one hand, it might be just a little prank. Monks and scribes were prone to such things, often including what was called a colophon at the end of a manuscript, in which they thanked their patron, boasted about what arduous work they'd done, and sometimes hinted that they hoped to be handsomely paid. In some Italian manuscripts of the fourteenth and fifteenth centuries, the scribes went so far as to suggest what they were planning to use the money for—wine and women.

But this message, cobbled together from catchwords, was nothing like that. It wasn't boastful, it wasn't lighthearted, it wasn't meant to be read by anyone but an initiate—a fellow writer, who knew his Latin. Beth knew that many manuscripts were produced, as this one might well have been, for patrons who could not themselves read the actual text. The book was a treasure, a measure and sign of their wealth and sophistication, and if it was read, it was read to them by an educated retainer. *The Beasts of Eden*, created for a rich and powerful Eastern dynasty, was even more likely to have been such a work.

But what did the rest of the catchwords say and how would they complete the message?

Beth turned on her heel and hurried back to her office. Elvis had polished off the sandwich and was working on an oatmeal cookie the size of a Frisbee.

"I've brought the letter catalogue up to date," he said. "Go ahead—ask for a letter, any letter."

"Not now."

Elvis looked hurt. The danger, Beth thought, of working with kids . . .

"I need you to bring up the list of catchwords."

"We just did that."

"No, not just the ones we've already deciphered and catalogued; I want the ones that are still remaining. All of them in the exact same order that they show up in the quires."

"Aren't we kind of getting ahead of ourselves? Didn't you say that the way to do this—"

"Forget what I said, okay? This is more important."

Suddenly Elvis looked stoked. "Hey, you look like you're on to something."

Beth didn't reply; she was riffling through the pile of photocopies on her desk, removing all the sheets that had, as a result of completing a quire, been embellished with two or three catchwords in the lower right corner.

"Aye, aye, Captain Kirk." Elvis crammed the rest of the cookie into his mouth and began to correlate the printouts Beth handed him with the same images on the computer screen. Then he highlighted the catchwords and moved them onto the master list. "You know that you're only going to have the Latin for these, right? We haven't completed the lexicon or the graphemical database yet, so we can't do the simultaneous translation."

"That's okay," Beth said, still not looking up from her work. "I'll muddle through somehow."

Elvis went back to his keyboard. "That is so cool," he said under his breath. "You're a total babe *and* you can read ancient Latin."

Even in the midst of this potentially huge discovery, the words "total babe" were not entirely lost on Beth.

CHAPTER TWENTY

CARTER DIDN'T KNOW who needed it more—Del or himself—but a few solid hours of hiking in the Santa Monica Mountains felt like just the right ticket.

Although they'd both always enjoyed going out on digs in remote places all over the world, Del was the one who couldn't abide city living. When he wasn't cooped up in a lecture hall or delivering a paper to a symposium some-where, Del was out in the woods, hunting, fishing, bird-watching. He had a separate meat freezer up in Tacoma, just to store the meat and game he shot—sometimes with a bow and arrow—on his various expeditions.

Today, the hiking conditions were quite different—eighty-five degrees or so, with an overcast sky and only the faintest breeze.

"You're sure you want to hike in this weather?" Carter had asked, and Del had said, "You bet!" without a mo-ment's pause. "If I don't get out of this city and into a little wilderness soon, I'm going to pop my gourd."

Carter wasn't sure if the hiking trails up into Temescal Canyon would really qualify, but it was the closest thing he could offer. He picked up Del at the fancy Wilshire

Boulevard high-rise where he was staying with his sister—
she'd married a movie studio executive—and as they drove
off, Del visibly shuddered. "You know they've got a guy
there who parks your car for you? And another one who
brings up your groceries? And a concierge—a concierge!—
to take your deliveries and your dry cleaning?"

"I bet the place is even air-conditioned," Carter said
with a smile.

"Damn straight it is," Del replied, "but I slept out on the
balcony last night."

Carter wondered what on earth Del's brother-in-law
must make of him.

As they pulled into the canyon parking area, Carter was
glad to see just a few other vehicles—a Pontiac, a couple
of SUVs, a private patrol car—parked there. Del wouldn't
go for lots of people blocking the trails, and, frankly, neither would he. He wasn't crazy about getting stuck, as he
had recently, behind a bunch of teenagers, bopping along
to their iPods and swigging from cans of Red Bull. He paid
five bucks for the parking pass, and as he stuck it on his
dashboard, Del shook his head sadly.

"You have to pay just to leave your car here?" he said.
"Up in Washington, we pull it off the road and go." He
slung his nylon backpack onto his shoulder. "How do you
stand it, Bones?"

"It's called civilization," Carter said, "and I made my
peace with it long ago."

Carter grabbed his own pack, which held nothing more
than some Gatorade, some sunscreen, his wallet, and his
keys, and they headed off across the picnic area, then up
onto the trail. Carter went first, and he could hear Del
taking deep breaths behind him, savoring the fresh air and
the tang of the dry sage scrub. They crossed a narrow
wooden footbridge over a trickling stream, and Del said,
"Hardly needs a bridge, does it?"

"This is L.A.," Carter said. "Be glad there's no toll."

But with every step that they climbed up into the hills,
L.A. fell farther and farther away. For once, you heard no
car horns, you saw no gas stations or 7-Elevens or Burger

Kings. You weren't looking over your shoulder, or into your rearview mirror, for what was coming up fast behind you. The Santa Monica Mountains, which pretty much bifurcated the sprawling city of Los Angeles, formed the largest urban wilderness in the country, and even Carter found it a necessary tonic. Ever since he'd moved west, he'd been poking around, every chance he got, into the various recreation areas and mountain trails. La Jolla Canyon. Escondido. Santa Ynez. The Circle X Ranch Grotto. Bronson Canyon. Zuma. Saddle Peak. There were dozens of places, some just minutes away, where you could get off the urban grid and, with a pair of sneakers and a bottle of water, get back into nature and leave your city troubles behind you. Right now, Carter had plenty of city troubles to leave behind.

He seldom went more than an hour or two without remembering Geronimo's tar-covered corpse or his strangely comprehending dead stare.

"Say," Del asked, as they paused to let a gray quail and her chicks skitter across the trail, "did they ever get a name for that guy who fell into the pit?"

"Yes, they did. It was William Blackhawk Smith."

"They say what tribe he was from?"

"Chumash."

"Not many of them left."

And now, Carter thought, there's one less.

They continued up the trail, Carter mulling over, despite himself, the events of the past couple days. After the body had been recovered, the medical examiner had immediately claimed it. But in order to avoid the protestors still holding their vigil out front, it had been zipped up into a body bag, loaded onto a canvas stretcher, and spirited out the back gate of the museum grounds at dusk.

As for the bones of the La Brea Man, Carter had managed to keep a lid on the latest discovery there—only he and Del knew that the man had been clutching something, something precious or important to him, in the moments before his death. While everyone in Pit 91 was focused on the dangling corpse of William Blackhawk Smith, Del had quickly removed what tar he could from the mysterious object, and then slathered the whole thing with the same plaster of paris that was now covering the rest of the bones. Carter was very grateful that he had. If word of this development had gotten out, Gunderson, who never learned his lesson, would have probably issued another press release.

"The trail marker said there was a waterfall a couple of miles up," Del said.

"Sometimes it's running," Carter replied, "but these days it might be dry."

"I'll take my chances," Del said. "Anything beats being down in the pit on a day like this."

Way up ahead, Carter saw a young couple—a Hispanic guy and a blonde girl in shorts that said JUICY across the backside—sauntering up the path. The trail was wider than usual here, and the boy was holding her hand. Carter remembered hiking in Scotland once with Beth, and taking her hand as they stood on a rocky crag. She'd called him Heathcliff and he'd called her Cathy, "my wild, sweet Cathy," for the rest of the trip.

This lower portion of the trail occasionally veered close to a service road, so you couldn't help but see the occasional ranger truck, or even an outbuilding or two, through the trees and brush. Carter wanted to get higher up, and further in, and he suspected that Del felt the same way. Even when they looked up into the hills, you could still see the back of a house, poking out here and there, on the side of a neighboring slope. Putting his head down, he started to climb higher and more deliberately, quickly passing the hand-holders and, at the first fork, taking the steeper and more roundabout path that led to the falls. Behind him, he could hear Del marching along, and every so often calling out a sighting.

"Yellow warblers at three o'clock. Orioles in the sycamore you're just passing."

Carter, not wanting to break his stride, would catch a quick glimpse and move on.

"Poison oak on the side of the trail. Veer to the left."

Carter knew a fair amount about flora and fauna, but Del, he knew, was a walking omnibus. There wasn't a bird or a plant or a critter that Del couldn't spot at a hundred paces, and reel off everything about it from its common name to its scientifically accurate title. He could tell you what trees grew where, what birds nested in them, which nuts and berries were edible, which ones would kill you. Once, Del had been bitten by an adult rattler out west—two hours' drive from the nearest hospital—and he'd lived to tell the tale. He still had the scar on his thigh to prove it.

"Now that's what I call a fixer-upper," Del said as they came up on an abandoned and boarded-up shack nearly hidden by the trees. Carter heard him leaving the trail to explore it. "You think I could afford it?" Del called out.

Carter pulled his water bottle out of his backpack, took a couple of swallows, then joined Del. The place looked like something from one of the Grimm Brothers fairy tales, with dilapidated wooden walls, a broken-down porch, splintered boards crisscrossing the window. Del stood in the shade and gathered his long white hair into a tight knot that he then bound with a thick rubber band.

"Doesn't look like it was ever a ranger station or anything like that," Del said. "It's just too damn peculiar."

Carter read the fairly predictable graffiti on the boards. SM LOVES MJ, with a heart around the initials. THE SAND-MAN RULES! (Whatever that meant.) A backwards swastika. (Like most young, would-be Nazis, this one was too dumb to get the symbol right.) In the shadows within, all he could see were cobwebbed rafters and the frame of an old wooden rocking chair.

That was rocking.

Carter lifted his shades and peered in more closely. Now he could see more—a filthy mattress off in the corner, a glass and a pewter plate beside it. A dusty lantern hung from a nail. But there was no one inside.

"You thinking of making an offer?" Del said. " 'Cause I saw it first."

"No, it's all yours," Carter said, still scanning the single small room. "But I think it might be occupied." The chair had stopped rocking, and was now as still and deserted as everything else.

"Occupied by what?" Del said, stepping up next to Carter and looking into the gloomy interior. "I don't see anything." He moved to his left and examined the rusted lock and chain that hung from the hasp. "Guess we'll have to call the real estate agent if we want to take the tour."

"Guess so," Carter said, moving away from the window. He didn't know why exactly, but he didn't want to hang around here anymore. He wanted to get back out of the shade and into the sunlight—even the hazy sun that was all the day had to offer.

"A waterfall sounds good right about now," Del said.

"Don't get your hopes up," Carter said as he waded through the tall grass and back onto the trail.

The ascent was steeper from here on up, and though it was a joke compared to the real wilderness climbs that Carter and Del had made, you still had to watch where you were going. The trail had rocks and roots and sudden declivities, and every once in a while there was a story on the evening news about somebody who'd been bitten by a snake or even—though this was extremely rare—attacked by a hungry mountain lion. Thinking back to Central Park in New York, Carter remembered plenty of mugging stories, but no mountain lions or rattlers.

Most of the time, they had a ravine on their left, with a slow-running brook spilling over mossy stones. Carter was encouraged to see that, even if it wasn't much, there was actually some water still running in it. Maybe they would find the waterfall operational, after all. Only one other person had passed them coming down the trail—a wiry guy using a ski pole as a walking stick, who'd said something in German. Otherwise, the day was so hot and muggy, the sky so overcast, that everybody must have gone to the beach or the movies.

Carter plowed ahead, and gradually the sound of the water running in the brook began to increase. A good sign. The path wound through shady patches of overhanging trees, oaks and sycamores, and then into open stretches of hot dusty soil, where the canyon suddenly rose up on both sides, its flanks covered with scrub and chaparral and clumps of yellow wildflowers. The air was scented with dry mesquite and sage and, alarmingly . . . smoke.

Carter stopped and, shielding his eyes with one hand, looked across the canyon. He couldn't see any flames or even any smoke, but if he listened carefully he could hear what sounded like a helicopter's blades.

"A brush fire?" Del said, drawing up beside him.

"Sounds like a chopper—"

"Or an airborne tanker."

"Yeah, on the other side of that rise."

They stood silently on the open trail, waiting. "Everything's so dry this season," Carter said.

Del, nodding, said, "Perfect conditions for a catastrophe."

After a minute or two, and without another word, they pushed on, the trail reentering a heavily shaded stretch. Up ahead, they could hear the promising sound of falling water. The year before had been a wet one, and the runoff must still have been sufficient. Carter ducked his head to avoid an overhanging branch. A pair of lizards skittered across the trail, their long blue tails shining.

About a hundred yards up, there was a cool, shady clearing, and a narrow little footbridge across the now rushing stream. But what Carter saw was confusing. That girl, the blonde one in the Juicy shorts, was sitting on the ground, with her legs splayed out in front of her. Her boyfriend was hanging his head over the rail, spitting, or vomiting, into the brook below.

Carter's first thought was, How'd these two kids get up here ahead of him? And then he remembered that there was a shorter, more direct trail, which they must have taken.

His second thought was more worrisome. Standing in the shadows, closer to the rock face where Carter could now see a torrent of clear water racing down a gorge and spilling under the footbridge, was a big man with light blond hair, cropped short in the military style. He was smiling broadly and brandishing a wooden staff. He said something Carter couldn't hear, and another man, whom Carter hadn't seen, stepped out from behind a tree. The second man answered, and they both laughed.

The girl, looking dazed, just sat there.

Instinctively, Carter crouched down, and when he turned to warn Del, he could see that Del had already moved off the trail and into the shade and had his own finger to his lips.

Something was very wrong with this picture . . . and Carter wanted to know more before he gave himself away.

The man with the buzz cut sauntered over to the boy, who was spitting what was now clearly blood into the water. "Lose any teeth?" the man said, almost solicitously.

The boy shrugged, like he didn't know, but kept his head down.

"Next time you might."

The man turned around to face the girl. "You know better now, right?"

She didn't answer him, either.

The other man, in a short-sleeved shirt that revealed some sort of tattoo on his forearm, picked up a fishing bag and said, "C'mon on, Stan. Let's get going."

But Stan didn't look ready to leave. Stan looked as though he were just getting started.

"You're not bad looking," he said to the girl. "You know that, right?"

She nodded, once, barely perceptibly.

"So what are you doing with this piece of shit?"

She had no answer to that one—and by now Carter had seen enough. He glanced over at Del, who lowered his head in assent, and Carter stood up, and in a loud voice said, "Hey, it's right here, Del! That waterfall!"

He barged into the clearing, making as much of a commotion as he could, and strode onto the little bridge, next to the Hispanic boy.

"You take a fall?" he said, putting his hand on the kid's shoulder and steering him away from the guy named Stan. "Let me take a look at that."

With his eyes, he swept across Stan and his tattooed partner, making damn sure they knew he knew what was up; Del emerged from the brush, holding a handy little club he must have just made.

"That's my friend Del," Carter announced to the two men as he took the boy over to the shaken girl. "He bats a thousand—want to try him?"

The two men exchanged a long look, and Carter dropped his backpack onto the ground. "Didn't I hear you were leaving—Stan?"

"Nah, I like it here." He squared off, ready to fight, when his friend grabbed his elbow and said, "What the fuck are you doing? We're done here—let's go."

Del moved around behind them and took a casual, but hard, whack at some branches.

Stan stared at Carter, then pulled a pair of Ray-Bans out of his breast pocket and put them on. "Does kind of smell like shit around here."

That was when Carter knew he'd won the standoff. He said nothing more as Stan and his pal moved back toward the trail and headed down the mountain. Carter knelt down next to the girl and said, "You okay?"

She looked up at him with watery eyes and murmured, "I guess."

"You have a cell phone?"

She shook her head.

"They threw it in the water," the boy said. Del was dabbing at the blood on his cut lip with a couple of leaves.

"You're going to be fine, both of you," Carter said. "Can you stand up?" he said to the girl. As he held her arm, she got up. "You feel able to walk down?"

She didn't say anything, but walked over toward her boyfriend. "You okay, Luis?"

But he wouldn't look at her.

"You okay?" she repeated, reaching out to touch him on the arm, but he pulled away.

"Just don't touch me, okay? Just let me alone."

Carter knew what was going on—he'd just been beaten up in front of his girl and he was in no mood to face her.

Del knew, too. "What's your name?" he said to the girl as he drew her away and toward the trail. "I'm Del Garrison."

"Lilly."

"Nice to meet you, Lilly." He guided her back to the

trail, with his club still in one hand. "It'll be a lot easier going down."

Carter picked up his pack and led Luis in the same direction. He was slight and not very tall, and his Nike shirt was spattered with blood in front.

They walked in silence, all their eyes on the loose rocks and dirt of the trail. There was no sign of the two men who'd attacked them, and Carter had heard enough that he didn't have to ask any questions.

Del, just to distract them, kept calling out over his shoulder what they were seeing or passing by. "That's called a popcorn flower over on your right. And deer weed all around it. Buckwheat brush on the ground up ahead, and twining snapdragon hanging down. Golden yarrow. Purple nightshade. Silver puffs." The list went on and on, and before long they were passing the abandoned shack. In the sky above it, a lone hawk circled slowly on the updraft.

Who had lived there? Carter wondered as they marched slowly past its boarded-up windows and padlocked door.

Only one other hiker passed them, going up the trail as they went down—a young woman in a big straw hat who gave them a very curious look—and when they got to the parking area, Carter said, "Which one is your car?"

Luis gestured at a red Trans Am with wire wheels. And four flat tires.

"Fuck!" Luis said.

"How'd they know it was yours?" Del asked.

"They didn't," Carter said, looking around at the other three or four cars—including his own—in the lot. All of their tires had been punctured.

"At least they're thorough," Del said.

"We can walk to Gelson's," Lilly said to Luis, who still wouldn't even acknowledge her. "I can call my mom."

"Maybe you should call the police first," Carter said, "and file a report. I've got a cell phone in my car."

"No!" Luis blurted out. "No fuckin' police report." He wheeled around and glared at Lilly. "Nothing happened—okay?"

"If you don't call, I will," Carter said.

Luis glared at Carter, too. "You do what you got to do. I'm out of here."

And he marched off toward Sunset in his bloody T-shirt and his jeans . . . with Lilly, who turned and held up her hand in a wave to Carter and Del, in slow pursuit.

"No good deed," Del said, "goes unpunished."

Carter nodded.

"But let's call Triple A first," Del added. "I know from experience; it could take them awhile to get here."

CHAPTER TWENTY-ONE

"**WHAT DO YOU** mean, it won't eat?" al-Kalli said in a cold fury.

Rashid, the keeper of the animals, visibly shook in his boots.

"I saw the man killed myself," al-Kalli said, rising from his chair behind the ornate desk in his library. "I saw him pulled down from the tree. I saw his body dragged into the lair."

Rashid, in a spotless white lab coat, nodded vigorously in agreement. "Yes, I am sure that is true. I am sure that is what happened." Rashid, who had been barred from the bestiary that night, had no exact knowledge of what had transpired. But knowing his master, he had a fairly good idea. And he had seen the remains inside the cave.

The largely uneaten remains.

"But the beast has not changed his habits . . . not since . . ." He did not know how to complete the sentence, nor did he have to. *Not since the beast lost its mate.* Rashid did not like even to advert to that sad fact, for fear it would rekindle al-Kalli's anger. He knew perfectly well who was considered at fault for that.

"And the other animals?"

Rashid swallowed hard and lied. "Admirable. They are all doing admirable," he said, using one of the favorite English words he had learned during his training at the American school in Cairo. In reality, several of the beasts were showing strange signs and behaviors. The bird was shedding long feathers with brittle quills, the larger beasts were exhibiting signs of labored breathing and had a lack-luster look in their eyes. The sudden expulsion from the compound in Iraq, the long journey to America, the new and unfamiliar quarters—in Rashid's view the creatures had never fully recovered. No matter what he did, no matter what new and innovative measures he tried—from changing their diets to altering the air temperature and composition inside the facility—he could not find the means to restore them to their former health and glory.

On many a dark night, he anticipated becoming a meal for the beasts himself. Al-Kalli, he knew, was not above it.

"I will be down to see the situation for myself later this afternoon. Go and tell Jakob to bring the car around."

"Yes, sir. Right away." Rashid backed out of the room all but bowing, and before he pulled the double doors closed, he could hear al-Kalli shout, "Admirab*ly!* Admirab*ly!*"

AL-KALLI WOULD HAVE liked to throw him to the beasts, but it wasn't that simple—Rashid and his ancestors had been caring for the creatures forever, and even though al-Kalli had his doubts about Rashid's intelligence and abilities, the man still knew more about them than anyone else could ever know.

And how, given the nature of his menagerie, could al-Kalli recruit anyone more knowledgeable, or trustworthy?

He picked up the phone to make a quick call to the Getty to tell them he was coming over to see how the work was progressing, but then put the phone back down. No, why alert them? Why not catch them unaware, and dis-cover in that way how diligently they were pursuing the project he had entrusted to them?

The armored limousine was waiting outside in the porte cochere, and Jakob opened the passenger door as soon as al-Kalli stepped out of the house. "The museum" was all al-Kalli had to say.

On the drive over, al-Kalli gazed out the tinted rear window at the hot, sunny day. It wasn't really so different from the Middle East. Without all this constant irrigation, even in the teeth of a drought, all of Los Angeles would retreat to what it naturally wanted to be—a desert. All but the palm trees would die, the lawns would turn sere and brown and blow away, the roses would wither and the bougainvillea would die on the vine.

And the people? The people would disperse to other, more hospitable climes.

A dog-walker with half a dozen different dogs on a tangle of leashes was walking along the opposite side of the street. The dogs' tongues were hanging out, and a couple of them stopped to lap at something on the ground.

So why, al-Kalli wondered, could his animals not thrive in this foreign, but not so very different, environment? He had saved all of them that he could, given the danger and the constraints at the time. He had spared no expense, he had done all that he could do to provide them with a safe and secluded and comfortable home. He had, in the larger sense, done everything he could to preserve the legacy of his ancient family, and to maintain its mysterious power . . . for he believed that all of these things were tied, in some ineffable way, to the beasts themselves.

And now the beasts were in jeopardy.

He knew, for instance, that Rashid had lied to him in the library. He wasn't blind. He could see that the other creatures were languishing, too. Their cries were not so loud, their eyes were not so bright, their fur was not so thick or their hides so tough. Something was happening, and he had to find a way to stop it.

At the Getty, his car was automatically waved through to a reserved area for distinguished visitors and guests. The plaza of the museum was crowded today with tourists clutching maps and cold drinks and their children's sticky hands. But as with most such people, they knew to make way for al-Kalli. There was something about him—his impeccable clothes, his regal bearing, his *aura*, he liked to think—that caused them to stand back and pause as he strode past. That Jakob, clearly his bodyguard, followed two steps behind was probably not lost on them, either.

When he entered the Research Institute, where Beth Cox worked, there was a flurry of interest and attention as he strode down the hall, past all the other offices and cubicles. Her door was open, and she was sitting next to a very pale boy who looked not much older than al-Kalli's son, Mehdi.

"Mr. al-Kalli," Beth said, startled. "I didn't know you were coming." She stood up, smoothing her skirt, while the boy continued to click away at the computer keyboard. "Elvis," she said, nudging him on the shoulder, "this is the owner of *The Beasts of Eden*."

Elvis ran off a quick trill on the keys, then looked up and said, "Hi. It's an extremely cool book." Then he went back to studying the screen.

Al-Kalli looked at the cluttered surface of the desk, but saw no sign of the book itself. What he did see were Latin dictionaries, rafts of printouts, and colored photocopies of various, random pages that he recognized from *The Beasts of Eden*.

It wasn't hard for Beth to read his mind. "The book is with the conservators right now," she said. "It's just one building away."

"What are you doing with these?" al-Kalli said, gesturing at the photocopies.

Beth hadn't really wanted to get into this so fast; she always liked to complete her research and come to some firm conclusions before sharing her discoveries with the world. Or, more to the point, with Mohammed al-Kalli. He was not a man you wanted to offer partial accounts to, or whose questions you wished to duck.

But he was already turning the photocopies around on her desk, and trying to ascertain why these particular pages were being worked on. Had he noticed that these were all the pages on which the quires had ended and the catchwords, pointing to the next quire, had been entered? Beth didn't really know how much al-Kalli knew about his treasure. He had never said very much, apart from conveying his obvious attachment to the book and his fear that, during the restoration process, it might suffer some injury. For all Beth knew, he was a scholar of eleventh-century manuscripts and was just waiting for her to make some small misstatement before pouncing.

"We're collecting the catchwords and putting them together," Elvis suddenly volunteered. "It's amazing how they're coming together into a kind of sentence."

Beth could have killed him.

"The catchwords?" al-Kalli said, in his dry, upper-crust English accent.

"The little words that run at the bottom of each section—Beth figured out that they were all connected." Clearly, he thought he was doing her a service. "It's like a treasure map or something."

Al-Kalli's eye brightened, and he fixed his gaze on Beth. "Is this true? You have found something in the book that no one else has ever discovered?"

Beth blushed and said, "It's possible." With one hand that was out of al-Kalli's sight, she pinched Elvis, hard, between the shoulder blades. He squirmed, but had the sense to say nothing more.

"What does it say so far? What have you learned?"

Elvis pretended to be absorbed in the computer screen, while Beth, reluctantly, drew out the stapled sheets on which the catchwords had been assembled. "It's not entirely complete, there are some words we might have misread or mistranslated, and I have not yet had a chance to—"

But al-Kalli had already snatched the pages from her grasp and was studying them. She glimpsed Jakob, the ever-present Jakob, loitering in the hall outside.

"These words connect, you say?" The catchwords, their rough English equivalents, and Beth's interpolated queries, were highlighted in yellow, and he began to put them together and read them aloud as he flipped the pages. "Brought here [question of volition] / to this land / an honored guest /

now a prisoner / laboring in obscurity / my name to sleep [vanish?] / beneath a cloth [blanket?] / blue sky and white clouds / pity the [too faint to decipher at present] / beasts [demons?] / in our Lord [Christian god? temporal employer] / for eternity / ivory grave [sepulcher?]." Al-Kalli flipped the last page again, looking for more, then raised his eyes to Beth. "I'm not sure I understand. What is this?"

Beth quickly explained the use of catchwords—so he wasn't secretly an expert in these matters, after all—and then added that these were possibly, or even apparently, a message encoded by the scribe, to be read—"possibly, again, we can't really say for sure yet"—by other scribes who later came into possession of the book.

"But who was he?" al-Kalli said, his enthusiasm visibly waning. "And why did he claim to have been a prisoner of my family?"

Funny, Beth thought, he spoke of his family—some distant ancestors from a thousand years in the past and half a world away—as anyone else might speak of his own parents or kids. He was indignant at the scribe's imputation.

"Is he implying that we forced him to create *The Beasts of Eden*? That he was ill used?"

"I wouldn't say that," Beth replied. "It was common practice for scribes and illuminators to complain about their patrons."

But al-Kalli's feathers still looked ruffled, and he appeared disappointed at what he had just read. What, Beth wondered, had he been hoping to read or find? A clue to some other treasure? From what she could surmise, the man was already as rich as Croesus. "I want to see the book," he said.

"Of course," Beth said. "I'll take you right over there." She was just as glad to get him away from Elvis, who might unwittingly start some other trouble. "Elvis," she said, before leaving, "would you call Hildegard and tell her we're coming over?" She didn't want what had happened to her—a surprise visit—to befall her favorite conservator.

The walk to the East Building, where the conservation work was done, was a short one, along a pathway shaded by a row of perfectly aligned London plane trees; if you looked directly at the one on the end, all the other slender trunks disappeared behind it. Al-Kalli, Beth noticed, was still clutching the sheaf of catchwords. Beth slipped her ID card into the slot at the door, and the electronic locks released. She escorted al-Kalli and the silent Jakob into the elevator, then down to the conservation workshop where the formidable Hildegard—a large woman in her sixties, who favored shapeless dresses in what could charitably be called earth tones—was laboring at a wide, stainless steel table, with filtered tensor lamps attached to its rim.

Beth knew she didn't like to be interrupted at her work, but she had not been about to deny al-Kalli a glimpse of his treasure.

Hildegard brushed a wisp of gray hair away from her eyes and greeted al-Kalli politely, if not warmly. The book lay on the table in front of her, and to Beth's horror—and she could only imagine how al-Kalli was reacting—its precious covers had been entirely removed and lay on a separate table behind her.

"How's it coming?" Beth jumped in, to forestall any explosion.

"Slowly. The boards are beech, which is unusual, but surprisingly solid and uncompromised. The inside of the spine shows sign of dry rot, and the thongs are as brittle as twigs, but in a manuscript this old it would be a shock not to find such damage."

"What have you done?" al-Kalli finally said, surveying his dismembered treasure. "You have torn the covers from the book? They have never been separated from the book, ever, in over a thousand years."

"There you're wrong," Hildegard said. She was not one to kowtow. "I'd say the front cover was removed, and restitched, at least twice. When, I couldn't say yet. But it might have been done by a jeweler or other artisan, someone who wanted to work on the ivory or reset the sapphires."

Al-Kalli laid the pages of catchwords on the edge of the table and went to the covers, which he touched with his fingertips the way you might gently graze a baby's head. Hildegard flashed Beth a look that said, *You know I don't like to be interrupted,* and Beth silently mouthed a *Sorry*.

"What else have you had to do?" al-Kalli said, resignedly now. "Has the book required a great deal of repair?"

Hildegard turned on her stool, her big brown skirt still hanging nearly all the way to the floor, and said, "Not as much as you might expect." There was a warmer tone in her voice now, not only because she could see how attached al-Kalli was to his manuscript—a sentiment Hildegard could well appreciate—but because he had asked her about her field of expertise, a subject on which she could happily expatiate for hours. As Hildegard ran through the various problems the manuscript had presented, and the ways in which she was remedying them—all of which Beth already knew—Beth picked up the catchwords and began looking them over again. With the disassembled manuscript right there in front of her, she felt as though she were suddenly much closer to solving the mystery.

One thing had always leapt out at her. It was the reference to the blue sky and the white clouds. Everything else was fairly prosaic, however intriguing—the notion that the scribe had been inveigled into an impossible task, the grumbling about feeling himself a prisoner of a powerful employer. Fairly standard stuff. But the touch of poetry, once it was coupled with the mention of the ornamented sepulcher at the end of the penultimate quire, gave Beth the feeling that she was suddenly very close to something.

So close she could barely wait for al-Kalli to leave. Only then would she be able to test the hypothesis even now forming in her head.

"The pigments in this book are interesting, too," Hildegard was saying. "We're using radiospectroscopy and X-ray fluorescence—don't worry, they're harmless—to get a better idea what they're made of."

"What were they generally made of?" al-Kalli asked with genuine absorption.

"Oh, that's a big question," Hildegard said, though it

sounded as if she would be pleased to answer it at length. The only thing she liked more than her work was coming across someone who seemed to want to know all about it. "In illuminations, like these," she said, guiding him to the illustration she'd been working on—a portrait of a snake-like creature with a blunt feline head and flicking tongue— "the coloring agents were usually vegetable, mineral, and animal extracts, though they were sometimes mixed with all sorts of things, from stale urine to honey to earwax."

That last item Beth had never heard about.

"But you'll notice that this book is rich in deep purples and blues, and that might be because of where it was made—ultramarine, which was made from lapis lazuli, was chiefly produced in Persia and Afghanistan."

The lesson on pigments alone went on for several more minutes, while Beth bided her time. She studied the catch-words again, then sidled over to the neighboring table where the bejeweled front and back covers lay. The sapphires, studding the slightly yellowed ivory, winked in the overhead light. Beth longed to pick the cover up, but she did not want to test her theory until al-Kalli was gone.

Jakob, looking supremely bored, rocked on his heels, his hands folded in front of him.

But Beth wasn't fooled; she had the impression that Jakob was always well aware of everything that was happening around him.

Beth pretended to be focused, too, on everything Hildegard was saying—she had moved on now to explaining why one side of a parchment page was always lighter and smoother than the other—while becoming, every second, more and more convinced that her own suspicions were right. When Hildegard finally took a breath, and al-Kalli consulted his watch—a gleaming gold Cartier from what Beth could see—she quickly thanked Hildegard for giving them so much time and guided Mr. al-Kalli and Jakob toward the door. She escorted them back up to the plaza, then took her leave. Even then, she deliberately walked away, back toward her office, for twenty paces, before turning around to make sure they were gone. Then she raced back down the line of London plane trees, back into the conservation building, and down to Hildegard's office.

Hildegard was already at work again and looked downright startled to see Beth.

"I need to look at that front cover again," Beth said, going straight to it.

"Why?"

"I need to look for something." Beth picked it up carefully and angled its edge toward the overhead light.

"What on earth are you doing?"

"I'm looking for a space between the beech board and the ivory."

"A what?"

"Just tell me—is there any space between these two, where something like a page of parchment could be concealed?"

"I've never heard of such a thing," Hildegard said, though her curiosity was sufficiently aroused that she quickly cleared a spot on the table in front of her. "Put it down."

Beth did, and Hildegard pulled the magnifying glass, which was mounted on a swivel, toward her. She studied the edge of the cover. "What makes you think we'll find such a thing?"

"The catchwords," Beth said.

"What about them?"

"They said that the identity of the artist would be lost forever, to sleep under a blanket of blue sky and white clouds."

Hildegard looked at her blankly.

"The cover of the book is made up of white ivory and blue sapphires. And together they make up a kind of ornamented sepulcher, which were the last catchwords in the book."

Hildegard didn't look sold, but she didn't look opposed to the idea, either. She took a scalpel from the drawer and probed the top of the cover.

"Nothing here," she said.

"Check the inside edge, where the cover would be attached to the binding."

She turned the cover sideways and bent her head low. All Beth could see now was the top of her gray bun, with a couple of long pins stuck through it.

"Well, I never," Hildegard finally said. With one hand, she inserted the scalpel half an inch or so, as if nudging something loose. Then she reached out and grasped a pair of long-nosed tweezers, with which she ever so slowly drew something from beneath the ivory cover. Beth's heart was beating fast as the tweezers emerged, with several faded parchment pages, fine as filament, clutched in their grip.

Hildegard sat back on the stool and gave Beth a very approving glance. "I'm not even going to look at these," she said. "You found them, and you should be the first person in centuries to read them."

Beth couldn't agree more.

CHAPTER TWENTY-TWO

GREER GRABBED A beer out of the fridge, wandered into the living room, and flopped onto the matching Barcalounger facing the TV. It was Naugahyde, and even though it got hot after you'd sat there awhile, right now it was cool and smooth and the little footstool part came up when he leaned far enough back.

His mother was parked, as usual, in the other one, with a cat in her lap and her hand in a bag of Pirate's Booty— another low-cal snack. Greer picked up the remote from the table between them, and was about to change the channel when she said, "I'm watching this."

Greer stopped and watched for a minute. It was something called *The Vorhaus Report*, one of those crappy cable interview shows with a two-dollar set and a moderator in a bad toupee. The guests tonight appeared to be some scientist—the chyron said CARTER COX, PALEONTOLOGIST— and an American Indian named James Running Horse. The Indian was wearing a three-piece suit, and he looked to Greer like he had maybe one-sixteenth, or less, Indian in him; Greer snorted, thinking this was just another scam the guy used to score some government money or affirmative action shit. Maybe even a piece of some new multimillion-dollar casino in the desert. Indians had it made these days.

He ought to tell Sadowski and his crew to look into it.

"What the hell are you watching this for?" Greer said.

"It's educational."

"You hate educational. You watch Home Shopping Network."

"Not always. I'm watching this now."

Greer sat back and listened for another minute or two. It looked as though they were discussing something about some bones that had been dug up in those pits over on La Brea. Wasn't that where somebody'd just died? Greer had caught something about it on the local news—another Indian had fallen in or something and drowned.

But the show didn't seem to be about this. It seemed to be about some really ancient bones that the Running Horse guy wanted returned, and the other guy—he was tall and in good shape, wearing khakis and an open-collared white shirt—wanted to study first. And they kept talking about something called NAGPRA.

"The NAGPRA provisions have been in place since 1990, for just such occasions as this," Running Horse was saying now.

"What are they talking about?" Greer asked. "What's NAGPRA?"

"Native American Graves something," his mother quickly put in. "It's about how when you dig up their bones or their . . . holy things . . . you have to give them back to the tribe."

Greer took a long pull on the cold beer. "Sounds to me like a case of finders keepers."

"It's more complicated than that," his mother said. "Just listen, Derek—you might learn something."

"But these remains predate any of the known tribes by many thousands of years," Cox was saying now. "Even if they were to be repatriated, to whom would they be given? What tribe? Where? These early peoples migrated, often over large distances."

"They should be given to the tribe of which he was an honored ancestor," Running Horse replied.

"Fine," Cox said. "But unless you let us study the remains, we won't even be able to determine that much."

"Then perhaps you should have thought of that before you disturbed his bones."

"We disturbed his bones, if that's how you want to put it, doing what we do—excavating the tar pits for the fossils of early North American animals. Mastodons, giant sloths, saber-toothed cats. We didn't exactly break into a sacred burial ground and start turning over tombstones."

"We Native Americans," Running Horse said, turning his attention to the neutral host seated between them, "have been treated like slaves, like chattel—"

Greer wondered if he'd just mispronounced "cattle."

"—for centuries, ever since the genocidal invasion of the European explorers. Our most sacred places have been defiled, our most precious objects—pottery, textiles—have been plundered, and even our bodies have been removed from Mother Earth, where they were meant to rest, and put on display in glass cases in museum galleries."

"The La Brea Woman is not on display," Cox shot back.

"And she's not in the earth, either," Running Horse replied.

It was getting heated—Greer liked that.

"Where is she, in fact?" Running Horse continued. "Is she in a file drawer? A cardboard box? A safe?"

Cox didn't seem to know how to answer that.

"There's a difference, isn't there," the host broke in, "between repatriation and disposition? Shouldn't we—"

"I'll tell you where she is," Cox said, totally ignoring the host's question and leaning toward Running Horse. Greer wondered if his mother was watching this because she thought this Carter Cox guy was handsome.

"She's in the air," Cox said. "And in the ocean. She's in the sky, and the clouds, and the rain. Isn't that what you believe? That we all return to the universe, to the Great Spirit? Then that's where she is. And her skeleton—what little we've got of it—is just the physical remains, the unimportant, insignificant, fossilized residue of a human life."

"Then why do you want it?" Running Horse countered, but even Greer could see that was a bad move.

"Because by studying what remains, we can learn more about her. About how she lived, and how she died. We can find out where we all came from, and maybe where we're all going. We can honor her—just as we can honor the La Brea Man now, too—in a way that simply burying their bones again will never do. We can honor them by paying attention not to their deaths—you've got to stop looking at these as dead souls—but to their lives. How they lived, how they survived, and how they prevailed, in a very hostile world. I can't think of any greater tribute we can give them."

"Than to lay their bones under bright lights and X-ray machines?"

Cox looked exasperated. "If that's what it takes, yes."

"The federal government thinks you're wrong," Running Horse replied, over the moderator's raised hand, "and I'm going to prove it."

"Thank you, thank you both," Vorhaus was saying, "but we are unfortunately out of time. It's been a very enlightening discussion, and a thank-you, too, goes out to our viewers for joining us tonight, on *The Vorhaus Report*."

The screen blipped and cut to a public service announcement a nanosecond later—guess the guy meant it, Greer thought, when he said they were out of time. "Can I change it now?" he asked.

"See what's on AMC."

Greer channel-surfed a bit—sometimes over his mother's protestations of "Wait—that looked good" or "What was that—was that *Law and Order*?"—but he couldn't find anything to watch either. At least on his computer he could get porn.

He tossed the remote into her ample lap—the cat hissed at him—and said, "I'm going out."

For a change, she didn't ask where.

But all he could think of right now was the Blue Bayou.

* * *

AS SOON AS the studio lights went down and *The Vorhaus Report* was officially off the air, Carter detached the microphone from the front of his shirt, shook hands with the host—he didn't have to bother with James Running Horse, who had conspicuously turned his back and stalked out of the studio—and went out to the parking lot.

He had deliberately parked his Jeep right below a halogen lamp, and his first thought was to check the tires. After that run-in at Temescal Canyon, he was only too aware of all the crazies loose in L.A.

He got into the car and started for home. At least at this hour—he checked the clock on the dashboard and saw that it was after 10 P.M.—there wouldn't be much traffic. The Santa Anas were blowing, hot dry winds off the desert, stirring up the scents of dry sage and dry mesquite and dry soil. Dry everything.

He put on the radio, but he couldn't really concentrate on it; instead, he kept turning over in his mind the last hour, much of it spent jousting with James Running Horse. He'd done his best to keep his temper, but he was so weary of this endless debate, this ongoing controversy between science and religion, which played out everywhere from the textbook wars over evolution to his own freedom to examine a precious and rare hominid artifact. He wished he'd said something more when Running Horse had demanded that the bones of this "honored ancestor" be returned to his tribe. Who was to say these bones were ever honored? Much of the evidence suggested that the La Brea Woman had had her skull crushed with a blunt instrument, and it was quite possible that her male counterpart had met an equally violent fate. Far from being honored, these people might have been murdered, or brutally sacrificed, and for all we knew today, their fondest wish, their *dying* wish, might have been to get away from their bloodthirsty fellow tribe members altogether.

On the private drive up to Summit View, Carter saw not a soul—even the patrol car was missing, off on its rounds perhaps—and only the porch light was on at his own house. He opened the door quietly, in case everyone was asleep, and crept up the stairs. The night-light was on in Joey's bedroom and he poked his head in there first. Champ, asleep on the crocheted rug that lay beside the crib, immediately raised his head, but upon seeing Carter just thumped his tail on the floor and waited for his ears to be scratched.

Carter looked into the crib and, just as he expected, Joey's little gray-blue eyes were wide open and looking right back at him. "One of these days," Carter said, leaning down to give the baby a wet smooch on his little forehead, "I'm going to catch you with your eyes closed. I'm going to come in so quietly that even you can't hear me."

Joey looked at him as if to say, *Highly unlikely.*

In the bedroom, Beth was propped up against the pillows with the TV on low, but she was fast asleep. Carter glanced at the screen—it was the same channel *The Vorhaus Report* was broadcast on, though now it was showing something about the dangers faced by illegal immigrants from Mexico. He picked up the remote, which was lying next to Beth's hand, and flicked it off. The second he did, she stirred and opened her eyes.

"When did you get in?" she mumbled.

"Thirty seconds ago."

"You were great, much better than that other guy."

"He had a three-piece suit."

She cleared her throat and sat up higher in the bed.

"But you're taller."

He laughed and took off his shirt. His arm, where Geronimo had cut him, was healing nicely. At least it had been a clean cut.

"Your boss'll be pleased."

"Gunderson's never pleased. He's just sometimes less unpleasant."

"You hungry?"

"Nah, I ate at the museum before going over to the show."

"Tell me you didn't eat at one of the specimen tables, with all the bones and stones around you."

"I ate with a very interesting guy that I've just recently met."

Beth groaned, "Don't tell me—the La Brea Man."

"You said not to tell you," Carter said, hanging up his shirt and then his pants.

Beth harrumphed. "I'm starting to think that James Running Horse had a point."

Carter went into the bathroom, showered, put some antiseptic on his forearm, and by the time he came out in fresh boxers and a T-shirt, the lights were off and Beth was fast asleep again. He debated going downstairs to read for a while, but suddenly the day caught up to him and he fell on his back onto the bed. The air-conditioning was humming softly, and the room was almost completely dark.

He closed his eyes, tried hard not to think about *The Vorhaus Report* or Gunderson or even the La Brea Man, and succeeded eventually in alighting on some harmless memories from his boyhood—fireworks on the Fourth of July. He yawned, stretched his long legs out on top of the sheet, and let his mind just drift. Firecrackers, corn on the cob, catching fireflies in the backyard . . .

How long he'd been asleep he couldn't even guess, but way off in the distance, as if from a world away, he thought he heard a dog growling . . . then a short bark. He was hoping it would stop—he was so damn comfortable—or that Beth would get up and see what was wrong. But when he heard it again, another bark, more frantic this time, but abruptly curtailed, he realized he'd have to get up himself and see what was wrong.

He dragged his legs off the bed, got up, and stumbled toward Joey's room. His bare feet stepped into something wet in the hallway, but in the dim glow of the nursery night-light all he could see was what looked like a dark stain on the white wall-to-wall carpeting. Oh man, he thought, this was going to be expensive to clean up, whatever it was, nor did he want to have to tell the owner of the place about it.

Best leave that to Beth, he thought.

Crossing the threshold, he tripped on something, something heavy and furry, and when he looked down, he could see that it was Champ, that he was lying on his side . . . and his throat was torn out, hot blood spilling toward the door. His breath stopped, and when he looked up again he could see eyes—three or four pairs of them—staring at him from all corners of the nursery. They were yellow and malevolent, and the worst of them, the ones that were fixed on him the most intently, belonged to the big gray coyote who had led the pack.

And who was now inside Joey's crib. Standing over him, panting fast.

How . . . Carter's mind could barely accept what he was seeing. A warm draft blew up the stairs and onto the back of his legs; he could hear the front door banging, loose and open, in the foyer downstairs. *Had he* . . .

He didn't dare move.

The other coyotes were perched around the room, one on the crocheted rug that Champ used to occupy, one on the window seat, a third in the corner near the closet, nosing now under the dresser.

Carter didn't even want to shout to Beth—he didn't want to do anything that might disturb, in some unpredictable way, the terrible tableau before him.

Not until he had figured out exactly what to do.

The leader's jaws were wet with blood—Champ's, no doubt—but Carter could see that Joey was so far unaffected. He was lying on his stomach, eyes open, in a blue sleep suit. His little toes curled, and Carter could see him now lifting his head to get a better look at this big stuffed toy that was sharing his crib.

No, Carter thought, *no . . . don't move. Please God don't move.*

The rank smell of fur and blood permeated the room.

The leader lowered his head, until his snout was just inches above the baby's head. But his eyes remained on Carter, as if taunting him.

Carter inched closer, hoping that he might get near enough to make a lunge for the baby and get him. But the coyote on the rug stood up on all fours, and with his head down and back arched, snarled loudly.

Carter looked around for anything he could swing, but there was nothing. Even the lamp on the dresser was only a little round ginger jar in the shape of Dumbo.

Joey gurgled, and perhaps sensing his father was in the room, started to make noise. Happy, meaningless burbles. He kicked his legs.

The coyote in the crib growled, and snapped in Carter's direction; his yellowed fangs, one of them badly broken, glistened wetly above the baby's back.

The others were on full alert now, and Carter could sense them moving closer from all directions. His mouth was so dry he could barely speak, but in a low voice he said, "Okay now, okay now . . . that's right, that's right," as he moved another few inches toward the crib. "Yeah, that's right . . ."

But just when he was close enough to pounce and grab his son, the alpha coyote raised its hackles, then vaulted over the bars of the crib, leaping straight at his throat. The impact sent Carter crashing back toward the door, his feet sliding on the bloody floor, his hands scrabbling at the beast's jaws. He could feel its hot breath scouring his skin and the fierce teeth biting and snapping. Carter slid down the wall, holding the beast just a fraction from his face, but he could feel the others now jumping in, one on each leg, another tearing at his shoulder . . .

"Carter!"

No, he didn't want Beth anywhere near this. She needed to get away, she needed to grab Joey and get away!

"Carter!"

His shoulder was still being shaken by the coyote. He flung it out, trying to free it from the animal's teeth.

"Carter! Watch it—you're going to kill me!"

The shaking stopped.

There was a bright light in his eyes, and Beth was saying, "Carter—wake up. Wake up, honey."

His legs kicked convulsively, one more time.

"You're having a nightmare."

He opened his eyes; he could barely swallow.

"You're having a nightmare."

Beth was kneeling over him on the bed, looking very, very concerned.

"Whew," she said when she saw that he was at last coming to. "For a second there, I thought you were going to punch my lights out."

He took a deep breath, and then another.

"You alright now?"

He nodded. The sheet had been kicked off and was trailing on the floor.

He propped himself up on his elbows and looked around the room, bewildered.

"Whoa," he said, exhaling.

"You can say that again."

"Worst dream I ever had."

"You want to talk about it?"

He sat up, legs bent. "No, not yet." He swiveled off the bed. "I just want to check on Joey."

He padded across the hall—the carpeting was clean and dry—and into the nursery. Champ was curled up on the rug, and Joey was just as he had pictured him in the dream, lying on his tummy in blue pj's. But he was alone, thank God, in the crib.

Beth followed him in and, seeing that Joey was awake, lifted him up and cradled him.

"See," she said to Carter, "fit as a fiddle. And getting heavier all the time. Here," she said, "you hold him."

Carter took the baby in his arms.

"I had this terrible dream, of coyotes," was all he said. Joey looked up at him with solemn eyes.

"Not surprising. They were howling in the canyon, and I have this terrible feeling they caught somebody's cat. They started Champ barking, too."

Carter nodded, rocking the baby. The muslin curtains were pulled back, and he could see outside into the deep dark canyon, where the dry trees and brush rustled in the night wind. And even now he could hear a coyote's distant wail.

CHAPTER TWENTY-THREE

GREER FELT LIKE a vampire, stepping out into the sun. He had on his shades and an Angels baseball cap, pulled down low over his brow, but there still wasn't much he could do about the hot glare coming off the beach sand.

Zeke, the bartender, was somewhere down there on one of those volleyball courts just off the Pacific Coast Highway. When Greer had gone to find him the night before, at the Blue Bayou, they'd said he was resting up for the big tournament that day. Something about a round robin, sponsored by Adidas.

Greer had been pissed; he relied on Zeke to get him anything from Percodan to cocaine, amphetamines to ludes. Zeke was a big dolt, but for some reason he got good stuff—and he was reliable.

Greer had ordered a drink and sat at the bar for a while, not even watching the strippers work the pole. All he'd really wanted was to be out among people, with lots of noise. He wanted his head to be filled with something, anything, that wasn't what he'd seen at the al-Kalli estate. It was funny, he'd seen all kinds of shit in Iraq—guys with their heads blown off or their guts spilling out, kids with missing limbs, an old lady cut neatly in two by an RPG—but the thing that kept him up at night, that intruded on his thoughts at all the worst times, was that creature in the private zoo. It was something out of a nightmare. His own nightmare, in fact: When he let his mind go back to that night in the palace outside Mosul, and he remembered the way that Lopez, and then the prisoner Hasan, had been snatched up and dragged off into the night, all he could see now was that beast. Now he knew what had done it, now he knew how close he'd come to being just another meal himself.

When the music changed, and Prince started singing about 1999, Greer swiveled on his stool. That was Ginger's music, and sure enough out she came, in an outfit of purple plastic and foil and strutting the way Prince used to do in his old videos. Greer knew the outfit wouldn't stay on long.

But his eye was drawn across the runway to a table on the far side, where he saw the back of Sadowski's head; he was sitting with that guy Burt from the shooting range, and a couple of other guys that Greer vaguely recognized. Where had he seen them before? He took a long pull on his drink, then thought, *Oh yeah, the recruitment party.* These were guys who'd been studying the Sons of Liberty membership materials. Greer had to hand it to the organization—they knew how to rope these assholes in.

"You want another?" the bartender who wasn't Zeke said, and Greer just shoved his empty glass at him.

Ginger was unzipping one purple pant leg, and a second later she was twirling the pants high above her head, then throwing them out into the crowd. She looked right at Greer, but in the bright lights that covered the runway—hey, nobody wanted to miss a thing—he doubted she'd even seen him.

Still, he felt a flicker in his groin and thought about buying a lap dance later. He wondered if he could get it on credit; cash was a little tight right now . . . though things might be looking up very soon.

After his visit to al-Kalli's estate, he figured he now had something on him—something concrete and real and valuable. Those animals had to be worth a ton, not only given the facility he'd built to house them, but the fact that they didn't exist—to Greer's almost certain knowledge—anywhere else in the world. It was as if al-Kalli had his own little Jurassic Park up there, and from the security precautions alone—not to mention the fact that he fed *people* to them—Greer had a strong conviction that all the blackmail material he needed was now in hand.

When he'd sat down to write the new shakedown note, he'd felt on much firmer footing than the last time. First he introduced himself as the man who'd so capably delivered the goods in Iraq, then he explained that he was "very well aware" (he'd been proud of that turn of phrase—it sounded very professional to him) of the "rare and valuable livestock" al-Kalli kept on the grounds. He knew enough not to come right out and start spelling out the terms of the deal—how much he'd need to keep quiet, how the money should be paid, where they should meet to make the exchange—but he did make clear that he was not a patient man and he expected to hear back immediately, "or word might reach the proper authorities." He still didn't know who those authorities would be, or how exactly he'd reach them, but he was damn sure it wouldn't come to that.

Since he didn't know al-Kalli's actual address, and didn't want to wait the week it would take those assholes at the post office to get the letter to him, he'd driven up there himself. He'd gone at night, so he'd be likely to catch that same gatekeeper—the black kid, Reggie—who remembered him from the first excursion.

"Hey, Reggie," he'd said, pulling up in front of the locked gates. "Got something here for Mr. al-Kalli."

"You off duty?" the kid had said, noting that Greer wasn't in his Silver Bear uniform or the patrol car.

"Yep," Greer had said, holding up the sealed envelope. "Just be sure Mr. al-Kalli himself gets this." As he handed it over, he made sure that Reggie also got hold of the fifty-dollar bill under it. "It's very important he gets this himself."

Reggie looked confused for a second and studied the bill. Then he slipped the money into the breast pocket of his shirt and said, "Sure thing. I'll put it in his hand myself, next time he comes through."

"You do that," Greer said, then backed out and down the hill.

He still hadn't heard back, but then, something like this was bound to take a little bit of time, while the mark thought about what to do, how to handle it, and all that. Greer did know one thing already, though—he knew not to trust al-Kalli in anything. He knew he'd do whatever it took—hell, he'd seen it happen—and if Greer wanted to come out of this rich and, better yet, still alive, he'd have to keep his wits about him.

One more reason that he needed some of the uppers that he'd come to get from Zeke.

Right now, Zeke was down on the beach, scrambling in the sand after a loose ball. His partner—they were both wearing matching yellow shorts and visors—had that pumped-up-on-steroids look. Why, Greer idly wondered, would you need to get pumped up to smack a ball over a volleyball net? Even though some of the soldiers had set up volleyball courts at the base in Iraq, Greer had always thought the game was kind of candy-ass. And those matching yellow shorts just confirmed it.

As he brushed the sand off the ball, Zeke glanced up toward the parking area and spotted Greer leaning over the rail. He raised his chin in acknowledgment, and Greer lifted one finger to the brim of his cap. When the game was over, and everybody had finished high-fiving each other—another faggoty thing to do—Zeke sauntered over to the concrete stairs that led up to the parking lot.

"Hey, man, good for you," Zeke said, bouncing the ball on each step.

"What the fuck does that mean?"

"You took my advice—got some sun."

Greer, from under his sunglasses, cap, and long-sleeved shirt, said, "Yeah, I'm just soakin' up the rays."

Zeke stopped at a white SUV, popped open the back, and tossed the ball inside. "Haven't seen you around the

Bayou lately," he said, rummaging around in a pile of sweaty clothes.

"I was in last night."

"Oh yeah? I was off."

"I know that. Why do you think I'm here now?"

Zeke pulled a fresh T-shirt over his head and said, "What do you need?"

"What are you holding?" Greer ran down a few things he might be interested in, while Zeke, nodding, dug around in the back of the car. He pulled out an Adidas bag, looked both ways to make sure nobody was around, then unzipped it. "Okay, this is what I've got." He had some Percodans, some OxyContin, a few Demerol. "I usually don't carry," Zeke explained. "It's all back at the club."

"This'll do," Greer said, taking out his money clip—an oversized paper clip—selecting what he wanted, and handing over the cash.

"We've got another match in a couple of hours. Want to watch?"

"I'll get back to you on that," Greer said, walking back to his own Mustang—damn, now that he saw it in the sunlight, he could see just how much of the green paint was falling off—and got in. There was a can of beer, not too warm, on the front seat, and he used it to wash down a few of his newly procured meds. There was a breeze blowing, and Greer just leaned back, gazing out at the blue sky and the blue water, the shimmering sand and the brown strip of smog, way off in the distance toward Catalina. Behind him he could hear the rush of the unending traffic on Pacific Coast Highway. This wasn't so bad, he thought; he should come here to get stoned more often. It was a lot more peaceful than the Blue Bayou.

Damn, why was he thinking about that shithole again? He still regretted what he'd done there last night.

He'd given Sadowski, of all people, an opportunity to dis him. After Ginger's set, Greer had crossed the room to join Sadowski and Burt and their new pals. That's how desperate he'd been to get out of his own head. They were way in back, and he'd pulled a chair over to their table and sat down before Sadowski knew he was there. The table was littered with glasses and bottles and, for no apparent reason, a map of greater L.A. Sadowski looked startled, and Burt quickly folded up the map; the two other guys just sat there, as if waiting to see what was supposed to happen next.

"Captain Greer," Sadowski blurted out, "where'd you come from?"

"The bar."

Sadowski said, "Yeah, cool. You remember Burt?"

Burt just regarded Greer with stony silence. There goes my membership in the Sons of Liberty, Greer thought.

"And these are Tate and Florio."

Greer nodded. "What's this? A new-members outing?"

"Uh, kind of."

Greer couldn't resist. "What was the map for? You looking to build a new clubhouse somewhere?"

"You got it," Burt said. "Something with a pool and a Jacuzzi."

Sadowski laughed nervously and said, "Yeah, Greer, see? You'll be sorry you didn't join when you had the chance."

Tate and Florio—two beefy guys who looked to Greer like they worked out a lot—kept their eyes down and their mouths shut. Greer started to get the sense that he'd interrupted some top-secret operation. Which made him want to press their buttons all the more.

"You know, you may want to keep your clubhouse out of the east side," Greer said. "Too many spics. And South Central, I don't need to tell you, that's all black. Definitely not a good place to hang. I see you guys more on the west side of town—maybe Beverly Hills, or"—and he cut a glance at Sadowski—"Bel-Air."

"Thanks for your input," Burt said, leaning forward in his chair, "but why don't you stuff it up your ass?"

Now Tate and Florio apparently knew how things stood, and they, too, glared at Greer. One of them—Greer couldn't remember which was which—had a fresh patch of gauze on his bare forearm. Greer was just about to ask to see the tattoo, when everybody's eyes moved to his right. Greer didn't have to guess why.

"How was my set?" Ginger asked coyly as she slipped onto Sadowski's lap.

The two newbies started falling all over themselves to tell her how terrific she was—Greer couldn't tell whether they were trying to make an impression on her or, oddly enough, on Sadowski—and Burt and Greer just held each other's gaze. It could have gotten ugly if Ginger—wearing just a purple bra and G-string—hadn't said, "Hey, Derek, want another lap dance?"

Greer wouldn't have said yes under any circumstances—besides, he didn't have the money—but it pissed him off, nonetheless, when Sadowski said, "No, baby, I want you to get to know these new friends of mine." He formally introduced Florio, with the bandage, and Tate, and even though they looked a little surprised that Sadowski would be encouraging them to get their rocks off with his girlfriend, Florio let himself be guided out of his chair and back toward the Blue Room.

Greer stayed put. There was just something about knowing he wasn't welcome there that made him want to stay. Burt stayed, too, with the kind of smile on his face that said he'd just as soon kick your ass.

Greer ordered another Jack on the rocks.

CHAPTER TWENTY-FOUR

*O*N THE MORROW, *I shall die.*

Even in the hot air of the backyard, Beth felt a chill run down her spine. For many centuries, these words had been hidden, secretly stashed beneath an ivory and sapphire tombstone. And she—right now—was the first person to read them.

And these were the first words that she read.

The printouts from the computer translation program were designed to be read laterally, with one-third of the page on the left devoted to an actual facsimile of the original Latin in which the letter had been composed, the middle column a clear rendering of what those graphemes or characters probably were, and the right side providing the best approximate translation of the meaning. Many of the passages were asterisked and numbered, indicating that the supplemental pages at the back would include, where necessary, more extensive alternative readings—sometimes because the ancient text was faded and/or indecipherable, and sometimes because the complex structure of the passage had left too many questions for easy analysis. Computers were fine for rote work, but they had no sense of literary style.

But these words were unasterisked, unnumbered, and perfectly plain in their meaning.

On the morrow, I shall die. Preserve [protect] my soul, O Lord.

Joey squealed and Beth looked up. They were outside, in the little grassed-in area that passed for a yard, with Champ on relentless patrol, sniffing at the low iron fence that surrounded them and occasionally lifting a leg to show any possible rivals who was boss around these parts. It was dusk, but the heat of the day was still strong. Beth, in her eagerness to get away from the Getty, to read these pages for the first time in the privacy of her own home, had left work early, dismissed Robin, who was delighted ("Cool—there's a band at the Viper Room that I wanted to see tonight!"), and gone outside with her briefcase and a tall glass of iced tea, which was precariously balanced on the wobbly little garden table by her side.

Of course, what she had done was a major breach of protocol. These pages, a translation of what now appeared to be the last testament of one of the world's most accomplished illuminators, should have been immediately revealed to the Getty authorities and of course to the owner of *The Beasts of Eden*. The originals should have been carefully catalogued and sealed, while a slow and deliberate plan of action—perhaps involving outside scholars and specialists—was assembled to analyze and study them. It all could have taken months, years. Beth had a somewhat greater patience with protocol than her husband did, but she did share with Carter one thing—and that was her thirst for knowledge, her passion for discovery. And this letter, which had taken many centuries to travel halfway around the world, she felt in some ineffable way was addressed to her.

On the morrow, I shall die. Preserve [protect] my soul, O Lord. I am the most fortunate, and this night the most unfortunate, of men. I have done greatness [great works] and I have done [committed] great crimes [mischief, transgressions]. Perhaps it is for [due to] this that I have come to [been conveyed to] this place of unimagined splendor and

equally unimagined barbarity . . . this palace of gold,
where the waters [rivers] run red [with blood] and even
glorious deeds lead to ignominious [shameful] death.

Beth paused. It was difficult reading, not only because
her eye was constantly coursing back and forth across the
page, checking the various columns to see that the computer had indeed read the Latin as she would have, and that
the translation was on point—but because the words themselves were so direct, so full of import and dire portent.
Were these in fact the last words of the man who had written *The Beasts of Eden*, and who (she was sure of it, though
she knew she'd get an argument from other scholars in the
field) had also done all the illustrations? Or would he survive whatever dreadful fate awaited him the next day?

Joey was happily crawling around on the grass, assembling walls and towers out of multicolored, squeezable
plastic cubes. She knew that mothers always thought their
own children were especially talented and precocious, but
still, she was impressed with the solidity and design of the
battlements—and battlements were what they most reminded her of—that he was building. Just now he was cap-
ping another tower, which, because it was standing on the
uneven ground, looked ready to topple any second. In
Joey's gray-blue eyes, she could see that he thought so, too.
He looked around and, wouldn't you know it, Champ
stopped his patrolling long enough to turn, pick up a big
red block in his mouth, and trot over with it. Joey added it,
like a buttress, to the base of his tower.

What other infant, Beth wondered, could ever have
done such a thing? Not for the first time, she thought about
having his IQ checked. Could they do that with a child so
young?

A fly landed on the papers in her lap, and she brushed it
away. The sun was starting to set behind the Santa Monica
Mountains, and the canyon below was growing dark, as if a
blot of ink was slowly spreading across the thick brush and
chaparral. She took a sip of her iced tea, wiped her fingers
dry on the cotton shorts she was wearing, and returned to
the pages in her lap.

*I have come to this place by God's hand, but without
achieving [procuring] his Grace. It was the voice of Peter I
heard, as it was heard by multitudes beside. Never had I
met Holiness [sanctity], nor seen it, nor heard it, until that
day in the fields. Peter bade us all to turn from combat and
strife and the undoing of fellow Christian souls; he bade us
turn our thoughts to our Savior and to the holy places He
had walked, the places now defiled by the Saracen unbe-
lievers.*

My God, Beth thought, was this what she thought it
was? Was it to be a firsthand account of a pilgrim—a
Crusader?—to the Holy Land? Peter, she knew, was not
meant to be St. Peter. But could it be the legendary Peter
the Hermit, a bearded anchorite who had emerged in the
late eleventh century to galvanize much of Europe and
send them off to reclaim Palestine from the infidels? If
that was true, then this scribe very likely spoke French,
Peter's native tongue and the language he used to stir up
much of Western Europe. The scribe's accomplishments
continued to grow: he could compose and write exquisite
Latin, he could provide illuminations that were breathtaking in their beauty and their power—and now, if she could
guess where this was going, he was an adventurer, too, a
man of action. More and more, she felt she was dealing
with a man in the mold of a Cellini, a Caravaggio, or a
Michelangelo. Not some cloistered fellow, who had seldom left the monastery's scriptorium, but an artist of the
first order, who had fully entered into the life of his time.

And if she was right about Peter the Hermit, then that
time could now be neatly pinpointed—it was 1095 when
Peter, newly returned from his first trip to the Holy Land,
traveled to Rome to beseech the aid of the Pope. Everywhere he went, Peter stirred up religious fervor and, in an
almost equal degree, bloodlust. Riding on a mule and
wearing a long frock girded with a thick cord, he regaled
the crowds that came to see him with terrible tales of the
atrocities visited upon Christians journeying to Jerusalem.
He called upon the angels to testify to the truth of his
words, and as he spoke he wept and beat his own breast

with a rude crucifix until he bled. He extolled the glories of Mount Zion, the rock of Calvary, the Mount of Olives, and Pope Urban II accepted him, as did thousands of others, as an anointed messenger from God.

So, too, did I hear the edicts of the Holy Father, who promised that all sins [mortal transgressions] could be thus expiated, and that no crime or deed of charge could be prosecuted against any such pilgrim.

Beth had to smile; her man was running true to form. Had he, like those other hot-blooded artists, committed some crime?

Further, no violence could be exercised against a Soldier of Christ without a verdict of anathema being brought upon the perpetrator.

If he had run afoul of the law, it must have been in a pretty bad way. But the scribe had secured his own protection; like so many others, he had enlisted in God's army, and anyone who interfered with him now risked anathema—or excommunication. For some, no doubt, the Crusades had been a divine calling, but for many others, the war on the Muslims had provided a kind of medieval Get Out of Jail Free card.

Having felt the sting of persecution [injustice] myself, I could well imagine the sufferings of my fellow Christians, and wished to bend my will to the achievement of God's greater purpose [higher plan]. We set out in the waning days of summer, a great army of the Lord, some among us knights on horseback, but many more on foot, with nothing but a staff and a satchel. In my own bag, I carried the tools of my trade, for I have long found that the skills of the artisan can prove more useful and more valuable than the weapons [ways; methods] of the warrior. In this belief, I was to be confirmed. These tools would save my life, though they may now have brought me to the end of it.

Beth glanced up; Joey was toddling after Champ, who had a bright blue block in his mouth. Joey was laughing, and Champ's tail was wagging, and Beth thought how strange it was that here, now, she should be reading what was probably a condemned man's final confession. Caught

up in the tale, she began to skip over the alternative readings and notes and let the narrative unfold.

We were led by several noble lords, among them Robert,
Duke of Normandy, Stephen, Count of Chartres and Troyes,
and Godfrey de Bouillon, descendant of the great Charle-
magne himself. He went on to recount many more barons
and princes who rode with this first crusade, all in the same
cramped, precisely executed style in which the entire letter
had been written. Under what conditions, Beth wondered,
had it been composed? Clearly, he had had only a few
spare sheets of parchment to work with, because the words
were very closely spaced, the lines very narrow. And where
was he at the time—confined to a dungeon cell, writing by
the light of a torch, or in the attic of a prison tower, huddled in the moonlight that penetrated the bars of his window? Was he resigned to his fate, or had he some hope, or
some plan, of escape?

Our journey, though favored by divine providence, was
a difficult one, and we were often besieged and attacked.
Beth knew the history of the First Crusade—some of the illuminated manuscripts she studied would allude to it—and
she had read the standard historical accounts in grad
school. But she had never read a first-person rendering like
this—had anyone?—and she quickly lost herself in it. Between the frontiers of Austria and the walls of Constantino-
ple, the pilgrim horde, which, according to most accounts,
numbered several hundred thousand, devoured everything
in its path, and the inhabitants of Hungary, Bulgaria, and
Greece proved less and less receptive, and finally hostile.
At a trumpet blast from the King of Hungary, a legion of
archers and mounted horse was unleashed upon us. Even
Peter was forced to flee to the Thracian Mountains, and it
was there we hid in misery until the Emperor Alexius
granted us safe conduct to his mighty fortress on the shores
of the Bosporus.

The sun had dropped another few degrees behind the
Santa Monica Mountains, and the words were becoming
difficult to read. Beth put the transcripts down in her lap
and looked up at Joey, who had knocked down his walls

and towers and was sitting surrounded by the fallen blocks. He was chattering gibberish to himself—he just *had* to be way ahead of the usual learning curve, Beth thought for the umpteenth time—with his head tilted up toward the bedroom window. "Da," she thought she heard him say—had he?—and she followed his gaze to the same window, where she could see, through the slats of the Venetian blinds, Carter's dark silhouette as he moved back into the room. He was home earlier than she'd thought he'd be. Still, it would have been nice if he'd come outside to say hello before going upstairs to change out of his work clothes. She'd picked up some swordfish steaks at the market and she was sort of hoping he'd be up for a barbecue.

"Want to go inside and say hello to your daddy?" Beth said to Joey. "Can you say that—daddy?" Joey looked at her with a big grin but said nothing. "I think you just did, ten seconds ago." Beth got down on her knees and crawled across the grass toward him. This made Joey laugh, and his loose blond curls shook in the evening air as Champ ran around them both, barking, in a big, wide circle.

With the transcripts tucked under one arm, Beth hoisted Joey up off the lawn and, together, they stood for a moment, watching the sun dip below the mountaintop. The ravine below their house fell into deep shadow; a flock of birds suddenly burst from the brush and flew off toward the ocean.

Beth nuzzled Joey's cheek—why had no one explained to her how sweet a baby could smell?—and turned toward the house. Carter hadn't turned on the lights yet.

In the kitchen, Beth flicked the switch and called out, "How would you feel about a backyard barbecue?"

But Carter didn't answer; he must be in the bathroom.

She put Joey into his high chair, turned on the local news—another forecast of hot and dry weather—and gave him his dinner. Champ sat on his haunches, expectantly, until Joey was done and she could feed him, too. The news was following a freeway chase somewhere down near Redondo Beach. That was one thing you could say for New York, Beth thought: traffic was so bad no highway chase could last more than a few hundred yards.

When the newscast ended, she turned off the TV and lifted Joey out of his chair. "Uh-oh," she said, "somebody needs a new diaper."

And it didn't look as if Carter was going to be in the mood for a barbecue. He must have flopped onto the bed and fallen asleep.

As she carried Joey upstairs, she noted that Carter still hadn't turned on any of the lights. She went into Joey's bedroom, changed him, and left him in his crib, then crossed the hall to the master suite.

"Carter?" she said softly, stepping into the darkened room. She'd expected to see him lying on the bed, damp from a shower. But no one was there. And there was a fragrance in the air—the scent of a forest, after a heavy rain—that made her stop in her tracks. It was the scent she remembered from New York, from the terrible and difficult days preceding Joey's birth. The days when their lives had been shadowed, even endangered, by the malevolence of a creature who went by the name of Arius.

She fumbled for the light switch and turned it on. The bed was unrumpled, the room was empty.

But the bathroom door was closed.

She put her ear to it and, holding her breath, listened for any sound within. There was a low swishing sound, of the plastic shower curtain crackling. "Carter?" she said, still hoping against hope that she would hear him answer.

But there was nothing.

She tried the handle; the door was unlocked. She opened it slowly, and yes, the shower curtain was billowing in the breeze from the open window. At dusk, a wind often came up off the valley below. But no one was in the stall.

Only the scent of wet leaves—more powerful here than it had been in the bedroom—suggested that someone might have been in here.

Someone who might even have exited, moments before, by the open window.

Downstairs, she could hear the sound of the front door opening.

"Honey?" Carter called out; she could hear his backpack

hitting the floor of the foyer. "Guess who I brought home for dinner?"

"You decent?" Del called out. " 'Cause if not, come on down!"

Beth closed the bathroom window tight, then stepped back into the bedroom.

"She must be upstairs with Joey," she heard Carter saying to Del. "There's beer in the fridge; help yourself."

Carter came up the steps two at a time, and when Beth turned to him, she knew he could tell something was wrong.

And then the scent must have hit him, too, because he quickly took her in his arms and looked all around. "You alright? Joey alright?"

She nodded.

Then he ran to the nursery, and came back with Joey nestled against his shoulder.

"When did this happen?" he asked. "Just now?"

"Yes. Right before you came home."

"Did you . . . see him?"

"No." She shuddered involuntarily. "It was only that smell."

He didn't have to ask how Arius might have gotten in. They both knew that he could come and go wherever he pleased. And now they knew something more—that whatever their hopes, and their suspicions, had been, he was still a presence in this world. And in their lives.

"You mind if I have one of the expensive foreign brews?" Del shouted up from the foot of the stairs. "I don't normally drink a beer that had to come all the way from Holland."

"Have whatever you want," Carter answered, still holding the baby and looking deep into Beth's eyes; they didn't have to say a word for each of them to know exactly what the other was thinking.

Little Joey looked from one to the other, with his usual expression—so incongruous for a toddler—of placid understanding.

"I should have called ahead," Carter murmured. "To tell you about Del."

Beth shrugged; she was used to Carter bringing home his buddies. At one time it had been Joe Russo—the baby's namesake. Now it was Del.

"And when do I get to see the kid?" Del called out. "God knows I didn't come all the way up here just to hang out with Carter some more."

Carter put his free arm around Beth's shoulders and shepherded his family toward the stairs.

Del was waiting at the bottom, one hand on top of Champ's head and the other holding a Heineken. "Now you're talkin'," he said.

CHAPTER TWENTY-FIVE

ALTHOUGH REGGIE STILL had the envelope that that other security guard, the one who'd shown up with Stan Sadowski, had given him, he'd already spent the fifty bucks. Sadowski had once handed him a Free Drink coupon for a place called the Blue Bayou, and after the free drink Reggie had used the money for a lap dance.

As for the envelope, he'd been waiting for the right opportunity to give it to Mr. al-Kalli himself—he'd read in a book on personal improvement that if you wanted to get ahead, you needed to make sure that you got on the boss's radar—but he just hadn't found it. Once the car had sped out so fast he could barely get the gate up in time, and the last few times al-Kalli must have come in and out by the back gate, over near the riding ring.

But tonight looked like it was going to be his night—the headlights of the Mercedes limo were approaching fast, up the hill, and Reggie dug the envelope out of his pocket. A couple of times he'd debated steaming it open and seeing what was inside, but he was afraid that al-Kalli would be able to figure out what he'd done. And from everything he'd heard, al-Kalli was one dude you didn't want to mess with.

Just those frickin' peacocks alone, with their screeching and squawking, was enough to give him the willies at night.

As the car pulled up, Reggie stepped out of the gate-house and raised a hand at Jakob, the driver. The tinted window rolled smoothly down, and Reggie said, "I have something for Mr. al-Kalli."

Always deal with the boss himself, never a middleman—that's what the advice book had said.

"Give it to me," Jakob said, holding his hand palm out.

Reggie tried to look into the back of the limo, but it was so dark in there he couldn't see a damn thing.

"My instructions were to—"

Jakob opened the door and Reggie had to step back just to get out of the way.

"Give it to me, whatever it is. Now."

Jakob towered over him, his eyes as black as his shirt.

Reggie handed it over, and Jakob turned it back and forth in his hand. "Who brought this?"

"One of the Silver Bear Security guys."

"When?"

"Um, I don't know exactly when." He didn't want to admit that he hadn't found a way to give it to al-Kalli immediately. "Maybe a day or so ago."

"And it took you till now to hand it over?"

Reggie wasn't sure what to say. What would that self-improvement book tell him to do?

Jakob got back in the car, and as the gates swung open, he said through the still open window, "What time do you get off tonight?"

"Six A.M."

"Don't come back tomorrow."

The car took off, and Reggie stood there, flat-footed, so long the gates nearly hit him when they closed again.

AT THE HOUSE, al-Kalli waited patiently in the kitchen while Jakob held the envelope up to the light, sniffed it for plastique, shook it gently for anthrax powder or any other substance. There was no return address, but that was to be expected. Jakob let some water collect in the kitchen sink, then opened the envelope just above it, ready to drop it and hit the disposal button in a second.

"It's probably nothing," al-Kalli said, impatiently.

Jakob thought he was probably right, and he carefully opened the envelope at one end, then drew out the single, typed page inside. He saw the salutation—a simple *Mr. al-Kalli*—and several brief paragraphs below it. There was a scrawled signature at the bottom, and below it the words *Capt. Derek Greer*. He made a small "huh."

"What is it?" al-Kalli said, taking the letter Jakob was now extending to him.

"It's from the one you hired, the American soldier, in Iraq."

Al-Kalli took a pair of gold reading glasses from the breast pocket of his suit coat and put them on. "He knows I'm here?" al-Kalli said, as he began to read.

Jakob didn't reply, but simply waited. Still, just watching al-Kalli's face told him most of what he needed to know.

In less than a minute, al-Kalli had put his glasses back in his pocket, folded up the letter again, and said, "We may have a small problem."

Jakob knew that when Mohammed said small, he meant large.

"What would you like me to do?"

Al-Kalli looked thoughtful. "We must first have a word with Rashid."

A few minutes later, they found him where he always was—in the bestiary.

But al-Kalli, already in a black mood, only grew blacker as the doors whooshed shut behind him.

The odor in the air was unhealthy, the cries of the animals strained and plaintive. Rashid himself, in a soiled lab coat, was playing a hose over the mottled hide of the basilisk. When he saw his employer, he quickly shut off the water and came forward, drying his hands on the tails of his coat.

"Mr. al-Kalli," he said, but before he could say another

word, al-Kalli had backhanded him, hard, across the mouth. His sapphire ring cracked against a tooth.

Rashid fell against the bars of a cage, and the creature within suddenly sprang upward, spittle flying in all directions.

Al-Kalli grabbed the spindly Rashid by the collar of his coat and dragged him clear. Rashid, in terror, simply slumped to the ground.

"Who have you been talking to?" al-Kalli hissed, and Rashid's eyes went wide.

"No one," he sputtered; there was blood smeared like lipstick across his mouth.

Al-Kalli drew back his hand and smacked him again, so hard Rashid's head spun on his neck.

"Someone knows about the animals."

"I have never . . . told anyone."

"Someone has *seen* the animals."

Now Jakob knew how serious the problem had become.

"Who have you let in here?"

"No one . . . only Bashir. To clean."

Bashir was a teenage boy, one step above an idiot, whom Rashid had brought from the bombed-out ruins of Mosul. He barely spoke, lived in a shed behind the bestiary, and was a virtual slave.

"Who besides Bashir?"

Rashid simply shook his head, in terror and denial. "No one ever comes here . . . unless it is to . . ." He didn't know how to complete that sentence, nor did he want to. The only other people who came here were prisoners, men al-Kalli planned to feed to the beasts. Was he about to become one of them? Rashid thought. Words of the Koran began to tumble like a fast-moving stream through his head.

Al-Kalli threw him away, like something soiled, and Rashid sprawled on the dirt floor of the bestiary. He knew enough not to get up; it was better to lie prostrate, submissive, defeated; it was true among the animals, and it was true among men.

Al-Kalli's gaze, filled with contempt and disgust, moved away from him. The scent of blood in the air, however slight, had agitated the animals. There were grunts and snarls, and overhead the furious beating of wings. As al-Kalli watched, his prized phoenix dropped off its lofty perch and swooped in a blaze of red and gold into the air, screeching like a whole flock of eagles. It flew madly from one end of the vast facility to the other, the tips of its glistening wings grazing the steel walls, its claws extended and flexing as if anxious to capture some living prey.

The other animals, watching its flight and perhaps envying the bird's relative freedom, let loose with a louder volley of howls and yelps and growls. There was a dense, musky smell in the air, and even Jakob instinctively loosened his jacket enough to make drawing his gun easier.

What was he to do? al-Kalli wondered, as the cries rose around him. His beasts were dying—the legacy of his family, for thousands of years, was about to vanish under his care. Under difficult circumstances, he had saved as many as he could, as many as he thought necessary to breed and sustain the species. But he was failing. Rashid was a fool, and, despite all his training, no more capable of caring for such exquisite treasures than the idiot boy, Bashir. These were creatures from a time before time, beasts that had walked among the dinosaurs, that had grazed the fields of Eden. It would be a risk—it would always be a risk—to share the knowledge of them with anyone.

But what was needed, al-Kalli saw more clearly now than ever before, was someone who knew that world. Someone who understood creatures of such great antiquity—someone who revered them as he did—and who might intuit what they needed to survive.

And if such a man existed, al-Kalli knew who it might be.

CHAPTER TWENTY-SIX

CARTER BENT LOW over the plaster of paris and with the tip of his scalpel delicately removed a piece the size of a dime.

"Neatly done," Del said, taking a sip of his cold coffee. "At this rate we'll be finished by Labor Day."

"What year?" Carter said, straightening up and, with his hands at the small of his back, stretching.

Del glanced up at the clock on the wall of the lab. "It's almost ten. How much longer you want to go?"

Carter wasn't sure. They were working on the remains of the La Brea Man, and they were doing it in the public lab on the ground floor of the Page Museum. This was the lab where the work was routinely done, behind a curved glass wall that allowed the general public, during normal museum hours, to watch the process. But these weren't normal museum hours, which was the only reason Carter was willing to risk using this lab at all. Working on something as sensitive as the La Brea Man—given all the controversy it had already created—was probably something he should be doing only in a place safe from public view.

It was just that the museum had no better lab than this.

"You getting tired?" Carter asked.

"I can go a while longer," Del said, tucking some strands of his long white hair back into his headband. "Long as we're not interrupted by any ghosts."

"I haven't seen any yet." But then, it would hardly be possible; they were working in a tiny island of light, in an otherwise dark and empty lab, in the middle of an otherwise dark and empty museum. Carter, too, had heard the rumors Del was referring to; the night watchmen had reported some strange goings-on. Moving shadows on the wall. Scratching noises. Once, some violent banging in the sub-basement. As far as Carter was concerned, either it was nothing at all or it was something the protestors were up to. Maybe they thought they could spook the museum into giving up the bones.

If that was the case, they were sorely mistaken.

Especially as he was making such notable progress on the bones of the left hand—the hand in which something, something still encased in the asphalt, was held. In fact, with another few moves of the chisel and scalpel, he thought he could separate the object from the hand itself.

"Put another tape on, and we'll work for the duration of one side."

Del turned and popped the Loretta Lynn out of the boom box balanced on the next stool. "What do you want to hear?"

"Something with electric guitars and no whining. The Stones, the White Stripes, the Vibes."

"I brought some Merle Haggard. Boxed set—*Down Every Road*?"

Carter laughed. "If that's what you've got."

And then he went back to work on the hand, while Del, on the opposite side of the lab table, continued removing flakes of plaster from the occipital lobe of the skull. During the day, the bones were carefully concealed under a black plastic sheath, but for several nights now, Carter and Del had taken to working on them for another hour or two after closing time. They hadn't ever gone this long, but as the skeleton became more and more revealed, Carter's compulsion to continue the work had grown. Beth, he knew, was less than enthused about his longer hours, but he promised her it would be over soon. And it wasn't as if she hadn't run into this kind of problem with him before.

He tapped the side of the plaster on what appeared to be the little finger of the man's left hand, and a tiny fissure opened up. He tilted the tensor lamp to give himself a better view, and yes, he could see that there was now a tiny, barely discernible line running between the bone and the still-coated object. If he was very careful, and a little bit lucky, he would now be able to separate the two.

"You getting along any better with your brother-in-law?" Carter asked. Del was still staying with them in their fancy condo on Wilshire Boulevard.

"As long as I stay out on the balcony, they're okay with it and so am I."

"The traffic noise doesn't get to you?" Carter used a fine camel's-hair brush to whisk away the plaster dust.

"They're on the twenty-ninth floor," Del replied, without looking up from his work either. "I get more noise from the planes. But no, it's not ideal. I'm looking for new accommodations."

Carter picked up the scalpel once more and gently increased the delineation between the bone and its prize. Merle was singing, in a rich baritone—Carter had to hand him that—about how all his friends were gonna be strangers.

"You up for another hike this weekend?" Del said.

"Sure."

"Maybe we can go somewhere they don't slash your tires."

"That would be a good idea." After their last hike in Temescal Canyon, they'd had to wait an hour in the parking lot for a tow truck to arrive. And Carter had had to shell out for a new set of tires.

He used the scalpel as a wedge, and just as the plaster cracked, and the bone and object cleaved apart, the overhead lights all over the lab snapped on.

"What the hell is going on in here?" Carter heard from the door directly behind him.

He didn't have to turn around to know who it was.

Gunderson, in a natty suit and bow tie, was standing in the doorway, with a red boutonniere in his lapel. Del quickly turned off the music.

"Do you know what time it is?" Gunderson went on.

Carter knew perfectly well. But what, he wondered, as he draped a clean cloth over the newly separated object, was Gunderson doing here?

"I was just leaving a concert downtown," he volunteered before Carter could ask, "and in view of all the security problems we've had of late, I thought I'd swing by." He strode over to the table. "And I'm very glad I did."

He glanced down at the plaster cast and quickly assessed the situation. "You," he said to Del, "I would not expect to know any better." But then he wheeled on Carter. "But how could you do something so obtuse?"

"This is the best lab on the premises, and we need to proceed with the work."

"In full public view?"

"We keep it covered and out of sight during museum hours. We've only worked on it at night."

Gunderson let out an angry breath and ran a hand back over his hair. "Dr. Cox, I know that the Page Museum considered it a coup to get you to come here. But I for one always had my reservations. I looked into the events that precipitated your departure from New York University, and I wasn't exactly relieved. Your unorthodox research methods not only led to a massive lab explosion—"

Carter wondered if he was going to run down all the sordid details.

"—but also caused the deaths of two of your colleagues."

Apparently he was. Carter looked over at Del—he'd never told his friend the whole story, and now he wished that he had. It's just that it was something he tried, without much success, to put out of his mind.

"Now it looks like you're up to your old tricks, and I won't have it in my museum."

When was it, Carter thought, that the Page had become *his* museum?

"I want this . . . specimen removed first thing tomorrow. I've already got the NAGPRA people swamping me with official queries and threats about our government funding. The last thing I want to do is give them any fresh ammunition." He threw one last look onto the remains, much of them still concealed by the plaster cast used to preserve them during the recovery and transportation to the lab, and then turned abruptly on his heel. "The museum closes at six P.M., gentlemen," he said on his way to the door. "The only person authorized to be in here is the night watchman."

The door, on an air-hinge, slowly closed and latched behind him, and Carter and Del were left alone again, in the now brightly lighted lab. Carter wasn't sure what to say.

"Two?" Del finally said. "I knew about your friend Joe Russo, but there was another guy who died, too?"

"Joe died from burns," Carter said, "in the hospital. A young assistant professor, Bill Mitchell, was killed at the scene."

"He was the one who started the laser?"

"Yes," Carter said.

"Without knowing about the gas pockets in the rock?"

"He wasn't even supposed to know about the project. He wasn't supposed to be in there."

"Where were you?" Del hadn't meant to make it sound so accusatory.

"Upstate, at a friend's house, for the weekend."

Del rocked on his heels, as if pondering the data, then said, "Well, it sounds to me like it was one royal fuck-up."

Carter couldn't deny it.

"But it wasn't your fault. You weren't even there." It was what Beth had tried to tell him a thousand times—what he'd told himself nearly as many. But it didn't matter. He would carry the disaster in his heart to the end of his days, and he would mourn the loss of his friend Joe Russo always.

"So," Del said, gesturing at the La Brea Man, "what do you want to do about our friend here?"

Carter wasn't sure yet. He could set up a makeshift lab in the sub-basement, but it would take a few days of preparation. What he did know was that he wanted to spirit one piece of the find away immediately; now that he'd removed the mystery object from the man's hand, he wanted to get to work on it first thing the next day. And he certainly couldn't do that in here anymore.

"Let's just cover it and leave it here until I can set something up."

They drew the black sheath over the remains and tidied up the work area, and while Del was busy looping the extension cord around the boom box, Carter wrapped the object in his clean handkerchief (thank goodness Beth encouraged him to carry one) and slipped it into the side pocket of his leather jacket; although it was much heavier than he'd thought it would be, enough to make that side of his coat sag, he was hoping that Del wouldn't notice.

On the way out, Carter suddenly stopped and said to Del, "I forgot something upstairs in my office."

"You want me to wait for you?"

"No, you go on home to your balcony. I'll see you tomorrow."

The security guard, Hector, let Del out, and then said to Carter, "Mr. Gunderson, he told me you're supposed to go now, too." He said it somewhat apologetically, as he and Carter had always been pretty friendly. In fact, when he and Del had eaten in the lab the night before, Carter had brought Hector a Big Mac and a large fries.

"I've just got to make one more stop," Carter said, and Hector looked dubious. "In the sub-basement."

Hector made sure the door was locked behind Del, then said, "You can't go down there now. The elevator's locked."

Carter hadn't thought of that. "But you've got the key, right?"

Hector looked as if he wanted to lie, but he knew it was too late.

"C'mon, Hector, we can be down there and back in five minutes."

Hector surveyed the empty precincts of the first floor—
the re-creation of the giant ground sloth rearing up on its
hind legs, the skulls of the dire wolves arrayed on the wall,
the skeleton of the saber-toothed cat snarling in its glass
display case—and must have decided everything looked as
though it might be alright for a while. Never underesti-
mate, Carter thought, the power of McDonald's.

"Okay, but we gotta be fast."

"We will be," Carter said, striding toward the elevator
bank before the watchman could have any second thoughts.

Hector got in, hitching his belt up over his paunch, and
inserted the master key into the control panel. Carter hit
the button for the sub-basement, where most of the fossil
collections were kept.

When the doors opened, the endless corridors, lined
with metal cases and file drawers, were in almost utter
blackness; only a couple of emergency lights were on, way
off across the floor. Hector said, "Hold the door open," and
he stepped out to hit the bank of light switches. All down
the corridors, fluorescent tubes flickered and hummed into
life, but even then the light was uneven and insufficient. It
was like entering a great, gray cave, one that didn't want
you there.

Hector said, "Maybe this isn't such a good idea. Maybe
we could come back tomorrow."

Carter wondered if Hector was one of the security personnel who'd reported the strange noises in the museum at
night. "It's right down here," Carter said, marching off. The
spot he was heading for was all the way at the far end of the
floor, but he didn't see any need to mention that just now.

His shoes had rubber soles, and they squeaked on the
linoleum as he walked; his shadow moved ahead of him,
and then behind, as he passed under each of the overhead
lights. Many of the green and gray metal cabinets, undisturbed for years, were coated with a fine film of dust. Hector followed a few steps behind him.

There was a burbling in his pocket, and he took out his
cell phone. Carter knew, before answering, that it would be
Beth.

"So you *are* still alive," she said, her voice faint.

"Barely, I'm down in the sub-basement."

"Where?"

He repeated himself; the connection was, predictably, pretty bad.

". . . coming home?"

"Yes, I will be coming home. I swear." As much for Hector as Beth, he said, "I'll be gone in a few minutes. Everything alright?"

"Fine." There was a burst of static, then he heard, ". . . an invitation."

"You're breaking up," he said. "We got an invitation?"

"Yes," she said. "From al-Kalli. Dinner, at his estate."

That was interesting, but Carter wasn't terribly surprised. Al-Kalli was expecting a lot from Beth—and for some reason expecting it fast—and this was probably just one more way to keep tabs on her. And so far, Beth had told al-Kalli nothing of the secret pages she had found under the front cover of the book; Carter had agreed with her that it was best to get them entirely translated and annotated before breaking the news, because once she had, it would be just one more thing al-Kalli would be breathing down her neck about.

"I hope I don't need a tux," Carter said. The lights down here seemed even dimmer than ever.

"I'm sure a . . . get you past the door." She said something else, too, but it was no longer audible.

"Beth, I'm losing you."

There was nothing at all but static now.

"I'll see you in about a half hour," he said, though he wasn't sure she could hear him either. He put the phone back in his pocket.

"You sure you know where we're going?" Hector asked.

"Absolutely," Carter said, though even he could feel the strange oppressiveness of their surroundings. It wasn't often that you found yourself deep underground, surrounded by millions of bones and petrified artifacts. He doubted that Hector ever made this floor a part of his regular rounds.

The object he'd retrieved from the grasp of the La Brea

Man hung heavy in the other pocket of his jacket, and he looked forward to coming back the next day and examining it—down here, away from Gunderson's prying eyes.

At the end of the corridor, under a bank of fluorescents, there was a wide table with a couple of glass jars holding some basic tools of the trade—chisels, scalpels, brushes, razor blades—and a pair of metal stools. It was here that Carter had examined the remains of the La Brea Woman.

"Why'd you need to come down here now?" Hector asked, a peeved note in his voice. "What couldn't wait until tomorrow?"

"I'll be done in a minute," Carter said, taking his keys out of his pocket and searching for the small one that unlocked the padlock on the top drawer of the cabinet.

"One of the other guards," Hector said, "he told me he saw Geronimo."

"Really," Carter said, noncommittally, finding the right key.

"Yesterday."

Carter fitted the key into the lock and said, "That seems pretty unlikely, doesn't it? Geronimo—William Blackhawk Smith," he corrected himself, "has been dead for over a week." Carter removed the padlock and put it on the worktable behind him.

Hector shrugged. "Funny things happen around here all the time."

And one of them was happening right now, Carter thought. Before he'd had a chance to touch it, the drawer containing the remains of the La Brea Woman was sliding open, as if on rails. Normally, these drawers were pretty sticky and you had to tug on them a bit. But not this one. This one was opening as if of its own volition.

The crushed skull lay back in the center of the drawer, its empty eye sockets angled up at the ceiling.

Hector, who hadn't seen the drawer open, came around to Carter's side now, crossed himself, and stared down at the ancient skull. "That's the woman they found in the pits? All those years ago?"

"Yes." Carter drew the white handkerchief containing

the object from upstairs out of his pocket. It would have been better if Hector had not witnessed this, but there didn't seem to be much of a choice. Carter removed the hankie, which fluttered to the floor, and placed the tar-covered stone, or whatever it would prove to be, in the drawer. This was the safest and most secure place he could think of.

Something stirred in the air, blowing the handkerchief, now smudged with tar, over their feet.

Hector's head snapped around. He pulled the flashlight off his utility belt and flashed it in all directions.

"It's just the vents," Carter said, picking up the handkerchief and tossing it into the drawer.

But Hector didn't appear convinced. "Something moved," he said, "over there." He motioned at the next aisle.

"If something did, it was probably a mouse."

Carter started to push the drawer closed again, but now it did stick. As easily as it had come out, that was how hard it was to get it closed. He asked Hector for the flashlight, who surrendered it reluctantly, then played the beam over the front and sides of the drawer. There were long lateral scratches on the metal, and even a couple of small dents at either end. Some of these cabinets were decades old, but Carter didn't remember this one looking quite so battered.

He tried closing it again, and this time the drawer almost seemed to push back. There was a screeching sound— the drawer refusing to return—and Hector said, "What's the problem? We got to go."

"I can't get the drawer closed."

"Don't worry about it," Hector said. "Nobody else is coming down here tonight."

"I'm not going to leave this open," Carter said, shimmying the drawer to either side. "These bones are too valuable."

"I won't let anybody down here," Hector insisted, his head swiveling in all directions. "Come on!"

And then, even though Carter had stopped trying to force it, the drawer began to shake. Carter stood back, staring, as the ancient artifacts rattled against the bottom and sides of the drawer. It was as if an unseen hand was rocking first the drawer, and then the whole cabinet.

"It's an earthquake!" Hector shouted. "We got to get out of here—now!"

Was that it? Carter hadn't been in California long enough to experience a quake yet. But this couldn't be a quake—nothing else was shaking. Not the floor, not the ceiling lights, not the table or stools.

Just this one cabinet, with the bones of the La Brea Woman—and the artifact he had just placed among them.

Hector had already taken off in the direction of the elevators, and Carter waited, watching. The air stirred again, and this time he wasn't so sure it was a vent, after all.

When the shaking subsided, as it did after a minute or so, Carter gently tried closing the drawer again, and this time it slid closed effortlessly—as if whatever force had been resisting him had given up, or run out of strength.

He put the padlock back on, and studied the scratched surface of the cabinet. What had just happened here? Had some unseen force been at play? He tugged on the padlock to make sure it was secure. Had he sealed something in that was trying to get out . . . or had he kept something out that had been trying to get in?

"I'm holding the elevator!" he heard Hector calling from the far end of the floor, his words echoing eerily around the closed walls. There was barely controlled panic in his voice. "But I'm not going to stick around forever, okay?"

CHAPTER TWENTY-SEVEN

HOW COULD SHE stay so fat, Greer wondered, with nothing but low-fat, low-carb, low-cal crap in all the cupboards? He rummaged around on the shelves looking for a can or a box of anything edible. A bag of baked, salt-free veggie chips fell out and onto the counter and his mother said, "What are you looking for?"

"What do you think?" Greer said.

His mother picked up the chips and stuffed them back where they belonged. "Just tell me what you want and I'll find it for you."

"What I want, you don't have."

"Then maybe you should try shopping for yourself sometime, buster."

She was in almost as bad a mood as he was. Greer had just gotten up—it was a little past noon—and he knew she thought it was a crime to sleep that late. But what else did he have to do? It wasn't as if he held a job anywhere. And the night before, he'd been back at the Blue Bayou till all hours, drinking, popping pills, and trying not to think about the one thing he couldn't stop thinking about.

Why hadn't al-Kalli called him yet? He must have gotten

the letter. Greer had put his cell phone number under his signature, and he hadn't gone anywhere without the phone now for days. He even slept with it on the pillow next to his head.

"How about cheese?" Greer said. "We got any cheese?"

His mother, who already had her head in the fridge, yanked open a plastic drawer and handed him a pack of low-fat—big surprise—American singles. If he could rustle up some bread, he'd be halfway to a grilled cheese sandwich.

The phone on the wall rang and his mother picked it up. She still had the TV blaring in the living room—Greer could hear a talk-show host noisily welcoming Katie Holmes—and right after "Hello," she said "Who?" And then she stood there, in what she called her housecoat—a big wide hunk of cloth in vertical, "slimming" stripes—listening to whatever crap the guy on the phone was no doubt trying to sell her.

Greer elbowed past her and found some cracked-wheat bread in the breadbox.

His mother was still listening to the caller. And then she said, "Yes, I am," in a markedly different tone.

Christ, Greer thought, she's *buying* it, whatever it is.

"I'm very pleased to hear that," she said. "I had no idea."

Greer nudged her to one side so he could put a frying pan on the stove; he thought about just nuking the thing in the microwave, but he wanted that crispy flavor you can only get on the stove. Man, this kitchen—kitchenette, to be more accurate—was small. Once he'd finished shaking down al-Kalli, the first thing he was going to do was move out and find a place of his own.

He poured some oil into the pan, and was just about to put the bread and cheese in, when his mother said, "Yes, he is—I'll put him on. And thank you."

She held out the phone to him, and Greer said, "Who the fuck you talking to?"

She slapped a hand over the receiver and whispered, "Watch your mouth in this house. It's your commanding officer, from Iraq. He was just telling me what a fine soldier you had been there."

Greer stared at the phone as though he'd never seen one before. His commanding officer, from Iraq? He didn't even know who that'd be. Major Bleich? General Schuetz? President Bush?

And why would he be calling here?

The oil in the pan started to sputter, and his mother reached over and turned off the burner, while urging the phone on him with the other hand. "I'll go in the other room and turn off the TV," she said. "And don't you be impolite with him. He might have some work for you."

Greer took the phone and, leaning his weight against the side of the stove, said, "Captain Derek Greer."

There was a pause, then a man with a slight foreign accent—maybe Middle Eastern—said, "Mr. al-Kalli received your letter."

Greer instinctively straightened up.

"And he would like to discuss it with you."

Greer's mind was racing. He'd always thought he'd be prepared for this call, but that was when he'd expected it to come in on his cell phone.

"How'd you get this number?" he finally said.

"Mr. al-Kalli likes to know everything he can about the people he deals with."

Now Greer knew perfectly well why they'd used this number, and why the guy had been chatting up his mother. It was classic technique—come at your enemy from the quarter they don't expect, catch them off guard, and let them know you're already way ahead of them in the game. Greer needed to do something to show that he wasn't thrown off balance.

"This is Jakob, right?" The man he'd given the box to in Iraq. "Glad to see you made it out of that hellhole alive."

"That's right," the man replied. "And yes, that was a very dangerous place." He said it in a friendly enough tone, but Greer still thought it sounded like he was saying, "*This* could be a very dangerous place, too."

There was a silence on the line, and in the apartment,

for that matter; his mother had shut off the TV, and if Greer had to bet, she was eavesdropping on every word he said from her easy chair.

"Why hasn't Mr. al-Kalli himself called?" Greer asked. "He's the one I need to talk to."

"And you will. Would you be free this afternoon?"

Greer knew he didn't have to check his busy schedule— all he had on for today was some physical therapy at the VA, but Indira would be just as glad not to see him there. "Sure. What time?"

"About three? I'll pick you up there."

Alarm bells went off in Greer's head. The last thing he was going to do was get into al-Kalli's car, with this guy driving. If he didn't wind up in the river, he'd be fed to that creature up in Bel-Air. "No, that's not gonna work," Greer said.

"Fine." It sounded like Jakob had known it wouldn't. "What do you suggest?"

Greer had already given this a lot of thought, but he'd never been able to decide on the perfect spot. It had to be public, it had to be outside, and it had to have a lot of people around, no matter what time of day it was. The best he'd been able to come up with was the Santa Monica Pier. At the roller coaster ride. For want of anything better, he suggested it now.

"Three o'clock," Jakob repeated, and then the line went dead.

Greer hung up, and a few seconds later, his mother, who had plainly been listening in, came back and said, "Well? What did he want?"

"They're doing a survey," he said, turning the burner back on. "They want to know how we're adjusting to civilian life."

"No. Really? I couldn't help but overhear you; you were making a plan for later today."

He slapped some cheese between two slices of bread and laid it in the pan. "It's a survey, I told you. Some of it you have to fill out in person."

She still stood there, not believing him.

"That's it, okay?" He tended to the sandwich. "I don't suppose we've got any no-fat pickles around, do we?"

EARLIER THAN HE had to, he left for the rendezvous point. He left his Mustang down below, right near the parking lot exit in case he needed to make a quick getaway, and then walked up and onto the pier. The whole place was one long, noisy, crowded amusement park, lined with arcades and rides and concession stands, and it was, as Greer knew it would be, mobbed with tourists and beachgoers. The roller coaster was out toward the ocean end, and he could hear the screams of the riders even before he saw it. A bunch of kids were already lined up next to the iron railing, waiting for the next run. Right now, the thing was hurtling around a sharp turn just overhead, the wheels clattering loudly on the wooden tracks.

Greer leaned against the railing and started to light a cigarette. He hadn't even put the match down before a lady with a broom and a trash bin on wheels said, "No smoking on the pier."

He took a puff anyway, then ground the cigarette underfoot. She waited till he was done, then swept it up and into the bin—but not before giving him a glare. Goddamn state, Greer thought. You couldn't smoke anywhere anymore. Pretty soon they'd be telling you that you couldn't smoke in your own apartment.

The roller coaster swooped down behind him, and even though this was the place Greer had said al-Kalli should meet him, he moved off a few yards, to the relative shelter of one of those quickie photo booths. A couple of teenagers were inside, and he could tell from their shrieks and cries that the girl was flashing her boobs at the camera while the guy egged her on.

Greer checked his watch; he was still a few minutes ahead of time. He meandered over to the side of the pier and looked out over the ocean. Gulls were idly soaring on the breeze, and you could see Catalina Island, lying like a sleeping beast, on the horizon. Greer had gone there once, when he was a kid; it was a school trip, and he remembered that there were buffalo. The herd had been brought out, a long time ago, when silent movies—westerns—had been shot out there. He remembered wondering, at the time, if he could go back and work as a cowboy there one day. Man, that was a long time ago.

He checked his watch again; he didn't want to be late, but now that he gave it some more thought, it wouldn't look good to be there too early, either. It would make him look too nervous, or eager. He'd been going over his strategy a thousand times—what he was going to say, how he was going to say it. He was going to start off sounding reasonable, reminding al-Kalli of the great job he'd done for him in Iraq, and the grave injuries he'd suffered while doing it. He'd even resolved to make his limp a little more pronounced than usual. But at the same time, he wanted to be sure that he didn't come off as weak or beholden in any way; he wanted al-Kalli to know that he, Captain Derek Greer, was a force to be reckoned with.

At three sharp, he went back to the roller coaster. They were just boarding another bunch. Greer moved out of the way and saw al-Kalli coming toward him, with Jakob close behind. A lot of other people saw him, too, and several stood back to watch him pass. It wasn't often that you saw, out here on the pier, a bald man in a cream-colored linen suit with a scarlet pocket square and gleaming alligator shoes, strolling toward you with an ebony walking stick in one hand.

Even Greer was impressed—which he knew he shouldn't be. The second he started feeling inferior, the game was lost.

"Captain Derek Greer?" al-Kalli said as he approached. He smiled and put out his hand. "A pleasure to meet you at last."

Greer took his hand, and noted that al-Kalli's was cool and dry, while his was warm and damp. Again, not good.

"I hope you haven't been waiting long."

"No, I just got here myself," he said, and when al-Kalli smiled again, Greer thought, *Damn, he knows I just lied.*

Al-Kalli looked around, as if appraising the pier and its attractions. "I've never been here before."

No shit, Sherlock, was what Greer thought. But what was it with this English accent? That night when Greer had crept into the zoo, he'd been too far away to hear what al-Kalli was saying. And though he'd been expecting him to sound like an Arab, or have trouble speaking the language at all, he sounded instead like that guy who played Lawrence of Arabia in the movies.

"Shall we take a look around?" al-Kalli said, as if he actually cared, and before Greer could reply, he'd sauntered off toward some of the other rides. Greer of necessity tagged along, with Jakob, in wraparound shades and a short-sleeved shirt that conveniently revealed his powerful arms, bringing up the rear. Greer wasn't sure how he'd imagined this playing out—maybe the two of them standing over by the ocean railing, speaking softly, in private, while the gulls wheeled above?—but this was definitely not it. Suddenly Greer felt he wasn't in control of the situation at all; worse, he felt like some poor relation who'd foolishly invited a big shot to meet him at some dive.

"Reminds me of a place called Brighton Beach," al-Kalli said. "Ever been to Great Britain, Captain Greer?"

"No, not yet," Greer replied, trying to keep the frustration out of his voice.

"It's just as tacky as this, but it lacks the California sun."

Greer knew that he had to take charge, or else al-Kalli would just keep snowing him with this bullshit. Setting himself squarely in front of al-Kalli, and using the line he had practiced at home, he said, "Have you had time to consider my proposal?"

But at home he had never imagined it getting a laugh. "Why," al-Kalli said, "are we getting married?"

Jakob snorted, too, and Greer felt even more like a fool.

"In business," al-Kalli advised him, "never appear too eager."

Christ, Greer thought, he's giving me blackmail advice. Al-Kalli stopped in front of one of the Skee-Ball booths and watched as a fat kid with a Lakers T-shirt hanging down to his knees rolled ball after ball up the alley.

"You sell yourself short," al-Kalli finally said, without even bothering to look at Greer—who had no idea how to take that remark. How could he have asked for too little? He hadn't even mentioned an actual price in the letter.

"Why stoop to blackmail when you have proven yourself, up until now, so resourceful?"

The kid in the Lakers shirt, unhappy with his final score, kicked the booth and stomped off, brushing past Greer like he wasn't even there. Greer was starting to wonder if the kid was right.

Al-Kalli had moved on, too, strolling with his cane in hand toward the bumper car rink. Greer caught up to him again at the rail.

"I know, for instance, how you gained entrance to my estate," al-Kalli said, his eyes riveted on the bumper cars careening around the course. "And that's been taken care of. But what, precisely, did you see? And how much do you really know? Your letter was somewhat vague on these points."

Now, Greer thought, they were finally getting down to brass tacks. "I saw enough," Greer replied, ever conscious of Jakob hovering just out of earshot.

"Enough for what?"

One of the bumper cars banged up against the rubber wall in front of them, and then got smacked by two others from either side.

Al-Kalli finally turned to face him, and his eyes glittered like beetles in the afternoon sunlight. "You don't seriously believe I would pay you hush money, do you?"

Greer was speechless.

"It would never end. I'd have you showing up with your hand out for the rest of my life." He turned his gaze back toward the bumper cars. "No, I'd much sooner have you killed."

"You could try," Greer said.

Al-Kalli laughed again. "Please, Captain, we both know your car—the green Mustang, with the cracked window, parked by the exit ramp—could easily have been wired by now. I could be done with you by nightfall."

This was not going at all as Greer expected. Maybe he should have mentioned an actual figure in the letter. Maybe al-Kalli thought he was going to be unreasonable, and yes, keep showing up for more money. But Greer wasn't like that; he was a man of his word. If he asked for a million, he'd take the million and then he'd be gone. Hadn't al-Kalli seen, from his actions in Iraq, that he was as good as his word?

"So what are you suggesting?" was all Greer could come up with. He felt that he needed time to fall back and regroup, but he wasn't going to get any.

Al-Kalli was already moving on, toward the video game arcade. The racket emanating from its doors was unbelievable.

"A job."

A what? Greer thought he might not have heard him correctly over the din. "What did you say?"

"Clearly, I need help with my security," al-Kalli conceded. "I've fired the gatekeeper, fired the Silver Bear company, and you, as it happens, are already compromised. I can either employ you or . . ." He shrugged, as if to suggest the Mustang could still blow sky high.

Greer was dumbfounded. He caught Jakob staring at him from a few yards off. Did he know what was going down?

"But you will need to tell me now," al-Kalli said, "so I can make my plans accordingly."

The bells and chimes and buzzers and whistles going off in the video arcade made it hard even to think. But Greer knew he had to.

Al-Kalli started to walk away, idly rapping the end of his walking stick on the wooden boards underfoot. Jakob followed him, and turned toward Greer as he passed him by.

Greer stood where he was, unsure of what to say or do.

They were fifteen or twenty feet away, before Greer, who felt himself suddenly fresh out of options, said, "Okay."

But they didn't stop or turn around, and for all he knew

they hadn't even heard. So he had to swallow his pride and shout, "Okay!" after them.

They were just disappearing around the corner of the next concession, on their way back toward the parking lot.

"Okay!" he shouted again, and a bunch of kids gave him a funny look. "I'll take it!"

CHAPTER TWENTY-EIGHT

*W**E WERE TWENTY-FIVE** days with barely enough food and water to sustain us, and in the dead of night, when we most needed his help, Peter the Hermit fled our camp, with William, Viscount of Melun, known to us as the Carpenter because of the axe he wielded so prodigiously in battle. The next day, the Frankish lord Tancred pursued and recaptured them, and upon their return they were made to give their public oath that they would not again abandon the cause of Christ and our pilgrimage.*

Beth knew that the scribe's account was true; she had checked the standard historical texts, and Peter's desertion was well recorded in the annals of the First Crusade. As was the scribe's account of the siege of Antioch, which immediately followed.

Though the walls of Antioch had been breached, the inner citadel and its defendants still resisted, and we found ourselves besieged in turn by a mighty army led by Kerboga, the Prince of Mosul, and twenty-eight Turkish emirs. We were offered but two choices—servitude or death—and so, under the Banner of Heaven we went forth to meet the enemy. It was in the first hours of that battle that I was

*made prisoner, and while those in my company fell to the
curved blade of the Saracen, I was spared by the Grace of
God and by the peculiar skills of my hand. A commander
of the infidels, judging by my tools that I was capable of
both art and writing, ordered that I be taken not as a prisoner, but as an honored guest, to his palace. It is here that I
write these last words, tomorrow to become but blood sport
in the garden of this dread ruler, once my patron and now
my executioner, the Sultan Kilij al-Kalli.*

Even though she might have expected it, Beth was still
stunned at seeing the al-Kalli name. Mohammed had not
been mistaken; *The Beasts of Eden* had indeed been created, nearly a thousand years before, for one of his direct
ancestors. Despite the remarkable odds against it, it had
been successfully passed down for countless generations
within the family, and preserved in miraculous condition—
though only now, and to her, had it yielded these terrible
secrets.

"Which tie should I wear?" Carter said, coming out of
the closet with two different ones draped around his neck,
and laughed when he saw Beth, still sitting on the edge of
the bed in her underwear, utterly absorbed in the pages.
"You're worse than I am," he said. "You've got to get
dressed or we'll be late."

She heard him, but she just couldn't change her focus
quite yet.

"Beth?" he said. "Earth to Beth? It's six forty-five."

"You won't believe what I just read," she said, and then
she told him about the mention of the Sultan Kilij al-
Kalli's name.

"Mohammed will be glad to hear about it," Carter said,
"if we ever get there."

She laid the printouts on the bed.

"Tie?" he reminded her.

"Oh—the one with the blue stripes."

"Of course, that all depends," he called out from the
bathroom where he'd gone to put on the striped tie, "on
whether or not you decide to tell him about your little
discovery."

That very question had been tormenting Beth; on the one hand, she hadn't yet been able to get the whole thing translated, and she didn't want to share what she had found until she absolutely *knew* what she had found. On the other hand, *The Beasts of Eden* did not belong to her; it belonged to Mohammed al-Kalli, and he had the right to know everything there was to know about it.

She could not put off telling him for very much longer.

She quickly finished dressing—a simple black dress, heels, a strand of pearls her aunt had bequeathed to her—and left Robin with all her final babysitting instructions. Joey was in his playpen, absorbed in his toys. Although they drove to Bel-Air in Beth's car, a white Volvo that was a little newer (and a lot cleaner) than Carter's Jeep, Carter took the wheel and Beth navigated. Once or twice they had to stop and consult their Thomas Guide.

"Dark up here, isn't it?" Carter said, as Beth confirmed that they were to bear to the left, and not the right.

Beth was surprised at it, too. They'd only been in L.A. for less than a year, and nothing so far had taken them into the heady precincts of upper Bel-Air. She felt as if they'd been driving up and away from the rest of the city, from all the ordinary people, like themselves, who led ordinary lives, and she imagined a celebrity or studio head or tycoon of one kind or another behind every towering hedge or shuttered pair of gates.

The houses up here were getting fewer and farther between, and most of the time all you could really see was the tip of a gable, the hint of a roofline, or, now and again, the back fence of a tennis court.

"Al-Kalli's should be at the very crest," Beth said, putting down the map. For the distance of several blocks already, the street had felt more like a private drive, and straight ahead they could now see a lighted gatehouse. As they pulled up, a squat Asian man in a blue uniform checked their name off the invitation list and told them to follow the drive—but slowly. "The peacocks sometimes stand in the road," he said.

"Peacocks?" Carter said to Beth as they drove, slowly, onto the grounds.

And sure enough, there they were—a flock of them, their tail feathers fanned out in a beautiful display of blue and gold, strutting around the lip of a splashing fountain.

"An awfully good replica of the Trevi," Carter said of the ornately sculpted fountain.

"What makes you think it's a copy?" Beth said, and Carter laughed.

"You could be right," he said. "What's next? The Eiffel Tower?"

At the top of the winding drive, in front of a massive stone and timber manor house, a valet in a red jacket stepped into the drive and gestured for them to stop. Another valet materialized out of the dark and swiftly opened Beth's door. Carter could see a dozen other cars lined up neatly in front of a garage wing. All the cars were Bentleys or Jaguars or BMWs, with the lone exception of a dusty green Mustang off at the far end. They were ushered up the front steps and into a spacious, marble-floored foyer, with a wide, winding staircase on both sides; ahead of them they could hear music, and a maid in a white skirt and cap escorted them out to the back garden, where a string quartet in formal attire was playing Brahms under the boughs of a jacaranda tree.

Al-Kalli, spotting them, stepped away from a small group of people and came forward with his hand extended. "I was beginning to fear that you wouldn't make it," he said, and Carter apologized for the delay.

A waiter with a silver tray of filled champagne flutes appeared and al-Kalli handed a glass to each of them. His ruby cuff links glittered in the pale glow of the standing lights that had been positioned here and there in the garden.

"Your house is beautiful," Beth said, and al-Kalli looked up at its mullioned windows and gray stone walls as if taking it in for the first time. "It's a pity you couldn't see our palace in Iraq."

Carter wondered to himself if it was still standing.

"But come and meet the other guests," al-Kalli said, "we'll be going in to dinner soon."

Beth had already noticed several familiar faces, including the wealthy museum patrons the Critchleys and her own boss, Berenice Cabot. The others, an interesting-looking mix of all races and ethnicities, had what appeared to be but one thing in common—money. They all exuded sophistication and style in everything from the cut of their clothes to the way they held themselves. Even as she approached them, she could hear a smattering of accents, a few words in Italian, a mention of the Venice Biennale. Beth and Carter were introduced to everyone as if they, too, were visiting royalty, and as Beth fell into the general conversation—she recognized one of the guests as a board member of the Courtauld Institute, where she had studied in London—she noticed that Carter was drawn off by al-Kalli to meet the one man who seemed not to fit in somehow. He was wearing an ill-fitting suit, and there seemed to be something wrong with his left leg. But then Mrs. Critchley launched into a story about a Mantegna, just on the market, that she thought "someone in Los Angeles really must buy," and Beth had to shift her attention back to the conversation at hand.

"This is Captain Greer," al-Kalli was saying to Carter as he drew the two men aside. "Formerly a member of the United States armed forces in Iraq, he is now in my employ, in charge of security."

Carter started to introduce himself, but the soldier stopped him short. "I know you. You're the paleontologist."

Even al-Kalli looked surprised. Impressed a bit, too.

"I saw you on TV," Greer explained. "You were arguing about Indian artifacts, with some guy named Running Horse."

"I was hoping nobody'd seen that show."

"Sorry—too late. But I can't say I remember your name."

"Carter Cox."

"Yeah, that's it."

Al-Kalli smiled. "Well, now that that's all cleared up, I will leave you two alone for a few minutes. Excuse me."

Why, Carter wondered, was he leaving them alone? Beth was off in the thick of things, and he was now marooned with this ex-army guy. Just looking at him, Carter could tell this guy was in a bad way. His skin had an unhealthy pallor and there was a dull gleam in his eye that Carter had seen before—usually in friends of his who'd burned out in grad school and gotten hooked on one drug or another.

When Captain Greer turned to a passing waiter to put his empty glass on the tray and take a fresh one, Carter noted that when he pivoted, his left leg moved oddly. Carter assumed it was a war injury, and if that was the case, if this was indeed a war vet and al-Kalli had hired him, then that was a point in al-Kalli's favor. Much as Carter had opposed the war, he didn't oppose the vets—that was just one of the myriad cheap and cynical sleights-of-hand the administration had pulled, conflating criticism of the war with criticism of the men and women forced to conduct it. Carter had nothing but respect, and sympathy, for the ones who had had to appear on the front lines.

"How long have you worked for Mr. al-Kalli?" Carter asked.

Greer glanced at his watch. "About twenty-eight hours, give or take."

Carter had to laugh. "Oh, so you don't know a whole lot more about this spread than I do." Carter looked around in all directions, at the back of the huge house, the rows of blossoming trees, the black-bottomed swimming pool, the gazebo—and said, "Just how big is this place?"

Greer shrugged. "I've had the tour, and yeah, there's a lot more to it than you can see from here." He gulped down the champagne the way you would normally drink a Coke. "A lot more." Then, appraising Cox, he said, "What are you doing here? You know al-Kalli?"

"My wife does. She's working on something for him."

"What?"

Carter wasn't used to the bluntness, and he wasn't sure how much to say in reply. "Oh, just a scholarly project."

Greer looked unsatisfied, and Carter thought maybe he was taking his new job as head of security a little too broadly. He also thought he was slugging down the drinks too fast.

A butler in a black tailcoat—Carter had never seen anything like that outside of the movies—moved across the flagstoned courtyard to al-Kalli's side, and then started circulating among the guests. "Dinner is served," he said to Carter and Greer in a low voice, as if it were a state secret, and with one hand gestured toward a pair of French doors that were now opened. Inside, Carter could see a long rectangular table, glittering with silver and china, lighted by flickering candelabra.

"Excuse me," Carter said, "while I go and retrieve my wife," but even as he turned he saw that Beth was being escorted into the dining room on the arm of al-Kalli himself. She cast Carter a confidential glance as she passed—a glance that said, *I'm as much at sea as you are, but I guess we should just go with the flow*—and Greer was the one who laughed now.

"That your wife?"

"Yes."

"Not bad," he said, "and I guess al-Kalli thinks so, too. He gets what he wants."

Carter knew what he was implying, but it didn't bother him. What he was wondering now was how he was going to get through a whole dinner with this guy, who was probably going to get increasingly stoned. Going into the dining room, he was immediately relieved to see that there were neatly written ivory place cards at every chair. He was looking for his own card, when he saw Beth being seated next to al-Kalli at the head of the table. He started to head in that direction, too, when the butler touched his sleeve and said, "The other side, I believe, sir."

For a second, Carter didn't understand, then the butler led him around the table so that he was seated on al-Kalli's right side, directly across from Beth, who was seated at his left. Carter sat down; the butler flipped his napkin open and draped it across his lap. These were sort of the seats of honor, and Carter was, frankly, a little surprised to be sitting in one of them. He and Beth had discussed the dinner invitation—especially its late delivery—and decided that al-Kalli must have invited them as an afterthought, after some prominent guests had dropped out at the last minute. Beth had said al-Kalli was probably going to use the occasion to pump her for information about how fast the translation and restoration work was going, "and maybe even try to instill a little guilt." Carter had figured he'd made the list strictly by virtue of being Beth's husband.

But now it almost looked as if the dinner had been pulled together, indeed on very short notice, as a means of becoming more intimate with the two of them. Al-Kalli was already leaning forward to tell Carter he had only that afternoon read a monograph he had written on the hunting habits of the *Tyrannosaurus rex.*

"Even for a layman," he said, in that upper-crust English accent, "it was a very thought-provoking piece."

"Glad you enjoyed it," Carter said, though he couldn't imagine why al-Kalli would have been reading it. It certainly hadn't been written for the layman; it had been published years before in an obscure scientific journal. "But I didn't know that you were interested in dinosaurs."

"I am," al-Kalli replied. "In fact, I'm interested in many questions of natural history—particularly those involving strange and extinct life forms." With that, he turned his attention to Beth. "Such as those depicted in a certain antique book."

A servant in a white jacket poured some white wine into one of several glasses and goblets at Carter's place.

"How is that coming along?" he asked Beth, and Carter dropped his eyes, lest it be too obvious what he was thinking.

"Very well," she said. "The graphemical database is almost complete."

"Meaning?"

"Meaning we can soon run the entire text against all the characters deployed in the manuscript and get the most accurate and expedited transcript." She did not mention that the process had been somewhat slowed of late by the discovery of a secret epistle, hidden under the front cover of the book, that she had been giving priority to.

"How soon?" he asked, and even though his tone was neutral, Carter could see the urgency in his expression.

"Within the next few days," Beth replied, and Carter hoped, for her sake, that she meant it.

Al-Kalli remained focused on her for a telltale second or two, then raised his glass to his other guests—Carter guessed there were a couple of dozen, with that Captain Greer way down below the salt—and announced, "Thank you all for coming on such short notice. I've been remiss all season, and I didn't want to go another night without seeing my dear friends and enjoying their company."

Mrs. Cabot, Carter thought, was one of his dear friends? That dithery old couple, the Critchleys? To Carter, it looked like a somewhat strange assemblage, with old-moneyed Europeans and South Americans, a few Middle Eastern types (one in the traditional Arab headdress), that new security chief, and of course, himself. But, taking the charitable view, maybe it displayed an admirably democratic streak in his host.

Though he doubted it.

The meal itself consisted of more courses than Carter had ever been served at one time, many of them with a distinctively Middle Eastern flavor. Al-Kalli was often explaining the ingredients and preparation to them—"Have you ever tried *fesenjan?* It's walnuts, sautéed in a pomegranate sauce" or "This is called *karafs*—seasoned with parsley, celery, mint, and other herbs—and my cook is the only one in America who knows how to make it properly." Carter had to take his word for that, never having had it before, and never, to be honest, likely to have it again. The food, he could tell, was exquisitely prepared, and most of the other guests were clearly enjoying it immensely—the man in the Arab headdress kept beaming at al-Kalli, and once bowed his head deferentially, with his eyes closed in bliss—but to Carter, whose palate was more accustomed to fast food and backyard barbecues, it was all pretty much off the charts.

Beth, however, seemed to be liking it—when it came to cuisine, she'd always been more adventurous than her husband—and all the emphasis on vegetables and yogurt and exotic herbs would, he knew, be dear to her heart. She believed in eating healthfully, and she had always contended that there were ways to do that without sacrificing the enjoyment that Carter claimed he could only experience from an ice-cold beer and a red-hot slice of greasy, New York pizza.

Carter remained unpersuaded.

When Beth wasn't talking to al-Kalli, she was talking to the man on her left, a distinguished, silver-haired gent who appeared to have some relation to the Courtauld Institute of Art. Perhaps that was why al-Kalli had seated him next to Beth. Which did not explain why Carter had, on his own right side, an heiress from Texas who strongly believed that "if everybody's so positive about the theory of evolution"—with a drawn-out emphasis on the word "theory"—"then why are they so afraid to teach Intelligent Design?" Because she had learned Carter was a scientist, she waited for her challenge to be refuted. And for a second, he almost did rise to the bait. He almost launched into an explanation of the difference between science and faith, between evidence and supposition, between the empirical and the assumed, between Darwin and the Bible, before reminding himself that he was off duty now, and that, no matter what you said anyway, nobody's mind was ever changed.

"Why not indeed?" he said, and eagerly turned, though he'd never imagined such a day would come, to al-Kalli for his conversation. However sinister the man might seem, he was at least well educated and urbane. And waiting. He seemed as eager to talk to Carter as Carter was to escape the idiocy of the Texas heiress. Was this all part of al-Kalli's clever design, too—seating him next to a buffoon, so he wouldn't have anywhere else to turn?

"In several of your papers," al-Kalli said, "you outlined your beliefs in the common ancestry of dinosaurs and modern-day birds. I found your arguments interesting—and not always in agreement with others in your field."

"No, I'm not always in agreement."

"But then, why haven't you drawn it all together into a book? You write compellingly, and you seem to have a rare knowledge of the animal kingdom, both past and present. Has it been for want of time?"

Carter had to mull that one over. He had written a number of published papers and monographs, and he had considered—virtually every day—undertaking a major synthesis of his views, but to some extent al-Kalli was right. Carter hadn't found the time—or more specifically, the money that would support him and his budding family—for the many months (years?) that it would take to compose and publish such a book.

"Because if finding the freedom to work on what you want is a problem, perhaps we can discuss that later."

Carter didn't know what he was getting at.

"My family does run a foundation—we never advertise its existence—to help with certain projects we find provocative or intriguing."

A servant refilled the last wineglass Carter had been drinking from. Carter took the interruption to think. "Thanks very much for your interest," he said to al-Kalli. With the way things were going with Gunderson at the Page Museum, he might be taking him up on it. "I'll keep it in mind."

"You do that." Al-Kalli signaled the butler, had a few words in his ear, then stood up at the head of the table and declared that dessert would be served in the garden, "along with a small musical diversion."

On the way out, Carter was able to sidle up to Beth and ask in a low voice if Robin needed to be relieved soon.

"No, she said she can stay as long as we need. If it's too late, she'll just sleep over."

Carter had sort of been hoping it *would* be a problem, and that he'd be able to use this excuse to leave early. Dinner parties weren't his favorite pastime, but if Beth was having a good time—and it looked like she was—then he'd find a way to stick it out. Even if it meant—as all indications were pointing to—sitting through a string quartet concert under the stars. The musicians were gathered in a semicircle on the edge of the courtyard, just where the stones gave way to the manicured green lawn. Little round tables had been set up, with long flowing linen cloths, and tiny white lights had been threaded artfully through the overhanging branches of the jacaranda trees. Thankfully, there were no place cards in evidence here, so he wouldn't be stuck with the Texas creationist again.

He was just guiding Beth to two seats at a table with the Critchleys (better the devil you know) when al-Kalli touched him by the elbow and drew him aside. Captain Greer, Carter noted, was standing a few feet away.

"I'm wondering if you would mind forgoing the concert," al-Kalli said, "so that I might share something—something terribly important—with you."

Skipping the concert was fine with Carter. He told Beth he'd be back shortly, and then followed al-Kalli into the porte cochere, where he found a four-seater golf cart waiting, and Jakob, whom he'd once seen at the Getty, at the wheel. Greer sat up front, perhaps so that he'd have more room for his bad leg, and Carter got in back with al-Kalli. Carter knew they weren't going golfing, but other than that, he was completely mystified.

As the cart took off along a graveled pathway, Carter could hear the opening strains of a classical piece that sounded, even to his musically untrained ear, like Mozart. The music wafted through the warm night air, growing fainter as they passed out of sight of the house. The cart rumbled over a wooden footbridge, past a stable where Carter could see an Arab boy leading a docile horse back into its stall. Just how vast was this estate? Carter wondered again.

They continued along, parallel to what was plainly a service drive, until they saw, emerging from a thick copse of trees, what looked to Carter like a white airplane hangar. Did al-Kalli keep his own private air force? It wouldn't have surprised him at this point.

Jakob steered the golf cart into a clearing within a few yards of the huge double door, then stopped it. He remained seated, as did Captain Greer, but al-Kalli got out and gestured for Carter to come with him. He walked off, taking a gold cigarette case from the breast pocket of his suit jacket. He held it out to Carter, who declined.

"Of course you're right," al-Kalli said, lighting one nonetheless. "It's a nasty habit, but I can't entirely give it up. And these I have specially made for me in Tangier."

He drew on the cigarette, his eyes narrowing but remaining firmly fixed on Carter. Then he exhaled, the fragrant smoke—it smelled to Carter less like tobacco than cloves and cinnamon—spiraling above their heads. "I pray I do not live to regret what I am about to do."

At first, Carter thought he must be joking—was he referring to having the cigarette?—but then he felt a sudden chill. Al-Kalli was referring to something else, and he wasn't joking.

"Then maybe you shouldn't do it," Carter replied. "Why take the chance?"

"Because I must trust someone. And I believe I can trust you."

Why he would think that—having spent no more than a few hours, total, in his company—Carter couldn't guess. Any more than he could guess what al-Kalli was contemplating.

"What I am about to tell you, you can never tell anyone. What I am about to show you, you cannot show to anyone else. Unless—and until—I advise you otherwise. First of all, is that understood?"

Carter hated to agree to anything so vague, and al-Kalli noted his hesitation. "Please do not fear—I am not running a white slavery ring or planning a terrorist attack. On the contrary, no one owes more to this country than I do. But will you give me your word, as one gentleman to another?"

"Yes," Carter replied. Although he hated to admit it, his curiosity had been piqued.

Al-Kalli nodded, drawing again on the cigarette. "You won't be sorry," he said. "Indeed, you will be very grateful that you did."

Carter doubted that, but kept quiet, waiting for more.

"I have in my possession, as you will soon see, the most remarkable collection in the world."

Collection of what?

"Walk with me a bit."

As they strolled beneath the boughs of the trees, along the winding gravel path, Carter caught glimpses, now and then, of the twinkling lights of the city, far, far below and way off in the distance. He was glad that he could see the lights because it rooted him in reality even as al-Kalli told him a story too fantastical to believe. A story that, had any-one else tried to palm it off on him, he would have dis-missed out of hand. But coming from al-Kalli, it had to be taken seriously—and even so, it was nearly impossible to credit.

For time immemorial, al-Kalli explained, his family had owned a menagerie. Or, as he called it, a bestiary.

"Yes, Beth has told me about *The Beasts of Eden*. She says it's the most astounding illuminated manuscript she's ever seen."

Al-Kalli paused. "It's not the book I'm speaking of. It's the actual bestiary; the book is merely a . . . guide."

Now Carter was confused. The book, so far as he knew, contained pictures and text describing such imaginary creatures as griffins and gorgons, phoenixes and basilisks. Medieval inventions, allegorical motifs. What was al-Kalli saying? Did he own a bunch of poor mutant animals, two-headed calves and three-legged ponies and other unfortu-nate creatures salvaged from traveling circuses?

"The animals in my care exist nowhere else. They have not existed for eons, if you believe the standard wisdom." He snorted. "If you believe the standard wisdom, most of them have never existed at all."

Carter began, for the first time, to question al-Kalli's sanity, and his own safety. Was he taking a moonlight stroll, with two hired thugs in a golf cart not far off, in the company of a lunatic billionaire?

Even if al-Kalli sensed his doubts, he went on as if he knew they would eventually be silenced. The animals had been carefully tended to, and bred, in the desert palaces his family owned not only in present-day Iraq, but in other remote regions of the Middle East—"most notably the Empty Quarter, as it is known, of the Sahara Desert." But with all the geopolitical changes in the region, "and of course the rise of Saddam Hussein, the situation gradually became untenable." The al-Kalli family had forged an unholy truce with the dictator that had held for many years, but in the end, Saddam's greed and lust for ultimate and unchallenged power had led to its unraveling. Without providing much in the way of detail, al-Kalli alluded to a catastrophe inflicted on his family, and a sudden, costly exodus. "What I was able to save of the bestiary, I saved. But you will soon see for yourself."

"Why?" Carter asked. "Why me?"

"Because who else on earth could understand, could appreciate, such a miracle?"

Carter was flattered, but still unsure what to make of any of this.

"But first," Al-Kalli said, "I know I have to convince you that I'm not mad."

Carter saw no point in protesting.

"I know what you're thinking, and I would think so, too." He dropped the cigarette butt on the gravel and ground it underfoot. "So, shall I prove my case?"

Carter glanced over at Jakob and Captain Greer, who were conferring in front of the doors to the hangar—or zoo, Carter suddenly thought—and considered his options. He could refuse, but what kind of a position would that leave him in? Al-Kalli would consider his own position already compromised, and might now regard Carter as a potential threat. And it certainly wouldn't help out Beth, whose access to *The Beasts of Eden* might suddenly be restricted or even revoked. On the other hand, if he were to accept al-Kalli's invitation, he would be entering into some sort of complicity with him—and al-Kalli didn't strike him as the kind of man who let you out of a deal very easily.

Al-Kalli waited, and in the distance Carter could hear the screeching cry of one of the peacocks. Maybe that was it—maybe al-Kalli thought peacocks were phoenixes.

Maybe he had a crocodile in his zoo and thought it was a sphinx. Maybe he had a snow white horse and called it a unicorn. Maybe all of this was some long-inculcated family delusion, and all Carter would have to do, once he'd passed through those sealed doors, was feign astonishment and swear a bond of eternal secrecy. How hard could that be?

And, if he were perfectly honest with himself, it would satisfy his own gnawing desire to know the truth. It was like some fairy tale now. What *was* hidden in Ali Baba's mountain cave?

"Okay, you're on," Carter said with a lightheartedness he did not feel.

Al-Kalli nodded in the direction of Jakob and Greer, and as he walked Carter toward the facility, the doors swung smoothly open, just as if someone had indeed muttered "Open, Sesame."

As Carter passed inside, powerful blowers overhead made his clothes flutter around his body; his hair felt like a thousand fingers were mussing it all at once. The air being expelled had the strong odor of musk and fur and dung on it. And the moment they were all inside, the doors swung shut again.

Jakob and Greer stood off to one side, as Carter took it all in. Al-Kalli, right behind him, whispered, "Not a word—even to your wife—of what you see here tonight."

Right now, Carter was just taking in the sheer size and scope of the place. The ceiling had to be a hundred feet high, and hanging just below it was a straw-covered aerie on a heavy chain. It was shaped like a huge shallow bowl, and it was swaying now, as if something had just launched itself from the perch. Carter scanned the roofline and though he saw nothing, he heard the grating cry of a swooping bird. He whirled around, just in time to see a red and gold blur, with a wingspan twice as great as a condor's, soaring over his head.

It was like no other bird he had ever seen—and al-Kalli could tell as much, from nothing more than the stunned look on Carter's face.

"There's more," he said confidingly.

Carter was still gazing up as al-Kalli guided him toward the western wall. Carter glanced at the two guards. Jakob appeared alert but unperturbed. Captain Greer, on the other hand, looked even jumpier than ever. Hadn't he told Carter that he'd only been working for al-Kalli for twenty-eight hours? If that was true, then all of this was nearly as new and shocking to him as it was to Carter.

All along this side of the building there was a shoulder-high concrete wall, painted white and surmounted by iron bars that rose at least another ten or twelve feet into the air. From behind the wall Carter could hear strange snuffling sounds, barks and grunts, and the occasional roar. He approached it cautiously, wondering what on earth could lie behind it. The first pen—there were several, each about a hundred feet apart—had a narrow chain-mesh gate, and then another gate, about a yard inside, so that together they formed a little sealed compartment; an extra security measure, Carter surmised, to allow someone to enter the pen—for feeding or observation purposes—without permitting whatever was imprisoned here any chance of a sudden escape.

But at first he saw nothing that could escape—only a wading pond, with fresh, clear water in it and several lily pads floating idly on its surface. The floor of the pen, rolling and uneven, was covered everywhere with a layer of broken rubble, pebbles and stones colored gray and green and rust. It looked like an immense mosaic, the pattern of which could only have been discerned by rising forty or fifty feet into the air and looking down. When Carter turned to ask al-Kalli where the inhabitants were, he saw that Jakob, his arm fully extended, was holding out to him a pair of plastic goggles. Al-Kalli himself was hanging well back.

Carter took the goggles.

"You might want to put them on," al-Kalli said, "just in case."

Carter did, though he could not, for the life of him, see why. He stepped back into the gated enclosure and looked again into the huge pen. Maybe a hundred yards in the rear, there was a shaded enclosure, but even there he could see nothing but shadows and gloom. What was he supposed to see? Was al-Kalli so deluded that he kept imaginary creatures in gigantic, empty cages?

But the bird, the bird he'd seen was real.

He studied the rock-strewn floor again, and this time he could see just one thing strange—a blurring above some of the stones. At first, thinking it was the goggles, he took them off, breathed on them, then wiped them clean with his handkerchief. They were a sturdy pair with a snug elastic strap, but when he put them back on, the blurring continued. In fact, he saw it now in another spot. Were there steam grates, or vents of some kind, under the rocks?

"It's not the goggles," he heard al-Kalli say.

And then, as if it were some optical illusion, the rocks themselves moved—but not randomly, as if they were being disturbed, but as if they were alive and integrated. He blinked several times, adjusted the goggles, but the rocks now were rising up, in not one but two separate places, and they were . . . standing. The fogging recurred. What was he looking at?

And what was looking back at him?

There were eyes behind the fog, sinister eyes that held steady under a thick, gray brow. There were two creatures, on all fours now, their entire bodies—perhaps six or even eight feet long—covered with spikes and stony protuberances, exactly like the rocks they'd been lying on. The noises they made, as they lumbered in his direction, were wet and hoarse and rasping. The one in the lead—like a gravel pit come to terrible life—raised its head, coughed, and, like a hail of bullets, the spittle splatted against the wall, clung to the bars of the gate, and dotted the lenses of the goggles. Carter fell back, wiping away the gray-green smear, in shock.

He could hear al-Kalli and Jakob chuckling.

"They used to be quite accurate," al-Kalli said. "Like cobras, they aim for the eyes."

Carter stumbled out of the gated enclosure and whipped

the goggles off altogether. Some of the mucus was stuck to his cheek, where it stung like a bad sunburn. Jakob handed him a hand towel.

"What is it?" Carter said, wiping away the gunk from his face.

Al-Kalli said, "I'm sure you scientists would have your own name for it. But in my family, we have always called it the basilisk."

The basilisk? Carter thought. That was a mythical creature—not the thing he had just seen walking toward him with slow, deliberate steps, the thing that even now was just a few yards away, behind a concrete wall. Basilisks were . . . he struggled to remember his mythology . . . creatures so monstrous their breath alone could kill.

"Are you beginning to believe me?" al-Kalli asked.

As if in mockery, the huge red bird, alighted now on the lip of its aerie, let out a stuttering cry that echoed down and around the cavernous walls of the bestiary.

"Shall we move on?" al-Kalli said. "We have only so much time before the concert is over and my other guests have finished with their dessert and coffee."

The entire menagerie was awake now and making itself heard. The basilisks were grunting and snorting—Carter wondered if there were more in there than the two he had seen—and as he was led toward the next double gate, he wondered if he should be putting the goggles back on.

"No," al-Kalli said, intuiting his question, "you won't be needing those again." Carter handed them to Jakob, while Captain Greer, his limp more noticeable now, brought up the rear. Reluctantly, it looked to Carter.

"But you may wish to stay back a bit from the bars," al-Kalli warned.

Carter did as instructed, and stepped only halfway into the next gate enclosure. This pen was as large as the one next to it, easily a couple of hundred feet in every direction, but where the first one had been barren and stony, this one was lush and filled with thick shrubbery and flowering plants. There was a dense carpet of weedy grass, speckled with dandelions. Fans in the ceiling directed a steady low breeze at the greenery, so that everything seemed to be in constant motion, gently undulating, swaying and waving in a delicate play of light and shadow . . . a play that was suddenly broken by a ferocious growl and a headlong rush at the bars. Carter barely had time to step back before a spotted beast, the size of a lion, had flown at the gate, its claws scrabbling at the iron bars. He had not seen it coming; he had no idea where it had even come from. It was as if it had launched itself from the lower branches of one of the ficus trees planted in the pen.

The creature snarled, its head back, and Carter saw a pair of fangs to rival those of any saber-toothed cat. But these fangs, even in his present state, he recognized were curved backward, like scimitars. The creature slipped down from the bars and stepped back, planting its paws flatly on the ground, the way a man, not a cat, might walk. Its claws were like twisted fingers, long and sharp and yellowed. Its forelegs were longer than its rear, so that it had the hunched look of a hyena, but a hyena with wings. Its massive shoulders were blanketed with a thick matt of feathery black fur, fur that right now, in the moment of its attack, had billowed out like a cape.

Again, Carter was thunderstruck.

"The griffin," al-Kalli said simply, brushing back his ruby cuff link to glance at his watch. "There is just one more—"

But they were interrupted by a man's voice, filled with fear and worry, carrying toward them. Al-Kalli looked displeased.

"Mr. al-Kalli, Mr. al-Kalli," the man was calling, barely able to catch his breath, "why didn't you tell me you were coming? If only you had told me you were coming!"

The man, a reedy Arab in an open lab coat, who looked like he had just fallen out of bed, came panting up to them. Carter noticed Captain Greer glancing at his new boss, as if wondering how this should be handled.

"You weren't needed, Rashid," al-Kalli said, and it was

as if he'd struck the man in the face. His features froze, but then, taking in the sight of Carter—this stranger in his domain—he composed himself again.

"This is Dr. Cox," al-Kalli explained, and Rashid nodded his head quickly. "He will be helping us."

"Helping us?" Rashid mumbled. "With the . . . animals?" He glanced at Carter with panic. "Are you a doctor, sir, of the veterinary sciences?"

"I'm a paleontologist," he replied.

It looked as if it took Rashid a few seconds to process that information—and after he had, he looked just as perplexed.

"Come along, Dr. Cox," al-Kalli said, turning toward the last gate at the far end of the facility, and striding off. "You have yet to see the pièce de résistance."

Carter, and the rest of the entourage, followed in al-Kalli's brisk footsteps and at the last gate, al-Kalli himself stepped into the gated enclosure. "This," al-Kalli said, leaving room for Carter to step in, too, "is the oldest and most prized of our collection."

It was resting now, half in and half out of an enormous rocky cave raised several feet above the dirt. It lifted its massive, scaly snout, its long, leathery tongue flicking dismissively at the air. Its yellow eyes stared coldly across the vast expanse of the pen.

"The manticore," al-Kalli intoned. "It's a corruption of an ancient Persian word for man-eater."

But Carter hardly heard him. He was looking at a creature more ancient than the dinosaurs . . . a reptile . . . and a mammal . . . a beast whose bones were the paleontologist's Holy Grail. It was a monster that had ruled the earth a quarter of a billion years ago, the *T. rex* of its day . . . the most ruthless and successful predator of the Paleozoic era . . . wiped off the face of the earth in the Permian extinction . . . and named after the terrible sisters of Greek mythology who were so frightening that simply to look upon them was to die.

And now he was looking right at it.

Not, as al-Kalli would have it, the manticore of legend. Not some mythical beast.

But what paleontologists had dubbed—based on a scattering of bones and teeth, some of the oldest and rarest fossils on earth—the gorgonopsian. Or gorgon, for short.

But these bones were walking, these teeth were wet, and these eyes radiated a malevolence as old as the earth itself.

CHAPTER TWENTY-NINE

SADOWSKI HAD PARKED the car a few hundred yards down the street from the gatehouse, where the low overhanging branches of a California live oak provided extra shadow. He'd been sitting there for over three hours, and every once in a while he'd been able to hear the sound of violin music being carried on the wind. But the music had stopped, and Sadowski began to hope the party would be breaking up soon.

In his lap, he had a map of greater L.A., folded open to the west side. There were little red Xs wherever he and Burt had decided would be good places to start. Several of the Xs were located right up around here, and Sadowski chose, on his own, to add a couple more. When he lowered his head, the night-vision goggles, strapped to the top of his head, teetered, and he had to flip the scope back up again.

He also had to take a leak.

He was just about to get out of the car when he saw the front gate to al-Kalli's estate swing open, and a gleaming Rolls, one of the old-fashioned kind, emerge. He pushed the map to the passenger seat, dropped the goggles, and lowered himself in the seat. The Rolls drove slowly past him, down the hill, with an old man in an Arab headdress sitting in the backseat.

Man, Sadowski thought, *I could take him out so easily.*

A few seconds later, a Jaguar convertible followed, with a sleek couple already arguing about something in what sounded like Italian.

Sadowski wondered if he should look into some audio surveillance equipment, too. Now that he wasn't working for Silver Bear anymore—now that that asshole Greer had gotten him shit-canned by sneaking around behind his back, showing up at the gatehouse with a fucking black-mail letter (oh yeah, he couldn't wait to tell him about everything Reggie, the gatekeeper who'd also been canned, had filled him in on)—now that he might be setting up a se-curity business on his own, well, he might have to invest in some more stuff. Wasn't that the kind of thing, though, that you could, what was it, claim as a deduction?

A few more cars came by, including an old white Volvo—definitely out of keeping with the Rolls and Bent-ley and Jaguar parade—with a tall, young guy at the wheel, who looked vaguely familiar, and in the passenger seat a very good-looking brunette, who instantly took his mind off the guy; she was turned toward the driver, smiling and saying something. Very fuckable indeed. Sadowski flashed on Ginger Lee; after he'd settled with you-know-who, he'd have to make a stop at the Bayou.

He was beginning to give up hope—had his information been wrong?—when he finally saw the beaten-up green Mustang approach the gate; actually, he heard it first, the muffler rumbling. The car lurched out of the gate and started down past Sadowski's car. The Silver Bear patrol unit was of course a thing of the past; now he was driving his own car, a Ford Explorer SUV that he was already two lease payments behind on. Buy American. But at least Greer wouldn't spot this car; he'd never even seen it.

As soon as Greer had passed, Sadowski swept the in-frared goggles off his head, put the Explorer into gear, and did a quick U-turn. Up toward the top of the hill, he hadn't had to worry about any private patrol cars; it was all Mohammed al-Kalli's property up there, and after firing Silver Bear, the Arab had been too wary to hire any other firm; as a result, nobody would be checking up on his perimeters. Down here, though, the patrol cars were making their usual rounds. Sadowski was passed by one from Bel-Air Patrol, one from Guardian, and even one from Silver Bear. He recognized the Silver Bear guy; he was a new recruit, very gung ho. Tonight, Sadowski was minding his own business, but on the next trip up here he'd have to make sure he got past these guys without being noticed at all.

Following Greer was easy. For one thing, he had no reason to believe he was being tailed; for another, he usually made the same rounds. The VA, the Bayou, sometimes a bar on Normandie, the apartment he shared with his mother. How the hell, Sadowski wondered, did he deal with *that*? He'd met Greer's mom once or twice, and if he'd had to live with her, he'd have had the old lady put down long ago.

But as they traveled down Sunset, Sadowski was able to rule out a couple of destinations—the bar, the Bayou. They kept heading west—Sadowski was surprised that Greer's heap was able to make the time it did—and he was starting to wonder where they were going. He'd already made plans in his head, ways that he could get the drop on Greer, catch him off guard and maybe even throw the fear of God into him. He was gonna catch him in the garage of his apartment building, going up in that crappy little elevator, or at the Bayou, maybe literally with his pants down. But now he'd have to improvise—and that had never been his strong suit.

At Bundy, Greer got in the left turn lane, and though Sadowski hated to do it, he had to wait in the turning lane right behind him as the oncoming traffic passed. He knew he was sitting higher up than Greer, and his windows were tinted, and he was slouching down in the seat, but this was just the kind of maneuver that his mail-away PI course had warned him against. You were always supposed to leave another car between you and the mark.

Not only that, Greer waited all the way through the yellow light—even though there were no more oncoming cars—before gunning it through the red. Sadowski had no choice but to gun his own car through, too, and a guy heading south gave him a blast on his horn. Oh, how Sadowski missed his patrol car; nobody'd ever honked at that.

And now he was wondering if Greer had made him after all. He purposely lay way back, let a Domino's delivery car get between them, and put on his night-vision goggles at traffic lights so that he could see ahead and make sure Greer's car was still in range. These goggles, the Excalibur Generation III, had built-in IR-LED and state-of-the-art automatic brightness control; he'd initially balked at the heavy price tag—over three grand—but they'd definitely been worth it. And they were way better than anything he'd been issued in Iraq.

Sadowski rolled down his window; the sound of Greer's shitty muffler made it even easier to tail him. And this late at night, the heat of the day had completely abated, and it was actually kind of cool out. It also looked like Greer was heading for the ocean. At the bottom of San Vicente, he turned left and Sadowski followed him all the way down Ocean Boulevard to the parking areas for the Santa Monica Pier. What the fuck was he doing here? Going for a ride on the Ferris wheel?

Sadowski pulled into a spot two rows over and waited for Greer to head for the stairs that led up to the pier. He considered confronting him right here, in the parking lot, but there were about a dozen spics partying around a new Cadillac Escalade. (How the hell did these wetbacks get the money for cars like that? Sadowski'd priced it himself, and even the lease payments were sky high.) No, he'd have to find a spot up top, on the pier somewhere, and maybe that wasn't such a bad idea, after all. Even though he'd only received the first couple of lessons for his PI course, it had said you should never cut a promising surveillance short. "Good things come to he who waits," it had said. And maybe Greer was going to lead Sadowski to a good thing now.

Or maybe it was just a new drug connection.

Greer was hobbling along, and trying to get a cigarette lighted in the stiff ocean breeze. His leg looked bad to Sadowski, and for a second he wondered if he'd taken a beating from al-Kalli or one of his men. But then why would he have been at that party? No, there was something else going down.

The pier, as always, was crowded. A live band, playing that New Orleans kind of zydeco crap, was wailing away on a makeshift stage and the video game parlor was jammed, with bells clanging and buzzers buzzing. Everybody was out enjoying the cooler ocean air. The hot, dry weather, and the drought, just made you want to hang out anywhere near the water. Of course, Sadowski and the Sons of Liberty were probably the only guys in L.A. who wanted the weather to continue just as it had been—at least for a few more days. "The less rain, the less to explain," was how Burt had put it at the last planning meeting. Burt had a real way with words.

Greer was moving slowly through the crowd, and out toward the roller coaster end of the pier. At one point, a cop on a bicycle pulled up and made him put out his cigarette. At another, Greer stopped and turned all the way around to watch a very hot girl in a frilly pink skirt go by: Sadowski just had time to duck behind a concession stand.

Greer started walking again, and Sadowski, who'd been out on the pier a few times—Ginger had insisted on seeing it right after she'd come to L.A.—knew that he could cut through the snack area and still catch up with Greer by the roller coaster.

But when he came around the corner, he saw no sign of him. There were lots of people in line for the roller coaster, which was thundering overhead and swooping down into a hairpin turn. A bunch of kids were screaming their heads off. But Sadowski still couldn't find Greer. Son of a bitch, had he doubled back? Or maybe he *had* come out here to hook up with someone—but where? Sadowski, who was taller than almost everyone around him, stood up on his tiptoes, brushed a couple of shorter guys out of his way—one of them looked like he wanted to start something, but his friend took a good look at Sadowski and pulled him out of harm's way—and came up empty. Shit. What did his PI course say to do when you temporarily lost track of your target?

Sadowski turned and was just passing one of those photo booths when a hand reached out, grabbed him by the back of the collar, and dragged him inside. He was off balance, too, and felt himself shoved down onto the little metal bench in front of the camera so hard the whole booth rocked.

Greer, swinging the curtain shut, said, "You are the worst fucking detective in the world."

Sadowski tried to get up, and Greer, leaning over him, shoved him back down again. There was barely room in the booth to breathe.

"You want to see me, why don't you just call my cell?"

"Fuck you," Sadowski said. "And the camel you rode in on."

"Now what," Greer said, "is that supposed to mean?" Sadowski's stupidity had always amazed and, to some extent, amused him.

"You know what it means. You and your party pal, Mohammed al-Kalli." Sadowski only knew so much, and he had to use it sparingly. The PI course said you could find out much more that way. "Did he pay you off tonight? Is that why you were up there?"

"I was up there, dipshit, because I'm working for him now."

"You're what?"

"I'm his head of security."

Now Sadowski laughed. "Yeah, and I'm . . . I'm King Kong."

Greer shook his head ruefully. "You just might be." He swept the curtain open. "You sure smell bad enough."

Greer stepped out of the booth and wandered over toward the wooden rail. Instinctively, he started to reach for a cigarette, then remembered. He could hear Sadowski, his ego bruised, shuffling up behind him. Greer had spotted the Ford Explorer that was following him almost immediately, and when he'd waited at that traffic light on Bundy, then gunned his way through at the last second, he knew he was right. But he hadn't been sure who was driving it. His first thought was Jakob. Even though al-Kalli had co-opted him and put him on the payroll, Greer wasn't sold at all. The whole thing was just too damn fishy. Why would anybody hire him? He wouldn't. He'd taken the thousand-dollar down payment on his salary, he'd come to the party, but he'd been watching his back. And he wasn't about to stop.

"You're not seriously working for that Arab piece of shit?" Sadowski said.

Greer leaned down and rubbed a little feeling back into his leg. He'd been standing on it too long tonight.

"Because if you are, you owe me a cut."

"Why would that be?"

"You wouldn't have known diddly-squat if I hadn't told you. You wouldn't have known he was up there, you wouldn't have gotten past the gate, you wouldn't have seen all those animals you told me about. The weird ones that supposedly ate a guy."

That was something that Greer did regret. He should never have shot off his mouth that night; he'd just been so shocked by what he'd seen, and what had happened, that he'd let it spill. And that, he knew, was never a good idea.

"Yeah, well, it turns out I might have been just a little bit high that night."

"What?" Sadowski was very suspicious.

"My meds needed some adjusting."

"You telling me now that what you said was bullshit?"

"Wouldn't be the first time."

Sadowski was getting twisted into a pretzel, wondering whether to believe what he was saying now or what he had said back then. Besides being his commanding officer, Greer had always been a slippery fuck. To this day, Sadowski suspected he'd been shortchanged for his part in the mission outside Mosul.

"I don't give a shit if it's true or not." Sadowski had come to a realization. "Reggie told me about your little shakedown action, and that's what got my ass fired. In fact, Silver Bear's starting to look back at all the other robberies that went down on houses I had the specs to. I could be in deep shit, Greer."

Greer always noticed when Sadowski dropped the instinctive "Captain"; he'd been doing it a lot lately.

But maybe he had a point, and Greer was feeling generous tonight. After all, he still had the thousand bucks, in cash, that Jakob had given him. He reached into his pants pocket, took out his paper-clipped wad, and peeled off a couple of hundred-dollar bills. He slapped them into Sadowski's hand, but Sadowski just kept staring at the wad that remained.

A couple of tourists, eating cotton candy, strolled past them.

"How much did he give you?" Sadowski said. "My cut is half."

"Since when?"

"From now on."

Greer should have seen it coming. But that didn't make it any easier to take. Something in him just kind of turned over, and he thought, *Better put a stop to this right here, or else it'll never stop.* Nor did he miss the irony of being shaken down on the very spot where he had brought al-Kalli for the same purpose. He looked out over the railing toward the dark ocean water surging below the pilings of the pier. From where they were standing, the drop had to be fifteen or twenty feet.

"That's how it's going to be?" Greer said, reaching down as if to rub his bad leg again.

"You got it."

And then he grabbed hold of both of Sadowski's pants legs and with one big heave lifted him up and over the railing. Sadowski made a desperate but futile grab for the railing as he went over, and plummeted headfirst, screaming all the way, into the water. There was a huge splash, and as the cotton candy couple turned to see what had just happened, Greer shouted, "Call the cops! A guy just jumped off the pier!"

He hobbled off, as if frantically looking for help, while the couple craned their necks over the railing. "Look," he heard the man say, "there is somebody in the water!"

Greer's only regret was the two hundred bucks.

CHAPTER THIRTY

EITHER CARTER WAS in an unusually amorous mood—breathing hard on her face and licking her hand—or it was Champ, anxious to go out.

Beth raised her head from the pillow—it felt heavier than normal—and glanced at the clock; it was later than normal, too. Nine forty-five in the morning.

Champ was standing beside the bed, his tail wagging back and forth as regularly as a metronome.

"Okay, I'm up." For a second, Beth wondered why Carter hadn't let him out, but then she glanced at Carter's side of the bed and she could tell he'd hardly been in it. After they'd come home from the party last night, she'd gone straight up to bed and Carter had stayed downstairs. "Something I've got to work on," he'd said before disappearing into the garage, where boxes of their books were still stacked against the walls.

Beth sat up, and she felt like something had just shifted inside her head. At al-Kalli's party, she'd had more to drink than she customarily did. It had become so hard to keep track. Every time she took a sip from one of her wineglasses, or cordial glasses later on in the garden, some servant had stepped up and silently refilled it. And the array of wines and spirits had been wide.

"Carter?" she asked aloud, hoping for an answer. Her voice came out as more of a croak than common, even for first thing in the morning. And there was no answer.

She slipped her feet into her flip-flops, pulled on her robe, and went to check on Joey. Who was lying on his back, eyes open, smiling up at her. Was this the best baby ever? she thought. She'd heard so many horror stories about colic, and crying, and parents who hadn't been able to get a decent night's sleep in months. But she'd experienced none of that. If it was this easy, she'd definitely have a couple more.

After washing up, she took Joey and Champ downstairs. The living room looked like an all-nighter had been pulled, with books and papers still scattered all over the coffee table and floor. Most of the open books and loose papers had Post-it Notes slapped haphazardly all over them. But where she might have expected to find Carter passed out on the sofa with a book spread open on his chest—it wouldn't have been the first time, not by a long shot—she found only the lamp still on and the sofa untenanted.

In the kitchen, she plopped Joey into his high chair, opened the back door to let Champ out—he was off like a shot to warn some squirrel or chipmunk off their property—and turned on the coffeemaker. Right next to it, where they usually left each other notes, was a yellow sheet from a legal pad, on which Carter had scrawled in his barely legible hand, *Gone to the office. Call you later! Love.*

As the coffee started to percolate through the filter, she thought, *Sunday. It's a Sunday. And he still has to go to work?*

Of course she did understand the impulse. If it weren't for the printed-out translations from the secret letter in *The Beasts of Eden*, translations which she took with her pretty much everywhere she went, she might have been tooling up to the Getty herself today. A fine pair, they were.

She was nearly done feeding Joey, and just starting to wonder what she wanted to fix for herself—a soft-boiled egg, whole wheat toast?—when she heard the sound of tires crunching in the driveway. With Carter home, maybe she'd make something fancy, like French toast or blueberry pancakes. Probably wouldn't be the worst remedy for a mild hangover, either.

But then the doorbell rang—had he lost his keys?—and she went to the front window, pulled back the curtain to peer out, and saw a mud-spattered pickup truck, with those big tires, parked in the drive.

Which could mean only one thing.

"If you're still in bed, Bones, get up!" Del shouted from the front portico.

Beth let the curtain fall back and went to open the door.

"Oops," Del said, seeing that she was still in her robe. "Hope I didn't wake you."

"Not at all. Carter's not here, but come on in."

Del was dressed for the great outdoors, in camo pants and hiking boots and a red bandanna tied around his prematurely white mane. It was like inviting Willie Nelson into the house.

"Hey, boy," Del said as Champ trotted up to bark a warning. He squatted down and extended the back of one hand. "Don't you remember me?"

Champ eyed him warily, glanced up at Beth to make sure everything was okay, then allowed Del to rub him on the top of his head. "That scar's healing up nicely," Del said, standing up again.

"Would you like some coffee?" Beth said. "I was just making it."

"Sure." Del stopped to look around the living room as Beth went into the kitchen. "What happened here?" Del said. "Did the study group break up early?"

"Looks like it," Beth called out as she poured a mug for Del. "How do you like your coffee?"

"Strong and black, just like my women."

She brought him the mug, and found him poking through the books and papers scattered around the room. "Thanks," he said, studying another one of the Post-its. "Looks like your hubby was working on some very odd theory here."

"Why do you say that?" Beth asked, as Del sauntered around the coffee table to take in another of the open volumes. There was a picture of a saichania skeleton, from the Late Cretaceous period, unearthed in the Gobi Desert. He took a sip from his mug. "Good coffee," he said. The next picture, in a book beside it, was an illustration of a lycaenops, a mammal-like reptile from the Late Permian, Del's own special area of study. He leaned down and flipped the pages to the next fluttering Post-it note. There was a black-and-white sketch, not bad really, of a homotherium, a scimitar-toothed cat that had hunted mammoth in Europe and North America before dying out, along with its favorite prey, at the end of the Pleistocene ice age. "Because he's examining critters from all different epochs, and all different orders, from all over the globe." Del couldn't resist trying to put it all together—was there something that united the things he was looking at? Some thread Bones was following that he, for the life of him, could not see? He'd have to ask him, if he could ever find him.

"I left him a couple of messages on his cell," Del said. "I thought we'd go hiking again, or even fishing."

"Fishing?" Beth said, with a laugh. "Carter?"

"Don't dismiss it," Del said, "the boy needs some R&R. He works too hard. I told him that even when he was just a grad student."

"I guess it didn't take," Beth said. "He left me a note saying he's at the office."

"Not when I called there," Del blurted out, then instantly regretted it. Oh man, had he just blown Carter's cover story? (But what the hell would he be covering up for?)

"You tried his office?" Beth said, trying to sound unconcerned.

"Well, maybe he's in the lab, or down in the basement with our pal, the La Brea Man."

That was probably it, Beth thought. "Say, I was just planning to make some breakfast. You like blueberry pancakes?"

"No, I don't like them," Del said. "I *love* them."

While Del lingered over the books and papers, Beth popped upstairs to put on some shorts and a tank top; fixing breakfast for Del, in her robe and slippers, felt just a little too domestic. But that was interesting what he'd said about the bewildering nature of Carter's research downstairs. Last night, when al-Kalli had escorted him back from wherever they'd been for the whole duration of the outdoor concert, he had looked altogether out of it. His eyes seemed focused on something that was no longer in front of him, but which he was seeing, nonetheless. And on the way home, when she'd asked what that had been all about, he'd just dismissed it by saying that al-Kalli had shown him some old bones from Saharan Africa that he'd wanted Carter's take on.

"So, were they important?" Beth had asked.

And it was as though Carter hadn't even heard her; he was just staring out the windshield of the car, driving as if on autopilot, already tuned back to some other frequency. The last time she'd seen him this consumed was back in New York, when the packet had arrived with the pictures of the fossil found in the cave from Lago d'Avernus. Like then, he had completely submerged himself in a world of interior theorizing and rumination. And much as she would have liked to continue to compare notes on the party while driving home, she knew enough not to take offense.

That was just Carter being Carter.

By the time she got back to the kitchen, Del had released Joey from his high chair and was down on the tile floor, playing with him. "His motor skills are exceptional," Del said, in what she knew was meant as a warm and cuddly comment.

"How are yours?" Beth said, taking some eggs from the fridge. "Want to run the egg beater?"

"I think I could manage that."

While the two of them prepared the pancakes and bacon—though Beth didn't eat it, Carter did—Beth asked about how Del was liking L.A., how he liked living with his sister and her husband, and the answers were what she expected.

"No offense," he said as the first pancakes were coming

off the griddle and the bacon sizzled in the pan, "but I do not understand how anybody can actually live in a place like this. Way too many people, way too many cars, way too much noise. You can't even hear yourself think." He took the syrup and a plate of pancakes from Beth and put them on the table in the breakfast nook. "And the air's so bad you can see it before you can breathe it." He pulled out a chair and sat down. "But these look good enough to eat."

"Go ahead and start," she said, though, glancing over her shoulder, she saw that she needn't have bothered. Del had already smothered a pile of pancakes in syrup and was digging in. He ate with the concentration and gusto of a man who customarily ate alone.

Idly, she wondered if she knew any eligible women who might be interested in Del. There were a few single women at the Getty, but they were far too sophisticated and polished. Even though he had a first-rate mind and a very kind disposition, they would never be able to see past the wild and woolly, Ted Nugent–style surface. They'd take one look and run for Beverly Hills.

"Carter tell you that we came across an abandoned cabin—well, more like a shack, really—on our last hike? I'm telling you, a few more nights on the balcony above Wilshire Boulevard, and I'll be ready to move in."

No, Beth wasn't likely to find anyone for Del among her immediate acquaintances. She put the bacon on the table and sat down with him.

The obvious elephant in the room was Carter—or, more to the point, the missing Carter. They tried talking about other things—the drought, the latest police department fracas, the ongoing debate about providing illegal aliens with driver's licenses—but they both knew they were just beating around the bush. So it was something of a relief when Del, swallowing the last strip of bacon and washing it down with his coffee, said, "What do you think? Should I try to track him down, or wait'll he turns up on his own?"

Beth had been thinking about it, too. And what she'd decided was that it was a perfect hot and sunny day, and nothing would feel better, or be more likely to help her clear her head, than a swim in the community pool. Most of the time, there was no one there, and even when there was, they tended to keep their heads down, absorbed in a paperback or zoned out on their headphones.

"I was thinking of taking Joey down to the pool for a swim."

"You've got a pool?"

"We don't, but Summit View has. It's just down the street."

She could see that his interest was piqued. "You could borrow one of Carter's swimsuits."

"Hell, no. I've got some Jams in the truck." He wiped his mouth, grabbed his plate, and said, "What are we waiting for? Let's boogie."

In no time, they'd cleared the table, gotten Joey into his stroller and Del into his Jams, and were on their way to the pool. Champ trotted along beside them, head down to the short brown grass (the watering restrictions had gotten tighter all the time). At the gate to the pool, where no dogs were allowed, they had to maneuver things so that Champ was left just outside—he stared at them mournfully from a patch of shade, his leash looped around a gate post—as they set themselves up under a big yellow umbrella. Even on a blisteringly hot Sunday morning like this, almost no one was at the pool. A couple of teenage girls, coated with lotion, were cooking themselves to a turn, and a man with long white legs and bare feet, his head buried in an open newspaper, was all the way at the other end.

Del, like some kid who'd been cooped up too long, peeled off his T-shirt, threw it on the chaise, and did a cannonball into the deep end of the pool. When he came up again, shaking off the water from his long, white hair, he looked to Beth like Poseidon, rising from the ocean depths.

"Come on in," he shouted, "the water's great!"

"In a few minutes," Beth said, resting her head against the back of the chaise and closing her eyes. "In a few minutes." But lying back now, in only her one-piece suit, with a faint breeze blowing across her bare limbs, she thought she might never move again.

The only sounds were the rustling of the dry leaves and brush in the canyon behind her, and the occasional splash as Del paddled from one end of the pool to the other. She rested one hand on the handle of the stroller, adjusted her sunglasses with the other, and wondered just where Carter was right now. Something had really captured his imagination last night, and she knew that he was off in pursuit of it now. Just as she would be, she had to admit, if the secret letter from the scribe had required her to.

Fortunately, it did not—and the translation was nearly done. The story it told was an incredible one—a master craftsman, plying his trade all over Europe and the British Isles, joining the First Crusade (most probably to escape the consequences of a violent crime), and winding up as an honored guest, then prisoner, of an Arab sultan. There was enough fodder in this letter alone for Beth to write and research an entire book—and the thought had already crossed her mind. The letter had described the unparalleled splendors of the palace—the endless banquets served by a legion of slaves, the marble halls and mosaicked floors of the vast public rooms, the silken draperies and rich carpets that graced the bedrooms, the white stallions bred and raced in the arena, the perfumed gardens, the thermal baths, the elaborate maze, all designed for the amusement of the sultan and his favored guests—but none of that had interested her as much as the comments the artist had made about his craft.

Here he wrote, as no illuminator ever had, about his art—not only about the techniques he used to make and apply his paints and inks (she wished there had been more of that)—but about the decisions he made in the composition and the rendering of his illuminations. At times, he sounded surprisingly like a painter of a much later century, particularly when he declared—and the force of his handwriting emphasized it—that throughout *The Beasts of Eden* he had "imagined nothing, but had taken his inspiration from the miracles and terrors before his eyes." He claimed to have painted only what he saw, which was both thrilling—for an artist of the eleventh century it was as bold as it was unprecedented—and at the same time absurd. You only had to look at the pictures themselves—mighty birds rising from flaming pyres, lions with wings, dragons breathing fire and smoke—to know that it was untrue.

But it was the brazenness of the claim, quite apart from its veracity, that had impressed her.

"Whew, that was good," Del said, clambering out of the pool and shaking himself like a wet dog. Beth felt the droplets landing on her feet and legs. "You ought to try it."

"Maybe I will." She took off her sunglasses and laid them on the hot cement, under her chaise. Del was letting himself drip dry; he stood there in the hot sun, with brown arms and neck and legs, and a torso the color of whole milk. Off in the distance, she heard Champ bark, and she didn't blame him.

"Watch Joey?" she said as she stepped to the side of the pool and put a toe in to test the water. The sunlight gleamed on the rippling surface. She had to say that much for Summit View—the pool and other amenities were kept in tiptop condition. She slipped on a pair of goggles to protect her eyes from the chlorine, then executed a quick dive into the invitingly cool water.

She stayed underwater as long as she could, gliding along with a few broad strokes of her arms. It felt so good she wanted to make her stay indefinite. When she did come up for air, she breaststroked her way to the far end of the pool, turned, and started on another slow lap. She wondered why she didn't do this more often, and for the tenth time she resolved to leave work a little earlier, come home, and get some exercise in the pool on a daily basis.

Maybe she could even recruit Carter to do the same. On days when he'd worked in the pit, he always smelled faintly of tar, no matter how diligently he'd scrubbed himself off in the trailer at the site. Chlorine would be preferable.

It might be nice, in fact, to get some kind of regular routine going; she worried sometimes that she and Carter worked so hard, and at such erratic hours, that they didn't have enough old-fashioned fun and relaxation together. In

New York, it had been possible to see each other for lunch sometimes, or to attend some of the gallery openings together after work, or even go off to their friends Ben and Abbie's country house on occasion (though their last excursion there remained vague and distinctly unpleasant in her mind). She shook off the memory by executing a flip turn off the end of the pool, and then freestyling her way back again.

Here in L.A., she thought, moving languidly through the water, their offices were much farther apart—you couldn't just jump on a subway for fifteen minutes—and they hadn't really had time to make many friends. She had a few people at the Getty, he had Del, but as a couple they weren't exactly part of any social circuit. Maybe it just came with having a baby. As she flipped again, she noted a pair of feet in the shallow end.

And, God knows, there was no way to meet anybody at Summit View. When you drove up and down the streets of the development, all you saw was immaculately done homes, with closed garage doors and tinted windows. They had neighbors on only one side, and to this day Beth had no idea who they were. Once she'd seen a Porsche pull out of their garage and race off down the hillside, but that was about it. She guessed she could ask the man, a Getty trustee from whom they were renting, who lived next door, but she hated to bother him with anything; he was giving them such a deal in the first place, she didn't want to even remind him that they were there.

She was starting to get winded—that party had really taken it out of her—and resolved to do just one more lap. At the far end of the pool, she put her hands up on the hot lip of the cement and rested for a while, just enjoying the hot sun on the back of her head and shoulders. Tanning, she knew perfectly well, was bad for you, but gosh, it was nice to have a little color.

She lazily turned herself over in the water and gazed down at the other end, where she could dimly make out the stroller, Del, and someone else. She knew it wasn't Carter; this was a man in white tennis shorts. The guy who'd been reading the newspaper, she figured. She took off the goggles and looped them around her wrist.

Wouldn't you know it, she thought. Just when she was thinking it was impossible to meet anyone at Summit View, Del was doing it.

Keeping her head above water, she kicked off and headed back. As she got closer, the man stepped out of the shade of the umbrella, and she could see that he was tall . . . and very blond. And she paused, watching.

She could barely hear, over the lapping of the water in the pool, their voices. The man was turning and walking toward the gate.

She kicked her legs underwater and, still watching, swam closer.

By the time she reached the ladder, she could hear the gate closing behind the man. Champ, who was leashed there, didn't bark.

She climbed up out of the pool and said to Del, "Who was that?"

"Got me," he said. "Sounded kind of foreign."

"What did he want?"

"Just being friendly. Said hello to Joey."

"By name?" she asked. "Did he know his name?"

"Huh," Del said. "Now that you ask me, I don't know for sure."

"Stay right there," she said, tossing her goggles on the chaise and grabbing her sarong.

She headed for the gate—the man's wet footprints were perfectly imprinted on the shaded portion of the cement. At the gate, Champ jumped up to greet her. She looked up and down the street, but it was as empty as always. She looked down again at the footprints; they had grown fainter all the time, and here they were just barely an outline. But just a step or two from the gate, where the bushes grew high, they abruptly stopped, altogether. Not a trace, not a drop more.

She looked up and down the street again, searching for a departing, or even a parked, car. But there were none; in Summit View, you were required to leave your car in your own driveway or garage.

She glanced down again for the footprints, but now they had all evaporated. It was as if no one had ever been there.

Champ strained at his leash, anxious to go inside the pool enclosure.

"Everything okay?" Del called out.

Beth wasn't sure how to answer that. The air smelled fresh, as if the sprinklers had just been on.

"Beth?"

"Yes," she called out over her shoulder. "Everything's okay."

When she went back inside, the two teenage girls, coating themselves with lotion, followed her with blank expressions.

"If I'd known you wanted to meet him that bad, I'd have asked him for his card."

"I just thought I recognized him for a second."

"Not the kind of guy you'd forget," Del replied, flopping back in the chair with a magazine on his lap. "But he could go a little easier on the aftershave."

CHAPTER THIRTY-ONE

CARTER GOT LOST three times on the way to al-Kalli's estate. He was in too much of a hurry, he knew that, and he'd barely slept all night. And the road to the top of Bel-Air was a winding one.

At the gatehouse, he'd had to explain himself twice to the guard, who'd then called the main house, and after a minute or two, waved him through. Even then, he'd had to wait while one imperious peacock had strutted slowly across the driveway.

Jakob had opened the front door, smirking, and ushered him through the vast entry hall and then out again to the back. They'd walked across the flagstoned terrace, then to the side of the swimming pool. Al-Kalli was doing laps, methodically. Carter was shown to a seat at a glass-topped table, Jakob departed, and a servant appeared out of nowhere to offer him coffee. Carter accepted, gratefully.

The morning sun slanted across the green expanse of the lawn, the shimmering blue of the pool, the purple blossoms of the jacaranda trees nearby. Birds twittered in the branches overhead, a light breeze stirred the leaves—it was idyllic, it was paradise, and Carter thought maybe it wouldn't be so bad to be rich.

Then he thought how strange it was that such a perfect setting should conceal such an astonishing thing as the bestiary.

Al-Kalli did one more lap, then drew himself up out of the pool in a swift, fluid motion. To Carter's surprise, he was naked, and his body, the color of beaten copper, was as hairless as his head. He was also trim and muscular. He scrubbed himself vigorously from head to foot with a striped towel that was folded on the end of the diving board, then pulled on a white robe and came toward Carter as he fastened the belt.

"Even I didn't expect you quite this soon," he said, sitting down at the table. He raised his chin and the servant reappeared, this time with a large silver tray. On it were two crystal bowls of sliced fruit, a basket of muffins and breads, a frosted pitcher of what looked to Carter like guava juice. While everything was placed in front of them, al-Kalli asked, "What else would you like? Eggs, sausages?"

"No, this is plenty," Carter said.

"When I was at school in England, I never could understand their passion for bangers and kippers and such stuff, especially first thing in the morning." He poured some cream into his coffee, sipped it. A drop of water hung from his sapphire ring, then dropped onto the table. "English taste, in many things, eludes me."

Carter had no strong opinion on the subject.

"But at least I don't have to ask what brings you here," al-Kalli resumed with a sly smile. "Did you sleep at all last night?"

"Not really."

"I'm happy to hear it. It means you were as impressed as I'd hoped you'd be."

"Impressed is not the word."

"Perhaps not. But there really aren't any good words, are there, to adequately describe the bestiary?"

"No, there aren't," Carter agreed. But he'd come here

with some important things to say, and he didn't want to hold off any longer. "I've been giving a lot of thought to what you said."

"And?"

"And I can't go along with everything you want. I can't agree to keep this discovery secret. What you have here is one of the greatest and most miraculous . . . zoos"—he still hadn't figured out what to call it and "bestiary" seemed strange—"in the history of the world. Do you even know what these animals are?"

"We know what my family has called them, for time immemorial."

"I've spent the whole night researching them, and though I'll need more time to study and confirm my initial take, I think I can tell you some things already. Would you like to hear?"

"Nothing would please me more."

"Your basilisk?" Carter said, raring to go. "It's probably what paleontologists would call a saichania. It means 'beautiful one' in Mongolian. It's from the family of ankylosaurs, armor-plated, plant-eating dinosaurs that lived in the Late Cretaceous."

Al-Kalli looked intrigued, and while spooning a piece of fruit from his bowl, said, "Interesting—go on."

"Your griffin? Your griffin is—and again, I'm going to need a lot more time to make sure I'm right—your griffin is what we'd call a homotherium. A kind of cat, a close cousin of the saber-toothed cat, extinct since the end of the last ice age, about fourteen thousand years ago."

"Or so you thought."

"Or so we thought." Carter had to laugh, too, though it came out sounding a little crazier than he'd expected. He had to key down; he had to get some sleep.

"And the phoenix?"

"Best guess? *Argentavis magnificens*. A full skeleton has never been found. It had a wingspan twice as wide as any living bird. It's in the vulture family, and it dates from the Late Miocene."

"It's a great deal more beautiful than any vulture *I* have ever seen," al-Kalli replied. He sounded slightly offended at the very suggestion.

"It is," Carter said. "It is. But how could we have known that? No one has ever seen one before." He was also talking too fast. He had to slow down; he had to calm himself.

"Have a muffin," al-Kalli said, tilting the basket toward him. "The cook makes them fresh every morning."

Carter took one, broke it in half, and began eating mechanically, without paying any attention. He hadn't even mentioned the most amazing discovery of them all. "And then there's the manticore, as you call it," he said.

"Ah yes, the pride of the bestiary."

Carter washed the muffin down, barely having tasted it, with half a glass of juice. "It's a therapsid, a kind of reptile that was a direct ancestor of the mammals."

"Are you saying it's a dinosaur?"

"No, no, this animal was something else, something earlier. We don't know much about it—its bones are extremely difficult to find, and the best place to look for them has been the Karoo Desert in South Africa, which is one of the least hospitable places on earth."

Al-Kalli poured some more coffee into Carter's cup, before refilling his own. "Then think how much easier it will be to study the manticore—"

"The gorgon," Carter corrected him. "Gorgonopsian."

Al-Kalli nodded, conceding the point for now. "Think how much easier it will be to study this gorgon in the flesh, and in the comforts of Bel-Air. Isn't that precisely the sort of opportunity a man like you would prize?"

And it was. Carter could never have imagined such a thing—*no one* could have. The whole scenario, from start to finish, was quite literally impossible. How could creatures like this have survived? Anywhere? How could they have been brought together, and preserved, by one family, however wealthy, however powerful, inhabiting a palace in a desert waste? How could they have been brought, of all places, to Los Angeles, California? To the movie-star precincts of upper Bel-Air? None of it made any sense.

Beth had told him some of the stories about the rich and mysterious al-Kalli clan—the sinister rumors of their barbarity, their occult powers, their lineage so old it was lost in the mists of time—but he had chalked it all up to superstition and hearsay.

Mohammed al-Kalli, he'd told her, was just a man—a man with a lot of money, there was no disputing that—but just a man. He wasn't a wizard, he wasn't Prospero, he wasn't Merlin.

Or—and this was a thought he'd been entertaining for hours—was he?

"I can give you everything your work here could possibly require," al-Kalli said. "Just name it and it's yours."

"Right now, I can't even answer that question. What I need, I guess, most of all, is simply a chance to go back to the bestiary and see the animals for myself. Again."

"You doubt what you saw last night?" al-Kalli said sympathetically. "That's quite understandable. But I'm not running a tourist attraction here. You appreciate, I hope, that no one outside of my family, and a few loyal retainers, has ever even seen the bestiary." True, al-Kalli thought, he had allowed that lowlife Captain Greer to see the place, but then, Greer was expendable—and soon. "If I'm going to permit this, I will need to know that you are prepared to accept my offer." He sat back in his chair, the sapphire ring catching the sunlight and glistening like ice. "I need to know that you're going to help me save the animals."

How could Carter refuse such a challenge? But how, he wondered, could he accept it? "I'm a paleontologist," he said, "not a veterinarian."

"I have a veterinarian—Rashid—you saw him. He has had the finest training available. But he no longer knows what to do. The animals are ailing; they are dying. And he does not know how to stop it."

"Then you need to find someone else, someone better, more knowledgeable."

"I can hardly bring these animals to the attention of your average vet. Even if I could, what would he know about them? Nothing. He wouldn't even know what he was looking at."

"I'm not sure I do, either."

"I have great faith in you," al-Kalli said, "perhaps more than you do. These are the last of the menagerie. When I left Iraq, I had to leave nearly everything I owned behind; God knows what Saddam and his troops did to the rest. Even the book, the book your wife is restoring for me now, I did not have time to recover; I had to make special arrangements, later, to have it brought out of the country." He put his coffee cup back in its delicate Limoges saucer, then leaned forward in his chair. "You, better than anyone else alive, know what these creatures are; you know how they lived, how they bred. Help me save them," he said, "and then, when that has been done, when the immediate danger is past, we can reveal our secret to the world."

Carter had listened carefully to every word, but still wasn't sure he believed it. Was al-Kalli playing him? Did he mean it when he said that he'd eventually share the bestiary with the world? Or was that just another ploy to ensure Carter's cooperation?

"I'm simply not ready yet to part with my creatures," al-Kalli said reassuringly. "Once the word is out, it will be difficult—probably impossible—to maintain any control over them. But give me some time, give me your help, and I will be."

His black eyes were bright with sincerity; his expression was sober but hopeful. Carter wanted to believe him—or maybe, somewhere deep down, he too wanted to hold on to the secret, just for a little while longer. Something of this magnitude, once it came to light, would indeed spiral out of control quickly. The animals would be spirited off to some state-of-the-art facility, God knew where, and scientists from all over the world would flock to study them. Would Carter continue to have access to them? Or would his role be summarily forgotten? The science he knew he could cut, but when it came to politics and bureaucracy and all the cutthroat stuff that professional advancement seemed increasingly to demand, he was hopelessly at sea.

"You will, while the animals are here, give me unfettered access to them?" Carter asked.

"Of course," al-Kalli said, leaning back and spreading his hands. He knew he had just won. "As far as I'm concerned, you can move into my house."

"And whatever I recommend, even if it does mean ultimately moving them or calling in some other expert, you will do?"

"Yes," al-Kalli replied, with well-feigned enthusiasm.

Carter didn't know how, under these circumstances, he could possibly refuse. Nor, frankly, did he want to. "Then let's get to work," he said, rising from his chair.

Al-Kalli smiled up at him. "Splendid," he said, clapping his hands for Jakob. "I'm so pleased." He knew that he'd won this battle the moment Carter had appeared that morning, but it was good to have it formally concluded. People, al-Kalli thought, could always be made to do what you wanted them to—and then, just as easily, they could be gotten rid of.

CHAPTER THIRTY-TWO

"**I DON'T BELIEVE** you."

That was just like his mother. Anytime he gave her good news—which, Greer had to admit, hadn't been all that often—she thought he was lying.

"Show me your pay stub," she said.

"They pay me in cash."

She put a cup of tea on the tray, right next to her toast and jam, and waddled back into the living room with it. "Hold this," she said, and Greer did, as she settled herself back into her chair. "Now, you can rest the tray across the arms."

He wished he had something to prove it to her—a company ID, a contract, a uniform. "Remember that guy from the army who called here the other day?"

"Yes," she said, spreading the jam and paying more attention to *The People's Court* than to him.

"The one I told you wanted me to complete a survey?"

"You were lying about that, too, I think."

Damn, her radar was really pretty good. "I was, a little. He wanted to know what I was doing now as a civilian, and I had to tell him I was having some trouble finding work."

That she heard. "Of course you couldn't find any—you didn't look."

Why did he bother? What had made him think he should even tell her anything? But he was going to plow ahead. He was going to get this out. "He told me about a guy—a very rich guy, up in Bel-Air—who needed someone to run his entire security operation. He put me up for the job, and I got it."

He was standing to one side of her chair, and she was looking at the TV, and the whole setup reminded him uncomfortably of the time he came home to tell her he'd been made captain of the baseball team and she'd been watching something on the TV—the big old one that still had an actual aerial on top—and instead of saying anything like "That's great!" or "Good for you!" she'd said, "Your father's run off again, and this time I think it's for good."

"When do you start this so-called job?"

"I already have. I told you."

She bit off a hunk of the toast—more jam than bread at this point—and shrugged. "Does that mean you'll be getting your own place?"

He couldn't tell how she meant that—whether she was hoping he would or hoping he wouldn't. She hadn't exactly welcomed him home when he'd returned from Iraq, but seeing as he'd been wounded and all, she could hardly turn him away. And then she'd gotten used to the extra cash his disability payments had brought in, for groceries and rent and utilities and stuff. If he'd had to guess, he'd have said she was kind of torn.

"Maybe," he said, letting her twist a little. "I'll see how far the salary goes." He liked the word "salary"; made it sound more authentic than the wad of bills Jakob had tossed him.

"If you've got a job," she said, having had a minute or two to think about it, "why aren't you there now?"

"It's not that kind of a job, where you punch in and out. It's an executive position."

She looked dubious.

"And I'm going there now, in fact." What was the use?

He turned and headed for the door. He grabbed his wind-breaker off the hook, and just before he closed the door, he heard her turn up the volume on the TV.

But she was right, whether she knew it or not—it was time he got a place of his own. This shit was definitely not worth it.

On the way to the VA hospital, where he'd been heading all along, he listened to a tape of Grand Funk Railroad—the old stuff was still the best—at full volume. His life, he thought, was coming together, but in a very weird way. What had started out as a blackmail plot—never a very good one, as he could never figure out exactly where the leverage was—had turned into a regular gig. He'd asked al-Kalli if his title was "Head of Security Operations," and al-Kalli had said that was fine with him. Now here he was, a decorated Iraq vet, working for an Arab billionaire, in L.A. yet, and guarding a bunch of . . . dinosaurs, for all he knew. That guy he'd seen on TV—Carter Cox—was a pa-leontologist, and that must have been why al-Kalli had let him in. The only other guy Greer had seen let into the bes-tiary had never made it out again.

And al-Kalli must actually think of him as more than just a security officer; why else would he have invited him to that fancy party? Although—Christ—that food had been some of the worst he'd had since his deployment.

At the hospital, he parked in his usual spot—a patch of shade off at the far end, just around the corner from the door—checked in at the front desk, and was halfway down the hall when the guard said, "Hold it, Captain!"

What, had he signed in on the wrong line? The army could find more ways to bust your balls . . .

"Got an advisory here," the guard said. "You're to re-port to the supervisor's office."

"I've got an appointment first," Greer said. Through the glass wall of the therapy room, he could see Indira tending to Mariani in his wheelchair. He wanted to talk to her—he needed to talk to her. Things had been bad for a while, but now that he was straightening out his life, he wanted to tell her that. He wanted to tell *someone* who would care.

"No, you don't," the guard barked, coming out from behind the semicircular counter he sat behind. "You're making an immediate left, and reporting to the supervisor. Last door at the end of the hall . . . Captain."

These pricks really killed Greer; the guy was in uniform, but Greer was damned if he could see any combat patches on him. Greer glanced into the therapy room again, and saw that Indira was looking out at him. He raised one finger and mouthed "Right back," then moved off down the hall.

The supervisor, Dr. Frank Foster, looked like he was in worse shape than some of the patients. He was a scrawny, walleyed guy with a glistening sheen of sweat on his pale face—even though the office air-conditioning was working fine—and the rabbity look of a smoker wondering where, and when, he could safely light up. Greer, gambling on his hunch, took out his pack of cigarettes and offered him one.

"Don't be ridiculous," Dr. Foster said, though his eyes did linger for that extra split second on the pack. "There's no smoking in this building, and you shouldn't be smoking anyway. Put them away."

Greer slipped them back in his pocket and tried to get comfortable in the hard plastic chair; it was sculpted for somebody, but that somebody wasn't him. And tempted as he was to ask what was up, he knew enough about the military and its protocols to keep his mouth shut and only volunteer whatever information he had to.

Dr. Foster swiveled in his chair, pulled a manila folder off a pile behind him, and slapped it on the messy desk. Greer noticed a telltale pack of matches mixed in with all the other crap. The tinny sound of a cheap radio, playing classical music, emanated from somewhere, maybe one of the desk drawers.

"We've made some corrections to your file," Dr. Foster said, "in light of some new information that has come our way."

New information? Greer wanted to ask, what new information? But didn't.

Foster riffled through some papers again, and said, "How long have you had your drug dependency problems?"

Greer stayed silent.

"And what drugs are you currently using?" He looked up expectantly, pen poised, waiting for Captain Greer to start spilling his guts. "Well?"

"The clinic has records, doesn't it?" Greer asked. "Ask my therapist, Indira Singh, what I've been prescribed."

"We know what you've been prescribed. We also have information that leads us to believe you're abusing other, nonprescription drugs. If you have drug dependency and addiction problems, problems that could affect the course of your treatment here, we need to know that."

"Now how would you know anything like that?"

"We're not at liberty to divulge that information, nor is it relevant. All that matters is whether it's true or not."

"It's not true," Greer said. "Okay? So we're done."

"Are you currently working?"

That one came out of left field. "Why?"

Foster shrugged. "We have to keep the records current, especially if your new employer offers any kind of private health insurance benefits. We're here to help the veterans, Captain Greer, but we also like to see that the veterans are trying to help themselves."

Greer was starting to smell a rat.

"So, are you currently employed, and if so where?"

A big rat with a grudge. Greer had to think fast, wondering how to play this one. His first inclination, as always, was to lie, and he saw no reason to depart from tradition now. "No." Even though he'd been planning to tell Indira, he was going to ask her to keep it under her hat.

The walleyed Dr. Foster just stared at him blankly. Greer wondered if his eyes were enough in sync, or if he saw two different images. "You have not recently been employed as a security officer?"

Greer laughed, as if he'd never heard anything so absurd. "Yeah, a gimp with a bad leg, no experience, and no references. Where am I supposed to be working? Wells Fargo, or Fort Knox?"

"We don't look kindly on the falsification of records, Captain Greer. If it comes to light that you have not been forthcoming, or that you have in fact provided us with mis-information, the Veterans Administration can, and will, take action."

"That's just what I'd expect them to do."

"The file is still open," Dr. Foster said, pointedly leaving it so on the desk. "I'd advise you to keep us up-to-date on the developments in your life, both medical and professional."

"I'll do that," Greer said, starting to lever himself up and out of the chair. "But I've got a therapy appointment to keep."

"Your therapy will have to wait today." He tore off a perforated form with a number of black boxes on it and said, "Take this upstairs to the main desk." Greer saw a lot of the boxes were already checked—for urinalysis, blood chemistries, etc. It didn't take a rocket scientist to figure out what this was all about.

"We're not here to punish you," Dr. Foster said, with all the conviction you'd muster to read aloud from an eye chart, "we're here to help you."

"I feel better already," Greer replied.

In the hall outside, he stuffed the form in his pants pocket; no point in getting any tests done today—he could think of at least three prohibited substances currently circulating in his bloodstream. And his blood pressure wasn't going to be so hot either—all he could think about was finding Sadowski, the fucking snitch, and killing him. Hadn't it even occurred to the moron that Greer had plenty of shit on him, too? He couldn't get him fired from Silver Bear—that had already been done. But how about that arsenal he kept, and the supersecret Sons of Liberty? What exactly was their agenda, and wouldn't the feds maybe like to be in on it? Greer even had the sense that they were planning their own little Waco to happen soon. That marked-up map he'd seen at the Blue Bayou, the new recruits, the meetings Sadowski had urged him to attend. Something was in the wind, and from what Greer knew of Sadowski and his mentor, Burt Pitt, it was going to be stupid, it was going to be destructive, and it was sure as hell going to be violent.

But he'd deal with that later. Right now he still had

some business to conduct with Indira. Chances were pretty
slim that he'd get another prescription out of her—Greer
was confident his name was on some internal watch list—
but it might be worth one last shot. And he still wanted to
talk to her. She was about the only straight person he knew,
the only one who might think this new job was for real and
that he wasn't just bullshitting.

Slipping quietly past the back of the reception booth,
where the guard was watching the main doors, Greer entered the therapy room. Indira had Mariani's wheelchair
pulled up to a table where she was having him squeeze
these metal hand clamps that were used to measure the
power of your grip. It was one of the few things Greer had
still registered well on. Mariani was squeezing one now,
Indira was watching the meter to record the results, and
Greer just stood off to one side waiting for her to finish.

A new guy, or at least somebody Greer had never seen,
was lurching along on a treadmill with a prosthetic left
foot. He had on headphones and a Yankees baseball cap.
When he raised one hand off the bar to acknowledge
Greer, Greer raised a hand back. Christ, Greer thought, at
least he hadn't wound up an amputee. What the hell was
that like?

"You waiting for the treadmill?" the guy said, slipping
his headphones down around his neck.

"No," Greer said. "I couldn't do two minutes on that
damn thing, anyway."

"Me neither," the guy said, panting, "not with this fucking contraption on. But screw it—you go to a regular gym
and everybody there wants to know what happened."

Greer knew exactly what he was saying. "And here, nobody cares."

The guy nodded, put the phones back on, and kept at it.

Indira wheeled Mariani over to the dispensary window,
then came back to Greer with her hands pressed down in
the pockets of her white lab coat. He could tell she knew
all about it.

"You got time to work with me today?" Greer said, pretending all was well.

"Have you gone upstairs for the lab work?" she asked.

"Next time," he said.

"I can't. You know that. The supervisor has to okay all your treatments from now on."

"I don't suppose you could tell me what started all this." He knew, but it never hurt to get independent confirmation.

"I don't know," she said, with evident sincerity. "But even if I did, I would not be allowed to tell you."

"Yeah? Then maybe I won't tell you that the stuff about the job was true."

"A job?" she said. "So you have a job now?"

Either she was a better liar than he knew, or she really didn't know anything about that. Another therapist brushed past them with a one-armed vet in tow. "I'm glad," Indira said. "It will do you good to be working again."

He started to reach into his pocket for a cigarette, then remembered where he was. "Yeah, well, we'll see how it goes. But the money's good, and I think there's actually a lot I can do there." It was odd, but he had indeed found himself thinking, seriously, even when he wasn't up at the estate, about al-Kalli's security needs. Having been waltzed onto the estate by Sadowski, he knew how lax some of the present measures were. He knew where the walls could easily be breached, he was learning where the motion detectors were and what areas they failed to properly cover. It was as if his mind had been waiting for just such a challenge, for something to think about besides his next score, or his next trip to the Blue Bayou. On the one hand he knew that al-Kalli was a cold-blooded murderer—hell, he'd seen him in action—and on the other, to his own great surprise, he wanted to prove to him that he'd made a smart move in hiring Greer.

"Indira," the other therapist called out, "I could use some help when you're free."

"I'll be right there," Indira replied.

"Okay, you gotta go," Greer said. "But I'll come back for those tests."

"Do that, Captain," she said, sincerely.

"And then maybe we can try again."

"Yes, of course, then we can schedule another therapy appointment."

That wasn't what he'd meant—and he wondered if she knew that or not. But for now, he decided to just let it go. "Right."

On the way past the security desk, the guard requested that he sign out, but Greer just kept on going.

"Captain Greer!" the guard shouted after him. "You have to sign out of the building!"

Greer, without turning around, raised the middle finger of his left hand and kept on walking.

He stopped just outside the front doors to light a badly needed cigarette. And to think about how he was going to handle the Sadowski situation. Maybe he shouldn't have dumped him off the pier, he thought, though the memory of it even now brought a smile to his face. Just the sound of his scream, and the big splash a second later . . . life didn't get much better than that.

The sun was beating down on the parking lot, and he was glad he'd parked in his secret shady spot around back. And since he hadn't spent any time getting therapy, or getting tested, he had an hour or two to kill. In the past, he'd have simply tooled over to the Blue Bayou, or maybe down to that beach parking lot where he'd watched Zeke play volleyball—he could get high in the front seat and mellow out. But instead he found himself seriously considering a run up to Bel-Air. He was wondering about how well secured that back gate was, the one that Sadowski had arranged for him to exit from. And he was sorry he'd ever told him anything about the animals up there. Information was a weapon, and that one he'd put in Sadowski's hands himself.

The roar of the traffic on the 405 was a steady drone, but it was otherwise kind of peaceful here. Only one other car was parked around back, one of those new Hummer 3s. Just the sight of them pissed off Greer. If he never set foot in another Hummer, it would be too soon. And now, here were all these civilians playing soldier—and that included that horse's ass bodybuilder now known as the Governator—

driving around Beverly Hills and the Palisades in cars that
were probably better armored than the buckets he'd originally traveled in back in beautiful Baghdad. He'd even seen
one that had fake bullet holes decaled across the back
bumper. At the time, it was all he could do not to reach
under the driver's seat and pull out his Beretta, which he
kept hidden there in a Weight Watchers box he'd retrieved
from his mother's trash, and blow some real holes into the
back of the damn thing.

But as he approached his own heap—now that he was a
working man, he wondered what it would cost to get the
thing painted—he noticed that the Hummer was occupied.
There was somebody in the driver's seat, and possibly
somebody beside him; the windows were too tinted and
narrow to tell. But something went off in the back of
Greer's head, some little warning bell—the same sort of
thing that would tell him not to open a closed door in Mosul, or step off the road to free a dog tied conspicuously to
a post in the middle of nowhere. That was how Gaines, a
softhearted black sergeant, had bought the farm.

He stubbed out his cigarette and, while keeping an eye
on the Hummer, approached his own Mustang. There was
the smell of cigarette smoke in the air, but it wasn't his;
where was it coming from? He glanced at a concrete
wall—clearly some kind of security addition—that jutted
out from the side of the VA hospital, about fifteen feet past
the parking area. Was there somebody behind it? Even if
there was, he'd already decided he could make it to his
car, and the Weight Watchers box, before anybody could
get to him.

He had the key in the lock when he heard the doors of
the Hummer opening and the sound of swift heavy footsteps. Shit. He turned the key too quickly, and the rusty lock
caught. He turned it again, glancing up, and he could see
Tate and Florio, the two new Sons of Liberty boys, bearing
down on him. Tate was in a tight black T-shirt, Florio was
wearing a red tracksuit, and both of them were carrying
what looked like brand-new aluminum baseball bats.

He wrenched the door of the car open, but it was too

late—Tate took a short swing, Greer ducked, and the bat took out the front window of the Mustang with a shattering explosion. Greer ran around to the other side of the car—fortunately these two were so stupid they'd come at him together from the same side—and waited while they regrouped.

"This can't be what the Sons of Liberty have been planning all along, can it?" Greer said, catching his breath. He knew he could never make a run for the hospital doors, or all the way out onto Wilshire Boulevard, without their catching up to him. But how was he going to get to his gun?

"Go around back," Tate told Florio. Florio lumbered toward the back bumper of the car, keeping his eyes on Greer the whole time.

Greer had no choice. He pulled open the passenger-side door and lunged across the front seat, scrabbling under the seat for the Beretta. Tate couldn't get in a swing from this angle; he dropped the bat with a clang on the concrete and reached for the back of Greer's shirt to haul him out. Greer could feel his fingers on the damn box; he could even feel the cold steel of the trigger guard inside. He braced himself against the bottom of the steering wheel with one hand while he groped to get the gun out, and then he felt Florio grabbing his ankles and trying to pull him out the other way.

"I've got him!" Tate shouted angrily. "Let the fuck go!"

Florio grunted and let go, and Tate grabbed hold of Greer's hair with both hands and dragged him out of the car, face-first and empty-handed. As soon as he felt his face scrape the concrete, Greer spun himself over—Tate was aiming a kick at his ribs and Greer was able to catch his foot and push it back. Tate flopped against the side of the car, but he didn't go down, and Florio was coming around fast to join him. Greer was scuttling backward like a crab, and figuring there was no way he was going to come out of this alive, when he heard a voice say, "What's going on here?" from somewhere behind him.

Greer kept scuttling toward the sound of the voice, and Tate and Florio were suddenly flummoxed like the dumb oxen they were. Greer smelled the cigarette smoke again.

"Security's been called," the man said. "Nobody moves a muscle."

Tate and Florio looked at each other—Tate said, "Shit!"—then bolted for the Hummer.

"I said hold it right there!" the man said, and Greer was able to whip his head around now and see that it was that supervisor, that Dr. Foster. The one he'd suspected was a secret smoker, only he was holding a cell phone now and not a cigarette.

The Hummer roared to life, drove right over the cement parking spot barrier, and rumbled toward the Wilshire exit. An entering van, horn blasting, had to swerve to one side to avoid getting hit. Greer took a deep breath and lurched to his feet. His left leg was singing like a choir.

"Captain Greer?" Foster said, his voice a little shaky, as he came closer.

Greer touched his cheek; there was a bloody scrape, but no serious damage.

"What was going on here?"

"What do you think?" Greer said. "Where's this security you called?"

"I didn't, I'm afraid," Foster said, opening his palm to reveal that it wasn't a cell phone at all—it was a transistor radio.

Greer heard a chorus of honks as the Hummer barged into the traffic flow and headed off toward Sepulveda.

Greer had to laugh. Jesus, that had been a close call— and he had to hand it to the doc. His timing couldn't have been better.

"Did you know those men?"

"Yeah, but we're not really friends."

Foster paused, then laughed nervously. "I guess not."

Greer reached into his shirt pocket and took out the pack of Marlboros. He put one in his mouth, then held the pack out toward Foster. "Go ahead. Your secret's safe with me."

Foster took a cigarette—his hands were still trembling a bit—drew a pack of matches from his own pocket, and lighted them both. "You know this is bad for your health," he said, as if he just couldn't stop himself.

They both inhaled deeply, and stared out at the stream of cars flowing past the far end of the parking lot. Like it or not, Greer felt that he owed the guy now; someday when he was clean, whenever that might be, he'd come in and get his blood and urine tests done.

CHAPTER THIRTY-THREE

IF CARTER HAD hoped his absences wouldn't be noticed, he soon discovered he was dead wrong. By the time he checked into his office late one afternoon, he had a stack of While You Were Out slips piled next to his phone. At least two of them were from his angry boss, Gunderson. And when he checked his e-mail, the list went on and on—everyone from a federal official writing to let him know that a NAGPRA form hadn't been filled out properly (he had already wasted countless hours on the bureaucratic red tape created by the discovery of the La Brea Man) to a scary hacker (how did these people find him?) declaring that "the blood of William Blackhawk Smith will be avenged." There was even a plaintive e-mail from Del, asking if he should pack up and go back to Tacoma or was Carter planning to resume work soon?

There was so much explaining he should do—Carter knew that—but there was so little he could actually say.

His mail, too, was spilling out of his in-box. He did a quick riffle through it all, and stopped only when he found the oversized envelope from Dr. Permut's lab at New York University. He and Permut had had their ups and downs, but when it came to analyzing and dating lab specimens, he was still the best in the game—and Carter had prevailed upon him to do him this one last favor. He ripped open the envelope, scanned the graphs stapled to the cursory cover letter, and found what he was looking for: the human bones Carter had retrieved from Pit 91 were approximately nine thousand years old, give or take a century or two.

And that was right in keeping with the bones of the La Brea Woman, discovered in a neighboring pit years ago.

It was something he could share—and was anxious to share—with Del, but at this hour he wasn't likely to be anywhere in the museum. It was dark outside, and all Carter could see when he looked out his office window was his own reflection—and he didn't look good. His shirt was rumpled and untucked, his hair needed combing, and his features looked drawn; he hadn't had a decent night's sleep since first seeing the bestiary, and he'd spent most of each day either researching the animals or observing them first-hand. Between the strain of the work, and the strain of keeping it all under his hat, he was starting to fray.

Even now, he knew he should just go home, get a good night's sleep, and the next day report back for work—at the museum, not at the al-Kalli estate—but he couldn't let go. Too much was happening, too much was in the wind. He felt guilty for letting Beth take up so much of the slack at home, and guilty for leaving Del in the lurch. Maybe now, he should just see where Del had left off the work on the La Brea Man, and drop off the carbon-dating report. Del would be as intrigued as he was by the results.

First, of course, he had to persuade Hector to take him down to the sub-basement, where he and Del had set up their makeshift lab. And though the standing orders from Gunderson limited Carter to the museum's normal operating hours, and as a result, he expected some resistance, all he got instead was, "Only if you promise to come back with your friend."

"My friend?"

"The man with the long white hair."

Del was there?

"He's as bad as you," Hector said, turning the key to unlock the elevator. "I tell him, you have to stop working now or I could lose my job, and he says, 'Hector, no one will know—and I will bring you a Big Mac when I go out later to get my dinner.' " Hector snorted as he let Carter into the elevator. "I can buy my own burgers," he said, "but I can't get another job so easy."

"I'll bring him back with me," Carter said, "I promise."

Hector snorted again, said, "I'll leave the elevator running," then headed back to his regular post between the dire wolves and the giant sloth.

Carter was elated. He could tell Del about the carbondating report in person, and at the same time he could apologize for going MIA. But what could he say by way of explanation? Del would know that for Carter to desert something as important as the La Brea Man, there would have to be something else of almost immeasurable significance hanging in the balance. And although that was exactly the case, it was the one thing Carter couldn't say.

The lights, insufficient though they were, were on, and in the far distance, back where they'd set up the work space, he could hear the faint strains of Tammy Wynette. As he walked down the corridor, his sneakered feet making barely any noise, he felt himself still haunted by the al-Kalli creatures. They constituted the most spectacular collection imaginable. And he could see, the more he studied them, where their ancient mythological names and reputations had come from. The basilisk, whose breath could reputedly kill, was in fact an ankylosaurid whose breathing passages followed an extremely convoluted passage within the skull, allowing the animal to cool and humidify desert air before it reached its lungs. The griffin—or homotherium—had passed into legend as a winged lion, but the wings were actually just a massive mane of thick black fur that billowed out as the creature launched itself at its prey. The phoenix, a prehistoric vulture, surely did not rise from its own fiery nest, but perhaps its chicks could be mistaken for spits of bright red flame; Carter had yet to scale the aerie to see if there were any. And as for the manticore—or gorgon, as the scientific community would one day acknowledge it to be—its baleful glare and fearful jaws were enough to ensure its reputation as the man-eating predator of lore.

But if Carter was to figure out what was ailing these creatures—and how to remedy it—he would need so much more time to study them. And as al-Kalli had made abundantly clear, time was running out.

Del's head was down as he worked in a pool of light shed by a goosenecked lamp they had brought down; an extension cord trailed off down the next aisle. The boom box was on top of the metal cabinet where the bones of the La Brea Woman were housed. Carter said, "Del," but he wasn't heard over Tammy. He came closer, and his shadow fell onto the disarticulated bones that Del was bent over. Del's head whipped up, his white hair flying, real surprise in his eyes.

"Jesus Christ," he said, breathing a sigh of relief, "you could have given me some warning."

"I did," Carter said, "but Ms. Wynette was louder."

Del plopped back on a high stool behind him with his hands in his lap. "Nice of you to drop by," he said. "After all this time, I'm glad you remembered where to find us."

"Okay, I get it," Carter said, knowing that he would be catching some flak. "I'm sorry I haven't been more on top of this."

"Just tell me it's not because you've been on top of something else."

"What are you talking about?"

"You're not horsing around with somebody—like maybe that Miranda kid who was working on the dig at Pit 91?"

"What in the world would make you even say that?" Carter replied.

Del shrugged. "I just couldn't think of anything else big enough to keep you away. Especially something that Beth wouldn't know about. She had no idea where you were last Sunday, and she called here looking for you today." He bent down and picked up a can of Sprite resting on the floor beneath the worktable. "It's just not like you, Bones."

And Carter knew he was right; it wasn't. But he should have planned for this confrontation. He should have come up with some excuse in advance. "I've had Gunderson breathing down my neck about the NAGPRA problems," he improvised. "Unless we want to wind up consigning these bones to some Native American burial ground, I've got to cross every *i* and dot every *t*."

"That's cross every *t* and dot every *i*," Del corrected him.

"Oh. Right."

Del gave him a long look and shook his head. "Anybody ever tell you you're the worst liar on earth?" He sipped from the soda can, then put it safely back on the floor, away from the exposed fossils. "But I figure you'll tell me the truth when you're ready."

"Mind if I ask you one question?" Carter said, stepping up to the worktable to survey what Del was doing.

"Shoot."

"How come you nearly jumped out of your skin when I showed up a few seconds ago?"

Del didn't look up, but cocked his head slightly, as if in embarrassment. "No reason," he said. "It's just that it does get a little spooky down here at times."

Carter laughed. "You? The guy who's crawled into caves on his belly? Who's slept alone on fossil beds in Kazakhstan?"

Del smiled. "Yeah, well, there's something about this guy," he said, referring to the tar-blackened bones before him, "that sort of gets to you after a while. You get the feeling his ghost is looking over your shoulder. A couple of times I've apologized out loud when I've had to scrape extra hard on the plaster and tar."

"Did he say you're excused?"

"Okay, that's enough," Del replied, indicating that the ribbing was at an end. "Why don't you roll up your sleeves and help me out here?"

"Glad to," Carter said, literally rolling up the sleeves of his white shirt.

"You can start by telling me what happened to the mystery object."

"The what?"

"The thing he'd been holding in his hand when he died. The thing that I can only presume you stashed somewhere for safekeeping." Del glanced across the table at Carter. "Tell me you do know where it is."

Carter nodded and turned around. He fished in his pocket for the padlock key, found it, then realized, with a terrible start, that he wouldn't need it. The padlock on the drawer holding the bones of the La Brea Woman—the same drawer where he'd concealed the mystery object—was open, hanging loose on the hasp. There were long, deep scratches on the metal cabinet all around it.

He pulled the loose padlock away and yanked open the drawer, dreading what he might find—or not find—there.

All that was left in the drawer was the white handkerchief in which he'd wrapped the object when he'd stashed it here. The bones were gone, the skull was gone. The paper lining of the drawer bore only the faint imprint of the skeletal fragments that had been safely stored here for so many decades.

Until Carter had intruded on them.

"I should have known," Del said from behind him; from his perspective, he would not be able to see that the drawer had been plundered. "It's a safe bet you wouldn't have let it go far." Carter heard him putting a new tape in the boom box.

Carter was flabbergasted. He couldn't imagine how this could have happened. He stood staring into the empty drawer, as if by doing so he could conjure up the bones again. As if he could will them back into the cabinet where they belonged.

The new tape started, Johnny Cash this time. Del had gone back to work on the bones of the La Brea Man. "Bring it on," Del said exuberantly. "Let us solve, once and for all, the riddle of the secret stone." Del's theory was that it would prove to be a sacred artifact of some kind.

Carter didn't know what to do, or say.

"Carter? You okay?" Del finally said.

"It's gone," Carter mumbled.

"What's gone? The stone?" Del quickly came to his side and stared into the open drawer.

"It's *all* gone," Carter said.

"What is? What was in here?"

"La Brea Woman was in here."

"Jesus," Del said as he absorbed the magnitude of what Carter was saying. He plucked the handkerchief up, just to see if there was anything left under it, then let it drop back into the drawer. "How'd they know she was here?"

"How'd who know she was here?"

"The protestors, the NAGPRA people." He looked at Carter as if wondering why he hadn't already put it together, too. "They wanted her bones back, too; they wanted to inter them in some sacred burial ground. And now they've got 'em." He scratched his head. "But how the hell did they get down here? Hector isn't exactly easy to get around."

Was that it? Carter wondered. Was it simply the supporters of William Blackhawk Smith and the Native American grave repatriation act? Was it only an elaborate and cunning theft?

"But why," Carter asked, "would they have taken her, and not him?" he said, glancing back at the bones of the La Brea Man laid out on the worktable. It would have been so easy to make off with it all.

Even Del had to think for a second. "They must have done it between the time you stashed the stone in the drawer and we brought the man's bones down. If you'd been around more, you'd have noticed it sooner." He was sorry it had come out that way, but in fact it was true—and Del, too, had had a stake in deciphering the mystery object. He was angry. "We've got to call the police. Maybe the FBI. I don't even know who'd have jurisdiction in something like this."

But that was the last thing Carter wanted to have happen. It would surely be the last nail in his own coffin at the Page Museum and, considering what had happened at NYU, probably his professional career. One disaster could be forgiven, two would brand him forever as either criminally incompetent, or cursed.

And he didn't believe that was what had happened, anyway. It just felt to Carter as though something else was going on here, something more . . . elusive.

"Let me have a day to figure this out," Carter said.

"To figure what out? Some crazy bastard snuck down here, jimmied the lock, and stole the bones. It doesn't take Detective Columbo to see what happened here."

"You're probably right." He turned to Del. "But let me think this through. Once it comes to light . . ." He didn't have to finish the sentence for Del to see what he was getting at. "Okay?"

Del swallowed his own eagerness to get the police on the case and said, "Okay, Bones. I get it." He shook his head sadly over the pillaged drawer. "But let's not give the bastards too much time to make their getaway."

"I won't," Carter said, though if what Del believed was true, the bones could be buried anywhere by now, never again to be found.

"And let's keep these," Del added, referring to the bones of the La Brea Man, "somewhere they can't find 'em."

CHAPTER THIRTY-FOUR

THERE IS LIGHT in the eastern sky; my time draws near. The door is guarded; the window is barred, and even if it were not, the tower is high and the ground below is rocks and sand.

My hand grows tired; I must sharpen another quill.

Beth could picture him all too well. Sitting by the narrow window at dawn, shaving the nib of a fresh quill (goose feathers were most commonly used, but for such close work as this he might have employed a crow or raven feather), then returning to his work for as long as he would be allowed, before the sultan's guards came inside to lead him to his death.

I know what awaits me, for I have seen it with my own eyes. I have seen the prisoner, his hands unbound, his feet free, led into the arena, where al-Kalli and his guests sit on high. Below them lies the maze, with its many pathways and great high walls, fashioned from the green leaves and thorny branches of the hawthorn bush. The maze is vast and intricate—the game would be over too soon if it were not—and the prisoner at first rejoices. He is free to run and to defend himself and there is no sign of his foe—though

*foe there is, for the snake that is Satan haunts this unholy
garden.*

For Beth, reading the English rendering of the secret
epistle, it was like looking a thousand years into the past,
like glimpsing a scene no one else even knew had taken
place. A scene whose truth, she believed, was undeniable.
When she had first discovered the letter, and begun to read
its fantastic tale, it had certainly crossed her mind that it
was an elaborate game or ancient ruse. But there was no
written record of any such equivalent performance from the
eleventh century; writing at all, and the mastery of Latin,
were such rare achievements that its practitioners were loath
to use them for anything but the most practical, and well-
paid, tasks. Vellum wasn't cheap, the work wasn't easy—the
sheer physical labor of mixing inks, stretching skins, prepar-
ing pens, hand-lettering each exquisite character—was immense, and the skills of the consummate craftsman were
considered a kind of divine gift which it would have been
sacrilegious to defile. No, the letter was real.

*The slave Salima still attends me and weeps now in the
bed.* Beth had read of Salima earlier—a concubine whom
al-Kalli had permitted the scribe to choose from among the
many in his private seraglio. But was she weeping at the
plight of the scribe, or was she, too, doomed?

*It will be her charge to take this letter to my accomplice
that he may place it in its secret grave. May she be spared
to do this deed.* Knowing no more than this, Beth could
only assume that the slave girl had survived—at least long
enough to convey the letter.

Someone was suddenly talking right in front of her.
"The bowers that you see here are made of steel and covered with three different varieties of bougainvillea," said
the tour guide as a dozen visitors stopped in front of the
one Beth was sitting under. It was a hot, bright day, but
here, in the shadow cast by the flower-draped sculpture,
she had been able to read in comfort and, best of all, seclu-
sion. Out here, she ran little risk of being interrupted by
Mrs. Cabot; only Elvis, her assistant, knew where she was
holed up.

"Let me get out of your way," Beth said as several tourists raised their cameras.

"No, no, you're fine," the guide, an older man, said. "These bowers should always look so good."

Beth smiled, but she got up anyway, clutching the pages in her lap, and walked over to the lip of the Central Garden below. It was made up of concentric circles, gravel paths winding around and around and culminating in a reflecting pool adorned by banks of azaleas. It was, it occurred to her, a kind of maze of its own. How strange that she should have found herself reading the scribe's letter in just such a place. The plantings here were not so tall or so thick as to obscure where you were, or how you could get out, but the design was unquestionably inspired by the classical maze.

And, now that she thought of it, it was here that she had first encountered Mohammed al-Kalli, when he'd come to the party to inaugurate her show of illuminated manuscripts. Though she didn't for one minute believe in such stuff, it was almost as if things were unfolding according to some plan.

Standing above the circular garden, the hot sun beating down on the shoulders left bare by her summer dress, she went back to the letter in her hand. There was not much left to go, and the suspense was killing her.

While the desert air is still cool from the night, I shall be summoned to the maze. Who shall the sultan invite to observe my death? What shall they eat and drink as I strive in vain to escape the beast? The sultan has said that the game has never lasted long enough for him to finish his repast.

Beth could hardly credit what she was reading. It read as if it were a real-life account of Theseus and the Minotaur; she struggled to remember the myth. Every nine years, the Athenians were made to pay a terrible tribute to King Minos, as part of an earlier truce; they were required to send a group of young men and women—seven of each, if she recalled correctly—to be devoured by the dreaded Minotaur, half man and half bull, who lived in a labyrinth from which there was no escape. Had the Sultan Kilij al-Kalli modeled his own maze on that legendary one? And what was the actual beast who haunted, and hunted in, his own deadly theater? A Minotaur, she knew, it was not; that was only a myth. But what was it really—a lion? A tiger? Something even more exotic—and dangerous?

The prisoner at first seeks a way out, going up one narrow path and down another, but only from on high, where the sultan sits, can the design be wholly known. And only from that perch [throne] can it be seen that there is no escape. The creature sleeps at the heart of the maze, in the shade of the towering terebinth tree.

The terebinth had been mentioned earlier, too, and Beth had done some research into it—enough to reveal that it was a massive indigenous tree, better known to botanists as the Palestine pistacia, that was known to live as long as a thousand years. Though sometimes called by other names, it was prominently featured in many scriptural passages: It was under such a tree that King Saul had been buried. It was in the mighty branches of the terebinth that Absalom, great in his own eyes, had been trapped and then murdered. And it was in the valley of Elah, thick with these always green trees, that David with his sling had brought down the Philistine champion, Goliath.

But as the prisoner approaches, the beast raises its head— it has a wondrous sense of smell, and an appetite for blood that is never appeased. The prisoner has no knowledge of the monster so close, but walks deeper and deeper into the trap, unable to see beyond the dense walls of the hawthorn bushes, with their thorny branches and bright white blossoms. As he ventures into the twisting garden, so too does the monster rouse himself from his torpor and stand on its four clawed feet. The prisoner, he searches for a way out of the green enclosure [trap], while the beast seeks out his offered prey. With my own eyes, as God is my great and eternal witness, I have seen many of the sultan's prisoners—men like me who have served him well and done him no disloyalty—thrust into the maze, there to be hunted down and torn to pieces. It is said that when the sultan has no more use for a man, there is but one use left, and that is to sustain this accursed creature, this beast he calls his manticore.

Beth let the hand holding the translation drop to her side. It was too bizarre, too unbelievable, what she was reading. And yet she did not doubt a word. It was as if the scribe were whispering these words into her very ear. And it certainly reinforced her initial feeling about the illuminations—that they weren't simple flights of fancy, but were drawn from living models. The artist, she felt, had faithfully reproduced the evidence of his own eyes.

Impossible as that, even now, seemed.

"There you are," Elvis called to her as he scuffed across the gravel path in his shorts and sandals. In the bright sun, he looked so pale as to be nearly transparent. "Mrs. Cabot's looking all over for you."

"Why?"

Elvis adjusted his wraparound shades and glanced about, as if he had never seen daylight up close like this. "Don't know exactly, but there's a lot of commotion. That Arab guy—"

"Mr. al-Kalli."

"He showed up about a half hour ago, with his bodyguard, and he wants everything back."

"The book?"

"That, and all the translation work we've done so far. He's already been down to Hildegard's lair and come back with the book itself."

"I can only imagine how Hildegard reacted."

"You don't need to—I can tell you. I had to bring him down there. She wasn't happy. But she reattached the front cover—for some reason it was still separate—"

At Beth's request.

"—and the minute she'd put the last stitch through the binding, he had his bodyguard—"

"Jakob."

"Right. He had him put it back in the big box it came in—"

Beth couldn't help reflecting that Elvis made it sound like repackaging a car stereo.

"—and then they came back upstairs and started looking for you." Having finished his summation, he removed a pebble from his sandal. "Hot out here," he said. "The Santa Anas must be blowing."

Beth folded up the letter, reluctantly, as there was just a small portion to go, and knew she had no choice but to reenter the lion's den. If al-Kalli was up in her office and he wanted all the work they had done so far, she would give it to him, gladly. The computer-driven translations of the bestiary text had been interesting, no question about it, but they had also been fairly pro forma. The animals, from chimeras to leviathans, all so naturalistically depicted in the illuminations, had been summarized and described in the accompanying text in the routine, Christian-iconographic manner of the age. The fire-breathing basilisk, for instance, had been portrayed as a symbol of lust and the Devil, and the Vulgate passage—*Super aspidem et basiliscum ambulabis*—had been duly included. (Translated into the New Revised Standard Version many centuries later, the passage read "You shall tread upon the lion and the adder: the young lion and the serpent you will trample underfoot," all of which Beth recognized as a standard reference to Christ's victory over Satan.) The griffin, because it had four clawed feet but the wings of a bird, was classed, as per Leviticus 11:13–20, among the unclean creatures. The phoenix, because its flesh was incorruptible and it rose, after three days, from its own ashes, was of course a symbol of the Resurrection. And the manticore, the lethal beast that none could withstand, "hungered after human flesh most ravenously," and, like the Devil himself, could never be sated. What was surprising was to find such Christian tropes and allegories in a book of Middle Eastern origin, but Beth attributed that to its foreign-born author.

She waited while another tour group began the climb back up the gently sloping hill toward the main museum complex, then followed them on the meandering path. The gardens of the Getty had been laid out with an elaborate plan designed to suggest no plan at all. Wooden footbridges crossed running streams dotted with boulders from the Sierra foothills, all arranged to create slightly different sound effects. Seemingly random collections of flowers—

deer grass, dymondia, geranium, lavender, and thyme—
were all strategically grouped by color and texture. Elvis
said, "You want me to print out a copy of all the files for
them?"

"Yes."

"What about the completed list of the catchwords?"

It was the list of catchwords, of course, that had led her
to the discovery of the scribe's secret letter, but what, if
anything, would al-Kalli be able to make of it? He'd been
unimpressed when Elvis had first blurted out something
about it. And even Elvis did not know about the letter; Beth
had scanned the text into their laboriously constructed
database on her own, after hours. Apart from Carter, the
only person who knew anything about it at all was Hildegard, and Beth was confident that she had kept mum.
Hildegard thought that most of the wealthy people who
owned these precious artifacts were precisely the wrong
custodians—and she seldom shared with them information
she felt they couldn't appreciate. Still, Beth would call her
later just to make absolutely sure.

The moment that thought occurred to her, Beth realized
that she had come to a decision without really meaning to.
Apparently, she had decided to hold on to the scribe's letter
after all. She was shocked in a way. It was wrong; it was
unethical. And it could lead to professional disaster. How
could she ever even publish her findings without disclosing
her source material and revealing how she had come by it?

But if she told al-Kalli about the letter and returned it to
him, there was a very good chance it would never again see
the light of day. She would never be able to have an analysis done of the paper and ink; she would never be able to
display it to the world, and she would never be able to
prove that its eyewitness account of the First Crusade, or
the scribe's imprisonment and death, were anything more
than some frustrated scholar's concoction. It was bad
enough that *The Beasts of Eden* might wind up locked
away from sight for another thousand years, but the idea
that this rare and powerful and terrifyingly authentic letter
should also vanish into oblivion was simply too much.

Maybe Hildegard was right—the wrong people possessed these treasures.

As she approached her office, she saw Jakob, holding the heavy box in which she had first seen the bestiary, waiting by the door, and she could hear Mrs. Cabot inside saying, "I'm sure she's on the premises. The garage attendant said her car is still here."

From the nervousness in Cabot's voice, Beth could tell things were going badly. She put on her brightest, most reassuring smile and swept past Jakob into the room.

"Mr. al-Kalli," she said, extending her hand—he was standing at the corner of her desk, as if he'd been surreptitiously looking over the papers spread out there—"it's a pleasure to see you."

Mrs. Cabot looked as if she could faint from relief.

"My assistant, Elvis Wright, tells me you'd like to see the results of the work we've been doing." In her heart of hearts, she was still hoping to persuade him to leave things as they were, and to let the book itself remain in the conservation wing.

He took her hand, but coldly. He was dressed immaculately, as always, in a midnight blue suit and a yellow silk tie fixed by a gold pin at the collar.

"The computer software is yielding a more thorough and accurate English version than we could ever have expected." *Keep emphasizing the progress being made.* "And faster than a whole battery of scholars could do it."

"Not fast enough, I'm afraid. I want everything you have done to date."

"I've already told Elvis to prepare that for you. He's next door compiling it all right now." Unable to restrain herself, she glanced at Jakob, holding the box—now containing the book itself—right outside the office. "But without the actual bestiary on the premises, it will be harder to continue the work in the way we would like. By completing the graphemical catalogue, and its accompanying translation, we had hoped to make the wonders of this work readily accessible, online, to scholars everywhere."

"Really?" said al-Kalli dryly. "That was never my hope."

Even after dealing with al-Kalli for some time now and suspecting the worst, Beth was still taken aback by his tone. "It wasn't?"

"What I wanted—what I needed—was to know what every word in the book said. If that's been done, and if the book itself has been suitably restored, the work is done."

"But you have no intention, ever, of sharing *The Beasts of Eden* with the world?"

Al-Kalli glanced at the door as Elvis entered, carrying a stack of multicolored cardboard folders, each one devoted to a separate quire in the book and the work that had been done on it. Elvis plopped them on the desk in front of al-Kalli.

"No," he said to Beth as he leafed through the folders, reading the tabs that indicated what each contained. Satisfied, he looked up at Jakob, who came in, placed the folders on top of the iron box, and then walked out again.

Al-Kalli reached into the breast pocket of his jacket and withdrew a slim, ivory-colored envelope. "But I don't want you to think I am ungrateful," he said, handing it to Beth. Then he turned on his well-polished heel, nodded to a speechless Mrs. Cabot, and left. There was a faint scent of Bay Rum in the air.

Beth stood stock-still, as did Mrs. Cabot, until Elvis shrugged and said, "It's not like we don't have our own copies of everything."

That was true. But without the actual book, Beth thought, what good did it all do? It was like a wonderful review of a movie no one could see, an authoritative article on a painting never to be exhibited, an exegesis of a text no one could ever read. Worse, without a public source, or an authentic artifact, to point to, it was like an exercise in the fantastic. None of it could, or would, ever be taken seriously.

She turned the envelope over in her hand. It was closed, to her surprise, with red sealing wax, on which the initials *MAK* had been impressed; she hadn't seen anything like it outside the movies, where people like Sir Thomas More got missives from the Archbishop of Canterbury. She broke the seal and removed two cashier's checks—the first, in the amount of one million dollars, was made out to the Getty

Conservation Institute. She passed it wordlessly to Mrs. Cabot. The second check, she had no idea what to do with. It was made out to her personally, in the amount of one hundred thousand dollars. Elvis craned his neck to get a good look at it, then whistled.

"Whoa," he said, "looks to me like that includes a hefty bonus for your executive assistant."

Beth wanted to say that she couldn't accept this, but al-Kalli was already gone. Mrs. Cabot came closer, and Beth held it out for her to see. "Should I just tear it up?" Beth said.

"It's a cashier's check," Mrs. Cabot said, "it'd be like tearing up the actual money."

"What should I do with it?"

Mrs. Cabot looked puzzled, too. She was running all the ethical standards through her mind, but it wasn't clear exactly which one was being violated. Al-Kalli wasn't asking Beth to lie about anything; he wasn't enlisting her official support in a dubious claim. He wasn't asking her to back up a suspicious provenance or declare something to be the work of an Old Master that had been previously attributed to a lowly apprentice. In fact, he was removing the object in question from all such considerations. So it clearly wasn't a bribe—it was a gift. But the Getty did have in place a clear and strictly enforced policy that required all museum employees to report anything at all that might represent, in any way, a conflict of interest. And on those grounds alone, the check had to be declared, cleared, and only then, possibly released.

"I say cash it, quick," Elvis whispered in Beth's direction, then scooted out before Mrs. Cabot could admonish him.

"I'll have to take this to the CFO's office," Mrs. Cabot said of the million-dollar check. "And I might as well take that one, too, for safekeeping," she continued, snatching it out of Beth's hand. "The museum counsel will have to decide whether or not you can accept it."

Mrs. Cabot left, too, now, and Beth suddenly found herself bereft in her own office—alone, in the late afternoon, without *The Beasts of Eden*, and without the king's ransom she had just been holding in her hand. She didn't hold out much hope of ever seeing it again—Mrs. Cabot would find a way either to have it returned or, if al-Kalli consented, deposited instead in the museum's coffers. Nobody ever became a museum curator for the money . . . but still, it had been nice to feel rich, even if it was only for a minute or two.

There was one thing, however, she did have left. Sliding open the bottom drawer of her desk, and lifting out a folder purposely mislabeled "Personal Correspondence," she removed the original, eleventh-century letter that had been hidden in the bestiary. As she held its fragile pages in her hand, she felt that maybe the label wasn't so misleading after all. It did feel as though it had been written to her, as if she were its most appropriate and appreciative audience. No one would ever have known it even existed had it not been for Beth's sleuthing. And if it hadn't been for her breach of professional ethics now, the letter would once again be in the possession of its rightful owner, on its way back to Bel-Air . . . and oblivion. She knew she should feel guilty about the ethical questions—her training in New York and London had always stressed the highest professional standards—but if she were perfectly honest with herself, she felt instead as if she had saved something precious from an all-consuming fire.

CHAPTER THIRTY-FIVE

EVEN THOUGH HE knew it wasn't true, the funny thing about the al-Kalli estate was that it had been laid out as if it *were* designed to withstand an assault. There was only one road that led up to it, it commanded the high ground from all sides, it was surrounded by a stone wall with only one other entrance apart from the main gate. Still, there were plenty of things Greer saw that could use improvement. For instance, there was no reason not to place some razor wire atop the back and side walls; yes, there were all kinds of codes and property restrictions for Bel-Air home-owners, but if you didn't actually ask permission, it couldn't be refused, right? And if you concealed the wire with some vines and shrubbery—which wasn't hard— what was the problem? That back gate, the one where Greer had first penetrated the grounds, also needed some serious attention. It should have had a dual-focus, night-vision surveillance camera mounted above it, and the feed should go either to a control center in the main house or at least to the front gate, which was manned twenty-four hours anyway. Greer had mentioned a few of these things to al-Kalli, who'd simply said, "Do what you think is necessary,"

and then kind of brushed him aside. Greer had the sense
that something else was really on his mind.

He could guess what it was. It was that weird damn
menagerie he kept. The place gave Greer, a guy who had
seen plenty of bad shit in his time, the creeps. From the
outside, you couldn't hear or see or smell a thing; it was
sealed up tighter than a drum. But at least once a day, Greer
felt he ought to look in as part of his routine patrol. This
morning, he'd found that paleontologist, Carter Cox, in
there with Rashid. Rashid, in his usual white coat, was trying to explain something about one of the animals—the
one that had spat the green crap on Greer's neck—and
Cox, Greer could tell, was just waiting for him to finish
with the blather so he could tell him what was really up.

"The air," Cox finally said, "is very pure—I understand
that."

"We have the best filters, imported from Germany,"
Rashid rattled on, "they are made for nuclear facilities."

Cox had glanced over at Greer, nodded, then replied to
the indignant Rashid. "The air is too pure," Carter said.
"That's part of the problem."

"How can good air be bad?" Rashid challenged him.

"These creatures have very elaborate breathing mecha-
nisms," he said. "They actually need to act as their own filters, to take in and process the particulate matter. It acts as
a kind of stimulant."

Rashid looked baffled.

"It keeps their airways and lungs clear and operative."

"The humidity does that," Rashid said. "We keep a constant level in the facility at all times."

Cox looked increasingly impatient. Greer had the feeling this Rashid guy was putting up nothing but resistance.
"The saichania—"

"The basilisk," Rashid corrected him.

"Okay, the basilisk is capable of humidifying the air for
itself. It needs to do that. If the air comes in too wet, it just
gets wetter once the basilisks take a breath, which is why
they're having so much trouble with their respiration."

Greer wondered how Cox could know any of this. And

yet he had the sense that he did. And even Greer could see that these animals were in a bad way. They lumbered around in their pens like they were drunk; they dropped clumps of fur on the carefully raked ground; the bird—if you could call that massive flying contraption a bird—left bright red feathers floating in its wake. Greer could never wait to get back outside again and clear his own lungs; the place smelled vaguely like an animal shelter where he'd worked one summer as a kid.

But those animals had been regularly put down.

When he was done with his rounds of the estate, Greer usually hung out on the grounds for a while; he wanted to look like he was earning his money and not just taking pay-offs to keep his mouth shut. And he thought, if he put his mind to it, he might actually be able to make something of this gig; he had a natural bent for security concerns (having broken into plenty of houses up until now), and if he did this right, maybe he could think about setting up his own kind of Silver Bear operation. He could hire other vets, even a couple of the guys he knew from the rehab clinic, line up a bunch of rich clients, and then just sit back and collect the money. Wouldn't Sadowski be pissed about that?

He'd been looking for Sadowski ever since those other fine Sons of Liberty—Tate and Florio—had tried to take him down in the parking lot at the VA. And now that he'd done pretty much everything he could do today at the estate, he figured he'd stop off at the Blue Bayou and see if he could stir up a little trouble there. He was dying to show Sadowski that he was on top of his game and not backing down.

The nice thing about the Bayou was that, no matter what time you came in, it was always midnight inside. The lights were low, except on the runway, and the music was loud, and the bartender Zeke always had a wide selection of choice pharmaceuticals. Greer took a stool, ordered a beer, and looked around at the few lame oddballs hanging around at this hour. On the runway, a girl with long blonde hair was down on all fours, with her ass high in the air, swaying to Aerosmith's "Crazy."

"Haven't seen you around as much," Zeke said, mopping up a wet spot on the bar.

"Been working."

Zeke laughed. "Yeah, right."

Why did everybody think the very idea was such a big damn joke?

"Haven't seen much of your old pal, either," Zeke added.

"You mean Sadowski?"

"Yeah. Maybe he's moonlighting somewhere."

Possible. "He's got so many talents," Greer said evenly, "it's hard to say."

"Ginger says he's got something big going down."

"She does, huh?" That was interesting. "She here by any chance?"

Zeke looked around the place. "She must be in back." The Blue Room. "With a customer."

Greer could wait. He drank his beer, watched the blonde girl skillfully play an old man until he'd dropped probably his whole month's social security on the stage, and wondered what Sadowski's big operation was. Were the Sons of Liberty planning a Bring-the-Family Fourth of July barbecue?

Ten minutes later, he saw a geeky guy with masking tape on his glasses—what was it with these guys, hadn't they ever even heard about Scotch tape?—being led out of the back room by his hand; Ginger was wearing an electric blue tube top, a matching thong, and glittering blue platform shoes. She was self-conscious, he knew, about her height and always liked to add a few inches.

She spotted Greer immediately, but she wasn't done working the geek yet. She held his hand that extra split second, like she just couldn't bear to let go, then smiled and sauntered away, letting him work himself up for another lap dance later.

"Hi," she said to Greer, sliding onto the stool next to his. "If you're looking for Stan, he's not here."

"Why would I be looking for Stan when you're right here?"

She raised a finger to Zeke, who brought her that green drink she favored. "Why's he so mad at you, anyway?"

"He's mad at me?" Greer asked.

"You cheat him?"

Greer wondered just how much she knew about their past activities—most notably, the home burglaries her boyfriend had helped set up. Knowing how bright Sadowski was, probably everything. But then Greer could kick himself for ever having told him about the zoo on al-Kalli's estate; that wasn't very bright, either. Yeah, he'd sort of been in shock when he first saw it, but that was no excuse. Information was power; never share it unless you have to. Greer knew that he needed to start following his own advice more closely.

"What is that stuff, anyway?" he asked, just to change the subject.

She took the glass away from her lips. "Crème de menthe," she said. Her lips were still frosted with it. "Want a taste?"

Greer didn't move, but Ginger leaned in and brushed his lips with her own. He'd tasted it once before, and that time, too, it had been on her lips. It was the last time she'd given him a lap dance. Maybe she remembered, too. Maybe that's why she'd just done it again.

"Zeke tells me Stan's got something big going down."

She made a fake frown, balled up a wet cocktail napkin, and tossed it at Zeke, who was standing down the bar.

"What'd I do?" he said.

"Tattletale." But she didn't look as though she really cared. "All I know is, he's too busy to pick me up after work anymore. He's too busy to fix the muffler on my car—he's been saying he'll do it for me all month. He comes over to my place at around four in the morning most nights, expects me to service him—I told him, there are plenty of girls out there who get paid for that—and he stinks." She made a face and said, "Phew!"

"He's been working out at a gym?"

"He's been working out his trigger finger." She sipped from her drink while scanning the two new customers who had just let a bolt of late-day sunlight stream into the club. One of them was black; Greer wondered if she'd still risk violating Sadowski's code and give the guy a lap dance. "All his clothes," she went on, idly, "smell like gunpowder and that other stuff—what is it?"

"You mean cordite?"

"Yeah, maybe."

Just hunting wouldn't do that. A couple of shots popped off in the great outdoors was nothing. If your clothes reeked of smoke and cordite, then you had to be in a firing range. And Greer knew which one it would be.

"I told him," Ginger said, "that a bunch of my girl-friends were going to Las Vegas for the Fourth of July weekend and I told him we should go, too. Elton John's doing a show there, and I was thinking of using some of his songs in my act; it would be really great for me profes-sionally."

Greer had to remind himself that Ginger did not con-sider herself a stripper: she was a dancer and performance artist (who just happened to take off most of her clothes). "You want to go to Vegas," Greer said, "I'll take you to Vegas." What might yank Sadowski's crank more than that?

"You will?" Ginger said, quickly calculating all the an-gles. "This weekend?"

"That's a little short notice."

"But that's when Elton John's going to be there. And Stan said there was no way he could go this weekend. The Sons of Liberty—I call 'em the Sons of Bitches," she said, with a laugh, "but he hates that. Anyway, he says the Sons of Liberty are staging their big operation, whatever that means. I asked if he meant a circle jerk, and he almost took a swing at me." She got serious. "I told him, if he ever did hit me, that was it. I've been hit before, and I never wait around for the second punch."

The two new customers had taken a table by the runway and were waiting for the next dancer to come out. Greer could see that Ginger was sizing them up and anxious to get back into action.

"Am I keeping you?"

"Huh?" She turned her face to him. "Oh, yeah, well, the manager gets pissed at me if I sit around too long."

Greer knew what she was getting at.

"You want to go back to the Blue Room?" she asked with a sly smile. "I could give you my pre-Vegas special."

"Save it for the Bellagio," he said, sliding off his stool and giving his left leg that extra second or two to kick back into gear. "I've got to be somewhere."

The Liberty Firing Range. Suddenly he had an overwhelming urge to do some target practice.

"You mean it about Las Vegas?" she said. "Because Stan and me, we're not exactly married, if you know what I'm saying."

Greer had to think about it for a moment but then he realized that, yes, he was serious. "Yeah. Let's do it in a couple of weeks."

"But what about Elton John?"

"He can come, too," Greer said, grazing her cheek with one finger and then heading for the door. He tried his best not to limp; he always hated the thought that somebody would be watching him walk away and thinking about his damn limp.

On the way to the Liberty Range, he had to stop and get gas. He never could do that without thinking about Iraq— about the towering oil derricks and the burning oil fields. Twenty dollars. Twenty-five. Thirty. The pump just kept on ringing. Christ, what was the point of going over there if they didn't just take all the goddamn oil that they wanted? The army should have just come in and put up a nice big— *very* big—electrified fence around all the drilling and processing plants, and left a battalion of soldiers to guard each one. Who cared what happened to the rest of the country? The Iraqis didn't seem to give a shit, and they sure as hell didn't want the Americans around anymore. Greer never could understand exactly what the point of that whole exercise had been, and when his leg acted up, as it was doing now, he understood even less.

Going to the firing range wasn't exactly as easy, or as safe, as heading into neutral territory like the Bayou. Here, if he found Sadowski, he'd find him armed, and surrounded by his fellow Sons of Liberty. One thing made sense now that Greer thought about it—if you're a Son of Liberty, wouldn't the Fourth of July be the perfect time to pull off your grand patriotic demonstration?

In the parking lot, he wasn't sure if he could spot Sadowski's car—there were half a dozen black SUVs, some Harleys, and a new Hummer 3—just like the one Tate and Florio had been driving. He felt like he'd just hit a trifecta. He drove down the block, turned around so that his car would be heading toward the nearest freeway entrance, then parked under a burned-out street lamp. There was no point in trying to bring his piece inside; there were metal detectors on the way in, and you had to surrender any firearms at the front counter—before you even got inside the security door. If you wanted to shoot some practice rounds with your gun, they'd give it back to you once you were inside, but Greer wasn't shelling out any money to step onto the range today.

At the front desk, there was no sign of Burt Pitt. An old man with a glass eye was running the place, and through the tinted bulletproof glass Greer could see only one guy on the range. So what accounted for all the cars outside? Greer could guess.

"If you want to shoot, I'll need to see your driver's license and one other form of photo ID," the old man mumbled, but Greer said, "Maybe later. Just want to get some stuff right now."

He picked up a wire basket and started to rummage around the stacks of ammo piled up by the counters, the scopes and mounts and visors and gloves. There was the muffled roar of gunshots from the range—Greer guessed that he was hearing a double-pump, twelve-gauge shotgun—but nobody was in the store area, either. The old man was counting the till, and Greer gradually made his way toward the back, where the bathrooms—and the safety instruction classroom—were located off a long hall, out of sight of the front desk.

The classroom door was closed, and the sign said

SAFETY SESSION IN PROGRESS. NO ADMITTANCE. Greer put
his ear to the door, and he could hear Burt's voice. But
what he could make out sure didn't sound like a routine
lecture on proper gun handling. Burt was keeping his
voice down, but Greer heard him say, "Timers all have to
be coordinated precisely." You didn't use timers on any
guns Greer knew of. Then his voice grew fainter. He must
have been pacing up and down the front of the classroom
while he talked. The next time he got close, Greer heard
him say, "And don't get some Japanese piece of shit—get
a Timex."

There was a round of laughter from inside—sounded
like maybe a dozen guys—and then Burt said, "If they
don't go off when they're supposed to, and where they're
supposed to, it'll be too easy to contain. Once it gets going, it's got to be completely unstoppable." He was standing right on the other side of the door; Greer stopped
breathing.

Somebody in the room asked something else that Greer
couldn't make out, and Burt replied by saying, "All the
forecasts are good—Santa Anas if we're lucky, hot and dry
either way."

"How about a break?" somebody called out. "I got to
make a pit stop."

"Good idea," Burt said. "I soaked through my Depends
ten minutes ago."

There was more laughter, and then, almost before Greer
had time to pull his ear away from the door, the handle was
turning. He whipped around and ducked into the nearest
door behind him—the ladies' room—just as he heard Burt
and the other Sons of Liberty taking their break. It was a
small room, with two stalls, a cracked mirror, and a withered bar of soap on the sink. Greer couldn't imagine that it
did much business. But then it occurred to him that it was
possible—if unlikely—that the Sons of Liberty included a
daughter or two. Shit. He ducked into the far stall, locked
it, and prayed.

Burt's voice was coming from the hall right outside—
"perfect conditions," he was saying "better than you could

ask for"—and then, as he went into the neighboring men's room, it became muffled, but still clear, and coming from overhead. Greer glanced up, where he saw a flat, dusty vent. A Son or two had entered the men's room with him. A urinal flushed. Burt was saying something about a test run he'd made. Greer gently stepped on top of the toilet seat and raised his head to the vent level.

"—and the choppers made it there in less than fifteen minutes. I timed it." His voice came in loud and clear.

"But we had some fun that day anyway," another man said, "didn't we?"

Greer knew that voice, too—it was Sadowski.

Burt chuckled. "Might have had more if we hadn't been interrupted."

Greer wondered what the hell they were talking about; he didn't remember Sadowski ever telling him anything that would correlate.

A third man said something Greer had trouble hearing—something about aliens. Somebody was taking a loud, splashing leak.

"If we set it up right," Burt said, "they will."

"Make sure you bring all the stuff and leave it the way you're supposed to," Sadowski said. He added something else that was lost under the sound of rushing water from the faucet. At least somebody's washing his hands, Greer thought; those Sons of Liberty didn't strike him as the most hygienic bunch.

"Incoming!" he heard loudly as somebody rapped hard on the ladies' room door. He just managed to duck his head as he heard a guy barge in. "It's empty," the intruder called out to someone else in the hall, then Greer heard a zipper being pulled down and the door to the other stall— thank God—being flung open. But what if this guy's pal joined him?

Greer teetered on top of the toilet seat, his left leg starting to quake; it was one thing to stand on top of it, it was another to have to crouch down and hold your balance.

The guy lifted the toilet seat with his foot, then let loose with a powerful stream that went on and on and on. *How many beers,* Greer thought, his palms flat against the cold tile wall, his leg cramping, *did this guy have in him*?

The bathroom door swung open again—Greer could hear several men horsing around in the hallway—and another man came in. Greer wondered what the hell to do—maybe he could put his feet down now, slowly, and the new guy would think he'd been there all along. There was no way he could burst out and run for it—his leg was going to need a few minutes just to get fully operational again.

But the stall door stayed latched; Greer held his breath as he turned his head. There was about a half-inch slit between the door and the side of the stall. Through it he could just make out the back of a guy standing in front of the mirror, lovingly combing and styling a thick head of oily black hair. On his forearm, he had a tattoo of the Liberty Bell.

It was Florio.

Which meant Tate was probably the guy still pissing in the next stall.

Which also meant that if they found him there, he stood almost no chance of leaving in one piece. Or leaving at all.

"You think it's gonna work?" Tate said, finally finishing off, then audibly zipping up.

"Who the fuck cares?" Florio said, patting down some stray hairs. "If it does, that's great. If it doesn't, so what? A lot of rich shits find out they're not so rich anymore."

Tate laughed and came over to the mirror. "Can I borrow that?" he said, reaching for the comb.

"No," Florio said, sticking it into the back pocket of his jeans. "What do you need it for anyway?"

Florio sauntered out, and Tate, unfazed, ran some cold water on his hands, then slicked his own thinning brown hair straight back on his skull. Greer felt the toilet seat he was perched on starting to tilt, and he prayed it wouldn't fall. Tate opened his mouth and put his face closer to the mirror, looking, it appeared, for something stuck in his teeth. The tremor in Greer's left leg was fast becoming a full-blown shake. Tate put a finger in his mouth and pulled a cheek to one side, inspecting something within. Greer's hand, sweating, started to slip on the tiles, and his left knee felt like somebody had just lighted a match inside it. The seat creaked, softly.

But Tate must have heard it because he glanced backward in the mirror.

"Somebody there?"

Greer let his legs slip down to the floor.

"Yeah," he grunted.

"Shit, I didn't know anybody was in here."

Tate bent down to look under the stall door. He could see Greer's feet facing the wrong way.

"Got a prostate the size of a softball," Greer muttered in mock frustration.

"That so?" Tate said, a tinge of suspicion still in his voice.

Greer knew he had to say something to allay it. "Tell Burt I'll be there when this fuckin' dam breaks."

The mention of Burt seemed to do it. "Yeah, well, don't take all night," Tate said, taking hold of the door handle, "we've still gotta get our final instructions."

And then he was gone—and Greer could lean forward with his head against the wall and let out a low moan of agony. His hands went to his leg and squeezed it tight, trying to block the pain signals from making it up to his brain.

He could still hear some commotion in the hall outside, and he waited till it died down. Then he fumbled in his pocket, found some Vicodin, and left the stall. He listened again for any noise in the hall—there was none now—then ran some cold water into his cupped hand and swallowed the pills. He opened the door slowly, poked his head out. The classroom door was shut, and he could hear muffled voices inside.

He walked past and back to the merchandise and display cases. The old man at the counter was collecting the lone shooter's safety gear and settling up the bill. As Greer moved past them toward the exit, the old man said, "Looking for something special?"

"Nah, just looking," Greer said. He went out the door and into the still hot night air. He limped down the boulevard, praying that the painkillers would kick in soon, and got into his battered Mustang. The only thing sparkling about it was the new window on the driver's side, the one he'd had to replace after Tate had taken it out with the baseball bat.

Tate. And his Hummer 3.

In that same instant, his hand reached under the seat and found the Weight Watchers box with the Beretta inside.

He put the car into gear and drove up slowly along the curb until he was just short of the Liberty Firing Range parking lot. Then, leaving it in gear, the door half-open, he walked casually into the lot. Stopping at the Hummer, he looked around, saw no one, and then, with the butt of the gun, tapped, hard, on the driver's-side window.

The horn started bleating, the headlights flashing.

Even though there was no way the glass in this Hummer would be the same bulletproof and shock-resistant consistency of the ones in Iraq, it had still withstood that first tap. Greer stepped back, and this time took a harder swing. The glass splintered, but held again. Shit. He bent his elbow back and really whacked it this time, right on the fracture, and the window dissolved into a thousand tiny blue pebbles, some spilling into the leather interior, some raining onto the concrete.

But now that he had the right method, he strolled around to the other side and took that window out, too. That blaring horn was deafening.

Then he stuck the gun back in his belt, ducked back into his idling Mustang, and—after carefully checking in his side mirror for passing traffic—pulled away.

As he sailed through the green light at the corner, he could hear angry voices spilling into the Liberty parking lot, and whether it was from the pills or the sheer joy, his leg already felt better.

CHAPTER THIRTY-SIX

CARTER HATED SECRETS, and right now his house felt like it was filled with them. Beth was in the shower, and he was putting Joey back in his crib. But his thoughts kept returning to the same secret things—the bizarre job that he had undertaken on the al-Kalli estate, the astonishing bestiary that he now supervised there, the bones that had gone missing from his basement lab at the museum. Normally, Beth would be the first person he'd turn to; she'd be the first—and possibly the only—one in whom he'd confide. There was nobody he relied on more, nobody whose judgment he valued more highly, nobody to whom he poured out his doubts and fears and quandaries more trustingly. But now he couldn't. Al-Kalli had sworn him to secrecy—and Carter even had the feeling that to tell Beth anything might be to endanger her somehow. As for the stolen bones, well, he felt as though he had made some colossal blunder, and that it was his responsibility to figure out what to do next. That, plus he was embarrassed. He couldn't imagine anything under Beth's supervision—especially something so irreplaceable—ever getting lost or damaged.

Joey looked up at him with those clear gray-blue eyes, his feet kicking merrily in the air, and Carter couldn't help but think of all the secrets and mysteries that would always attend him, too. The doctors had told Carter, in no uncertain terms, that he would not be able to father a child, but here was Joey. And though Carter and Beth had thought that by leaving New York, they could also leave behind the terrible ordeal with Arius, who had stalked them for months, he now suspected (or *knew*? did he know and was he just denying it to himself?) that he had been wrong about that, too. He wondered if that was what life was like—that everything you ever did, everything that ever happened to you, every decision you ever made haunted you the rest of your days? Los Angeles was supposed to be a fresh start, but were fresh starts even possible?

Joey burbled something that sounded suspiciously like "Dada," and Carter laughed. "You talkin' to me?" he said, in his best De Niro. "You talkin' to me?"

Joey laughed and batted his arms against the mattress. But he didn't repeat the experiment.

Carter leaned down into the crib and, with his eyes closed, kissed him on his smooth, untroubled brow. The skin was cool and dry and fragrant, and for a few seconds Carter just stayed as he was, bent down like a crane fishing in a pool of water, feeling Joey's little mitts pull at his hair and his earlobes. This, he told himself, is all that matters. This . . . and Beth. He focused entirely on the moment, banishing all other thoughts. This . . . and Beth. This . . . and Beth, until, for one split second, he suddenly flashed on a green forest, fragrant with rain.

"Did you have to change him?" Beth asked from the doorway.

Carter opened his eyes and turned around. Beth was in her blue robe, toweling her hair dry. "Change him?" Carter said, the image of the forest fading fast. "No. He's fine."

Beth came to his side and gazed down into the crib. "He is, isn't he?" she said.

But something in her tone didn't sound right. "You say that like you're not completely sure."

Beth shook her head—was she just shaking her hair dry?—and said, "Of course I'm sure. What a thing to say!"

Carter, chastised, remained silent. But he still thought he'd heard a discordant note. And neither he nor Beth moved for a few seconds, as if by standing there they could dispel any doubt.

Finally, Carter said, "Where's Champ?" Outside, the long summer day was finally drawing to a close and it was nearly dark.

"I think he's in the yard," Beth said. "Maybe you should bring him in." She didn't have to say anything about the coyotes for Carter to know what was in her mind.

He nodded and left the room. He went down the stairs of the house where he felt, despite the many months that they'd been there, a bit like an intruder. Everything was nice—well appointed, freshly painted, plushly carpeted—but it wasn't his, and it wasn't even decorated with his stuff. His old rocking chair, his scarred coffee table, his cinder-block bookcases—they'd all, quite reasonably, been left behind. It was hardly worth the cost of shipping them, much less to a fully furnished place. And that, too, had been part of their plan for a fresh start. Get rid of the old stuff, with all its scratches and dents and memories, and begin again with new and foreign and unencumbered belongings.

A hot, dry wind was blowing again, and the short grass in the yard crackled under Carter's feet. The canyon below was bathed in moonlight, the far slope of the Santa Monica Mountains outlined against a starry sky. New York has nothing like this, Carter reflected, though that didn't mean he missed his view of the Washington Square Arch any less. He sometimes wondered if it had something to do with his work—spending so much of his time in the study and contemplation of long-dead things, did he need the fix of human activity at the end of the day? Did he need to rub elbows with the crowd, to feel the pulse of life around him? To exchange the dry bones (the question of what he was going to do about the missing bones of La Brea Woman coursed through his mind for the zillionth time) for warm flesh?

Off in the distance, he could hear the sudden burst of

backyard fireworks, one day early. He knew that the police and fire departments were on high alert; there had been nothing but warnings all week about the drought-dry tinder, and the dangers of setting off a wildfire. Carter had never been anywhere near such a blaze, but he'd seen the news footage of previous blazes on CNN. And the sad interviews afterward, with people who had struggled to save whatever they could—their pets, their photo albums, their family silver—from the devouring flames. One guy had narrowly escaped on a bicycle, clutching, of all things, a massive bowling trophy.

He looked around the small, fenced yard, and heard Champ before he spotted him. Most of his body was under a bush, apparently trying to root something out. All Carter could see was his bushy blond tail.

"Champ!"

The dog's tail wagged, but he was still intent on what he was doing.

"Come on, Champ. Time to go inside."

Carter went closer, but all he could see was the dog's arched back and wagging tail. "What are you doing?"

Carter put his hands on Champ's haunches and gently dragged the dog out of the brush. Champ didn't resist, but he didn't cooperate, either. He just allowed himself to be pulled, like a statue, backward on the patchy grass. In his jaws, Carter could now see his prize—it looked like the bones and carcass of a recently deceased squirrel—and Champ was clearly not planning to let go.

"Oh, man, what do you want that for?" Carter said. "Don't we feed you better than that?"

Champ glanced at him, but appeared to be utterly unpersuaded.

"Come on, boy, let go," Carter said, squatting down and trying to dislodge the remains. But Champ growled, and Carter let go, wiping his fingers in the dirt.

What was the best way to win this war? Carter wondered. Should he go inside, get something the dog liked—maybe a big wad of peanut butter?—and get him to drop this treat for an even more appealing one?

Champ shook the desiccated carcass, as if making sure there wasn't any life left in it, and that's when it suddenly occurred to Carter—Champ might be the answer to at least one of his problems. Why didn't he think of it sooner?

He jumped to his feet, ran into the kitchen, got the peanut butter—he just brought the whole jar outside—and let Champ bury his face in it. With the toe of his sneaker, Carter kicked the now neglected squirrel over the edge of the yard and down into the ravine below.

"You want to go for a ride?" Carter said to Champ, who was too busy with the Skippy to pay any attention. When the dog took a break, Carter put the leash on him and went back inside. He bounded up the stairs to the bedroom, where he found Beth propped up against a stack of pillows, with her nose in a sheaf of papers. "I'm going to go out for a little while," he said.

"Out?" she said. "Now?"

"There's something I forgot at work."

"At the Page? Why can't it wait till tomorrow?"

"Tomorrow it's closed, for the Fourth."

"It'll be closed now, for the night."

"I know the guard; he'll let me in."

"This really can't wait?" Beth said, though she knew her husband well enough to know that whatever it was, it couldn't.

"Be back in no time," he said, before adding, "and, by the way, I'm taking Champ with me."

He was thumping back down the stairs before she could even think to ask why he'd want the dog along.

Fortunately, Champ loved going for a ride; Carter had only to open the side door of his Jeep and Champ leapt up onto the front seat, ready for anything.

And would he be ready for what Carter wanted him to do? Carter put the car into gear, backed out of the driveway, and hoped that this wasn't the craziest idea he'd had yet.

At the museum, the parking lots were closed, so he had to leave the car on Wilshire. He had a plastic passkey to the employee entrance, and he led Champ inside. He knew Hector would be on duty somewhere, and he didn't want to give the poor guy a heart attack by coming upon him unexpectedly.

"Hector?" he called out. "It's Carter. Carter Cox."

There was no answer.

"Hector? You here?"

Champ was fascinated by all the smells from all the feet that had trampled over the museum floor that day, and Carter was encouraged to see his head down, nose fixed. Maybe this would work, after all.

He led the dog toward the rear elevators, past the lighted display of the dire wolf skulls, past the open lab, past the entrance to the lush atrium garden where Geronimo used to like to wander, and tried calling out again. "Hector? You around?"

He heard the jangling of a key ring, and a tentative voice saying "Who's there? Don't move!"

"Hector, it's me—Carter. Don't freak out."

Hector, breathing a sigh of relief, emerged from behind the life-size replica of the giant sloth being attacked by a saber-toothed cat.

"What the hell are you doing here?" Hector said. "The museum's closed. And Mr. Gunderson, he gave me special instructions about you." Then he noticed the dog. "And are you crazy? You can't bring a dog in here."

"I had to," Carter said.

"Why? Why you need to bring a dog into the museum, at night?"

Carter recognized that he was going to have to do some fast, and persuasive, talking, if he hoped to get Hector's cooperation. "I need him to help me find something."

Hector waited, unimpressed. "Find what?"

Carter knew that this was an important moment—if he let Hector know what was missing, and Hector shared his secret with Gunderson, all hell would break loose. But if he didn't tell him, it would be impossible to do what he had to do.

"Some bones are missing, from the collection downstairs. Some very important bones."

Now Hector started to look concerned. Anything that

went missing, especially if it could be tracked to his watch, potentially spelled trouble. "You report this?" he asked, hitching his belt back up over his belly.

"Not yet," Carter confessed. "I was hoping I could find them first. Or at least figure out what happened." And then, in a low blow that he regretted giving, he said, "You've been so helpful about granting me access downstairs, even after hours, that I was hoping we could solve the problem before either one of us had to answer any questions from Gunderson, or the police."

Hector wasn't stupid, and he immediately surmised where Carter was going with this. Cooperate, and maybe the problem could be made to go away, or stick to the rules and risk all kinds of shit coming down. Why, he wondered, had he ever let Carter, and that friend of his with the long white hair, slide? He didn't even like Big Macs that much.

"What do you need to do?" he said, and Carter inwardly exulted.

"Not much. I just need you to take us downstairs again, to the lower level, for a few minutes."

Hector hesitated, wondering if this was in fact a way of getting himself into even deeper trouble, then turned toward the elevators with his keys in hand. He would stick right by this guy—and his dog—and make damn sure nothing else went wrong.

Carter and Champ followed him into the elevator, and Carter, afraid of saying the wrong thing, kept his mouth shut all the way down. When the doors opened, he said, "You can just wait here, if you want," but Hector wasn't going to chance anything else going wrong.

"I'm coming with you," he said. "And that dog better not do anything—and you know what I'm talking about—down here."

"He's completely museum-trained," Carter said, though the small joke got no response at all.

Hector turned on the overhead lights, which flickered to life, row after row, like waves receding into the distance. The light they threw off was pale and ghostly and caught a million dust motes drifting through the air. Even

Champ, normally an avid adventurer, waited sheepishly by the elevator.

"Come on, boy," Carter said. "We've got work to do."

Carter set off down the center aisle, with Champ staying close by his side. Hector followed right behind them. They walked past seemingly endless rows of identical cabinets with shallow drawers, all containing countless artifacts and fossilized remains gathered over the decades that the La Brea Tar Pits had been excavated and explored. The bones gave off a dry and arid aroma, and Hector coughed once or twice as they passed them by.

As they approached the makeshift lab that Carter and Del had set up at the farthest reach of the floor, Champ tried to trot ahead. Clearly, he smelled something different here—maybe the scent of Del, or the tarry bones of the La Brea Man that had, until just a short time before, lain exposed on the worktable. Now those remains were secretly stashed on another floor, in a locked closet used for chemicals and solvents.

But it was what remained in the burgled drawer that Carter was after. The broken padlock still hung from the hasp, and as Carter slid the drawer open, he saw the crumpled handkerchief that he had used to conceal and transport the mysterious object that the La Brea Man had once held in his hand. The cloth was all that was left there, but it was still encrusted with bits of the tar and tiny flakes of bone or stone from the object itself. It wasn't much, Carter realized, but it was all that he had to work with.

"Wasn't that where the woman's bones were?" Hector said, concerned.

"Yes."

"And those, aren't they the oldest bones in the whole museum?"

Hector seemed to be appreciating the gravity of the situation by the second.

"Not the oldest," Carter replied, "but the most significant."

Hector whistled under his breath, as Carter delicately lifted the handkerchief out of the drawer—he didn't want to disturb or taint its odor in any way—and then held it down to Champ's nose. At first, the dog tried to turn away, as if uninterested, but when Carter put a finger through his collar and pulled his head back to the cloth, Champ took a good whiff.

Then he looked up again at Carter, as if to say, *Yeah?*

"I want you to follow that scent," Carter said, knowing of course that the dog couldn't understand a word. But that's what people did, wasn't it? You spoke to the dog as if he could be made to comprehend your meaning . . . and damned if it didn't work sometimes.

Champ turned and looked around, as if wondering exactly what to do. Carter led him a few feet back down the aisle—the only way any thief could have gone—and then pressed the handkerchief to his nose again. Champ took another strong sniff and trotted a few feet ahead, dragging out the length of his Extendo leash. Carter reeled him in, gave him another shot at the wadded-up cloth, then let him go again—and this time Champ seemed to be fully involved in the game. He put his head down to the cold linoleum tiles, then up in the air, then back down to the floor. Occasionally he would stop and sniff at another cabinet; how different could any of these artifacts and fossils really smell? Carter wondered. He could only count on the freshness of the sample to help Champ distinguish it from all the others resting in their silent graves all around them.

"This is the stupidest thing I have ever done," Hector muttered. "This I will lose my job over for sure."

"Maybe not," Carter said as he followed along in Champ's wake. "Maybe not."

But when the dog started to retrace their steps directly to the elevator, Carter, too, began to wonder. Was Champ just leading them back out the way they came? Was that all he thought he was being asked to do?

But then the dog stopped, turned, and, with his head close to the floor, moved to the left, past the elevator bank and around the corner. "What's back there?" Carter asked over his shoulder.

"Not much," Hector said. "A storage unit, some machinery, a stairwell."

Champ had wrapped his long leash around a steel column, and Carter had to hurry up to catch him. The dog was
standing in front of a sealed metal door with a red slash
painted on it warning that an alarm would go off if the door
was opened.

"Where's this lead to?" Carter asked.

Hector had to think for a second, and looked up as if to
see what they might be under. "The garden," he said.

"You mean the one in the middle of the museum?"

"Yes."

Champ put his nose to the bottom of the door, and
pawed at the metal.

"Can you open it?"

Hector stepped around him, using a passkey to disable
the alarm—to Carter, it looked like the alarm hadn't been in
operation, anyway—then pried the door open with a re-
sounding screech. It sounded as if the door hadn't worked
in ages, either. Inside, it was pitch black and a cobweb
brushed across Carter's face. Hector played his flashlight
beam over the interior until he found the light switch. A
bare bulb hung down from the ceiling, illuminating a rusted
lawnmower, several gardening tools, some rubber boots, a
stack of dented paint cans. It looked as if no one had been
down there, much less passed through with a pile of stolen
bones, in a very long time. But Champ was eager to go.

"Okay, boy, I'll take your word for it," Carter said,
though he wasn't really so sure.

Champ neatly threaded his way through the detritus,
and he was halfway up the first flight of stairs before Hector had managed to close the door behind them. Carter was
looking at the dust on the steps to see if there was any sign
of a footprint, or anything at all to suggest a recent intruder, but in the dim light from the overhead bulbs—not to
mention the haste with which he was trying to keep up with
Champ—it was all he could do to see the steps themselves.

Champ stopped on the landing to make sure he had his
pack in tow, then trotted up the next flight of steps, which
culminated in another sealed door. At this one he whined,
as if anxious to capture his prey just beyond. Hector, huffing

and puffing, climbed the last steps, released the alarm, then yanked the door back with a loud screech. Carter was instantly overwhelmed by the smell of wet leaves and thick foliage, and by the sound of swishing sprinklers.

Champ leapt out into the garden so fast that the leash came out of Carter's hand. There were modest lamp poles with amber lights every few yards along the pathways, but otherwise the garden was lighted by the moon, which shone down through the open, unobstructed roof. Carter could hear the plastic leash handle clattering after Champ as he dragged it down the cement walkway, then over the little footbridge that crossed the meandering, koi-filled stream. Though it was not as strictly planned as the Pleistocene Garden on the grounds outside, where nothing but plants indigenous to the area during the last ice age were grown, here—in this secluded atrium, surrounded by the curving glass walls of the museum all around it—visitors still had a sense of the quiet, natural landscape that this place had once possessed. A gnarled gingko tree rose up in one corner, slender palms rustled in the night wind, the furtive splashing of turtles—who enjoyed their own little nesting ground—joined with the constant rushing of the waterfall toward the back of the garden. And it was there that Carter spotted Champ, trying to drag his leash up a small escarpment overgrown with ferns.

"Okay, hang on," Carter said, but Champ didn't turn. It was as if he were trying to enter the streambed from the miniature waterfall.

Carter unhooked the leash from his collar—there was no way the dog could escape from the enclosed atrium—and Champ instantly ran down the path to a spot that afforded easier access, then went up the slight rise to the source of the waterfall again. For a second, Carter thought he might just be thirsty, but then he saw it—lying there, atop a larger, flatter stone in the center of the stream.

The object from the La Brea Man's grasp.

But now, perhaps because it had been partially cleansed by the running water, it gleamed, like the mano—or grinding stone—it had clearly once been. On its surface there were long diagonal scratches, made with another, possibly redder stone. Champ, unable to reach it, was hovering over the small pool from which the waterfall descended. Carter, not quite able to see everything from the pathway, stepped off the cement and, wrapping his arm around the base of a slim pine spruce, hauled himself up. He had to nudge Champ to one side just to make room for himself; this was an ornamental garden, and it wasn't designed for off-road adventures. But the ground around his feet didn't look as ornamental and undisturbed as the rest of the garden. Carter could see that some brush had been cleared to one side, and the dirt here looked freshly turned.

Champ barked, as if confirming his discovery, and Carter, suddenly realizing what he was standing on, instinctively stepped back.

"What's there?" Hector asked from the walkway below.

Carter wasn't sure how to answer that. But then he said, "A grave, I think."

Hector crossed himself.

Carter looked again at the mano stone, sitting in the stream like a kind of marker, and then at the turned earth on the bank where he stood. It was as if he had stumbled upon a prehistoric burial site.

"What do you mean, a grave?" Hector said. "Whose?"

That much, Carter knew. It was the grave of the La Brea Woman, who had died just a few hundred yards away, over nine thousand years ago—though who had dug it here, and how, he couldn't even guess.

"Damn," Hector muttered, "this is something we got to report."

"Not yet," Carter replied. First he needed to know more about how it had happened. And then, he would need some time to think through its consequences. "Just let me handle it. Okay?"

Hector looked dubious, but at the same time glad to be off the hook. "You'll say that it isn't my fault? You'll say that I did my job?"

"Yes," Carter said, reaching down to ruffle Champ's fur in gratitude, "I'll keep you out of it entirely."

Hector's mind appeared at rest.

But Carter's was not. As he surveyed the marking stone, the last and most precious thing in the world to the La Brea Man, and then the earth that still bore the trace of bony fingertips, his own mind was decidedly in turmoil.

CHAPTER THIRTY-SEVEN

FOR SADOWSKI, IT felt as if this night would never end. It was the night before the Fourth of July and it felt a hell of a lot like Christmas Eve, back when he was a kid. He remembered not being able to get to sleep or even stay in bed, and one year, when he was about five, he'd crept into the family room early, started unwrapping his presents, and gotten a good walloping for it when he was caught. But he was all grown-up now, and he had no excuse.

He couldn't even talk about any of this to Ginger. It was all top secret. Not that she'd have understood it anyway. All she could talk about lately was going to Las Vegas to catch that faggot, Elton John, at some casino. "It's for my act," she kept saying, and Sadowski kept promising he'd take her some other time, though the point of taking a stripper to Las Vegas, on your own dime, eluded him. There were more strippers and more hookers per square inch in Las Vegas than anywhere on the whole fucking planet. Why bring your own? It'd be like carrying a six-pack into a bar.

"Stan, aren't you ever coming to bed?" she asked now, from under the covers. "You're keeping me up."

There were only two rooms in the apartment and there

wasn't a real door between them—just a couple of lou-vered panels that swung back and forth. Sadowski had the TV on—another one of those *Cold Case* files—and he was swigging his fifth or sixth beer of the night. "I'm not sleepy," he shot back, and she instantly retorted, "Then why don't you go back to your place, because I am."

She had a point—though he would never have admitted it. He'd only come over here to get his rocks off—and he'd already done that—and there was only one reason not to go back to his own place now.

All his gear was there and he knew, if he did, he would start fiddling with it again.

He watched TV until the show ended—it was another one of those where the DNA from a semen stain caught up with the guy ten years later—and then, when he was satisfied that he'd made his point and kept her awake long enough, he tossed the can into the garbage pail, burped loudly enough to elicit a disgusted groan from the bedroom, and headed out.

The night air felt good—it was relatively cool, maybe high sixties, but it was still dry. The only thing that could have spoiled their plans was rain, and there was absolutely no fucking chance of that. During the commercials on *Cold Case*, he'd kept flipping back to the Weather Channel, just to hear more about the arid conditions in the L.A. Basin and the advisories for anyone planning some Fourth of July festivities: "The whole county is a tinderbox," one blow-dried blonde declared, "so don't even think about set-ting off those Roman candles or cherry bombs, folks."

Well, it wasn't any goddamn cherry bomb he was plan-ning to set off.

Driving home in his black Explorer, he was careful not to go too fast or make any mistakes that some cop on patrol might pull him over for. Even a guy his size would never pass the Breathalyzer test with a six-pack under his belt. (Once, he'd been pulled over and failed the test after hav-ing only three.) No, easy does it, he kept telling himself. Easy does it.

His own place was a dingy apartment above a mechanic's shop, accessible by a wooden staircase off the alley. Ginger had never been there; nobody had ever been there. And that was just the way he liked it. He'd replaced the landlord's door, at his own expense, with one made of vulcanized steel, with a kick-proof base panel and a dead bolt that could withstand anything short of a battering ram. Inside, he had a warren of small, dark rooms, the last of which had its own locked door on it. He took his key ring out of his pocket, opened it, and flicked the switch on what he called his War Room.

A bank of ceiling lights came on, bathing the room in a stark, white glow. On the walls he'd mounted topographical maps of L.A., along with some free gun posters he'd gotten from Burt at the firing range. In the center of the room, there was a beaten-up desk and chair, and behind that a couple of green metal lockers he'd salvaged from a gym being demolished up the street. That was where he kept his field gear.

Should he just suit up, he thought, and get it over with? He knew this would happen—that if he got anywhere near his stuff again, he would want to get started.

But he also knew what Burt had told them all, a dozen times: "If it goes off too soon, it'll go nowhere." The whole idea was to carefully plant the incendiary devices in all the places marked on the map, and time them to go off so the resulting blaze would be unstoppable. As soon as the fire department moved its resources to stop one, another one would start up, just beyond where a firebreak might have been formed. Burt knew all about this stuff—he'd been a volunteer firefighter in the Northwest, and he'd made a thorough study of the L.A. geography and terrain. If everybody in the inner circle did exactly as he was supposed to do, then the whole west side of Los Angeles, from Westwood to the Pacific Palisades, would go up in the biggest fucking conflagration the country had ever seen. And the Sons of Liberty would have done in one night what the Minutemen hadn't been able to do in years: put the illegal aliens—and the terrorist threat from our unguarded borders to the south—in the dead center of the national radar screen.

Burt had all the rest figured out, too—how it'd look like

some wetbacks or foreign agents had done it (this was part of the plan that Burt had kind of kept under wraps), and the war to reclaim America's borders, and its proud white heritage, would be well under way.

Sadowski couldn't resist popping open the lockers and looking over his equipment one more time. Army fatigues (he considered this work to be a continuing part of his national service), flashlight, canteen (filled with Gatorade to keep his electrolytes high), a forty-caliber Browning Hi-Power pistol (its grip made from the wood of the last surviving Liberty Tree), and most important of all, his fireproof asbestos sheath; this was what the smoke jumpers up north used, just in case they found themselves caught in the middle of a fire. Burt had shown them what to do. As fast as you could, you made a depression in the ground, then lay down in it with the sheath zipped up (from the inside) from your feet to your head. If the fire lingered, you'd probably cook to death—"like an ear of corn in aluminum foil," Burt had joked—but if you were lucky and it swept on past quickly enough, you'd make it out alive.

In a rucksack, under a wadded-up mosquito net, there were a half dozen incendiary bombs on timers, all of them housed in empty Kleenex boxes—the boutique style. It was amazing how cheaply Burt had been able to make them; all he'd needed was some battery-operated alarm clocks, a bag or two of fertilizer, some of those Fire Starter sticks for home barbecues. Sadowski wondered why there weren't more arsonists; you could create some major havoc for not much money, and with very little chance of ever getting caught. Most of the evidence against you went up in the blaze. (Burt had bragged that he'd been arrested several times, but never convicted, for fire-related crimes.)

There was a portable TV in the corner, perched on top of a mini fridge, and Sadowski turned it on. *Cold Case* had been replaced by another of his favorite shows, *American Justice*. The host, Bill Kurtis, was someone Sadowski thought he could really get along with; he seemed like a regular guy. Sadowski took a cold beer out of the fridge and plopped himself down on the rickety desk chair. It was a rerun—about some woman in Texas who'd run over her cheating husband in a parking lot—but it was still good. And it took his mind off what he had to do—at precisely 1700 the next afternoon—in the swanky hills of Bel-Air.

And wasn't his old army buddy—Captain Derek Greer—going to get a good swift kick in the ass out of that? Sadowski hoped—though it wasn't likely on the Fourth of July—that he'd get to see him up there, at the Arab's place. It would be so much sweeter if Greer actually knew who had fucked him.

CHAPTER THIRTY-EIGHT

EVEN THOUGH IT was the Fourth of July, it was business as usual around the Cox household, Beth reflected. Carter had run off to the Page Museum to catch up on some urgent paperwork—or so he claimed—and Beth had managed to prevail upon Robin to come to the house for just a few hours to watch Joey, so she, too, could go to work. With the museum closed for the day, and the staff all off at backyard barbecues and pool parties, Beth thought she'd never find a better time to run in, enter the last few paragraphs of the scribe's secret letter into the computer database, get the translation . . . and find out, at last, how the drama had come to an end.

Traffic was heavy—it was another hot, dry day, and everybody in L.A. seemed to be heading for the beach—but fortunately Summit View wasn't far from the Getty. And of course there were no cars, other than those belonging to a few of the usual security personnel, in the garage. Beth had an assigned spot, but it wasn't as close to the elevators as some of the others, so she took one of those. The parking garage was at the foot of the hill, and the tram, which took visitors all the way up to the museum complex, had no one else on board. As the sleek, air-conditioned car made its way up the curving track, Beth looked out over the 405 freeway—the cars inching along, bumper to bumper—and toward the neighboring hills of Bel-Air. Way up at the top, though well hidden from view, was the al-Kalli estate . . . and on that estate was the book Beth considered one of the most remarkable in the world. A book that might now remain unknown, and unseen, forever.

The very thought still pained her.

Stepping out into the wide, travertine plaza, she saw only one other person, a security guard whom she knew. She waved to him and he waved back. Her own staff card allowed her to enter the building where her office was located. The carpeted halls, never noisy, were now completely silent; no phones were ringing, no copying machines were humming. It was all that she could have wished for.

Until she approached her own office. Lights were on, and spilling into the hall. And she could hear the clatter of computer keys, at a dizzying rate of speed. A rate that she knew only one person in the world would be capable of—her assistant.

When she stopped and looked inside, Elvis, his back to her, was staring at his computer monitor while his fingers flew across the keyboard and his head bopped to the jangling tune accompanying the program on his screen.

"Elvis," she said, "what are you doing here?"

From the way he whirled around, it was clear that he was more than startled; he looked guilty. Beth's eyes strayed to the computer—was he downloading porn?—but what she saw there looked a lot more like some super-high-tech version of "Dungeons and Dragons." A wizard with a white beard was traveling up a winding road, toward a castle with several gates, while numbers flashed in the lower left corner of the screen and words scrolled across the top.

"Did I know you were coming in today?" he asked.

"No," she said with a laugh, "because I didn't know it myself."

There was a creaking sound from the computer—one of the castle gates was lowering its drawbridge—and Elvis said, "Shit—can you give me a second?" He whipped around in his chair, glanced at the screen, tapped in a barrage of keystrokes, which were greeted with the sound of a heavy bell tolling ominously, and then the screen went blue.

"If you're just playing some video game, why would you need to come here?"

"Because, well, it's more complicated than that." His skinny white arms poked out of his short-sleeved shirt. "It's a network kind of thing—players from all over the planet—and the setup here is a lot faster and a lot more powerful than the crap I've got at home."

"But didn't it occur to you that it's a beautiful day? The Fourth of July? You could be outside." She realized that she had just channeled her mother.

And Elvis must have realized it, too. "Thanks, Mom," he said with a smile. "But if you don't mind my saying so, look who's talking."

Beth had the manila folder with the printout of the scribe's letter in her hand, and clearly she wasn't out on the beach, either.

"Welcome to Geek Central," Elvis said. "I brought Doritos and Dr Pepper," he added, gesturing at the junk food on his desk. "You want some?"

"No, thanks." Shaking her head, Beth went around her assistant's desk and on into her own office. "I'm going to log on myself."

A few seconds later, she heard from Elvis's desk the faint blast of a trumpet and the creaking of the drawbridge lowering again. "Could you turn that down?" she called out, and Elvis replied, "No problem—I'll put it on the phones."

Beth had really hoped to be alone, and wondered how she had wound up with the one assistant in all of Los Angeles who would rather be in the office on a national holiday than out smacking a volleyball somewhere. But she lowered her blinds—the afternoon sun was blinding—and then spread her papers out on the desk. She called up the graphemical database on the computer, then split the screen (as Elvis had taught her to do) and started scanning and transferring the remaining passages of the Latin text. She still felt lazy and vaguely unprofessional for relying on a computer to translate the Latin writing for her, but between the difficulties presented by the cramped handwriting and of course the archaic language, she knew that this was the safer and more expeditious route. And she could—and did—routinely check the work over afterward and smooth out the many rough edges.

And there were only a couple dozen lines left in the scribe's hidden missive.

While she waited, she thought about giving Carter a quick call. She didn't like what she was feeling around the house lately—a feeling that there were things in the air between them, things unspoken, and she wondered if Carter felt it, too. She'd never kept anything major from Carter—the way she was keeping her decision to hold on to the scribe's letter from him now—and she suspected that the tension might stem from that. Or maybe she was imagining the whole thing—Carter had always been one to burrow deep into whatever intellectual puzzle he was trying to solve, and maybe he was just being true to form. And given that she, too, was sitting in her office on a hot, sunny Fourth of July—as Elvis had just pointed out—who was she to throw stones?

Her thoughts went back to that very morning, when Carter had been in the kitchen, feeding Champ several strips of raw bacon.

"Since when did he graduate from kibble?" Beth had asked, as she carried Joey to his high chair.

"From now on, this dog gets whatever he wants," Carter said, though he didn't explain why Champ had suddenly earned such privileges. And when Beth had asked about his late-night trip to the museum, Carter simply said, "I think I was able to put something to rest." But again, he didn't elaborate.

Even if Beth had been in a mood to confess her own transgression, Carter's taciturnity would have turned her off.

Still, she thought, it was ridiculous to deal with a communication problem by not communicating. She picked up the phone and called Carter's cell. He picked up after several rings and said, "Everything okay?" His voice was faint and muffled.

"Where are you?" Beth said. "It sounds like you're in a bunker."

"You're close," he said, "I'm in the closet."

"That's not how it sounds!" she heard another man's voice call out.

"Del's there, too?" she said. "Why?"

"We're working on the La Brea Man, in a location undisclosed to the NAGPRA protestors. A storage closet." He did not tell her why they had had to resort to such measures. "What's up?"

She could tell he wanted to get back to work. "I was just checking in. Do you have any interest in going to that party later?" They'd been invited by the Critchleys, the elderly Getty donors, to a Fourth of July dinner at their Brentwood estate; Mrs. Critchley's forebears had come over on the ship that landed right after the *Mayflower*.

"Do you?" Carter asked, sounding dubious. "I mean, if you think it's important to put in an appearance . . ."

He left the question, a legitimate one, hanging. On the one hand, Beth thought it wasn't a bad idea, politically speaking, to show up. On the other hand, it wasn't the most enticing invitation. She heard a mumbled question from Del, and Carter saying, "Maybe the solvent needs more time . . ."

"Why don't I call you later?" Beth said, and Carter said, "Huh? What was that?"

The bar on her computer screen was showing that the graphemical analysis was nearly done. "I'll call you from home. We can decide then."

"Okay," he replied.

She could tell his attention was focused elsewhere. "Bye."

She hung up, wondering if she had just bridged, or widened, any communication gap. It was like that a lot over the last week or so.

A soft chiming sound went off on her computer, signaling

that the job was complete and she could now print out the results. She hit "Print," then quickly got up from her desk. In another few minutes, she'd have the answer—or as much of one as she'd ever be likely to get—about the fate of the mysterious scribe and illuminator. Elvis had his head down as she passed through his outer office—on his screen she could see an open field, with a dragon at one end—and in the room where the printers and copiers were kept, even the lights were off. The moment she entered, a sensor flicked them on again, and she was able to retrieve the printouts from the bin.

On the way back, she was already reading them.

The guards have entered the courtyard below, it said. *Salima will delay them so that I may offer a last prayer for the success of my plan.*

A plan? Beth thought. Had he actually hoped somehow to escape?

The secrets of ink making, he wrote, and for a moment Beth thought the database must have gone haywire—why else would he be digressing into such a subject now?—*are the secrets, too, of the poisoner.*

Ah. But was he planning to poison the guards somehow once they'd come to transport him to the monster's maze?

From the sap of the acacia tree and sal martis *[no equivalent found],* the printout read, but Beth knew that the latter term referred to green vitriol, or copperas, a common ingredient of iron-gall ink, *bound with gum arabic and sundry other ingredients, may be made a deadly brew. This I have decanted within the holy vessel long worn about my neck, a vessel that even the sultan will not now deny me. The silver body of our Savior is a hollow shell, yet indeed shall it hold my salvation.*

Beth thought she could discern his intent.

At the moment of surrender, I shall obtain my release, and so, too, have my revenge. May the manticore, in his haste to drink my hot blood, drink the coursing poison, too.

She felt, suddenly, as if she were reading a speech from some bloody Jacobean tragedy.

And may my curse, the curse of Ambrosius of Bury St.

*Edmunds, descend upon the Sultan Kilij al-Kalli, upon all
of his descendants, and upon all the unholy beasts whom
the Lord designed [alt: intended] to drown in the Flood.
Now and forever, world without end, amen.* And with that,
the letter ended, the printout simply recording a row of as-
terisks followed by *Document complete.*

Beth sat stock-still in her chair, wondering if she could
possibly have read all that she just had. It wasn't just the
revelation of the scribe's final scheme; that was ingenious
enough, even though its outcome would never be known.
No, what had shocked her even more were two things: the
fact that he had inscribed his name—at last she knew who
this unparalleled scribe and illuminator was!—and the
curse that he had entered as a kind of colophon at the end.

It was so very similar to the curses laid by the mysterious scribe whom she believed had created all the manuscripts currently on display in the Getty exhibition hall.

The scribe that she had been trying to identify for so
many years.

How could she have been so blind? How could she not
have realized that she was dealing with the work of the
same master? She went over it all in her head, all the things
that would have kept her from even imagining it to be the
same man. First there was the Middle Eastern origins of
The Beasts of Eden. It had never occurred to her, until dis-
covering the secret letter, that the author of the book could
be anyone but a subject of the sultan, or at least an artist of
regional repute. And then there was the sheer fortuitous-
ness of it all: what were the chances that an Iraqi plutocrat
would show up at the Getty and bestow upon her—of all
people—the masterpiece, the capstone, in the career of the
itinerant illuminator whose identity she had labored so
long to determine? All those countless hours of research,
in dusty archives and hushed libraries from London to
New York, Oxford to Boston, and it was here, in Los Angeles, on a hot sunny day, that the answers should fall, as if
from the sky, into her very lap.

It was almost too much to accept.

And to believe it truly, she would need to confirm it with her own eyes. She would need to compare the original letter with the handwritten text in the manuscripts she had assembled for display. She scooped up the printouts, along with the ancient letter itself, and hurried out of her office.

"Where are you off to?" Elvis said as she shot past.

"The manuscripts exhibit."

"You haven't seen it?" he said, mockingly. "You put it together."

In the plaza outside, the leaves of the London plane trees were rustling in the dry wind that swept the Getty's hilltop site, but there was no one, not even a security patrol, anywhere around. The sound of Beth's heels echoed across the stone courtyard as she marched to the North Pavilion, where a red and gold banner above the entrance proclaimed THE GENIUS OF THE CLOISTER: ILLUMINATED MANUSCRIPTS OF THE ELEVENTH CENTURY. At the access panel, she entered first her own security code, and then the code to unlock the doors. She heard a faint buzzing, and quickly entered the hall. The heavy glass door slowly closed, and clicked shut, behind her. The motion sensors responded by turning on the overhead lights.

But they did not provide much in the way of illumination. The manuscripts were so precious, and so prone to fading, that the ambient light was kept to a bare minimum. Instead, each manuscript was gently cradled in its own display case—two dozen or so, ranged around the three rooms of the exhibition hall—and indirectly lighted by small tungsten halogen lamps inside the glass. The effect was to make the manuscripts shine like beacons, their burnished gold glittering like autumn leaves, the lapis lazuli gleaming like the Mediterranean, the red and blue and purple gemstones in their covers and bindings sparkling like a kaleidoscope. The first time Beth had seen the exhibition completely installed, she had stepped back, breathless at its beauty.

But now she went straight to the nearest display case, one that held a sacramentary, illuminated for the Cathedral Priory of Christ Church, Canterbury. The book was open to its frontispiece, depicting the Holy Spirit descending upon the Apostles at Pentecost. But now she looked at it with fresh eyes. Now she looked at it not as the work of an anonymous, though brilliant, traveling artist, but as an example of the work of a man who went by Ambrosius of Bury St. Edmunds. Could she see in it the same techniques, the same flair, that she had been studying for weeks in *The Beasts of Eden*? There was indeed a fluidity to the motion of the Apostles, their hands raised toward heaven, that suggested the work of the master, but it did not equal the artistry of his last great work for the Sultan Kilij al-Kalli.

She moved past it, to the first display case in the next room. And here she found an herbal, a treatise on plants and their medicinal uses, created for the English abbey of St. Augustine's. A flowered stem, its crimson leaves now faded to russet, extended itself all the way across the page, while the text—drawn, as was the custom, from the ancient Greeks rather than practical observation—flowed all around it. The imagination of the design was striking— Beth couldn't help but think of the splashy layouts in glossy fashion magazines—and the text, she could see now, bore the same unmistakable slant of the writing in the al-Kalli bestiary. Yes, she thought, it was all coming together!

But she would not be satisfied until she had seen another colophon, that final salutation by the scribe, and she knew exactly where to find one. A good example was on display in the last room, in a copy of the Apocalypse from East Anglia. At its end, she knew, there came a curse.

As she stepped into the room, the light sensors automatically responded, but this was still the gloomiest and most remote part of the exhibition. The display cases here were more widely spaced, and the shadows deeper and wider. And even though Beth had become accustomed over the years to working alone in empty museum halls, sometimes even late into the night, she wasn't always impervious to the spooky aspects of the job. She reminded herself now that it was only late afternoon outside, that the sun was shining, that Elvis was sitting up in their office, playing some idiotic computer game. And that she would be done very soon—she would study the colophons, one against the other, and lay to rest any doubt whatsoever. And then her quest would be at an end, her discovery complete.

Still, she went quickly to the last case in the room, where the Apocalypse—better known in the Protestant tradition as the Book of Revelation—was on display. The illustration was of a seven-headed dragon, writhing in an ocean of fire. And she knew, from her work on the exhibition, that the final words of the biblical text were a warning to anyone who dared to alter or subtract anything from the Apocalypse; to do so, the book declared, would be to write yourself out of the book of life, for all eternity. Below that, separated by a miniature of a child being raised to heaven, came the colophon—in the form of a curse that echoed the final lines of the Apocalypse itself. In elegant Latin, it said that anyone daring to injure or deface the book before them would be stricken from the book of life, too.

Although she hardly needed to, Beth took the last page of Ambrosius's letter from the folder under her arm, placed the rest of the papers on the floor, and then held the page up to the pale light emanating from the display case. The curses, in their very nature, not to mention the rhythm of the prose, were strikingly similar; the ornate character of the lettering was virtually identical, and the handwriting itself, tight and slanted to the left, was unmistakable. Ambrosius of Bury St. Edmunds—artist and soldier, scoundrel and Crusader, an unknown genius whose bizarre journey had taken him from the cloisters of Canterbury to his terrible end in a sultan's maze—was the author of both, and the Michelangelo of his age.

And only Beth knew who he was.

She had hardly had time to savor her victory before she heard, in low tones from the shadows at the rear of the gallery, "Don't be afraid."

And suddenly she was as afraid as she had ever been in her life.

It was as if the shadows were coalescing, taking shape . . . the shape of a man—tall and elegant, with perfectly chiseled features, in a suit that seemed made of the darkness itself—who now took a silent step forward. His white-blond hair, which swept away from his forehead, glinted in the overhead lights. His eyes were concealed behind small round glasses with amber lenses.

"But you are afraid," he said, in that strangely foreign accent.

The gallery was suffused with the scent of a forest, right after a light rain.

Beth wanted to turn and run—and as if the intruder had sensed that, he stopped where he was—but she could barely move.

"Consider this," he said. "If I had wanted to harm you, or your son, wouldn't I have done it by now?"

Her worst nightmare was now real: Arius was alive; Arius was here. All the times she had tried to persuade herself that it was just her imagination playing tricks, all the times that she had told herself that she was making something out of nothing . . . she'd been wrong.

And in her heart, she had always known it.

She wanted to say, "Why are you here? What do you want?" but her mouth was too dry—and it didn't seem she had to. He answered as if she had.

"I've always been here, and what I want—what I have always wanted—is your welfare."

Her welfare? Beth's memories of Arius had always been muddled—it was as if they existed behind some veil, some superimposed scrim through which she could only catch glimpses of strange and confusing events—but protecting and caring for her was certainly not the way those memories came back to her now. Not at all. The memories—sensory impressions, really—were, all of them, dark and deeply troubling. Just seeing him here made her skin crawl.

Without his having visibly moved, he seemed again to have moved perceptibly closer. The smell of rain-washed leaves was stronger. And even though the light in the room was dim and ambient at best, he seemed somehow to have gathered it all to him. He stood out against the black shadows, in his black suit, his face subtly glowing, as if from a fire within. The amber lenses concealed the color of his eyes, but Beth had a recollection—a vague and terrible recollection—of eyes that churned and changed and penetrated, like knives, whatever they looked at.

"And to prove what I'm saying, I am here now only to give you a warning."

"Of what?"

"Go home, now, to Joey."

Beth felt jolted as if by an electric shock. "What's wrong? What's wrong with Joey?" In the flood of her concern, even her fear was subsumed.

"There's still time. But go. You need to be with him now."

With no reason to believe him, Beth did; with no reason to do what he was suggesting, she had an overwhelming impulse to race out of the gallery. But nothing would make her turn her back on Arius; it was as if she weren't even capable of it. There was something riveting about his very presence, something hypnotic even in his partially concealed eyes.

He stepped back, and the shadows fell more fully over his face.

Was he deliberately doing that?

"I will," Beth said, her voice soft and faltering, "but tell me: why? What's going to happen?"

Again without moving, he seemed to have receded farther into the room. The white light meant to illuminate the final pages of the Apocalypse barely touched his perfect features and the waves of his white-gold hair.

But his head tilted to one side, as if he'd heard something, just a split second before Beth heard the whoosh of the gallery door opening, three rooms away, and a footfall approaching. "Hello? Ms. Cox? Are you in here?"

It was the security guard, the one she'd waved to at the tram plaza.

She didn't answer at first—and she wondered why. Was it because she was actually seeking to protect Arius from discovery?

"Ms. Cox?" The voice was coming closer, and even though the lights in the exhibition hall were on, a flashlight beam was sweeping the darkened corners.

"I'm in here," she finally said, turning her head.

The guard—she only remembered that his name started with a *G*—rounded the partition and said, "Everything okay? We registered an intrusion in the security office."

Beth looked back toward Arius, but he was gone.

"I entered my code," she assured him.

"I know—we had that. But security was tripped again, after that." He played his flashlight around the dimly lighted room and poked his head behind a couple of the standing display cases. "Must have been a glitch, I guess."

Now she could see the name on his laminated badge—Gary Graydon.

But where had Arius gone? There was only one way out of the gallery, and how could he have slipped past the guard unnoticed?

"What's all that on the floor?" Graydon said, and Beth glanced down at the papers she had utterly forgotten were lying around her feet. She bent down and picked up the folder with the other pages of the secret letter in it. She slipped the page she was still holding—she'd forgotten she was holding that, too—inside, and after casting one last look around the gallery, said, "I'm done here."

"Good," Graydon replied. "We've got enough on our hands already today."

"What do you mean?" Beth said, leaving the gallery with the guard close behind.

"The wildfires."

Beth stopped, "Where?"

"Where aren't they?" Graydon said. "They're springing up all over town, from Bel-Air to the Palisades. Even with all the warnings about fireworks and the drought conditions, it looks like some people never listen."

Beth didn't need to hear any more. Clutching the folder tightly under her arm, she hurried out of the gallery, and then, with Arius's warning to go home ringing in her ears, sprinted across the empty plaza toward the tram.

CHAPTER THIRTY-NINE

CARTER WAS SO absorbed in the work that at first he didn't even feel the cell phone vibrating in his pocket. He'd turned off the ring the second he came into the museum; he didn't want anyone—especially Gunderson—finding out he was there, on a national holiday yet, concealed in a storage closet, in the sub-basement, working on the most volatile discovery the La Brea Tar Pits had ever yielded. He'd never be able to finish explaining.

"Look at this fracture line," Del was saying, indicating with a scalpel a crack in the skull near the temporal lobe. "Tell me that's not from a blow."

The phone vibrated again, and this time Carter noticed. "Hang on," he said.

The connection, as usual down here, was terrible. But it was Beth, and she sounded agitated. She was saying something about . . . Arius.

"Slow down," Carter said, instinctively turning away from the table and stepping out in the corridor. "You're breaking up."

"Arius," she said again, "was here, at the Getty."

Was it just another scare—several times they had thought

there was evidence that Arius had survived, and was stalking them—or was it for real this time? Despite all their suspicions and fears, neither of them had ever seen or encountered him for sure.

She was saying something else, but it was coming through in bursts of static.

"I can't hear you," Carter said, wondering if she could hear him, either. "Are you okay? Is Joey okay?" That was the crucial thing.

"Yes."

He heard that. Then something that he couldn't make out. Then: ". . . on the tram. I'm going home right now, to Joey. The fires are spreading."

"What fires?"

". . . from fireworks maybe . . ."

Fourth of July fireworks had already started a wildfire? It was only late afternoon—he'd thought the danger would have come after nightfall.

"Not in Summit View . . . ," she was saying, "but above Sunset, the Palisades . . . Bel-Air."

At the mention of Bel-Air, his ears pricked up. There were fires, approaching Bel-Air? The al-Kalli estate? The bestiary?

"I'll call you at home," he said, but already he sensed that the line had gone dead. "Beth—can you hear me?" He could tell that the line was still open, but he had no idea if he was transmitting. "I'm leaving now. I'll see you at home as soon as I can get there. Beth?"

But the line was definitely dead.

He stuck the phone back in his pocket, went back into the converted storage closet, and said, "I've got to go—right now."

Del looked stunned, and a little bit pissed; Carter knew that Del had been irritated lately by Carter's elusiveness and seeming lack of commitment to the project at hand. More than once Carter had wished he could simply explain it all to him—not only because he hated to be so evasive with one of his oldest friends, but because he would have welcomed Del's insights and opinions. Sitting up in Bel-Air, of all places on earth, was, without a doubt, the most astounding discovery in the history of the animal kingdom, a revelation second only to Darwin's, a glimpse into the earliest origins of reptilian, mammalian, and avian life, and no one would have understood all that more deeply than Del.

"What do you mean, you've got to go? We've got the whole place to ourselves today—you know how much work we could get done in the next few hours?"

"I do, and I'm sorry."

Del shook his head and sighed, then dropped the scalpel on the worktable. "Someday, Bones, you're going to have to tell me what's really going on."

"I will," Carter said, "I swear."

Carter was already turning to leave when Del said, "So where are we going now?"

And it was only then that Carter remembered he didn't have his car there; Del had picked him up, and they had planned to go for a hike after working for a few hours at the museum. Del had said there was something he wanted to show him.

Del laughed at the look on Carter's face. "You forgot, didn't you?" he said, jangling his car keys in the air. "I'm driving."

Carter was speechless, wondering what to do next.

Del laughed again, and after quickly covering the remains, grabbed his backpack off the floor, and said, "Now, my friend, you are in my power! You will have to reveal your secret destination."

Del headed out the door and marched down the corridor, his white hair flying. "Don't forget to turn out the lights," he said over his shoulder.

Damn, Carter thought—of all the days to carpool. He snapped the lights off and followed Del, who was heading not for the elevator—that would have required enlisting Hector's help again—but the stairs to the atrium garden.

The garden where the bones of the La Brea Woman were now lying in an unmarked grave.

Another secret he had never shared with Del.

Outside, where Carter finally caught up to him, a hot

Santa Ana wind was blowing. The air was parched and brittle. Del hopped up into the cab of his dusty truck, an all-terrain vehicle perched on monster tires, with a gun rack on top and a dinosaur decal on the bumper, and Carter clambered into the passenger seat. Carter was calculating fast—would it be worth it to have Del drive him home first, where he could pick up his own car, or should he just have him drive straight to Bel-Air? He glanced over at Del, who had the motor rumbling and the truck in gear.

"Where to, boss?"

"Bel-Air," Carter said.

"Yeah, right. Where really?"

"Really."

And Del could tell he meant it. "The mystery gets better and better."

Carter rolled down the window as they drove out of the parking lot. Red, white, and blue bunting, wrapped around the streetlight poles on Wilshire Boulevard, flapped and rustled in the breeze. A bright sun beat down from behind a veil of wispy cirrus clouds. Carter was wondering what, if anything, he should reveal to Del when they got to al-Kalli's estate. There was no reason he had to tell him, or show him, anything of the actual bestiary. Sure, he'd be curious, but Carter could always hold him off for now, and maybe, just maybe, he'd run into Mohammed al-Kalli himself and be able to persuade him that Del was a trusted and very valuable colleague, one whose advice and counsel might be of great help to the animals. That would be the best outcome of all . . . however unlikely it seemed.

Traffic was light as they drove, but twice they had to stop for fire trucks, their horns blaring, as they raced past. In the distance, Carter could hear other sirens blaring, too. The streets had an uneasy calm about them, a feeling Carter remembered from the Midwest when tornado weather came. He turned on the radio, and the sounds of a bluegrass band wailed from the powerful speakers. Carter quickly changed to an all-news station, and the announcer was saying something about a blaze that had erupted about fifty miles south of Los Angeles, near Claremont. "San

Bernardino County has put all of its firefighters on alert for the Fourth of July," the announcer said, "and, unfortunately, it looks like they won't be sitting idle."

At least those fires were far off. But even here, as Del piloted the truck toward Bel-Air, the air had a faintly acrid odor.

Carter fished in his pocket for his cell phone to call Beth. By now, she'd be safely home, but he wanted to make sure. He dialed, but he could barely hear a ring; he tried again, and this time he checked the battery. It was nearly dead; maybe that was why he'd had such trouble downstairs in the museum. He'd just assumed it was because of the location.

"Calling Beth?"

"My battery's gone."

"Wish I could help you out," Del said, "but you know I don't even carry one."

Carter did know that. Del always said that when he wasn't near a phone, he didn't *want* to be near a phone.

"You want me to stop and find a pay phone somewhere?"

"No, that's okay," Carter said. "We're making good time. Just keep going." The sooner he arrived at the al-Kalli estate and made sure that everything was okay—he was a little worried that the air filters might need adjusting—the sooner he could go home for the night. Some holiday this was turning out to be.

At the gates to Bel-Air, several expensive cars were backed up, waiting to pull out onto a crowded Sunset Boulevard. Carter had never seen more than the lone Rolls-Royce or Jaguar waiting there at one time.

"Friends of yours?" Del asked as he drove the truck past a Bentley with an elderly couple in the front seat and two big black poodles hanging their heads out the back.

"Intimate."

"Do I just keep going?" Del asked, and Carter said, "Yep, all the way to the top."

Del clucked his tongue. "You do travel in the right circles, Bones."

Carter didn't answer.

"But you want to tell me *why* we're going up there?" Del said.

And Carter felt that he couldn't simply stonewall him anymore.

"There's a man up here named Mohammed al-Kalli. I've sort of been working for him."

"Moonlighting?" Del said with a puzzled smile. "Doing what?"

"He's an amateur . . . naturalist."

Del laughed. "A naturalist? Come on, Bones—nobody's been called that for a hundred years. You're going to have to do better." He slowed the truck. "Right or left up here at this fork?"

Carter pointed to the right, and Del switched to a lower gear for the steeper climb. Carter thought about what more he could say; he knew he was just making things worse, and more mysterious, by being so evasive.

"He's a very wealthy man—"

"That much I could figure," Del said, glancing around at the increasingly rarified precincts they were driving through.

"—and he has asked for my advice—my help—with some animals he's been keeping." Already Carter thought he had gone too far; al-Kalli would have his head if he knew.

Del mulled that one over as he drove. "Some animals?" he said contemplatively. "What kind of animals? No disrespect, Bones, but the only animals you know anything about have been extinct for a very long time."

Carter had skated right up to the edge of the truth, but until he had to—or until al-Kalli had given him his express permission—he didn't feel he could say any more. "Bear to the left up here," Carter said, and Del steered the truck past a tall, perfectly manicured hedge that ran for hundreds of yards. "You'll keep on going until you see a stone gatehouse," Carter said, "at the very top."

He didn't reply to Del's last observation, and he knew perfectly well that Del was still waiting.

As they came up toward the crest, the gatehouse appeared at the end of the road. Carter could see Lee, the Asian guard, standing outside it, shading his eyes with his hand as he looked off toward the east.

"Next stop," Del said, breaking the silence, "Jurassic Park."

Carter cut him a glance, but Del didn't look like he'd actually figured anything out. How could he? He was just making a joke. But if only he knew how close to the truth he'd come.

Lee turned and held up his palm as the truck approached the gate; of course he wouldn't recognize the vehicle. When Del stopped and rolled down his window, Carter leaned toward the driver's side and said, "Hey, Lee."

"Oh, Dr. Cox," Lee said. "Was Mr. al-Kalli expecting you?"

"No, I'm just here to catch up on some work." Carter knew that even the security staff was told nothing about the bestiary. It was strictly on a "need-to-know" basis, and as far as Carter could tell, that "need to know" didn't extend very far: it took in Rashid and Bashir, who tended to the animals, Jakob the bodyguard, and that new guy, Derek Greer, the ex–army captain with the bad attitude. Carter wasn't sure if al-Kalli's son, Mehdi, even knew, though it would have been one hell of a secret to keep from an inquisitive teenage boy.

"You can smell the smoke, even up here," Lee said, pressing the lever to open the gates. "The peacocks, they're going crazy."

Del gave him a look, as if to say, *Peacocks?* and Carter just gestured for him to move on.

"Make damn sure you don't drive over any," Carter said. "Al-Kalli is very attached to his birds."

"Curiouser and curiouser" was all Del said as he maneuvered up the long, winding drive, past the splashing fountain and into the forecourt of the great gray house. Two cars were there already: al-Kalli's long black Mercedes, and a cobalt blue Scion, with a surfboard lashed to its top. The huge oaken door swung open, and although

Carter might have expected to see al-Kalli, it was instead Mehdi, with a couple of his young friends. They were carrying towels and coolers and wearing flip-flops, and as they piled into the Scion, Carter asked, "Where's your father, Mehdi?"

While loading his gear and without turning around, Mehdi said, "Somewhere over there," lifting his chin toward the western portion of the estate. Mehdi had a way of making you feel like a servant.

The bestiary was in that direction, and Carter didn't doubt that was where he was. Even with all the air-conditioning equipment and temperature controls working fine, the animals would be sensitive enough to register that something was going on, and al-Kalli would be worried. Rashid, if Carter's guess was correct, was probably in a panic.

And now, here was Carter accompanied by an unofficial interloper.

"Just come with me," Carter said to Del, getting out of the truck. "And promise me you won't do or say anything until I tell you to."

"You know, Bones, it's a lucky thing I'm not the type that gets easily offended."

"I was counting on that."

With Carter leading the way, they trotted around the garage wing of the courtyard and then across the sweeping green lawn.

"Doesn't look like this guy has been observing the drought restrictions," Del said.

"Al-Kalli lives by his own rules," Carter said.

"Looks like he can afford to."

As their footsteps clattered across the wooden footbridge, they heard a loud, strangled cry from a grove of trees. Glancing over, Carter could just make out one of the peacocks, its purple and blue tail fanned out in all its glory.

"There's more of those?" Del said from close behind.

"Maybe a dozen," Carter said. "I've never counted."

They passed the stables, which looked as if they were almost empty. The stall doors were open, and a sleek white horse was being led out by Bashir, the stable boy. He raised a hand in greeting as Carter and Del jogged past, then went back to leading the visibly skittish horse.

"Where'd this guy get all his money?" Del said, barely huffing or puffing.

"It's very old money." The top of the bestiary building was just coming into view past a scrim of trees. "From Iraq."

Del whistled. "Friend of Saddam's?"

"Nope," Carter replied. "His sworn enemy."

As Carter slowed down, Del did, too. "Someday," Del said, "when we're not on the run, you can explain it all to me. Sounds like a hell of a story."

"It is." But Carter was already on the alert, approaching the white walls of the bestiary; the golf cart was parked just outside.

"What's this?" Del said. "A high-tech barn?"

"Kind of." Carter turned to Del. "Now, you're just going to have to trust me. I want you to stay out of sight. Get behind those trees," he said, indicating a pair of ancient eucalyptus trees with thick, gnarled trunks, "and don't come out until I signal you to."

Del chuckled, like what kind of a game was this. "Okay. But what do you want me to call you from now on—Bond, James Bond?" He thought Carter must be joking.

Carter stepped closer and looked him straight in the eye. "I mean this, Del. I shouldn't have brought you even this far. These can be dangerous people. You've got to do what I'm telling you."

Del got it; the look on Carter's face was unmistakable. "Okay, Bones. I hear ya." And he moved off behind the trees.

As Carter approached the bestiary doors, he could smell smoke, but this was just the cigarette kind. He even knew who was probably smoking.

"Captain Greer?" he called out, and Greer stepped out from the other side of the building, cupping his cigarette in his hand.

"What are you doing here, Cox?" Greer asked. "It's a holiday. Take a break."

"I could ask you the same thing."

"And I wouldn't answer."

Carter never knew what footing he was on with Greer; they usually engaged in this same sort of macho banter, but with Greer there was always an edge of danger to it. Carter couldn't tell if Greer regarded him as a threat of some kind, or just another one of al-Kalli's lackeys.

"Is he inside?" Carter asked, and Greer nodded.

"But you don't want to cross him right now," Greer added, stubbing out his cigarette on the gravel path. "He's tearing Rashid a new asshole."

Carter wasn't surprised. Ever since Carter had begun working with the animals, he had seen, many times first-hand, the contempt, and even physical abuse, with which al-Kalli treated Rashid. And it never failed to occur to Carter that, unless he was somehow able to restore the animals to perfect health, it was just a matter of time before that same fury was directed at him. He did not doubt that al-Kalli had it in him to take any measure he chose, however dire, against those he considered his enemies, or his incompetent subordinates.

"I expected the animals to be restive," Carter said. "Maybe I can do something." And he went to the doors and pressed the release button; Greer limped along close beside him, and it occurred to Carter that Greer was trying to make it look to al-Kalli as though Greer was escorting him in, doing his job as security chief and monitoring everyone's comings and goings. Around al-Kalli, no one was ever off duty, or on a sure footing.

Certainly not Rashid. Just as Carter entered the bestiary, he saw al-Kalli lift his open hand and deliver a stunning slap to Rashid's cheek, a slap that sent him down to his knees.

"*Why* don't you know?" al-Kalli was shouting, as Jakob stood by, arms folded across his chest. "This is your job! This has been your family's job for centuries! I paid for the best training in the world!" He put his foot on the man's chest and shoved him backward onto the dirt floor. "I should have fed you to them years ago!"

"But no one knows about creatures like these," Rashid pleaded, his open lab coat spread around him. "There are no books, no papers to read." His eyes suddenly took in Carter and Greer. "But here is Dr. Cox!" he said exultantly. "Perhaps he can help! Yes, Dr. Cox may know!"

Al-Kalli turned around, and the look of absolute contempt on his face barely changed. He wasn't wearing his customary suit today—just a pair of perfectly tailored dark trousers and a crisp white shirt with billowing sleeves; ruby links gleamed like flame at the cuffs. His bald head shone in the bright overhead lights. "Dr. Cox, you've come at an opportune time," he said, sounding like an English aristocrat welcoming the family physician to the manor house. "The animals are restless and agitated today."

"I thought they might be," Carter said. "Their sense of smell is highly developed, and even the hint of smoke from the wildfires might have alarmed them."

"I thought we had an air filtration system for that."

"We do. But it's even possible that they're picking up some sort of vibrations through the earth. Some animals can sense earthquakes coming—perhaps these can sense the fires."

Al-Kalli shook his head derisively. " 'Perhaps' they can do this, 'it's possible' they can do that. I'm sorry to say it, but you're starting to sound as bad as this worthless scum Rashid."

Carter couldn't stand it a second longer, and he started to move toward Rashid with his hand extended to help him up.

"Oh, I wouldn't do that," al-Kalli said in a low but menacing tone. "We have an old saying, 'Let the dead lie where they fall.' "

Jakob stepped between them and unfolded his arms.

"I told you, when I hired you," al-Kalli went on, "that I would give anything at all to the one who could restore my creatures to health."

"We've made progress already," Carter said, though he did not try to circumvent Jakob.

"What I did *not* tell you," al-Kalli went on, completely

ignoring what Carter had just said, "was that I would show little patience with those who failed. That's only fair, don't you think?"

While Carter debated how to reply, he saw al-Kalli look with amazement toward the open doors of the bestiary. Jakob reached into the waistband of his black trousers, but before he could pull out the gun that presumably rested there, Carter heard a voice call out, "Don't even *think* about it, raghead!"

Carter turned around, as did Greer, and what he saw was a man in army fatigues, a big man with close-cropped hair and a knapsack slung over one shoulder, striding into the arena with a gun hanging loosely from one hand. Even worse, fanning out behind him were two more men, also in army gear, each one holding, incongruously, an aluminum baseball bat.

Only Greer seemed to know instantly what was going on.

"Sadowski," he said, shaking his head, "this time you've really fucked up."

"That so? Sure doesn't look that way to me." Sadowski looked around at the vast facility. "This that zoo you were talking about? 'Cause I don't see any critters."

Al-Kalli leveled a glare at Captain Greer. "You know this man?" he said. "You told him about this place?"

At that moment, Carter recognized him—this was the guy he and Del had run into on the hiking trail in Temescal, the guy who'd attacked the girl and her boyfriend. He also knew there was a strong possibility that if everyone wasn't very, very careful over the next few minutes, somebody could wind up hurt, or worse.

"He served under me in Iraq," Greer said.

"Whatever your name is—was it Sadowski?" al-Kalli said, addressing the intruder, "you're trespassing, and I would be within my rights to kill you on the spot."

Sadowski raised the gun a few inches and, in answer, fired a round into the dirt in front of al-Kalli's feet. But al-Kalli, to Carter's astonishment, didn't so much as flinch; he behaved as if he were invulnerable.

The animals heard the shot, though, and suddenly there

was a howl from the griffin's cage, a rumbling snort from one of the basilisks. The phoenix, from its perch high above them, let out a piercing scream, a thousand times worse than the cry of the peacocks, and even Sadowski looked up, rattled.

"What the fuck is that?" he said. The monstrous bird was still concealed in its straw-filled nest.

"You don't want to know," Greer said. "You and your boys just want to get out of here . . . while you still can."

Carter didn't know what he feared more—harm coming to one of the people present, or harm to the animals, surely the last of their kind, that had by some miracle survived for millennia.

"What *is* your plan, soldier?" al-Kalli taunted him. "Or are you as stupid as most Americans—blundering in where you have no business, and with no idea of how to get out again?"

"Oh, I've got a plan," Sadowski said. He glanced at a massive black and chrome wristwatch. "And trust me— you're going to find out all about it."

"And what do we do until then?"

Carter heard a metallic screech, and saw Rashid, who had quietly gotten to his feet, yanking a lever in the concrete wall.

Sadowski shouted, "What are you doing?" at him, but Rashid simply turned and ran toward the glassed-in office at the far end of the bestiary, zigging and zagging with his cupped hands attempting to protect the back of his head. Sadowski cursed, and fired another round, the wild shot sparking off the bars of the griffin's cage.

The phoenix screamed again, and this time Carter knew it would emerge from its aerie. He looked up just as its massive hooked beak poked over the edge of its nest and its claws, in preparation for flight, wrapped themselves around the rim of the platform. Sadowski and his two accomplices stared upward, slack-jawed.

With a sudden, even ungainly, lurch, the phoenix plummeted from its nest, then spread its wings, the width of a school bus, and soared above their heads. The two soldiers behind Sadowski fell back a few steps, and as the bird came lower, heading, Carter suddenly realized, for the open doors behind them, one of the two—the one with a bell tattooed on his bare forearm—took a furious swing at it with the aluminum bat. The end of the bat caught the claws with a loud crack, and the bird, squawking in pain, wheeled in the air and beat a retreat toward the other end of the bestiary.

"I got it!" the tattooed man cried, his voice filled with as much terror as exultation. "I got the bastard!"

But the phoenix wasn't done—it simply coasted in a great slow circle, then with one more beat of its red-feathered wings, a beat that sent a shivering wind through the whole facility, it shot back toward the open doors. Sadowski fired, missed, but the bird had its prehensile claws extended; there was a look of fire in its eyes and its vulture-like head was tucked into its body. It went straight for its attacker, and before he could even think to swing the bat again, the phoenix had snatched him up in its claws—one of the talons appeared to tear completely through the man's body—and then, with its wings folded back like a missile, it flashed through the open doors and out of sight.

Dust from its exit filled the air. And all that was left of the tattooed man was an aluminum bat lying in the dirt.

"Jesus fucking Christ," Sadowski said in a tone of mechanical disbelief, and Greer said, "Didn't I tell you you'd fucked up?"

The other man with a bat stood stunned, looking at the spot where his accomplice had been just seconds ago. Then, throwing his own bat on the ground, he turned without a word and ran out the doors . . . leaving Sadowski to fend for himself.

It was only then that Carter thought to look at the row of cages—and saw that the lever Rashid had pulled had opened all of their gates at once. The animals had not yet realized their freedom, but they would, soon. Greer must have reached the same conclusion because he suddenly made for the lever.

Sadowski shouted, "Hold it!" and fired again, and this

time Greer collapsed, blood spurting from his right thigh. "God *damn* you, Sadowski! That was my good leg!"

"I told you not to move!"

But something now *was* moving—and it was at the farthest cage, the one that held the gorgon. Carter saw the tip of its enormous snout protrude from the open gate, as if it wasn't sure if this was a trap or not. Then its head came out entirely, and swung, like a huge pendulum, from one direction to the other, taking in the whole arena.

Jakob stepped between al-Kalli and the emerging monster, drawing out his gun, but al-Kalli angrily batted it out of his hands. "What do you think you're doing?"

Jakob looked at a total loss; he'd thought he was doing his job.

"It won't harm *me*."

It was then that Carter realized just how mad Mohammed al-Kalli really was.

The beast approached slowly, still swinging its ponderous head from side to side so that its bulbous eyes, situated far back on either side of its skull, could take in the whole landscape. It was like watching a tank rumble cautiously across land-mined terrain.

Jakob walked backward, never taking his eyes off the animal, and toward Sadowski, who was speechless and immobilized.

But al-Kalli actually took several steps forward. He opened his arms, the white sleeves billowing, and said something, not in English, to the beast.

Carter knew that the creature would be attuned to movement, that it would notice whatever was in motion, so he tried to make his own retreat as subtle as possible. When the animal's snout was pointed directly at him, temporarily limiting its vision, he took a giant step back. And then, seconds later, another. He glanced backward, over his shoulder, but Jakob and Sadowski were already gone.

Greer, too, was hobbling toward the doors, using one of the aluminum bats as a makeshift cane and leaving a trail of blood in his wake.

The doors to the outside were still wide open, the waning

sunlight casting a golden pool on the hard-packed earth just inside the entrance.

Al-Kalli spoke again, in Arabic it seemed, and Carter detected movement behind the gates where the basilisks and the griffin were kept. At any moment they, too, could stagger from their enormous pens and into the greater world beyond.

The gorgon, with its stumpy legs splayed out from its body like a gigantic toad, stopped a dozen yards or so from al-Kalli. As both a reptile and a mammal, a bizarre precursor of the dinosaurs and the large land mammals to come, it displayed a strange collection of traits: Its skin was green and scaly, like a crocodile's, but it was also tufted here and there with clumps of grizzled black fur. Its eyes were large and lizardlike; it had no visible ears, just hollow indentations well behind the eyes; canine fangs, shaped like sabers, grew down from its upper jaw; and a long, thick, serpentlike tail dragged along the ground behind it.

Al-Kalli spoke again, in the soothing tones you might use to calm a nervous stallion, and he even held up one hand as if he were prepared to stroke the neck of the waiting beast.

Carter had never seen the creature so clearly as he saw it now; usually, it was lurking in the back of its pen, or hidden altogether in the enormous rocky grotto provided at its rear. It didn't like to be fully exposed; it shied away from the light. But now, as he studied its stance—its terrifying head held high, its broad, clawed feet planted firmly on the ground, its jaws parted—he knew what was about to happen . . . and even if he'd found a way to warn al-Kalli, to tell him that he was exposing himself to the most ruthless predator the planet had ever known, the man would never have listened.

And there wasn't time, anyway.

Carter saw the gorgon lower its body, gathering strength, and then, like an enormous jumping bullfrog, it leapt into the air and landed, claws extended and already tearing at him, on top of al-Kalli. He screamed once, but the gorgon quickly put a stop to that, dropping its jaws and snapping his head off with a swift, sideways ripping motion; the head rolled to one side, the mouth still open, the eyes still staring, as the gorgon shredded the flesh it still squatted over.

Carter, knowing there was no time to waste, made a run for it, racing toward the open doors. The gorgon would make quick work of al-Kalli, and be right back on the hunt again. He bolted outside, and nearly crashed into Del, who was just about to run in.

"What's going on?" Del said as he grabbed Carter's shoulders. "What's in that place?"

"Later—I'll tell you later," Carter gasped. "We've got to get out of here!"

Del said, "I've got a guy who's bleeding bad, behind the trees."

It had to be Greer. Carter glanced over at the golf cart, now a pile of wreckage, tumbled onto its side—the work, undoubtedly, of the escaping phoenix—and no longer usable to transport the injured Greer.

Carter followed Del for a couple hundred yards to where Greer was propped up against a tree, tying a tourniquet, made from his own shirtsleeve, around the leg where Sadowski had shot him.

"I knew something like this would happen!" Greer snarled. "I fuckin' knew it!"

"We've got to get out of here, now!" Carter said, grabbing Greer under one arm and hoisting him, groaning, to his feet. With Carter holding one arm and Del the other, they were able to drag him away from the bestiary and back toward the house. But by the time they reached the wooden footbridge, Greer was screaming in agony, begging for a brief rest.

"Okay," Carter said urgently, "but we've got to do it under the bridge."

Del looked puzzled, then followed Carter's gaze. What he saw he would never have believed—there were creatures that had been extinct for eons roaming the green lawns and eucalyptus groves, armor-plated dinosaurs (some kind of ankylosaurids?) lumbering between the trees, rubbing their spiky backs against the bark of the trees. Not far from them a powerful, spotted catlike creature, with a glistening patch of black fur that bristled and swelled like wings above its shoulders, prowled the gravel pathway. As Del watched in amazement, the hyenalike beast (could it be a homotherium, he wondered, thought to have disappeared at the end of the Pleistocene, fourteen thousand years ago?) stealthily approached one of the peacocks preening in the late-day sun, then pounced on it with the fluid movement of a flying tiger. Purple feathers flew in a frenzied cloud.

Del looked at Carter, as if for confirmation of what was before his eyes, but Carter just nodded, and hauled Greer deeper beneath the footbridge. Greer cupped a hand in the stream and rubbed the cold water over his face to keep from going into shock. Under his breath, he muttered an unending stream of curses and epithets.

"We can get some help and come back for you here," Carter said, but Greer shook his head and said, "I'll never last—I'm losing too much blood."

"You want to try to move again?" Carter said, though he doubted Greer would be able to make it far.

"I have to." Greer propped himself up again with the aluminum bat, and after Del checked to see that the animals were still far enough off—the cat was still dining on the peacock—they skulked back toward the empty stables, then down the sloping hillside to the forecourt of the house . . . where Del's truck and al-Kalli's black Mercedes were still parked.

"Let's get him in the truck," Carter said, and as Del threw open the door on the passenger side, Greer tossed the bat away and said, "I can do it—I can do it." He hauled himself up onto the seat, a thick ribbon of blood coursing down his leg.

"Take him to UCLA hospital—it's the closest!" Carter said to Del, and Del said, "Where are you going?"

But Carter already had a plan, if he was lucky. He ran to the limousine, ducked his head inside, and yes—Jakob had left the keys in the ignition; why not, when the car was parked on a gated estate with its own security force?

"I'm going home!" Carter shouted across to Del. With the wildfires spreading—and now a pack of primeval predators roaming free—he only wanted to get to Beth and Joey and make sure they were safe. Nothing else mattered to him now.

CHAPTER FORTY

BY THE TIME he got to the back gates that provided the service entrance to the estate, Sadowski was huffing and puffing so hard he thought his chest would explode. He swung them wide open and, once safely outside, stopped and leaned against the wall, his head down, his palms flat against the vine-covered stone.

Jesus H. Christ, what had happened back there?

The plan was just to stage a little raid, kind of like the one al-Kalli himself had sponsored back in Mosul. But Sadowski had been cheated on that one—he knew that Greer took home a whole lot more, in that big sealed box, than he'd ever shared up with the other guys on the mission—and this was going to be Sadowski's chance to even up the score. And maybe screw up whatever new moneymaking deal Greer had struck with the Arab now.

But that just wasn't how it had turned out so far. Man, was it not. Florio was dead—that gigantic bird had stuck a claw right through his chest cavity—and there was no telling what had happened to Tate, that cowardly piece of shit. Sadowski swallowed hard—his mouth was so dry he had almost no spit—and glanced at his watch. What was supposed to have taken no more than ten or fifteen minutes had consumed the better part of an hour. And if he didn't get out of there fast—very fast—he'd be cooked right along with everything else that fucking Arab owned.

Those goddamned animals included.

He took a long, ragged breath and looked down the road, fully expecting to see the Explorer gone. Everything else had gone wrong, why not that? But there it was, parked where he'd left it, in the shade of some old oaks.

And if he wasn't mistaken, that was Tate, sitting in the driver's seat and fiddling under the steering wheel . . . trying, no doubt, to hot-wire the engine.

Sadowski slung his backpack higher on his shoulder and tromped over to the car. Even with the door open, Tate didn't hear him coming, and only looked up from under the dashboard when Sadowski shook the car keys and said, "I ought to leave you here to burn."

"Stan!" Tate exploded, with patently fake enthusiasm, "you made it! That's great—I mean, I was really worried!"

Sadowski grabbed him by the collar and dragged him out of the front seat. He tossed his Browning onto the passenger side, but before he stepped up into the car, he sniffed the air. The acrid smell of smoke was already wafting up from the dry scrub a few yards down the hill. He checked his watch—the first firebomb had ignited at precisely the right time, but the flames were moving even faster than he'd planned. He could see them now—orange licks crackling through the brown grass and racing up the trunks of the dry trees. Like fireworks going off, the tops of the oaks and eucalyptus trees burst into balls of flame, first one tree, and then the next, and before he could even get the Explorer into gear, a huge flaming branch crashed down onto the road about ten feet in front of the car.

"Wait for me!" Tate shouted, running around to the passenger side.

But Sadowski was already backing up, hoping to get enough room to maneuver around the burning branch.

"Wait! Stan!" Tate was shouting, as his hands scrabbled at the side of the car. "Give me a break!"

He should have thought of that, Sadowski figured, before he ditched his bat and left him alone in that zoo from hell.

He switched gears and started forward again, but Tate had run right in front of the car, screaming and waving his arms back and forth. Billows of black smoke were starting to drift across the road and over the stone walls of the estate. Sadowski shook his head and motioned for Tate to get out of the way. He blasted the horn, but Tate threw himself on the front of the car and clung to the hood ornament—a Liberty Bell that Sadowski had special-ordered from Philadelphia.

Sadowski drove ahead a few yards, Tate still hanging on, when everything suddenly went crazy—a whole tree must have toppled onto the hood of the car. The windshield shattered, the roof caved in, and a thousand angry red sparks zipped around the interior like fireflies. Any second the gas tank could explode!

The door was dented and jammed; Sadowski had to shove his shoulder against it three times before he could even get it open. Toppling onto the pavement, he scrambled through a maze of burning leaves and twigs. He didn't even know which way he was running—the smoke was too thick and he could barely stand to open his eyes—but he knew he just had to get away from the car. The explosion, when it came, knocked him head over heels. He lay where he fell—there was earth under him, not concrete, that much he could tell—but there was no time to dig any kind of trench or hole; with his eyes shut, he dug the asbestos sheath out of his backpack. He fumbled to open it, then pushed his feet down into one end, pulled the rest of it up and over his head, and with singed fingers yanked the zipper up from the inside. If the fire passed over him quickly enough, and he could just catch enough oxygen, he'd survive. If it lingered, he'd wind up like Tate, who was surely nothing but a cinder in the middle of the road by now.

CHAPTER FORTY-ONE

EVEN AS HE pulled the door of the limousine shut, Carter knew this was no ordinary car. The door was heavier and more solid than any door, of any car, that he had ever felt. It closed with a thump like the sound of a bank vault being sealed. And when he looked at the front console, his suspicions were confirmed. There were enough meters and screens and dials to fill the cockpit of a 747. This, he guessed, was what you'd call an armored car, fully equipped and state-of-the-art—exactly what you'd expect a man like Mohammed al-Kalli to travel in.

The *late* Mohammed al-Kalli.

He put that thought from his mind as quickly as possible—there'd be time enough later to mull over all the horrors he had seen that day; right now, he just needed to pilot the car down from Bel-Air, across the freeway, and up again into Summit View; on an ordinary day it would take fifteen minutes. Today, however, as dusk began to fall and wildfires loomed, there was no telling how long it would take.

For a vehicle of such size and weight, Carter found that it steered with the ease and delicacy of a nimble sports car.

He made a tight circle in the forecourt of the house, and as he passed the front steps, he saw the door swing open and Jakob, his arms holding a big iron box, standing in amazement. Carter glanced in the rearview mirror and saw that Jakob was shouting, then he dropped the box and groped for something at his belt. Carter couldn't hear what he was saying—the car was virtually noiseproof—but he knew damn well that it wasn't a good idea to wait around to find out.

He touched the gas pedal more firmly, and the limo smoothly accelerated down the drive; he hesitated even to guess what kind of horsepower this engine could muster—or what all the brightly lighted controls were for.

But one of them had to be a phone. Without taking his eyes off the driveway for more than a second or two, he glanced at the console, saw something that said COMMUNI-CATIONS, and assumed that would be it. He pressed the black button, expecting perhaps a voice prompt, but instead he got nothing. He pressed it again, and this time an ear-splitting siren went off, a sound that was so loud, so prolonged, and so forlorn in its way that it might have been the cry of some ancient beast, like one of those whose lives he'd been working to preserve in the bestiary. The siren blared for several seconds, then went dead, and just when Carter thought it was over, it went off again. Several peacocks suddenly skittered across the drive, their tail feathers dragging, crying out in alarm—and when Carter rounded a turn, passing the fountain, he saw, off to the right, a roseate glow in the sky. The windows were thick, no doubt bulletproof, and tinted black, but even so Carter could now make out flames, rising and falling, moving like a glowing tide through the trees on the western border of the estate . . .

. . . And moving before them, lurching oddly but swiftly across the hillside, a huge dark shape.

The klaxon went off again, its plaintive wail piercing the air, and the dark shape seemed to change its direction, heading straight for the armored car.

Oh my God, I'm drawing the gorgon, Carter thought. He slapped at the dashboard controls, while steering the limo with one hand down the hill. The siren seemed to stop, but a blue light continued to flash. Carter had no idea what it meant—global positioning? Silent alarm?

He could see the gatehouse a few hundred yards ahead, but the gorgon was clearly tracking him now, and had even begun to adjust its course to cut him off before he got there. Carter gunned the engine—the Mercedes responded like a thoroughbred—but the driveway was narrow and curved, and suddenly he saw a white horse—with Bashir, the stable boy, riding him—right in front of the car. He hit the brakes, and the car ground to a halt just as the horse reared up in terror, throwing the boy to the side of the driveway. Before Carter could roll down the window and call out to him, the boy was running, running for his life, and the horse . . . the horse was whinnying and pawing in the air, at first at what looked like nothing, at a great black shadow, but which Carter could now see was something more. The glow of the approaching flames caught the dark green scales and the lacerating tail, snapping like a monstrous whip, of the gorgon—how could it have covered the distance so quickly?—as it savagely mauled the horse with its claws. Carter pressed the steering wheel everywhere, and the horn blasted, but the gorgon was undeterred. The horse turned to run, its white mane stained with blood, but the gorgon pounced on its back like a monstrous rider and the horse went down with its legs splayed out, broken, to either side.

Carter hit the accelerator and tried to drive around the beast, but instead he caught its swishing tail, the front tires bouncing over its fleshy tip, and the gorgon swiped with one paw at the chassis of the car. Its claws screeched across the black metal and it swung its heavy head away from the dying horse to snap fiercely at the rear bumper.

The gatehouse was just ahead, but there was no sign of Lee, the guard, and the gates themselves were closed . . . but Carter counted on the car to plow on through. He pressed down on the gas, sat back in the seat with both arms extended, his hands gripping the wheel, and hit the gates flying. The metal clanged, blue sparks shot up from the lock, and the gates flew off their hinges. The limousine spun half a turn into the road outside, its tires squealing, before Carter was able to gain control of it again and shoot off down the hill.

No air bags? he wondered. Then thought—an armored car is built for running right through barriers. An air bag could actually incapacitate the driver. Al-Kalli's car was made to thwart any ambush and keep on running.

But all Carter wanted the car to do now was get him through the increasingly surreal landscape—the wispy clouds in the sky were tinged with a fiery glow, the air was bitter and acrid, the palm fronds were rustling like parchment high above—and deliver him to his wife and son. He drove down the winding road as fast as he could go, encountering dozens of other cars quickly exiting through their own private gates and drives. All the way, he had one eye on the road before him, the road back down to the city, and one eye on the rearview mirror; don't turn around, as the saying went, something might be gaining on you. What he had left behind him, he knew no one would ever believe. And what, if anything, would be left of it once the fires had swept through, he could hardly bear to contemplate.

CHAPTER FORTY-TWO

HE'D NEVER BEEN the praying kind—God, when he thought about Him at all, was just some old guy in the sky to whom he might one day have to apologize—but wrapped in his fireproof blanket, the air like a furnace baking all around him, Sadowski was praying with all the earnest devotion of some medieval monk. He was sucking desperately at the oxygen in the sheath itself, and holding each breath for as long as he could, but he still didn't know if he'd be able to outlast the fire. Fortunately, he must have been lying on a spot where the grass had already been burned away, and no bushes or shrubs were too close by, because the waves of fire seemed to pass over him swiftly, seeking new fuel. *God,* he was thinking, *please don't let me burn alive. Please don't let me die here. I wasn't really going to let Tate die out there—I'd have let him back in the car, I swear. And I wasn't going to shoot Greer, either—much as he deserved it. The people I killed in Iraq—well, that was war, and they were Muslims anyway. They don't believe in you—or they believe in some crazy other version of you that isn't true—and I can't believe it's a sin, no matter how you look at it, to kill somebody who's trying to kill you first.*

All around him, he could still hear the crackling of the underbrush as it burned, and the occasional thump of a tree branch, severed from its trunk, crashing onto the street. Man, those incendiaries that Burt Pitt had designed sure as hell did their job—so well, in fact, that they'd nearly cost him his ass. He wondered if the others would go off with as much success—members of the Sons of Liberty had spread them all over the place, in ragged lines all across the Santa Monica Mountain Range and Topanga State Park, up and down from the Riviera Country Club to the Palisades Highlands and Summit View—and they had all been timed to cause maximum damage. Fifteen minutes after one set went off, and the fire department's resources had been diverted to deal with the blaze, another set would go off miles away. There wouldn't be enough firefighters or equipment on the entire west coast of the United States to stop the cataclysm that would follow.

And wouldn't America wake up on the fifth of July with a whole new attitude about the threat posed by open borders?

The air in the bag was gone, and he could feel his own hot sweat pooling in the small of his back; his clothes were stuck on him like a wetsuit. The noise around him had subsided, and he thought it might be safe to pull the zipper down an inch or two and test the air. The second he did, a film of black ash fell onto his face, and he sputtered to get it off his lips and out of his mouth. But there wasn't any fire to be seen, at least not through that tiny opening, and he had started to pull the zipper down a little more—damn, it was sticking—when he heard what sounded like footsteps, approaching from the street. Tate, he thought—he'd survived it somehow after all. And while his first impulse was to cry out for some help—come on, the danger was over now, couldn't they just act like buddies once again?—he wasn't sure that Tate wouldn't harbor some grudge. He might take advantage of Sadowski's defenseless position—wrapped in a bag with a stuck zipper—to beat the shit out of him.

The footsteps had stopped, and Sadowski wondered what Tate was thinking. Was he wondering why Sadowski hadn't outfitted him with an asbestos sheath, too? Had he been burned—badly—by the fire? Was he going to be really hard to look at?

And what should he, Sadowski, do? Should he play dead? Or should he say something, or stir inside the bag, to show that he was still alive in there? His fingers instinctively reached for the gun that he now regretted having left in the car.

The footsteps came closer, but they sounded heavy and hard. Maybe Tate was on his last legs. That wouldn't actually be so bad; if he died, Sadowski could take his wallet and ID off of him, and his body would probably never be identified; there'd be a lot of unidentified remains by tomorrow, Sadowski figured.

Either way, Sadowski hoped he had a full canteen on him; his throat was parched and he'd left his own water supply in the Explorer.

Sadowski didn't hear anything more, but he sensed someone very close by, and even through the small aperture he could smell something now—but it wasn't like human sweat or flesh, even of the slightly cooked kind. He knew those smells pretty damn well, from the white phosphorus attacks they'd laid down on the insurgents in Iraq. No, this was a different smell, but it, too, took him back to the desert . . . to the day that Captain Greer had talked them all into that little extracurricular mission outside Mosul. It was the smell he'd encountered in that empty zoo in al-Kalli's palace . . . where the bars of the cages were bent like they'd been hit with battering rams . . . and Lopez, the poor dead son of a bitch, had helped to press on the wings of that iron peacock . . . to reveal the box that Greer claimed he had never opened.

He decided not to call out. Or move. Or give any sign of life at all.

But the footsteps came closer anyway. And something was strange about that, too. It didn't sound like two footsteps at a time . . . but four.

Sadowski tried to pull the zipper closed again, but it was stuck firmly in place.

And the smell—of scorched fur and rugged hide—got much stronger.

Sadowski froze, not so much as breathing anymore.

But something was breathing—and it was directly above him now. As he peered through the hole in the bag, he saw a green eye, as big as a baseball, looking back down at him. He felt a trickle of urine stream down his leg.

The creature snorted—its breath was as fetid as a garbage dump—and Sadowski felt a broad paw grazing the top of the bag . . . looking for a way in.

Jesus, Mary, Mother of God, God Almighty . . . Sadowski couldn't think the words fast enough. And he couldn't think of anything else he could do; he could barely move his arms and legs anyway.

The gentle pawing became more firm, and Sadowski could swear that he heard the click of the creature's claws suddenly extending; one of them, an evil, crooked talon, hooked itself inside the tiny opening at the top of the bag and drew the zipper down as smoothly as a tailor. Sadowski lay there like a sardine in an opened can, while above him he saw what looked like a giant hyena, a mottled beast with hanging fangs and a thick matting of black fur all across its shoulders and neck.

Sadowski wanted to jump up and run, but his feet were still tangled in the bottom of the sheath, and when he tried to kick them free, the creature reared up on its hind legs, the black fur flying out like a cape, like the wings you'd see on a vampire bat. And then—just as Sadowski had mustered enough spit to scream—the beast threw back its head and let out a howl of its own, more bone-chilling than anything Sadowski had ever heard, and loud enough to drown out his own cry altogether.

Then it fell forward—jaws open and claws out—its black fur wrapping itself like a reeking veil around his thrashing head.

CHAPTER FORTY-THREE

SUNSET BOULEVARD WAS predictably snarled, the traffic inching along as policemen, stationed at the major intersections, tried to redirect the cars and keep the lanes moving at all. Carter ached to hit the klaxon again, and then use the limo like a snowplow, just shoving everything ahead of him out of the way; he had no doubt that this car could do it. Everytime he stopped dead, he studied the screens and dials on the dashboard, and eventually he found the phone connection.

"Number, please," an automated female voice said.

Carter, relieved, recited his home phone number.

But instead of connecting him, the voice said, "Unrecognized caller. Please say your name."

What would it recognize? Al-Kalli? Or, more likely, Jakob? And did he need Jakob's last name?—because he had no idea what that was.

Carter tried "Jakob."

The automated voice did not respond.

He tried "Mohammed al-Kalli."

But again, there was no reply.

"Please say your name," the voice finally repeated.

And this time, in total frustration, Carter simply said his own.

"Unrecognized caller. Please say your name."

Carter gave up. Maybe they had some code name; maybe it could actually recognize Jakob's voice itself. The blue light, next to the siren, was still silently flashing. What the hell was that, anyway—LoJack?

"Good-bye," the automated voice chirped.

"Yeah, right," Carter replied, "have a nice day."

A cop waved him through a blocked intersection—he managed to go about three car lengths—before he had to stop again entirely. He lowered his head to peer up through the tinted windshield at the sky; the wispy cirrus clouds that he had seen earlier were eclipsed now by plumes of smoke, rising like funnels from every direction. It reminded him of the pictures he'd seen from Kuwait, when the fleeing Iraqis had set the oil wells on fire.

What the hell was going on? Was the whole city of Los Angeles going up in flames? He was reminded of the guys in army fatigues—Sadowski and his pals—who had shown up at the bestiary, and of something their leader had said: "Oh, I've got a plan," or something like that, and then he'd glanced at his watch, as if making sure he was still on schedule. It seemed both impossible and incomprehensible—why would anyone do it?—but Carter had to wonder if what he was seeing was more than random wildfires, started by careless picnickers or kids with fireworks. Was it some insane and orchestrated plan?

He crawled forward, another thirty or forty feet, just as a helicopter swooped overhead; more images of Middle Eastern warfare teemed in his head. And his fear for the safety of Beth and Joey suddenly grew, exponentially. Were they home? Were they waiting there for him? Or had they fled to safety somewhere else?

A fire truck, sirens blaring, maneuvered itself across the intersection, right in front of Carter, and then, with a police escort clearing the way in front of it, started driving along the shoulder toward Sepulveda. The right side of the fire truck was riding up on the sidewalks and curbs, but Carter saw his chance and he took it; he gunned the Mercedes and caught the fire truck's wake, following along close behind. A firefighter, manning the ladder at the rear, waved him off, shouting, but Carter couldn't make out what he was saying—though he could certainly guess the gist of it—and he didn't care, anyway. He was determined to get to Summit View, and this was the only way to do it. Several times cops, too, hollered at him through bullhorns, and once, Carter got so pissed off he purposely hit the klaxon again, a blast louder and more powerful than anything you'd hear from even a sixteen-wheeler. He also noticed that one of the LED screens read INTERCOM ENGAGED. He touched the screen and then said, "Testing."

His voice boomed out over the jammed traffic lanes.

Oh man. What did this car not do?

"Official business," he said. "Please clear the way."

That must have given the cops a surprise, he thought—and at the next corner, they slowed down and fell back to attend to an accident. Carter didn't doubt that they'd made note of his license plate, though, and that al-Kalli—if he'd lived—would have been hearing from them soon.

Al-Kalli. When Carter thought about what he'd seen not an hour ago—the man's head rolling, and still sentient, if Carter's guess was correct, across the dirt floor of the bestiary—he couldn't believe it; it was as if Carter's own mind could not process the information, could not accept everything that had happened, and everything he had witnessed, that day.

And though it wasn't late even now, dusk had come early—the sun was shrouded behind an increasingly dense pall of smoke and cinders. Passengers sitting in the stalled cars that Carter passed looked stunned, terrified. Some had abandoned their cars altogether, and were running down the center lanes, carrying dogs in their arms, or car seats with squalling babies still in them. In the brown grass along one side of the road, he saw several people kneeling around a Hispanic man with a Bible who was leading them, heads down, in prayer; black ash swirled around their heads. Terrible shades, he couldn't help but think, of 9/11.

He fumbled at the levers of the wheel until he found the windshield wipers and fluid; as the blades went back and forth, the window at first got sootier and more smeared, but then, with another jet of fluid, it began to clear.

The radio—he finally thought of trying the radio, but when he found it, and got it on, it was tuned to some Middle Eastern music station. Although he needed to keep both hands on the wheel, every chance he got he reached over and played with the controls until he found a news station. But even then the reception was terrible, and staticky. "Fires . . . Temescal Canyon ablaze, fanned by Santa Ana winds . . ." There was another burst of static, and then a fire official's voice saying, "Please stay in your homes unless and until an evacuation order is given." Carter continued to listen as the announcer read off an endless list of freeways that were impassable, roads that were closed, neighborhoods that were endangered. But nothing, thank God, was said about Summit View—at least so far.

The fire engine had turned off in another direction several blocks before, and Carter now was simply barreling along the shoulder, often with one or two tires off the macadam, and eliciting blasting horns and angry shouts and bullhorned police warnings. Over the car's loudspeaker, he occasionally repeated his claim of official business, and once—at a particularly tricky juncture—announced that he was the mayor; the powerful black limousine with the fortunately tinted windows made a convincing case.

But when he got to Sepulveda and approached the entrance to Summit View, he found the long driveway blocked by a couple of fire trucks and several police cars. A stream of cars, some of them hastily loaded with stuff, was coming down off the hill and being shepherded toward the Valley. He had to stop short, and a young cop wearing a white paper face mask banged on his closed window with the butt of a flashlight. Carter rolled it down.

"You can't go up there," the cop barked, the mask billowing out, "we're evacuating."

"I have to," Carter said, "I live there! My family's up there!"

"Not anymore they're not. Everybody's coming down."
He waved to the left. "Now move it."

He walked away, but instead of turning in to the file of
cars slowly moving toward the Valley, Carter moved forward. The cop saw it and, pulling down the face mask,
hollered, "What did I just tell you?"

Carter rolled the window up. The cop was running after
him, and in his rearview mirror Carter could see that he
was actually unsnapping his holster. Carter was fairly confident that this was a bulletproof car, but that still didn't
mean he wanted to test it.

"Stop!" the cop shouted, and two or three other policemen, dead ahead, got out of their cars to see what was happening. They had parked bumper to bumper, to blockade
the right lanes of the drive. Carter would have to go around
them. He steered the limousine over the curb, up onto the
lawn, and then through the towering palm trees that lined
both sides of the drive.

Carter heard a shot, glanced in the mirror, and saw the
young cop, feet squarely planted, firing his pistol into the air.

And one of the patrol cars that had been blocking the
drive started up after him, bumping over the curb with its
lights flashing and siren blaring.

Was all of this for nothing? Carter thought. Was Beth in
one of the cars that was already snaking its way down the
hillside? He kept shooting glances over to his left, looking
for her old white Volvo, but he didn't see it.

Nor did he see, until it was almost too late, the big green
SUV that was barreling down the hillside, trying to circumvent the traffic on the drive. The SUV blasted its horn,
and Carter blasted the klaxon in reply, its piercing wail re-
verberating around the hillside with a frightening echo; the
SUV, perhaps startled, veered to the side, so close that it
grazed Carter's side mirror. Carter saw a panicked woman
on a cell phone in the driver's seat, a couple of kids in the
back, and then he saw her swerve to miss a tree behind
him, and he heard the crash.

She'd run right into the front of the police car; the
hoods of both cars were crumpled, and there was a cloud

of steam escaping from them both. Two cops jumped out to assess the damage, and Carter drove his own car back onto the main drive. While the lane on the other side of the cement median strip had a dozen or so cars still backed up, the lane going up the hill was clear, and Carter took its turns as if he were on the autobahn. The Mercedes purred, like a pent-up animal delighted at last to run free.

But the air, as he ascended, was darker and dirtier all the time. Smoke from the east was drifting over, and it was as if night was falling by the minute. Carter passed only one or two other cars racing down, one of them an open Miata with a bronze statue of a naked nymph on the passenger seat. Far ahead, he saw a red fire captain's car, and he could hear the speaker on the top telling people to evacuate now. He cut sharply into a side street, then shot back up through a service drive that led toward the top of the development. Via Vista, his own street, connected with it just a block or two up.

Ash was falling like snowflakes on the immaculate houses and parched lawns and empty streets.

Tires screeching, Carter wheeled the limo onto Via Vista, where only one row of houses stood along the crestline, the dense canyon falling steeply away just behind them. All that could be seen of the massive power towers that rose up above the trees and thick brush were the red signal beacons flashing at their top; the Santa Monica Mountains, perfectly visible on most days, were now just an immense black shadow, far away. Carter raced up the hill, past the tennis courts, past the swimming pool, toward the lighted windows of his own house. Beth was home, he thought, Joey was home! He would gather them all up into the Mercedes, along with Champ—he couldn't forget Champ!—and get the hell out of there, while there was still time!

The car lurched to a halt in the drive, right next to his Jeep, and he leapt out while the engine was still turning off. He ran across the front lawn—he could hear Champ barking inside—and threw open the door.

"Beth! Where are you?"

But there wasn't any answer. Champ jumped up onto his pants.

"Down, boy!" He pushed the dog aside and raced up the stairs, shouting, "Beth! Beth!" The dog bounded up after him.

He ducked his head into the nursery—the crib was empty—then into the master bedroom—empty, too.

He stopped to catch his breath, then heard a voice—Beth's, from downstairs—calling, "Champ! Champ!"

"We're here!" Carter shouted, then ran back to the top of the stairs.

Beth, at the bottom, was holding a leash; her hair was slapped up under a baseball cap, and she was wearing a Getty sweatshirt and gray sweatpants. She looked shocked to see him.

"Where did you come from?" she blurted out. "I've been waiting—"

"No time—let's go," he said, leaping down the stairs again, three at a time.

"Joey's in the car, but your Jeep is blocking the drive! I couldn't—"

He grabbed her tight, kissed her on the top of her baseball cap, and said, "Follow me."

The door to the garage was standing open. He ran in and lifted Joey out of his car seat.

"What are you doing?" Beth said. "Just move the Jeep out of the way!"

"Trust me," he said, running outside now, past his Jeep and toward the limo. If any car could get them out of this maelstrom . . .

He yanked open the rear door and waved Beth and Champ toward it. The dog made a running jump, Beth quickly clambered in, and as soon as she was seated, he handed her the baby. Even Joey, the imperturbable baby, looked concerned; black ashes clung to his blond curls.

Beth didn't even have time to ask where this car had come from.

Carter threw himself behind the wheel, backed up wildly halfway across the cul-de-sac, then started back down the hill. In the time the car had been out, the soot and ash had piled up on the windshield again, and he hit the fluid and wipers. But the debris was so thick, the wipers could barely move. Carter leaned forward to see ahead, then opened his window instead, and put his head out. It was like a scene from hell.

The sky was filled with clouds of black smoke, lighted from below by the advancing flames. The streetlamps, on light sensors, had all gone on, casting pale golden pools of illumination on the debris collecting around the base of their poles.

Carter fumbled at a few switches again, then found the high beams and turned them on. He had slowed down, looking for the turn back down the hill, when he saw something move, just a few yards in front of the car, and hit the brakes.

At first he couldn't tell what he was looking at—then he was able to see that it was a kind of animal exodus. In the crosswalk yet! A small herd of deer was skittering across the street, flanked by several coyotes, who were, miraculously, so intent on escape that they weren't even molesting the deer. A pair of raccoons tumbled over the curb. A skunk followed.

"Why are we stopping?" Beth said, cradling Joey in her arms. Champ barked at the closed window.

"Some deer," Carter said, before slapping the klaxon control again and sending up a mighty bellow. The deer fled, the coyotes scattered, and Carter started down again.

He hit the klaxon, over and over, to warn away the animals, but then a cloud of smoke and flame suddenly billowed from the eastern hillside, blinding and choking him; he pulled his head into the car, hit the button to close the window, and felt the car lift gently on one side, the undercarriage scraping along cement, before colliding with something he couldn't see at all, and coming to a full stop.

He tried to reverse, but he could hear the tires spinning.

He jumped out to see what was wrong, and watched as

the tops of the palm trees on the other side of the road burst, one after the other, into fiery balls, like puffs of dandelion blowing away in the wind.

The limo had driven right up onto the high curb in front of the pool complex—designed to let parents pull up and easily disgorge a horde of kids—and was perched there, with the left-side tires several inches off the ground. The road below looked dark and impassable . . . and the pool, though it looked like the black lagoon, was right there.

"Get out!" Carter shouted. "Out of the car!"

Beth kicked her door open, got out with Joey in her arms. Champ leapt out, barking frantically at the falling ash and advancing flames.

"The pool!" Carter said. "Get into the pool!"

The klaxon went off again, and Carter clamped his hands to his ears. He leaned into the front seat of the still running car and turned off the ignition, but the klaxon went on for at least ten seconds more, and that blue light on the dash kept flashing.

By the time Carter ran to the pool himself, Beth was already wading into the shallow end, with Joey held tight against her bosom. Champ waited by the lip of the pool, barking a warning.

"Come on!" Carter urged the dog, jumping in himself; the water was so coated with debris that it didn't splash, but simply sloshed like muck around him. Carter waded toward Beth and Joey, throwing his wet arms around them both. Champ still hesitated, lying by the side of the pool, front paws extended, whimpering.

The klaxon blared again.

"I thought I'd turned that off," Carter said, trying to catch his breath.

"What?" Beth said, coughing herself and unable to hear him over the siren.

Joey, his head against her shoulder, stared at his father with an ineffable expression of . . . what—sympathy? concern? definitely not fear—in his blue-gray eyes. Carter didn't have much other experience with babies, but Joey struck him, at all sorts of times, as . . . different. Shouldn't he be crying now, for instance? Or at the very least, agitated? Even his breathing seemed unobstructed.

The klaxon, blissfully, turned off. But with it gone, Carter could hear the unadulterated whooshing of the Santa Anas, whipped to a frenzy by the encroaching fires, and the crackle and snap of the dessicated foliage on the hillsides across from the pool. It was getting harder and harder to keep his eyes open, and harder to see anything even when he did. Beth's face looked like it had been coated with that black grease snipers smeared under their eyes; she was blinking at the cinders caught in her lashes.

He put his mouth to her ear, cupped it, and said, "Give me Joey."

She nodded, and wearily did.

"Now," Carter said, "you should duck your head under the water, go all the way down, then come up quick. It might clear your eyes."

She nodded again, took a labored breath, then disappeared under the black surface. When she came back up again, fast, she was shaking her head from side to side, the wet hair flying, and her eyes were tight shut.

"Did it help?" he said.

"Yes . . . yes. But . . ." Her gaze traveled over the pool to the street beyond, where the Mercedes still lay stranded on the curb and a sheet of flame, visible even through the pall of smoke, was cascading down the slope, engulfing a two-story stucco house.

Carter wondered if their own house had already gone up, too.

"Do you think we're going to die here?" she said, baldly, and Carter vigorously shook his head; despite everything, the thought had genuinely not occurred to him. No matter what came next, no matter what happened, he was going to make sure that no harm came to Beth or his son.

"We'll be okay," he shouted over the roar of the wind and the fire. "If the fire comes this way, just go down in the water." He didn't actually know if this plan would work, but it sounded good in theory . . . as long as the pool didn't

crack and send the water, with everything in it, flooding
down into the canyon.

"Now you clear your eyes," Beth said, nodding down at
the brackish pool. "It does help."

She reached out her arms to take Joey back, and Carter
did lower himself into the water. The deeper he went, the
clearer the water felt, and the cooler it had remained; for a
few seconds, he lingered there, enjoying the relative silence, the feeling of being clean and unsoiled, the respite
from the madness he knew was still swirling above.

But when he came up, wiping his eyes clean, he saw
Beth looking out at the hillside with a fixed expression. He
looked where she was looking, and then he saw it, too. A
hulking black shape, bigger than a rhinoceros but moving
as if it were one, lumbering down the hillside. Its scales
glistened green, like a salamander's—the reptile reputedly
immune to flames—and it paused, between two ribbons of
fire flowing like lava, and waited.

The klaxon burst out again, and the beast lifted its head,
roaring. Even through the smoke, Carter could see its bulbous dark eyes battening on the limousine, which lay
stranded like a beached whale . . . or perhaps, in the eyes
of the gorgon, an adversary.

With renewed purpose, it bounded down the slope,
moving around and through the flames with surprising
agility. And as Carter and Beth watched, it went straight for
the Mercedes, lowering its massive head and butting the
hood with such force that the whole car was pushed up
onto the broad sidewalk. The klaxon, either damaged or
simply finished with this cycle, went dead, and the gorgon
raised itself on its stubby hind legs and roared.

Beth began to shiver uncontrollably, and Carter gathered her close. "I know what it is," he said, and she looked
at him with terrified incomprehension.

What it was, Beth thought, was a picture from *The
Beasts of Eden,* come to terrible and unbelievable life!

The creature bellowed again, and then, perhaps smelling
the water, used its jaws to rip the iron fence posts up from

the ground. With its legs splayed out to either side, it calmly trampled over the wreckage.

Had it seen them, Carter wondered? Had it picked up their scent?

The creature came to the lip of the pool, and instead of lapping at the water, it knew enough to plunge its thick snout well below the debris and drink the less polluted water that lay below.

Champ, still crouching on the hot cement at the lip of the pool, stood up, tail raised, and barked loudly.

Carter prayed the creature, with its head still down in the water, wouldn't hear. But when it raised it again, Champ let loose with another angry challenge, and the beast swung its ponderous head from one side to the other, taking in everything that lay before it . . . including Carter, Beth, and Joey, still huddled together in the water.

"Stay low," Carter mumbled to Beth. "Move slowly, toward the deep end."

Maybe the beast wasn't a swimmer.

But then it lifted one front paw in the air, laid it on the surface of the water, and lowered it slowly, until clearly it had touched bottom. With its head turned to keep track of Carter and his family, it dropped the other front leg into the water, then, satisfied, plunged its enormous body into the pool like a gigantic crocodile scuttling off a riverbank. The displaced water rose like a tidal wave, carrying Beth and Joey up over the rim and onto the cement, while Carter was thrown against the wall beneath the diving board. The dirty water gushed over his head, and he sputtered for breath. The beast swam toward him—one stroke would bring its fangs within easy reach—and Carter hoisted himself up and out of the pool. He glanced over—Beth was carrying Joey and racing for the poolhouse—and Carter, instead of following, waved his arms and made sure to keep the gorgon's attention focused on him.

"Here!" he shouted. "Keep looking here!"

The cement was blazing hot, and slick with wet, sizzling cinders, but Carter ran around the rim of the pool, past the gorgon, which immediately changed course, and then onto the fallen railings. He had to dance through them, careful not to snag his foot or break an ankle.

"Catch me!" he hollered, without turning around, then hurried around the sidewalk to the driver's side of the limo; the car was now perched on all four tires again.

The klaxon went off, nearly shattering his eardrums, as he piled into the driver's seat, slamming the door shut behind him. The car was so well armored and insulated that the noise, once inside, was tolerable . . . but barely.

And for once he was glad to have the klaxon blaring. It was what must have allowed the gorgon to follow him here in the first place; maybe he could use it now.

He started the car, revved the engine loudly, and waited for the beast to take the bait.

Which, seconds later, it did. Through the side window, Carter saw it planting its broad, clawed feet on top of the iron fence posts and coming for its enemy, the car. Black water was streaming off the creature's flanks and matted fur, and its long tail lashed back and forth, blowing the smoke and ash away like a fan.

Carter flicked on the headlights and flashers—anything to make himself more of a provocation to the gorgon—and then, when the beast was almost upon him, he let the limo roll down the sidewalk, between the lampposts on one side and the burning hedges on the other. He could see the gorgon in his rearview mirror now, nimbly tracking him.

Carter waited for a spot where the curb was lower, and then jerked the car off the sidewalk; it jounced down onto the littered street, its headlights sweeping across a panorama of burning trees and swirling smoke. All the houses to the east were wrapped in flames, and as he watched, the chimney of one collapsed in a tumble of bricks and dust.

The gorgon had followed him into the street, its baleful glare unwavering, picking its way through the fallen branches and scorched leaves. Carter, though he could barely see through the filthy windshield, sped up . . . wondering all the while, what should he do now?

The klaxon, which had been blissfully off for a minute,

blared again, that blue light on the dashboard relentlessly flashing. For all Carter knew, the car was also being tracked by satellite. Jesus, he thought, al-Kalli had probably outfitted it with machine guns, but he had no idea where they were or how to operate them.

All he knew was that he was leading the monster away from his family.

He prayed that the poolhouse would provide a refuge.

But then the gorgon roared again, in answer to the klaxon, and he saw it, in his mirror, scurry forward on its splayed legs. It was angry—did the car's siren sound like a challenge from some primeval opponent?—and he feared it was about to attack.

He was right.

Before he could maneuver around the trunk of a flaming palm tree, the gorgon had suddenly scrambled forward, and with strength Carter could never have imagined, launched its massive body into the air. The roof of the limo was suddenly crushed by its bulk—the interior light exploding, the windows shattering into a rain of glistening shards, even the sound of the klaxon, though still going off, muffled and shrill. In any other car, Carter thought, he'd be dead by now, but the reinforced chassis still held together well enough for him to scrunch down in the seat, his head grazing the roof and his damp hands gripping the wheel. The creature was on top of the car, and had already batted one massive paw through the missing window on the passenger side. Its claws, as big and yellow as ancient ivory tusks, sliced at the leather upholstery, feeling, no doubt, for its adversary's innards. A creature like this was used to disemboweling its prey, and then waiting patiently for the blood loss to render it defenseless. If the victim was still clinging to life while the gorgon began eating it, that was all to the good; a gorgon liked its meat to be as fresh as possible.

But Carter knew something else about it, too: It would cling to its prey no matter what. It would never loosen its hold, or relinquish its kill to some other predator.

And in that he might have found the answer he was looking for.

The road dipped ahead, and Carter could see there the turnoff he'd been looking for, the path back down the hill and out of the development. But now he drove past it—he could hear the gorgon above his head, growling with rage and hunger, only a few inches of armored steel keeping it from crushing him—and gradually began the ascent toward the other end of Via Vista.

A wall of flame descended the eastern hillside, but the western side, at least up here, was not yet burning; the canyon was dark and deep and, though covered with a haze of smoke, it had not yet caught fire. Carter increased his speed, the gorgon still managing to envelop the limousine in its deadly embrace, its tail dragging like a heavy chain on the pavement. It slowed the car, but not so much that Carter, switching gears, couldn't pick up steam as he drove toward his goal—the cul-de-sac, just like the one at his end of the street, that lay ahead.

He suddenly felt the sleeve of his shirt rip, and he saw a long, hooked talon making another swipe at his arm. The roof of the car crumpled even more—the gorgon must have shifted its weight—and the driver's-side door groaned and then popped out onto the pavement, clanging and clattering as it fell away down the street. Carter glanced up and out, and at that moment the monster lowered its head to try to peer inside.

Its mouth was open, revealing rows of serrated teeth, interrupted only by two saberlike fangs that hung down from the upper jaw; they were gleaming with saliva, and one was broken off at the tip. The unblinking eyes were so large and convex Carter imagined he could see himself reflected in them.

But what did the gorgon, a ruthless predator nominally extinct for 250 million years, make of all this? Clinging to the crushed chassis of a limousine, with a human—Carter had no doubt the creature could smell his flesh and the blood pounding in his veins—harbored inside? Was it really able to think at all—or was it just acting on instinct, driven like a shark to kill and eat, to flee from the danger of a raging fire, to attack and devour all enemies?

Carter certainly hoped that last one was true—that the gorgon would do anything to make sure this gleaming black beast would die in its grasp. The klaxon sounded again, more subdued by the mutilated metal, and the gorgon bellowed—exultantly, it seemed, to Carter. It thought the enemy was dying, that the fight would soon be over.

But not too soon, Carter thought—not too soon!

He gunned the engine again, enough to pick up even more speed, but not enough to shake the gorgon loose. He wanted to keep the beast right where it was, enjoying the death throes of its prey. He raced up the hill, the siren blaring, the gorgon roaring, and headed for the crest of Summit View, the cul-de-sac where everything stopped; beyond it, below it, lay nothing but the canyon.

Twice he had to swerve around fallen debris, and once around the smoldering wreck of a sports car, but the monster's tail seemed to serve as a kind of rudder, keeping the beast on board and the limo on track. The roof strained and squealed, then burst its rivets and caved in another few inches. Carter, nearly horizontal in the broken seat, could barely operate the steering wheel and gas pedal. But the end of the street was fast approaching; he could see the last lampposts lighting the way.

Carter leaned toward the left, planted his foot on the floor where the missing door had been, and as he saw the black, empty crest ahead, he pressed on the gas pedal, then braced himself for what might be his last act on earth: Head low, arms tight, he threw himself out of the racing car, flying into a pile of burning brush, then tumbling and turning and falling through the smoke and ash and glass. He felt a shoulder pop from its socket, heard a bone crack, but even as he rolled away he was able to catch a glimpse of the Mercedes, its red taillights glowing, as it shot toward the cliff with the gorgon ripping at the steel and its head raised in triumph.

As Carter banged up against something hard, the breath was knocked from his lungs; he saw the car plow through the low metal barrier at the top of the street, and then sail off the edge of the cliff. The gorgon's tail swung high in

the smoky air as the creature—and its doomed prey—
plummeted into the canyon below.

Then, before he could even catch another breath of the
scorched air, everything went hazy, dim, and finally . . .
black.

CHAPTER FORTY-FOUR

BETH PULLED THE curtain back and took a peek into the garden.

Agnes Critchley was out there, just as she'd expected, pruning her roses.

She let the curtain fall back, and sighed. She felt guilty about trying to avoid her—after all, the Critchleys had been nice enough to take them all in after their rented house in Summit View had gone up in flames—but she just wasn't up to another chat about gardening and pest control right now. Living in the Critchleys' guesthouse was a blessing, but it did have its price.

Joey was in his playpen, happily banging plastic blocks together, while Carter tried to work the end of a ruler into the cast holding his fractured left arm together.

"You want some help with that?" Beth asked.

But Carter shook his head. "It's best if I learn to do these things for myself," he said with mock solemnity.

"Anything I can do for you instead?"

Carter laughed. "What? Is Agnes outside?"

Beth nodded, caught.

"So you're a prisoner until she leaves?"

"Something like that."

Joey, hearing his father's laugh, laughed, too, and tossed a red block out of the playpen.

Beth stooped to pick it up, and Carter said, "If you really need something to do, you could help me lace up my hiking boots."

Beth frowned. "That would be aiding and abetting something that I think is a bad idea."

"I know that," Carter said, "but I've got to get some exercise. You want me to get fat?"

"I wouldn't mind," she said, though secretly she had to admit that she would. She bent down and started lacing up the boots—tightly—so there wouldn't be any other accidents. She had had all the drama, and all the terror, she ever wanted in her life. She had seen things that would haunt her for the rest of her days. Her hair hadn't exactly gone gray overnight, but there were definitely a few strands here and there that she had had to touch up.

She could feel Carter looking down at her as she tied the boots, and she knew, without even asking, what he was thinking. Ever since the Fourth, he had looked at her with a depth of affection, and protectiveness, that made everything before it pale in comparison; it was as if she and Joey had been restored to him by some divine providence and he was determined not to take any chances with them ever again.

It was a miracle, she supposed, that he was willing to leave her today to go hiking. Instead of worrying about his recuperation, she should have been encouraging him to go. It was a good sign, really.

"That alright?" she said, pulling the laces snug one more time.

"Perfect," Carter said, tapping the new boots on the floor. Everything they owned had been lost in the fire. Their clothes, their books, their furniture, their photos . . . along with, most notably for Beth, the secret letter from Ambrosius of Bury St. Edmunds. When Beth had run home that day from the Getty—which had withstood the walls of flame like the impregnable fortress it was designed to be—she had, tragically, brought it with her.

And now it was gone.

As was, presumably, *The Beasts of Eden,* too. Al-Kalli's estate had been razed . . . and with him in it, from what Carter had told her.

All Beth had now was a collection of files and translations, notes and printouts, all pertaining to a mythical object that no one could see and that she could never again produce. The most beautiful and original illuminated manuscript the world had ever known, by the greatest and most innovative artist of the eleventh century, whose masterpiece would never be seen.

Champ barked, and ran to the door. Beth could hear Del exchanging pleasantries with Agnes Critchley outside.

"David Austin English roses," he was saying. "They do need their water."

"Yes, they do," Agnes trilled back. "They're thirsty fellows."

How did Del know anything about roses? Beth was always amazed at the variety of topics Del could expound upon.

She opened the door, and Del—his white hair tied up in a blue rubber band, wearing shorts and a loose Lakers T-shirt—said, "I'm selling magazine subscriptions to work my way through college . . ."

Beth gave him a hug, and Joey squealed. He liked his Uncle Del.

"Anybody here ready for a hike?"

Carter stood up and with his right hand hoisted his backpack onto one shoulder. "Rarin' to go."

"You sure it's okay if I take him away for a few hours?" Del said to Beth.

"Just promise to bring him back in one piece."

Del shook his head. "He's not in one piece now—you expect me to fix him?"

Carter threw his plastered arm around Beth's neck and gave her a tender squeeze. He loved the smell of her hair, the feel of her shoulders, fragile but firm. "I'll be back in a couple of hours. We'll barbecue."

As he turned to go, he took one look back, and Beth was

already bending down to take Joey out of his playpen. "You want to go and see the lovely roses?" she was cooing.

He left the door open—the garden was large and immaculately manicured, not only by Mrs. Critchley, now off in another quarter, but also by a regular crew of Mexican gardeners. Del's truck was parked on the quiet street outside the gates.

"Where we going?" Carter asked as he tossed his backpack into the cab and climbed in.

"Temescal," Del said, settling behind the steering wheel.

"Isn't that completely burned out?"

"Probably. But that's why I need to go there."

"Need?"

"Got something to show you."

Carter couldn't argue with that. He had shown Del plenty . . . from creatures who had thrived ages before the dinosaurs to the burial site of the La Brea Woman . . . and her long-lost partner.

A few days before, on the pretext of going to the Page Museum for a teleconference, Carter and Del had met with James Running Horse, the leader of the NAGPRA protestors. They had wanted the remains of the La Brea Woman and Man to be buried in a spot sacred to Native Americans, and Carter felt he had been led, by means that were still a mystery, to a fitting resolution. He'd started by showing Running Horse the broken mano stone that had been discovered in 1915, when the bones of the La Brea Woman had been excavated.

"It's a mano, used for manual chores like—"

"I know what it is," Running Horse had said, witheringly.

Carter let that pass. "But look at the striations on it, and the way that it has been broken in half."

"So?" Running Horse replied. "Lots of these are found broken."

"Not like this," Carter said. "Not against the natural cleavage plane, and not defaced like this. This was done deliberately, as punishment or retribution."

Running Horse said, "The Native American Grave Protection and Repatriation Act is not about manos or arrowheads or pottery shards. It's about bones, Dr. Cox. Human bones."

"So it is."

"So show me where you have stashed the bones of my ancestors, and I will take them and put them where they belong."

"They're already there," Carter said.

"Where?" he shot back skeptically.

"I'll show you."

Del turned and walked across the closed lobby of the Page Museum—Carter, not wanting to start up any further ruckus with Gunderson about what he was planning, had picked a time when the museum was officially closed— and into the atrium garden.

It was a beautiful afternoon, late in the day, and birds were twittering in the branches of the gnarled gingko tree. The garden, open to the blue sky above, was cradled within the glass walls of the museum, and today, more than ever before, Carter felt what a magical place it was. Small and tranquil, traversed by a single quiet footpath, its running stream inhabited by nesting turtles and glittering orange koi . . . it was as close to the primeval landscape of the region as any of present-day Los Angeles was likely to get. It was like stepping back into a tiny patch of the Pleistocene epoch, and as Carter led Running Horse toward the waterfall at the back, he hoped that some of that feeling was rubbing off on him, too.

"Very nice," Running Horse said, "but I've been in here before."

Carter wasn't sure the magic had worked yet. He paused beside the burbling waterfall, and let Running Horse soak up the peace and the harmony of the place. Del hung respectfully back, like a funeral director.

"I want you to do something for me," Carter said.

Running Horse didn't look amenable. His dark eyes were obdurate and his chin was set.

"I want you to take that stone, the one right there, from the center of the waterfall."

Running Horse looked at the waterfall splashing down a short rock face and into a small elevated pool. "Why?"

"Because I want you to see something."

Running Horse stepped off the pathway and onto the grassy earth. He was wearing a long-sleeved white shirt, and he stopped to roll up the sleeve before leaning close to the little fall and retrieving the glistening rock.

When he turned back, Carter was holding out the mano the La Brea Woman had been found with. "Now compare them," Carter said. "Put them together." It had come as a sudden revelation to Carter—and he hoped it would have the same effect on Running Horse.

Running Horse took the woman's mano and joined the two together between his hands—the pieces fit perfectly.

"And look at the defacing marks," Carter said.

Running Horse lifted the stones and studied them more closely. He could see that the slashes and cuts neatly meshed.

But he still didn't understand what all of this was leading to.

"The bones of the La Brea Woman were brought here, and buried here," Carter said, "by some means I do not begin to understand."

Running Horse remained silent.

"And that stone was placed there, in the waterfall, as a marker. A tombstone."

Running Horse waited still.

"We—that's Del and I—have buried the bones of the La Brea Man beside them," Carter explained. "We believe that these two people were together in life, and that they were killed, perhaps because of some transgression, together at the end. The stones prove it."

"Here?" Running Horse finally said, in a voice still fumbling toward comprehension.

Carter gestured at a spot of freshly smoothed earth, away from the path, in the shade of a tree.

"This is where they lived," Carter said, "and this is where they died." Carter gestured at the lush foliage and babbling brook. "This is a world they would know, even today."

Running Horse stood silent, contemplating all that he had just been told. Carter and Del moved away to allow him some time to commune with his thoughts, and when he turned toward them again, he said simply, "Then let it be." He replaced the broken mano in the waterfall, and nestled beside it the other half. Under his breath, he chanted some words, unrecognizable to Carter, then bent down and touched the recently turned earth with the flat palm of his hand.

When he stood up, he didn't offer to shake hands with Carter, or speak any words of reconciliation, but he didn't challenge him or argue anymore either. He walked out of the atrium garden, letting the glass door close slowly behind him, and Carter had neither seen nor heard anything from him since . . .

And there had been no further disturbances in the museum at night.

"You see the *L.A. Times* today?" Del asked now, as he steered the truck through the morning traffic on Pacific Coast Highway.

"Nope," Carter said, laying his cast on the center armrest. They sure made trucks a lot nicer than they used to.

"There's a big photo of that Derek Greer, the man of the hour."

Carter knew he should have been following the news more closely, but he just couldn't bear to. There was too much he didn't want to think about.

"He's the one who pointed the cops to those Sons of Liberty bastards," Del went on. "The leader, some guy named Burt Pitt, was caught at the Mexican border, of all places. Now I guess he wishes the borders were more open than they are," Del said, with a grim chuckle.

Even as they drove along PCH, a ribbon of highway that hugged the ocean shoreline, Carter could see, in the hills and palisades, burn scars where the fires had swept down through the chaparral before running out of fuel on the concrete roadway and the broad beach beyond. But in their terrible progress the flames had destroyed hundreds of houses, consumed untold millions in property, and taken dozens of lives.

But what Carter was looking for, as he scanned the cliff-sides, was something else.

Del had the radio on—a country-western station, of course—and he tapped his fingers on the wheel in time to the music. The singer was claiming that there was a reason God made Oklahoma, but Carter hadn't been paying attention, so he didn't know what it was.

At the turnoff to the Temescal Canyon hiking trail, there was a chalkboard sign saying that, although the trails were open, it was advisable only for experienced hikers to proceed. "Fire danger still exists," the sign said. "Report any indications of fire immediately."

"And hey, look at that," Del said, pointing to another sign in the lot where the parking validations used to be dispensed. "Parking fees have been waived." Nothing pleased Del more than a bargain. "God help me, I'm starting to love this town."

Carter had never seen such a turnaround. For a guy who had hated L.A.—its noise, its commotion, its traffic, its phonies with cell phones welded to their ears—Del had made a near miraculous conversion. And it was the Fourth of July—or *Götterdämmerung*, as Del liked to refer to it—that had made the difference. On that day, he had seen things in Los Angeles that no other place on earth could ever have offered. He had seen creatures—living and breathing and hunting—whose petrified bones he had studied all his life. He had seen, on al-Kalli's lawns, a glimpse of a prehistoric world hundreds of millions of years old. And even in the fires—the raging, deadly, uncontrollable conflagration—he had seen the power of nature unleashed, and he had seen the city scourged, like Sodom, and in his eyes reborn to a rough kind of beauty. He rooted for Los Angeles now.

Which explained, Carter thought, the purple and gold Lakers T-shirt.

Del hopped down out of the driver's seat, his green

canvas knapsack slung over his shoulder. Carter got out more carefully—his body was still plenty battered and bruised. In the fall from the Mercedes, he'd sprained both ankles, broken one arm, dislocated one shoulder, bruised several ribs, and scraped the skin off both shins. He didn't look so good in his hiking shorts, but then, there didn't seem to be anyone around to notice. The parking lot was empty, and as they started up the trail, they saw no sign of any other hikers. Or even much wildlife. Everything was preternaturally quiet, and the air still smelled of cinder and ash. The fires had beaten jagged and unpredictable paths all through the Santa Monica Mountains and the nature preserves, cutting wide swaths down the sides of some hillsides, while leaving others unscathed. Even in Summit View, where Carter had been found unconscious by a fire crew, some of the houses had been reduced to a pile of ash, while others, just across the street, had sustained nothing but smoke damage.

He'd been back there only once since the fire. He'd had Beth drive him to the crest of Via Vista, or what was left of it, and he'd looked over the side of the cliff, where the Mercedes had disappeared. Several hundred yards down, turned over on its back like an eviscerated turtle, he could see the black and twisted wreckage of the car; he half expected the klaxon to still be making some feeble noise.

But there was nothing; no sound, and no sign of the gorgon who had ridden it down. The trees and brush down there were largely intact, as were large parts of the parklands to the north. Had it crawled off to die in the brush? Had it been cornered, and consumed, by a sudden change in the fires, a gust of Santa Anas that had blown the flames all around it?

Or was it still out there, somewhere, foraging in the tens of thousands of acres that made up the vast preserves, learning to survive in this altogether new world?

For all the misery it had nearly brought him, Carter hoped that it was—and that, when he was in better shape again, he would be able to go in search of it.

"You see those photos," Del asked, without turning around on the trail, "the ones from the cell phone cameras? They were showing them again last night on the news."

"I've seen them," Carter said—grainy shots, taken through the smoke, by people stuck in their cars on back roads, of a huge and lumbering creature crashing through trees and, in one case, slinking through a culvert under a freeway. A fire department helicopter, bringing a huge bucket of water up into Bel-Air, got its own long-distance shots, but from so high above, and through all the swirling smoke, it looked as much like an armored vehicle of some kind as it did a creature of legend and lore.

And no one, from the witnesses to the authorities, had any idea what to make of it, or what to do about it if they did. The city administration had its hands full with the more immediate problems—thousands of displaced people, a conspiracy of arsonists to round up and prosecute, sporadic but continuing smaller blazes, disaster relief to claim from the feds (and then find some way to dispense). The Godzilla stories had been put on the back burner, as it were, everywhere but the tabloids and the Fox network.

"So what did you want to show me?" Carter asked, stepping carefully over the rocks and boulders strewn across the hiking path; many of them looked as though they had come loose in the fire and just recently tumbled to rest down here.

"My home away from home," Del said, "if it's still standing."

Carter had no idea what he was talking about until they came to a fork in the trail and Del headed to the right, to the more arduous route—the one that Carter now remembered they had taken on their previous expedition up here. He also recalled passing an abandoned old cabin covered with graffiti. If Del imagined that it was still standing . . .

All around, Carter could see the charred remains of the trees and brush that had once afforded so many animals, from gray quail to the occasional bobcat, a refuge and a home. But now the landscape was more desertified than ever, with only an occasional weed or patch of grass poking its head up above the layer of ash and cinder that coated the ground.

The cabin, which had at least sported a roof and walls the last time they had come past here, was now nothing but a pile of charred timbers, melted glass, and broken bricks. The blackened branches of a scorched sycamore reached out toward it as if in consolation.

"Any special reason you wanted to come back here?" Carter asked. "Were you expecting some mail?"

"You laugh," Del said, "but I was living here lately."

Carter stopped. "You were what?"

"Living here," Del said, treading carefully through the ruins, his eyes on the ground.

"Why? What was so bad about your sister's million-dollar condo on Wilshire Boulevard?"

"It was a million-dollar condo on Wilshire Boulevard. It gave me the willies just being there. Out here, I didn't have a valet trying to park my truck, I didn't have horns honking all night down on the street, I didn't have my brother-in-law freaking out every time I tried to play some Willie Nelson on his sound system."

"Out here you didn't have a sound system," Carter pointed out.

"I had a battery-operated boom box," Del said, stopping in front of a blob of twisted black plastic, the size of a toaster now. "And this was it."

Carter now understood why they were there and he, too, looked around at the rubble and ash at his feet. "Anything else I should be looking for?" he said.

"I had a propane stove, a few clothes, not much." He kicked over one of the fallen timbers. "Can't imagine anything else made it through the fire either."

Carter helped to make a desultory search through the wreckage. Here and there he saw the glint of a twisted spoon, the metal buttons from a workshirt, a sliver of glass. He was just about to give up when a lizard skittered across the toe of his boot, and looking down, he saw the sunlight pick up a trace of something blue. He crouched down and cleared away some of the debris. Under it all, he saw a turquoise stone, and when he pried it from the earth, it came up on a tarnished silver chain. There were several more turquoise stones attached to it . . . making a necklace.

Carter held it up. "This yours?" he asked Del, brushing away some of the clinging dirt.

Del came closer. "Nope," he said, turning it over in his fingers. "Never saw it before in my life."

But Carter already knew he had seen it himself. He had seen it that terrible day in Pit 91, the day when Geronimo—a.k.a. William Blackhawk Smith—had jumped down and slashed him with the knife. The day Geronimo had died, swallowed alive in the tar pits.

He heard the cry of a bird overhead, and saw a hawk circling . . . just as he'd seen one the first time they'd come here.

And he knew at that moment whose home this had originally been.

"But it's not an ancient artifact of any kind," Del said, handing it back. "That chain is machine-made."

He wandered off in search of any other remnants of his life, and once he was gone, Carter put the necklace back in the dirt, and covered it over. The hawk, perched on a limb of the sycamore now, cried again.

In the end, all Del was able to retrieve was a pair of army field binoculars, miraculously spared by the fire; they were still in their steel case, and under a bunch of bricks. "Not a total loss," he said, stepping free of the burned boards and cinders, and climbing back toward the trail.

Carter turned to follow, but not before casting one more backward glance at the last remains of the cabin, and the hawk keeping watch from the blackened branch above it.

They continued on up the trail, toward the waterfall near the top, but it was all so different now; where the hillside had been dense and thickly overgrown, now it was spare and wide open. Most of the trees were down, but those that remained were just skeletal figures, black and bare of leaves. The scrub brush was just clumps of furze, affording almost no cover for the myriad creatures that would once have taken shelter below it.

At a turn in the trail, Carter stopped to catch his breath. Beth was right; he had to take it easy. He had been lying around for a couple of weeks, his body had taken a pretty bad beating, and the sweat was starting to trickle down into the cast on his arm. Del, who'd been pushing on, noticed and came back.

"You need a break?" he said, offering Carter his canteen.

Carter nodded, while showing Del that he had his own water bottle in his knapsack. He took a swig, and then another, while gazing out over the devastated canyon below.

"You don't think you're still going to see them, do you?" Del said, and Carter knew exactly what he was talking about. He and Del had discussed the creatures from the bestiary often—what precisely they were, what Carter had been able to learn about them in the brief time he'd had on al-Kalli's estate, whether or not the fire had consumed them all, entirely. The beasts that had probably died on the grounds of the estate in Bel-Air—the basilisks, the griffin— would never be found, Carter was sure. Al-Kalli's teenage son, Mehdi, and his attorneys had sealed off the place, and Mehdi would make sure that his family's secret treasure— even if now it was only a pile of bones—would remain a secret forever.

As for the gorgon, Carter wasn't so sure. But he hadn't told Del—he hadn't told anyone—about his encounter with the creature in Summit View. That was his own secret—his and Beth's. One day, when he was back in shape, when the world had returned to some kind of normalcy, he would pursue the matter, he would try to find out what had happened. He would confess it all to Del, and together they could mount their own private expedition.

But not just yet.

"Here," Del said, handing Carter the field binoculars. "I'm going to head up to the crest. Why don't you take a breather?"

Carter hated to admit it, but Del was right. He should take a break.

"Thanks," he said, sitting down in the dirt. "You might be right."

"I'm always right, Bones."

Del set off toward the waterfall, and Carter took a deep breath and looked out over the canyon; the Santa Monica Mountains rose up on the other side, their ravaged flanks showing the sweeping path of the flames. Beyond them, and just visible past their peaks, lay the tranquil blue of the Pacific, shining in the hot summer sun.

Carter kneaded his calves, where the skin was still tender, and flexed his ankles, still sore from their sprains. He stretched his long legs out in front of him. The sun felt good, like a hot pack. He wondered what Beth and Joey were up to. Had Beth dared to venture outside and run the risk of a gardening conversation? The Critchleys had made it clear that they could stay as long as they liked—in fact, Carter thought they rather liked having a Getty curator in their guesthouse—but Carter knew that he had to start looking for a new apartment soon. The housing on the west side was at a premium right now, with so many displaced Angelenos, but there were some buildings not all that far from the Page Museum and the La Brea Tar Pits that were still advertising summer specials.

He'd look into it when he went back to work on Monday. For now, he would just enjoy the downtime.

Off in the distance, he could see a few spots on the mountainsides where the chapparal had not been burned off, and a couple of others where there were even signs of new growth; yellow flowers had popped up, in profusion, in one area to the northwest. Even from here, Del would know exactly what they were. He'd miss having Del around, he thought, but he knew that his friend's university leave was running out, and he'd have to be heading back up to Tacoma soon.

A tiny spot of red, flickering like a flame, appeared among the distant yellow flowers.

Carter's heart stopped.

His hand reached into his knapsack, fumbling for his cell phone.

Was it a hot spot? A place where the fire, even now, was still burning?

But then the red spot . . . moved.

He put the cell phone on the ground and picked up instead the field binoculars Del had left with him.

He kept his eyes on it while unsnapping the steel case, taking out the binoculars, unfolding them.

The red spot moved again, and this time he noticed that it seemed to move with some deliberation, traveling from one clump of the yellow flowers to another.

He put the binoculars to his eyes, quickly trying to focus them.

He found the scorched crest of the mountain, then moved down, and across, to find the yellow flowers.

He twisted the dial again, gently, to gain greater focus.

And there it was, the red spot—only now he could see that it was larger than he had thought, and that it could expand and contract.

When it moved again, he saw that it had a shape—the shape of a bird.

A huge bird.

And now his heart beat faster than ever.

He followed its path as it spread its wings, caught a sudden updraft, and drifted on the wind to another patch of flowers. He lost it for a moment, glanced over the top of the binoculars to get a fresh fix, and then found it again.

Its hooked beak, its scarlet feathers, its massive wingspread were all unmistakable.

Instinctively, he stood, never letting his lock on it waver.

And he thought again of the ancient lore of the phoenix, the immortal bird that rose, renewed, from its own blazing pyre . . . and he could see how it might have appeared that way. With its wings folded, it looked like a beam of light, but when it spread them again, it was like a bouquet of flames, opening up and out. It moved with all the incandescence and unpredictability of fire.

Had Del seen it, Carter wondered, from his perch higher up the trail?

The bird paused—Carter couldn't see what it was doing, its body obscured by shadow—before it suddenly raised its head and Carter could again see its glittering eyes. Had it sensed something, even from this great distance? Did it know it was being watched?

It seemed impossible, but then, the creature itself was an impossibility.

It unfurled its curved wings and glided off the mountainside, traveling from light to shadow, its crimson body like a beacon of flame against the black and defoliated mountainside. And then, suddenly, it changed course, sweeping toward a gap in the mountain range, toward a wedge of blue ocean far off on the horizon. With one beat of its wings, it swooped into the narrow pass, and with another it went nearly through. Carter tried to adjust his focus, but he was losing it. The phoenix was becoming just a tiny scarlet dot, like a spot of blood from a pricked finger.

It beat its mighty wings one more time, and by now, though he had lost it in the distance, Carter knew that it must be over the ocean . . . sailing out of sight, sailing toward the sun.

He put the binoculars down . . . and wondered if he, or anyone, would ever see it again. A part of him—the paleontologist, the man of science—desperately wanted to; nothing so wonderful should ever be lost to the world. Not again. But there was also another part—a part that was strangely closer to his heart, his spirit, a part that had been alive in him ever since childhood—that hoped the phoenix would vanish for good, flying into the sun forever.

Author's Note and Acknowledgments

Much of the action in this book takes place in two Los Angeles locations: the J. Paul Getty Museum in Brentwood and the George C. Page Museum of La Brea Discoveries, a satellite facility of the Natural History Museum of Los Angeles County.

While most of what I write about these places is accurate, a lot of it, I'll be the first to admit, is pure conjecture. The characters, too, are wholly fictional.

That said, these two institutions are, to my mind, the jewels in the crown of L.A., and I hope that this book conveys my boundless admiration for both.

Bestiary is also filled, as you have no doubt noticed, with a great deal of information about everything from illuminated manuscripts to paleontology. Again, much of the information is based on scrupulous research . . . while some of it is founded on nothing but fictional license. I will say this: For the paleontological material, I have relied heavily upon a fascinating volume called *Gorgon: Paleontology, Obsession, and the Greatest Catastrophe in Earth's History* by Peter D. Ward (Viking Press, 2004) and on several books available in the Page Museum's public bookstore. Anything I got right, I owe to these sources; everything wrong is entirely my own fault.

The same principle holds true for the sections dealing with medieval manuscripts. But I do owe a huge debt to one man: Christoper de Hamel, without whose books, *A History of Illuminated Manuscripts* (Phaidon Press, 1986) and *Medieval Craftsmen: Scribes and Illuminators* (University of Toronto Press, 1992), I would not have known where to start.

Now, a note about the text: Readers of this book will occasionally come across references to a character named Arius and his mysterious relationship to Beth and Carter Cox. Anyone whose curiosity is sufficiently piqued by these references may wish to read my previous novel *Vigil*, in which all is made abundantly clear.

I'd also like to thank some real people, for their unflagging help and support: my editor, Natalee Rosenstein; my agent, Cynthia Manson; and my cousin, Rob Masiello (yes, I know, we spell the family surname differently), who bailed me out repeatedly with his extensive knowledge of firearms and related security issues. (Again, any mistakes are all mine.)

Finally, I'd like to thank my wife, Laurie, for seeing me through yet another of my great big book ideas. It's never easy.

ROBERT MASELLO is an award-winning journalist, a television writer, and the author of many previous books, including *The Spirit Wood*, *Black Horizon*, *Private Demons*, *Raising Hell*, *Fallen Angels*, and *Vigil*. His articles and essays have appeared often in such diverse publications as *New York Magazine*, the *Los Angeles Times*, *Newsday*, *Glamour*, *People*, *Elle*, *Town and Country*, *TV Guide*, and *The Wilson Quarterly*. He has also written for such popular TV shows as *Charmed*, *Sliders*, *Early Edition*, and *Poltergeist: the Legacy*. Currently the Visiting Lecturer in Literature at Claremont McKenna College, he lives in Santa Monica, California, and may be reached through his website at www.robertmasello.com.